THE GAP

NINIE HAMMON

THE GAP

Prologue

Thursday, October 21, 2022
4 a.m.

THE ANGUISHED SCREAM sounded like cloth ripping.

No, not mere cloth, canvas — the canvas sail of some great tall ship, a windjammer staggering in a storm, the fierce gale tearing apart its mainsail.

Or maybe not canvas, not a sail at all. Maybe just a curtain — the one in the temple in Jerusalem that ripped from the bottom to the top when Jesus died.

The scream could have been the cry of either a man or a woman — but it was surely someone in extraordinary distress, a great grief expressed in a single vocal exhalation.

Gabriel Chambers sat bolt upright in bed when he heard it. The sound swelled bigger and bigger in his head until it exploded — shattering all his defenses and freeing his imprisoned Boogie Man. Oh, the monster had escaped a few times over the years, but this was different. This time the sound ripped apart the carefully constructed cage where Gabe had kept it locked away — because *this was how it'd started*. As a little boy, lying here in *this* room, in *this* bed, in *this* house, he'd been suddenly awakened in the midnight dark by an ear-piercing scream and …

Gabe toppled head first into darkness, tumbling over and over into a mind space occupied by a pale, ephemeral reality, nightmare images and impressions and emotions, a fragmented horror that could not possibly be real. Except it was. At the very core of his being, Gabe was convinced that it was.

Screaming.

A continuous shriek slicing into his temples.

Terror, heart hammering.

Hide!

No, get away! Run!

Dark passageways with the screams nipping at his heels like rabid dogs.

A strobe of light captures an image, a … thing.

It is so unutterably horrifying that it is burned onto Gabe's eyeballs and forever after he will look out his eyes at the world through that image burned into them.

A creature smeared with black blood, a pale, slimy thing, that's a skin-crawling, dead gray with … veins in it.

In flashes of strobing light, it slithers toward him and a tentacle — blue, gnarled and lumpy like a knotted rope — grabs him, wraps around his neck. He writhes to get free. More tentacles. So many he's tangled up, can't escape.

Other creatures come. They crawl down the walls like spiders, dozens of them, hundreds, all sizes. They slither out of the shadows across the floor toward him, all around him, writhing in the black blood, crawling over each other, so many they cover the whole floor. And then they cover him. He sees their open mouths and vicious sharp teeth, curved backward like the fish, so when they bite into his flesh there'll be no escape. Their

*teeth will rip his face off his head. He can only whisper a dying scream
— "Nooo!"*

"Noooo!" Gabe screamed — a cry that tore out of his throat
in a hoarse whisper. Clamping his hand over his mouth, he sat
panting in the tangled sheets, listening.

Another scream. Not a night terror, a human voice. Gabe
was fully awake now, a grown man, not a little boy. And this
was a real scream, not like the one in his childhood dream
that'd fundamentally changed *who he was.*

When Alexandra Harrington heard the scream, it startled
her, caught her by surprise, and she froze in place. She
thought about that night, too, about her sick little boy who
heard the scream and ran from it … and he'd been running
ever since. But this scream was not that. She'd known all those
years ago what it was Gabe had really heard, and she knew
now who was screaming and why. She understood the pain
and sorrow that rode the scream out into the world, too, and
she was sorry about that, genuinely sorry.

Olivia Harrington wasn't awakened by the scream. She
hadn't been asleep, was lying awake for no reason whatsoever
except that, according to her doctor, "as you get older, you
need less sleep." If that was the case, she might as well give up
going to bed altogether. She'd been awake that other night,
too, four decades ago. She'd gone to help and got swept up in
the moment, did a thing she had regretted every single day for
forty-five years.

The scream wailed, warbled, and then trailed off into
what sounded like a strangled sob. Olivia sat up, swung her
feet carefully off the bed, and started feeling around on the
floor for her house shoes. She hadn't even found them yet
when she heard the second sound. Not a scream this time, a
yell from the same voice, a cry with a word in it. A name.

Haaannnnnnaaaah!

That was Cyrus. *Here we go again. Only this time, might be he got to her too late.*

Family members hurried down hallways in the pre-dawn darkness, climbed shadowy stairs to the big room on the third floor with windows that opened onto an endless expanse of prairie where the sun would paint the eastern horizon a pinkish-golden glow in a few hours. No one saw the figure in the darkened alcove outside Hannah's bedroom door, and it melted effortlessly into the shadows as soundlessly as it had come, so ephemeral that maybe it was never really there at all.

Chapter One

FRIDAY

OLIVIA KAVANAUGH HARRINGTON looked out the window over the crepe myrtle blossoms and watched the hearse pull slowly — maybe even reluctantly, but she was probably imagining that part —down the winding driveway to park at the front door.

Hannah was home now.

More to the point, there was about to be a dead body in the house for three days, and the uproar that was causing would have been comical if it hadn't been such a serious occasion.

Why, Olivia had heard one of Jordan and Marilou's girls whine that there should have been a trigger warning — a *trigger* warning, for crying out loud! — to let the family know about the corpse. That child actually expected the world around her to cater to her tender sensibilities — more than expected, demanded it. Believed she had a *right* to it, that life was obligated to tippy toe around her, being oh so careful not to hurt her feelings. Or to make her feel threatened by some kinda "micro aggression."

The old woman made a *humph* sound deep in her throat. Micro aggression my ass.

Olivia hadn't clawed her way through a full century of living — exactly one hundred years on Sunday — in all the different places and situations and circumstances the good Lord had planted her by getting her panties all in a wad every time life threw something her way she wasn't expecting. Not a one of them young ones would have lasted ten minutes in a High Plains sandstorm where the wind was apt any minute to blow the whole house away.

There was a knock on her bedroom door. Firm. *Knock-knock.* Not tentative like her son, Cyrus, who always rapped his knuckles light on the door like he didn't really want to disturb anybody. That was the point of knocking, wasn't it?

She was moving slow this morning, ten o'clock and she hadn't yet got out of bed. Didn't sleep in, though, just lay there as the morning wore on, hearing the sounds of *family* downstairs. The ones that lived close had come yesterday afternoon and last night, but the rest would be streaming in all day today — and probably tomorrow, too, during the viewing.

"Come on in, Gabe. I seen they brought Hannah. You getting her settled in the parlor? You seen Cyrus?"

"Yes and no. Yes, we're getting her settled in the parlor, and no, I haven't seen Uncle Cyrus."

Olivia's grandson, Gabriel Chambers, always seemed to take up more space in a room than his physical presence displaced. She'd never figured out how he managed to do that. Oh, he knew the effect he had on people. It was calculated. She could tell. At fifty-three, he looked forty, still as handsome as a movie star even if he had lost most of his hair. Didn't shave his head, though. Just cut it real short so's it was hard to see where hair stopped and scalp began. She never let on, but he was her favorite among all the grandchildren ... and all the greats. She wasn't sure anymore how many generations there were now.

He looked more haggard than usual this morning. He never got more'n three or four hours of sleep at a stretch and probably didn't even go to bed at all last night. Folks thought he stayed up 'cause he was one of them people didn't need much sleep, but she knew he didn't sleep 'cause he *couldn't* sleep, least not for very long 'fore he got jolted awake. She'd long suspected that was the way of it, but after he moved back into his old room in the big house with her six months ago, she was sure. That boy was *not* gonna like what Olivia was about to do. Oh, lordy no he was not, for a fact! Shoot, none of them was gonna set off fireworks and ask Olivia to be the grand marshal of the parade over it, but Gabe was like to be slapped down the hardest. She could tell somethin' was bad wrong with him, worse than all them other times. His own fault, though. He's the one got his own fanny in a crack and she wasn't under no obligation to get him out of it — even if he'd asked for help, which he hadn't. She'd settled in her mind her plan was the right thing to do, and not liking it didn't change nothing. Problem was that what was right and what felt good hardly ever rubbed elbows with each other. Her own granny used to tell her that knowing what to do was wisdom, actually doing it was virtue, and the gap in between the two was utter anguish.

"Three-D moved that end table and the old leather couch to give the guys from Whittiker & Ramírez more room."

"You hadn't ought to call them boys that."

"Three-D? Dumb, Dumber, and Dumbest. Hey, if the shoe fits. Cal had the body under that beautiful patchwork quilt you worked on for two winters, on a bier — some kind of bed on wheels like a gurney. I had to fix a wheel, but it's all good now."

"They bring the flowers?"

"Smells like a florist shop down there. They hauled *everything* out here in a van, took two trips. Joaquín brought pedestals to put plants on, and then set the rest all around on the floor. All they have to do is set up the monitors—"

"What do they need monitors for? She done flat-lined for sure."

"For pictures of Aunt Hannah, shown in a continuous loop. Steve is going to scan a bunch of them in and show them on screens in the four corners of the room. Leanne said she wished someone had warned her yesterday she was going to have to find pictures and she'd have started digging around in Aunt Hannah's things. She sent a couple of the cousins to go through those boxes in the attic. They were glad to get out of the room where Hannah was."

Olivia liked it when Gabe was in charge of things. He could get more done in an hour than most of the rest of them could in a day — well, except for his mother. Alex could work anybody under the table.

"Why'd you do it?" he asked, then stepped over to her bed and sat down on the edge of it. "Why'd you demand we hold ... what? An Irish wake? I figure you must have had a reason, and since you knew it would hit the family like a drip of water in hot grease, you must have had a good one."

"I wanted the whole family to gather, everybody under one roof. It ain't like there's that many of us —what? three dozen or so." Shoot, Olivia had friends who'd had eight, ten, twelve kids — who'd all got married and had kids of their own, and them kids had kids and ... no telling how many there was of them now. She'd just had the two, Cyrus and Alex. She and Landon had *wanted* more, a big family like Landon's had been. They'd stayed in that big ole house, expecting to fill it up with the sounds of kids running up and down the halls. Waited year after year after Alex was born, but it just didn't happen.

"We'd have all stayed here if that's what you wanted without bringing Aunt Hannah to the party."

The Circle H Ranch was home. The house on the sprawling acreage had been added onto so many times Olivia'd long since forgot when and what for. It sat in the middle of the only grove of green for ten miles in every direction, fifteen miles from Muleshoe, the county seat of Bailey County, Texas. The homestead, as her late husband liked to call it, had bedrooms all over it — some of them *real* little. Most were on the second floor, fourteen of 'em, and she'd forgot how many bathrooms. There was a grand front staircase, and two sets of back stairs in the north and south corners of the house. There were also stairs that only went from the second to the third floor, and that circular staircase made of solid cherry that come up from the floor in the parlor through the ceiling into the front second-floor hall. And there was an elevator. If the house'd been listed as a vacation rental — counting roll-away beds, cribs, hide-a-beds and couches — it'd have said "can field four baseball teams." Wasn't never in danger of being no tour bus destination, though, out in flat west Texas, the High Plains, where the sky sat in a blue bowl overhead and the prairie extended out from the front door to the horizon.

She'd lived in other places over the years, but them places with hills and trees and such that blocked the sky, they always made her feel like somebody'd closed her up in a shoe box and stuck it the back of the closet.

"It was the right thing to do, bringing Hannah and everybody here, right for poor Cyrus — them married just shy of sixty years — he needs all the support he can get, him like he is."

<h1 style="text-align:center">Chapter Two</h1>

Eighty-two-year-old Cyrus Kavanaugh opened the door and stepped into Hannah's walk-in closet. It smelled like leather shoes and her perfume and whatever that odor was on clothes you got from the dry cleaners. She'd picked up a whole bunch of clothes from the cleaners last week, and they were still hanging in that plastic bag.

Cyrus needed his black suit clean. He'd have to wear it Sunday for … something. What was it? He couldn't remember. Hannah would know. He'd ask Hannah —

Hannah was dead!

The reality of it hit him in the chest and he couldn't catch a breath, couldn't move or think. His precious Hannah was gone. His ever-present guilt settled around him — it was *his* fault! Of course it was.

His eyes welled with tears that poured in twin rivers down his cheeks, but he didn't even bother to wipe them away. How could he have done a thing like what he'd done to his precious wife? How could he have … what? Suddenly confused, he didn't know where he was or why he'd come here. Something in the closet …

He shook his head to clear it. The world still seemed fuzzy, wrapped in cotton, but he remembered now why. That pill his sister, Alex, gave him, to "take the sharp edges off," she'd said. It would let him catch his breath for a little while, but then the sharp edges would return. The slicing pain that hurt so bad he doubled over from it. It'd be back. But right now, just for right now, he could breathe.

And while he could breathe, he needed to make sure he hadn't made a big mistake. It would matter to Hannah how she looked when she was "laid out." Oh my yes, his Hannah would care about such a thing! She'd want to have her hair done right, and that makeup that the man sprayed on — like with a paint sprayer — and it made her wrinkles go away. Some of them, the little ones anyway. And she'd want to be in her very best dress. Trouble was, Cyrus didn't have any idea which of all the dresses that surrounded him in the closet had been Hannah's favorite. She loved clothes, was always buying something new. He turned slowly around, eying all the different colorful fabrics and designs and was sure he had screwed up. When they'd come to him yesterday, he couldn't even breathe yet, had had the air so totally knocked out of him when they said she ... and then the world went crazy. They'd asked, the funeral director Calvin Whittiker had asked what Cyrus wanted her to wear. Had told him he should pick something out. He might as well have told Cyrus to whistle Dixie out his left nostril. Cyrus didn't know ...

Maybe he should have gotten something new — let the girls, Millie, Cynthia, and Marilou, his sons' wives, go buy something. He should have told them to get the best dress they could find, he didn't care what it cost — and Cyrus Kavanaugh didn't say that about many things. He could get ten cents out of both sides of a nickel. Of course, if he'd gotten the girls to get her something brand new, they might have got something Hannah woulda hated.

That'd been yesterday afternoon, he supposed, and he'd gone to the closet in her bedroom, looked at the dresses in the closet, and just grabbed one. The blue silk one she had worn to Cassidy's wedding five years ago. She'd preened in front of the mirror for a long time trying that one on, and he'd thought she looked wonderful. He always thought that.

But now, when he thought back on it, he realized he hadn't taken the proper amount of time to select the very best, her favorite. Was it too late to change it now? Could they … take off what she was wearing and put something else on her? She was dead and …

Hannah was dead. He'd found her in the middle of the night on the floor beside the bed, lying in a puddle of spilled orange juice, her hair all sticky with it. And he'd screamed. Screamed and screamed. They'd had their first fight in what … thirty years, maybe, that night over that stupid koi pond. He'd yelled at her, at least he thought he had. Had *threatened* her? No, he wouldn't have done a thing like that. The image of finding her lying there hit him full force, literally knocked him off his feet, and he sank to his knees on the closet floor. His Hannah had been at his side for sixty-two years. Every day. She was there, like the sky was there and the prairie was there and the house was there.

Now, she wasn't there anymore. Bending at the waist from the pain, his forehead touched the carpet, his face near her shoes. He didn't remember selecting shoes, so he supposed they didn't put shoes on her.

No shoes!

Bare feet.

He gasped and sat upright. He had to make them put shoes on her! She couldn't lay there with her feet bare. Why, Hannah would have been mortified to be lying there with no shoes. Searching frantically, he picked up one shoe after another. Discarded pair after pair. She was wearing that blue dress, and he was sure that it had matching shoes. It did, didn't it? Which ones? The closet light high above wasn't bright enough, so he got slowly, painfully to his feet and went out of the closet into the bedroom and opened the drawer of the nightstand beside the huge four-poster bed — that Hannah wouldn't be sleeping in tonight. Or tomorrow night. Or all the other nights out there …

He looked down at the silver metal thing in his hand. What was it? What did it do? Why was he holding it?

He'd go ask Hannah what it was and how … No, he couldn't ask Hannah. There was a reason why not, but he couldn't remember it. He needed to go to the bathroom, but when he passed the open closet door, he remembered — he had to find Hannah's blue shoes. But he didn't know why.

There were lots of blue shoes in the closet, so he dropped the silver thing and snatched up a pair and took them into the bedroom.

There was a light knock and then Andy Schaeffer, Cassidy's husband, opened the door and peeked around it. When he saw Cyrus, he walked in and stood looking at him. What? What was it? Was Cyrus's fly unzipped? He glanced toward the mirror and saw that his hair was askew, his shirt rumpled and untucked. Hannah would have said he looked "untidy."

"Grandpa Cyrus, you alright?" Andy asked. "Your mother asked me to come check on you, said Aunt Alex had put you to bed for a nap, gave you something to help you sleep. What are you doing up?"

That's why he looked so unkempt. He'd been napping. Cyrus didn't remember napping. He looked down at the shoes in his hand and thrust them at Andy.

"Take these."

Andy took them. "What for?"

Cyrus had no idea who the shoes belonged to.

And then he did. Oh, dear God, he did!

Stifling a sob, he said, "They need to put these shoes on Hannah."

"You want them to change the shoes Grandma Hannah's wearing?"

"She's not wearing any shoes, she's barefoot."

"How do you know that?"

He didn't.

"These are the shoes that match the dress she's wearing," he heard himself say and that was it! That's why the shoes were important. "So if she *is* wearing shoes, they're not the right ones."

"Grandpa Cyrus, her feet are covered up. You can't see—"

Cyrus tried to snatch the shoes out of Andy's hand. "I'll take them—"

Andy held on. "No, Grandpa Cyrus, that's okay. You go back and lie down. I'll take the shoes."

"You'll make sure they put them on her?"

"I'll—"

Some child downstairs squealed and Andy must have recognized the cry, because he turned quickly toward the hallway "That could be Chap … I'll make sure they change her shoes."

"Not *change*. She's not wearing—"

But Andy was already gone and Cyrus stood in his bedroom doorway, listening to the pandemonium downstairs. The children — his grandchildren and great-grandchildren and the nieces and nephews … couldn't their parents make them behave?

But that was the thing. The parents thought their kids *were* behaving, at least the way they defined it.

Them hollering and running around, making noise, interrupting conversations, in your face all the time … and if you said anything, their folks would shrug and say, "Just kids." He knew they thought he expected too much from children, but how could it be too much when he and his sister managed it, and all the neighbor kids had managed it. They stood respectful in the background and didn't demand to be in the middle of every adult interaction, cavorting around in the center of the room, everything about them.

How many times had Hannah said to him, "Children should be seen and not heard." Just to him, though. Even Hannah had given up making any impression on the younger ones. She'd tried—

Hannah was dead. Lying there barefoot. They needed to put shoes on her feet. He turned and went back into her bedroom to the closet, where a flashlight lay on the floor. He picked it up and turned it on and began to search for shoes.

Chapter Three

CHAPMAN SCHAEFFER WAS HIDING behind the big chair so he could see what was going on. His mother had shooed him out of the room, but he wanted to see, so he sneaked back in when she wasn't looking. Nobody was looking. They were all staring at the thing that Chap's daddy, Uncle Gabe, Uncle Sam, and Uncle Lawson were trying to fit through the front door. It was like a bed on wheels — they called it a beer — and there was something on the bed but he couldn't see what.

Uncle Gabe had trouble getting the beer up over that thingy on the floor where you close a door. When he tried, one of the wheels came off, and a man Chap didn't know said a bad word. He was the Funeral Home Man, and he was wearing a black suit and a white shirt and his face was red like his tie was too tight. He didn't say the word very loud and maybe the others didn't hear, but Chap did.

He was four years old, and he could hear special good. Aunt Leanne had told him so, said something about little pictures and big ears that didn't make sense, but when he asked her what it meant, she wouldn't tell him. He had told her his mommy was going to give him a baby sister for Christmas — he didn't want a baby sister, he wanted a Nerf

Ultra One Motorized Blaster! — and Grandma Danni had laughed and said he'd spilled the beans. But he didn't spill anything or he woulda got in trouble and Mommy woulda put him in timeout.

Uncle Gabe went into the kitchen and came back with some tools, a scoo-diber, and those big pinching things Chap didn't know the name of. It didn't take Uncle Gabe long to put the wheel back on. And when they pushed it through the door and into the parlor, Chap knew that what was on the beer was Grandma Hannah, because Mommy had said there would be a dead lady in the parlor and she must be it.

Chap didn't know how she had gotted dead. She wasn't all mashed up like that deer he'd seen on the side of the road with its insides laying out on the ground. Daddy said the deer had got hit by a car, but Aunt Hannah didn't get hit by a car because all her insides were still inside her, as far as he could tell. He didn't know what other way there was to get dead.

Aunt Alex saw him behind the chair, but she didn't tell his mommy, just took his hand and led him out of the room.

"You need to stay out of there right now," Aunt Alex said.

"Why? Is it because of the dead lady? Can I see? I never seed a dead lady."

"The person who died is your Grandma Hannah."

"Grandma Hannah's the dead lady?"

"Don't call her a dead lady, sweetheart, that's not nice."

He didn't know what was not nice about it because she was a lady and she was dead, but he didn't ask. Sometimes you got in trouble and got sent to your room or put in timeout for asking questions.

As soon as Aunt Alex left him on the back porch, Chap went back into the parlor. He didn't try to hide though, just stood without talking and nobody saw him. Grownups were so tall that lots of times they didn't see little kids — even if you were right in front of them and you had to be careful not to get trumpled.

The Funeral Home Man pulled back the blanket, a raggedy old thing made outta a bunch of different pieces of fabric, must not have had enough of any one of them to make the whole thing. The dead lady looked like Grandma Hannah alright — and Aunt Cynthia started crying. Just busted out crying like somebody pinched her or she mashed her finger. All his aunts started crying then, and all the uncles looked sad.

His mother saw him and he thought he was in trouble, but she just came over to him — she was about to cry, too, but hadn't started yet — and took his hand and led him to the beer with the dead lady and picked him up so he could see.

"You remember Grandma Hannah," she said, and her voice was all soggy-like. He did, but the woman he remembered must not be the same person, because that lady always had a mad face and her hair was frizzy like the Chia Pet he got for Christmas. This was just a doll.

"She's home with Jesus now," his mother said.

Chap had heard about Jesus in church. He was the man wearing a bathrobe in the paintings, or just had something over his private parts and was hanging on a telephone pole. He thought Jesus lived in the church, but maybe not. Wherever he lived, Grandma Hannah wasn't there with him because she was right here on the beer.

Mommy set him back down on the floor and that's when he saw it. It was the prettiest thing he'd ever seen. On Grandma Hannah's finger, a ring with a big red stone, and all colors of other rocks around it, and it sparkled and twinkled even in the dim lamp light. He'd never seen anything that pretty. Not ever. He *wanted* it. Maybe he could ask for it and his mommy would give it to him, but he didn't think she would. The dead lady wouldn't care, would she, if she had gotted dead like that deer on the side of the road, she wasn't ever going to wake up and open her eyes — Daddy said the deer wouldn't. If she didn't open her eyes, why would she care if that red-shiny-thing wasn't on her finger?

If Chap had it, he would put it in his secret place, the wooden box that somebody made for him with his name on the top of it cut into the wood. All his precious things were there. The Indian arrowhead he found in the backyard, and the shells he found at the beach, and the bottle cap that had got smashed by something and was flat. And the black rock that looked just like a dog turd. He would put the red shiny thing there.

If he had it, that is.

Maybe he could get it.

He had to try.

Chapter Four

"GRANDMA LIV …?" Gabe said, and she knew she'd blinked out on him. She did that more and more often these days — but what can you expect from synapses that'd been firing for a hundred springs with their sandstorms, summers with their broiler-oven heat, autumn with bushes and tumble weeds "flocked" in lint from the cotton gins, and ugly winters that didn't have no saving grace whatsoever. Wintertime on the Texas High Plains pure-D sucked.

"I was just thinking about Cyrus's daddy. He never laid eyes on the boy." She knew she'd told Gabe that story a thousand times, but she didn't care. It wasn't about him needing the information. It was about her needing to say it. "He never even seen a picture. Didn't none of my letters get to Okinawa."

SHE KNOWS what it means the instant she sees them. Of course she does. Two soldiers in dress uniform coming up the sidewalk to the front door. She turns and runs away — out the back door and out onto the prairie, knocking over yucca plants, scaring up jackrabbits and ground squirrels … except she doesn't. She can't make her body obey, can only sink to her knees on the floor she'd been sweeping and watch through the mesh screen as death comes calling.

"BEN WASN'T AS handsome as your granddaddy." Landon Harrington had been a looker! "That's where you got your good looks." She cocked her head to the side and looked up at him. "Shame you didn't inherit my hair."

Olivia had a mane of hair that'd been pale blonde until it turned, now it was as pure white as the cotton that hung down out of the bowls in the fall. She wore it up in a bun, but when she let it down, it still flowed all the way to her waist. She was inordinately proud of all that hair, always had been vain about it, but vanity wasn't her worst character flaw. She figured it was a misdemeanor when a whole lot of the rest was felonies.

Her son, Cyrus, didn't inherit Olivia's hair, neither. He had red hair and freckles, just like the father he never met. All three of Cyrus's sons were redheads, or had been until their hair fell out — Lawson was completely bald and Jordan was half way. Only the oldest, Samuel, escaped the curse, though at sixty-one, his russet hair had faded and was streaked with silver. Cyrus's wasn't, though. His full head of hair was as thick and red today as it'd been when he came squawling into the world more than eight decades ago. Quite a few of the grandchildren and great grandchildren on that side of the family had hair in varying shades of red, but none of them had hair the deep, claret-wine shade of red that Cyrus had inherited from Benjamin. None of them had Cyrus's freckles, either, at least not as many. Olivia'd feared sometimes when he was a little boy that just one more freckle would pop out some-where on his body and that would put Cyrus over the limit and all the spots would run together.

Olivia's only daughter, Alexandra, born ten years after her brother, Cyrus, had hair as black as Cyrus's was red — "black Irish" hair, so reflective that in bright sunlight it looked almost silver. Her eyes were a striking robin's egg blue just like her daddy's, and she'd passed that down to her oldest son, Gabe. Alex had been married and divorced three times. The girls, Sydney and Brooke, snared their mother's black hair, but not the blue eyes. Gabe's son Spencer, and Spencer's daughter, Avery, all had pale blue eyes, but only Avery's were the same special shade of robin's egg blue. Gabe's two daughters, Casey and Juliana, had black hair like their grandmother, Alex, but both the girls looked more like Gabe's ex-wife than they did their father.

"You didn't answer my question."

"What question?"

"Why you demanded to have Hannah brought here?"

"You know why," Olivia snapped. "'Cause they was gonna cut her up and wasn't but one way I could be sure they didn't do that."

"It's not like they were carving up a side of beef. Just an autopsy. It's standard procedure where the cause of death is uncertain."

"Wasn't nothing uncertain about it. It ain't like this was the first time. She took too much insulin, just like them other times. All that wine she drank in the evenings, one of us shoulda took over a long time ago—"

"And tell Aunt Hannah she couldn't drink? Good luck with *that!*"

"She wasn't in no shape to be giving her own insulin shots."

"Sheriff Hastings just wanted—"

"I don't give a fart in a whirlwind what the sheriff wanted. Ain't none of mine getting cut open. That's the beginning and the end of it."

She never talked about why she felt that way— how they'd told her when they sent the bodies home from the war that they'd removed all the internal organs first, just sent home the outside, like a pumpkin rind. She didn't know if that was true or not, but it'd so horrified her, she had practically stood over the dead bodies of every family member who died since then with a shotgun to keep them whole.

"Cal snatched her out of there just in time. Dr. Carpenter had completed the external examination and was getting ready to start—" Gabe started.

"Way I heard it, Doc got far enough to see wasn't no wounds or bruises or such — you know, 'foul play' — and only the one puncture wound where she gave herself her bedtime shot."

"Which means that's the one she screwed up — too much. Insulin overdose is listed as the official cause on the death certificate, right now, anyway, but the blood toxicology test results won't be in until next week."

"Won't matter a hill of beans by then — Hannah'll be dust in the wind." Olivia yanked the conversation back to Gabe's question. "I brought her here because this is her *home!* I never should have let them take her outta here in the first place."

Cyrus and Hannah had lived with Olivia in the Harrington House on Circle H Ranch for a few years when their boys were in high school, but they'd moved back from Dallas to live there permanent maybe twenty-five years ago. They'd said they'd come to "look after Mama." Olivia'd been in her eighties at the time and hadn't needed nobody's lookin' after, thank you very much. Olivia figured the real reason was Hannah'd wanted to be cock of the walk like her mama'd been, and she couldn't do that in Dallas. Hannah'd come from Odessa oil money, and when she was growing up, she had watched her mama reign supreme over her own small-town kingdom. Hannah'd wanted to be a big fish in a little pond, too, and she certainly had been that when she come to Muleshoe, ruled whatever roost there was to rule, set up her very own "Museum of the Southwest" — she'd intended to drag the little town into notoriety whether the residents liked it or not.

All told, just about every member of the family had lived in the Harrington House at one time or another, different ones of them at different times, and it was good to pull them all together to grieve. They'd become too far flung over the years, and Olivia longed to have all her chicks in one nest. This one last time. Surely to goodness it'd be the last time — she was a hundred years old, for crying out loud. Of course, the timing was a little inconvenient. She wasn't sure whether it was the good news or the bad news that they'd all be together when she detonated the bomb that was likely to put a world of hurt on their lives, some of them anyway. But Hannah had dropped over dead and it was what it was. Just have to make the best of it.

"Grandma Liv, you couldn't have kept a dead body here for four days! Bible says even Lazarus 'sinketh.'"

"Don't you go quoting Scripture like you know any more about the Bible than what it says in the table of contents. Then you best have my funeral the day after I croak, 'cause I don't want to be hauled away to some funeral home—"

"You're going to outlive us all."

She made another humph sound in her throat. "Son, I stopped buying green bananas twenty years ago."

Chapter Five

"YOU OWE ME FIVE BUCKS," Avery Chambers said to the girl sitting in the passenger seat of Avery's Honda CRV, the window down and her blue/blonde hair whipping in the wind.

"You take plastic?" Madeline Shepherd replied.

"If you didn't have five dollars, why'd you take the bet?"

Maddie gave Avery a condescending look as she pushed the button and rolled up her window.

"For the same reason everybody takes a bet — because they're sure they'll win. Who'd take a bet they thought they'd lose?"

Avery thought, *Well, my Grampa Gabe, for one,* but didn't say it. Besides, that was unkind and might not even be true.

Avery'd been betting on a sure thing, though. When she'd described to Maddie how you could see the Harrington House on Circle H Ranch from five miles away, Maddie'd said, "That's impossible." And Avery'd said, "Wanna bet?"

Now, as Maddie gazed out the windshield at the shape on the horizon across what Grandma Olivia called "miles and miles of nothing but miles and miles," Avery studied the girl's profile. Her blonde hair was streaked with blue— different shades — dark, light, aqua, teal. She looked like a tropical fish. A nose ring, a lip stud, couldn't see the tongue stud but it was there, and Maddie'd claimed she had studs in "other places" that Avery had no desire to see. From the side, you could trace the tangled green vine tattooed on her neck as it snaked down into her collar. Maddie's whole body was tattooed, or so she claimed, with full sleeves on her arms and legs. The detail that bright sunshine revealed in the tattoo on her left forearm was amazing — a woman's face distorted in terror, as realistic as a portrait. Avery figured Maddie had designed the tattoos herself since she was an art major, and the little bit of her work Avery'd seen was dark and frightening — mostly faces contorted by fear or anger or pain, skulls and dragon-like creatures.

Nodding toward the horizon ahead, Avery said, "Grandma Liv says the prairie's so flat that when your dog runs away you can see it for three days."

Maddie burst out laughing, almost choked on her coconut pineapple bubbly, barely kept herself from spewing the sparkling water all over the dashboard.

"She also says she's seen a sandstorm chew the paint right off a car."

"Oh, that part couldn't be true. I'd take that bet."

"She lived through the Dust Bowl on the Texas High Plains, so—"

"The Dust Bowl? Wasn't that like during the Depression — like 1915 or something? How old is your grandmother anyway?"

"It was in the 1930s, and actually she's not my grandmother. She's my grandfather Gabe's grandmother, so that'd make her my great, great, great ... my family doesn't keep track of those things, a bunch of greats. And she will turn one hundred years old on Sunday."

Maddie was suitably impressed. "I never met anybody that old. Can she talk?"

Avery laughed, thinking of the bright-eyed little woman who inhabited every childhood memory of that big old house.

"She's as sharp as a needle! She doesn't hear very well even with hearing aids anymore, but other than that there's not a thing wrong with her ... well, other than being a hundred years old. And she tells the best stories. She actually remembers hearing the President on the radio call the Japanese attack 'a day that will live in infamy.'"

"I never heard of Japanese terrorists. What were they pissed off about?"

"Not terrorists, Pearl Harbor. You know, the Japanese bombed the naval base in Hawaii, started World War II."

"If you say so. I sucked at history. I hated the teacher, Mr. Carter, made me stay after school. But I got him back. I poisoned his dog."

"You *what?*"

Avery was absolutely dumbstruck. The other girls on their floor in the dorm at Texas Tech University said Maddie was weird, screwy, that she gave them the creeps. Avery'd just thought she was withdrawn and shy. But *poison* a dog?

Maddie saw her reaction and immediately started back pedaling.

"I wasn't trying to kill it or anything like that," she said, talking fast. "I just wanted to make it throw up, that's all. You know, it was a great big dog, and I knew there'd be a lot of puke that Mr. Carter'd have to clean up." She paused. "I'd never hurt a dog."

Making a dog throw up fell within Avery's definition of hurting it, but she didn't say so.

Maddie kept talking, changing the subject.

"The only reason I remember the date of 9/11 is that ... well, duh — 9/11. Making airplanes into flying bombs, that was a pretty clever idea, don't you think? Killed a whole lot of people, not as good as an atomic bomb or anything like that, but a lot."

Avery heard admiration in Maddie's voice.

"Grandma Liv remembers that, too, the atomic bomb. Not just when they dropped it, but when they were making it. She lived in Alamogordo, New Mexico at the time, and that was close to the White Sands Proving Grounds where they tested it. She said everybody in town was used to hearing explosions, but that day there was this gigantic *BOOM!* She said the ground shook, her cabinets flew open and glasses fell out and broke."

"She remembers all that?"

"I told you, there's not a thing wrong with her mind, except maybe she remembers things like that better than where she left her glasses. She said she ran to the window and saw this huge mushroom-shaped cloud rising up out of the desert into the sky."

"Did she take a picture?"

"I doubt she owned a camera."

"Camera? Oh, yeah."

"And besides, you didn't take pictures of stuff like that. She said that was the weirdest part of it, that nobody talked about it, never said a thing. That's the way it was back then."

"If it happened today, there'd be a hundred videos on Instagram before the smoke settled out of the air."

"Uncle Cyrus was a little kid and he cut his foot bad on the broken glass. You could ask him and he'd show you the scar. Not now, of course. It's his wife, Aunt Hannah, who died. They'd been married like sixty or seventy years. I'm sure he's devastated."

Maddie leaned back in the seat but couldn't stretch her long legs all the way out. She was at least six feet tall, maybe taller, totally dwarfed five-feet-two-inch Avery — had six inches and a hundred pounds on her. The passenger seat was shoved forward so Avery could stuff Velma into the floorboard of the back seat. Velma was a mannequin, Avery's "companion" so she could park in spaces beside the science building reserved for vehicles with two or more riders. Normally, Velma lived in the trunk, but Avery'd moved her to fit in Maddie's duffel bag, which was big enough to carry a walrus.

Maddie'd looked sheepish when Avery'd asked her about the duffel, said it was her "go-bag" as she heaved it into the trunk. Whatever she carried in there, it was heavy.

"You bring that zaza?" Maddie asked. "I got some edibles."

"Good. Smoking anything, and I mean *anything*, even a vape pipe is verboten in Grandma Liv's house. I've got a bag of gummies. A few of my aunts, uncles and cousins will have some — particularly Aunt Juliana. Hers is straight fire."

"Anything stronger? E? Molly? Snow? Freddie?"

Avery was horrified. "You use *fentanyl?*"

"No, of course not," Maddie said too quickly. "I've tried … some things, but you can't trust that rainbow shit. It's dangerous. You never know what you're gonna get."

What had Avery done! Was this *stranger* going to be shooting up in the bathroom?

"You didn't *bring*…?"

Maddie picked up on the alarm in Avery voice.

"No, no it's not like that—"

"Because my family's mostly straight arrow." It was possible there was more drug use than Avery knew about, but she hadn't shed "kid sister" status yet with the older ones, wasn't "in the club," so nobody was open about it.

"Just brought a little weed to vibe on. That's all."

Avery relaxed. She used weed just like everybody else did but shunned anything stronger.

"… and a few shrooms."

Before Avery could protest, Maddie added, "Which I will leave in the car."

Avery's roommate's boyfriend claimed magic mushrooms had given him the most "mind-expanding" experience of his life. Avery was pretty sure she was happy with her mind the size it was.

Avery's phone dinged with an incoming text and she reached for it.

Maddie beat her to it.

"Stay alive, don't text and drive," Maddie parroted from some commercial.

"I don't text when I'm driving — *in Lubbock,* but out here — look at it." She gestured toward the emptiness. "There's nobody to run into. You can see a car coming from a mile away."

She reached for the phone again, but Maddie held it out of her reach.

"I'll check it for you."

She did not want Maddie reading her private text messages, but there was nothing she could do without wrecking the car.

"It's from Rye," Maddie said, no intonation of any kind in her voice.

Rye was Mariah Alvarez, Avery's roommate. They'd been BFFs since elementary school, though they lived five hundred miles apart. Mariah grew up on a ranch outside Laredo. She'd have come with Avery to the funeral, but she had to go home to help her family move.

Maddie read the text aloud. "How's it going with the weirdo?"

Can you saw *awk*-ward.

Maddie's thumbs moved quickly over the keyboard.

"What are you doing?"

Maddie didn't answer until she'd finished what she was typing and hit send.

"Replying. I said 'The weirdo's fine, but I think I'm pregnant.'"

"What? You didn't really—"

Rye's answer was instantaneous. Maddie held out the

screen but Avery could only glance at it, saw many question marks and exclamation points.

"Put it on silent mode. I don't want to listen to the dinging." Not true. She didn't want Maddie to read any more of her texts.

"She knows it was a joke," Maddie said as she turned off the phone. "I thought it was pretty funny." She was either being a very good sport about it or she was lying. Safe money was on Door Number Two.

Maddie changed the subject.

"Tell me about these people, your grandmother and your uncle and all."

"It's a long story."

"My family's story isn't long. Real short. My mom was a crack whore, and I don't know who my father is and she didn't either."

Avery managed not to gasp, just kept her eyes on the road. She hadn't been expecting … *this*, when she gave in to Madeline Shepherd's pleading to take her home for the weekend, even for a funeral, just to get out of Lubbock. Maddie'd sounded so desperate, and scared — a reaction way out of proportion to the situation. Sure, there *might* or might not be a serial killer afoot in the city. The police weren't saying for sure yet. But in the past six months they'd found the bodies of two young women killed in the same way — smothered with a plastic bag. A Texas Tech student had gone missing a week ago, and now the campus was crawling with police officers asking questions. Avery had to admit she was creeped out by a serial killer, even a maybe one. But Maddie was pure-D *terrified*, kept pointing out that the one thing the three girls had in common was that all of them had blonde hair and blue eyes — just like Maddie. Well, Avery was blue-eyed and blonde, too, as were half the girls on the Tech campus! And they weren't all hiding under their beds in terror.

You'd think Maddie would have been more … hardened,

used to violence, growing up in the foster care system in Chicago. On a full ride to Tech courtesy of an art scholarship, Maddie didn't really fit in with the other girls in Chitwood Hall — southerners, mostly Texans, and Avery had felt sorry for her. But she barely knew Madeline. What had Avery gotten herself into?

"Come on — who are these people I'm about to spend the weekend with?"

"Well … let me just say that putting them all together in the same place — with a dead body —for three days will be a lot like shaking up hornets in a Mason jar."

Chapter Six

OLIVIA LOOKED toward the door when the briefest of knocks was followed by Alex marching into the room. Alexandra Doreen Harrington Stephens Watson Hamilton — and then back to Harrington again — didn't walk, she marched.

"Mama, did you send Juliana and Cassidy up into the attic to dig through all those stored boxes?"

"Wasn't me. I—"

"There's no telling what's in those things — all kinds of records and papers." She looked over at her son, Gabe. "Your first tooth and kindergarten diploma, stuff like that."

Alex blew a puff of air up at the lock of hair that habitually hung down over her forehead in the widow's peak her son had inherited — and had enjoyed until his hairline inched back over the top of his head and down into his collar.

"You keep all the old pictures in the boxes in the back of the basement behind the Christmas decoration boxes, don't you?" Alex continued. "No telling what Juliana's going to find if she starts digging around in the attic."

Olivia felt like she'd been struck by lightning. The boxes in the attic! She hadn't given them boxes a thought in — what? Thirty-five, forty years. She shook her head in denial. No …

wasn't nothing there … couldn't be. Wasn't nothing to leave except … what had she kept? She hadn't just thrown everything away. She wouldn'ta done that. She'd a kept up with something, put it somewhere besides with the rest of the family papers. But where? She couldn't remember. And that wasn't just because she was old. She'd always been like that — you coulda followed Olivia Harrington through her life along the trail of her lost possessions — coats, car keys, gloves, earrings, sweaters, scarves. She had never in her life kept up with a pair of sunglasses for more than three days. So what might she have left in one of them boxes in the back of the attic?

"You tell them kids to stay outta them attic boxes!" she said, louder and more forcefully than she meant to. When both Gabe and Alex looked surprised, she tried to backpedal. "Ain't nothing there but … like Alex said, kindergarten graduation diplomas and Vacation Bible School finger paintings. The pictures they's looking for is in the basement. Send the kids down there." She managed a smile. "Might be they'll find a naked-baby-in-the-bathtub picture of their father. That'd be worth the price of admission."

Gabe and Alex both fake-smiled and nodded, but Olivia'd already stepped in it.

Olivia gave Alex a knowing look, grabbed her gaze and held on, tried to convey all kinda information.

"If they're already up there digging around in those boxes of papers in the attic," she said quietly, "you need to go help them."

"I can't, Mama, I have to—"

"Listen to what I'm saying, Alex. You need to be there when they start tearing into them boxes. You understand me?"

Olivia could tell she sorta did, but she was reluctant to make the connection between what might be in them boxes and *that night.*

"On them television shows, they call it *'damage control.'*"

"Damage control? Grandma Liv, what are you talking about?" Gabe asked.

But Alex *got it.* Her eyes grew huge, her look questioning. Olivia gave the slightest of nods.

"I'll help them," Alex said. "I don't mind. Cynthia or Millie can go find sheets for the rollaways." She turned on her heel and practically ran out of the room.

"What just happened?" Gabe asked. "There was a whole conversation between the two of you that I wasn't privy to."

"Just you never mind about that." Actually, Gabe had been there, too, when it all happened, but he didn't know it. Alex'd seen to it that he thought he'd dreamed the whole thing.

Chapter Seven

ALEX HURRIED out of her mother's room, down the hall, and took the back stairs to the third floor two steps at time. Probably not a whole lot of seventy-two-year-old women could do that, but Alex wasn't like most seventy-two-year-olds. She was thin and athletic—a beautiful woman. Still. Large robin's egg blue eyes and angel-wing eyebrows. Her face was a perfect oval, with full lips (they hadn't started thinning yet), a high forehead beneath her black hair — Lo'real said she was worth it. There weren't many women who could still turn heads — older men's heads, at least — at age seventy-two, either, but she could. And without all kinds of stitching and tucking and artificial remakes, thank you very much. Oh, she'd had a boob job after she divorced Brooke's father thirty years ago, had the silicone gel implants replaced every so often — like changing the oil in her car — and got her face nuked when she was in her forties. Laser peel. They told her it'd be like a bad sunburn. Right. You'd have to lay out on the beach all day, in July, on the planet Mercury to get that kind of burn.

Alex had come to think of herself as the poster girl for "late bloomers." When she was in high school, she would have registered as pretty, certainly, but she was way outshone by the flashier girls — the popular cheerleader types. But as the years passed, she ... what? Got prettier? Maybe. The loss of her chipmunk cheeks with age made the cheek bones more prominent, and wearing her hair fashionably and learning how to apply makeup, that'd helped. Mostly, she passed up high school cheerleader types in the looks department because they all got fat. Every woman she knew, okay, eighty percent, left high school, went blissfully off into adulthood and gained thirty pounds or forty or whatever. And as their bodies ballooned, their facial features just ... melted away. Alex didn't. She got pregnant, put on weight, had the baby and lost the weight. Had it been easy? She doubted it but didn't remember. She'd just done it. As had every new mother in China or India or Africa. But not in America, no sir. Not in the corpulent continent. According to statistics, just about every person in America could stand to lose twenty pounds. When she looked into her old friends' eyes, she felt such compassion — there was a person, a real *person* underneath the pounds. A person who was struggling, doing the best they could in an awful circumstance.

... and now that stupid rock star, or rap star ... what was her name, it had a lot of z's in it, was flaunting her folds and bulges, demanding that the world celebrate her as some kind of *role model.* Like just about everything else these days, it was a complete twisting of reality. That woman wasn't beautiful, desirable, or *healthy,* she was morbidly obese. If she wanted to tell herself she was a sex goddess, that was her business — everybody's entitled to their own fantasies. But to suggest that the rest of the world walk out into wonderland with her, to *demand* that all humanity share her delusion ... that was lunacy.

Alex ground her teeth, furious. She felt so sorry for the poor people who went to war with their weight *every day,* who tried so hard, worked out, starved themselves, battled heredity along with their doughnuts. And now some celebrity was telling them that all their effort was for nothing, they were wasting their time, should just give up and eat a Twinkie! And bless their hearts, they followed along like lemmings to the sea, believed it because they wanted so desperately for the lie to be true.

A little piece of Scripture popped into her head, from the decades of her life that her mother had seen to it every member of the family had a bum on the pew on Sunday morning. Something about telling people "what their itching ears wanted to hear." That nailed it. The obese "role model" didn't mention to her followers that, oh by the way, excess weight would take years, literally *years* off their lives! That while they were "owning the perfection of their natural bodies," they weren't likely addressing the deeper psychological issues that could be causing the obesity. And meanwhile, they were courting diabetes, high blood pressure, osteoarthritis, heart, liver, and gallbladder disease, and strokes. They were destroying their joints and their self-esteem — taking up two seats on an airplane — limiting what they could do every day of their lives, making simple tasks like tying their shoes a chore ... and Miss Name-Full-of-Z's was saying all that was *good* thing? Somebody ought to—

Stop!

Uh oh.

Alex stopped dead in her mental tracks, could see the flashing lights and hear the siren — she'd been pulled over by the Diatribe Police, her self-appointed tirade patrol. She had always cared so *passionately* about things — about right and wrong, about goodness and justice and ... but she'd learned early in her career that unleashing a blistering onslaught of painful rhetoric when something violated her personal values might validate her self-righteousness, but it was not the best way to climb the corporate ladder. And *that* did matter to her. So Alex disciplined herself to keep her mouth shut, got pulled over by the DP often in the beginning, spent a night in diatribe jail after she went off about Benghazi in the newsroom and her best reporter quit the next day. Alex wanted the American dream more than she wanted to win arguments, though, taught her children that anything was possible if you worked hard enough. And it'd taken *work*, she'd put in ridiculous hours, nights and weekends for years, decades, but it'd paid off when she'd moved into the corner office with "Managing Editor" on the door.

For all the good it did her now.

Passing a mirror, Alex stopped and looked at her face, turned it to one side, then looked at the other and bemoaned the Great Brown Spot Attack. She had looked down at her hand one day, saw a brown spot on it, like a big freckle, and within six months, her whole body was covered with the things. Age spots. Sun spots. Liver spots. Different names, same affliction. Freckles were cute on a four-year-old, but on a seventy-year-old, not so much. Her doctor'd called them actinic lentigines — harmless. She thought they made her skin look like she was an apple rotting on the inside.

Stepping back, Alex looked at herself full length. The light in the hallway was dim, of course, but it was bright enough for her to verify that you couldn't tell anything yet. Well, most people couldn't. Her hair was thinning, big handfuls of it on her brush at night. She hadn't been prepared for that, but she didn't think it was noticeable. She was still beautiful — spots and all — she was slender and looked healthy and athletic.

Unfortunately, she was also dying.

Chapter Eight

"HERE'S THE TLDR VERSION." Avery told Maddie. "Grandma Liv was born in ... well, 1922 if she turns a hundred on Sunday. She grew up in Tahoka, Texas, got married ... I can't remember his name. They had a little boy, Uncle Cyrus, but his father never saw him, was killed in the South Pacific in World War II."

"Is your Uncle Cyrus one of those shriveled up dudes in the wheelchairs you see at Veterans Day parades, look like raisins?"

That offended Avery, but she didn't let it show. Actually, she hadn't ever really thought about age and her family because the older ones had so much life in them. Most of them anyway.

"Uncle Cyrus has ... issues." She felt suddenly protective of the old man and didn't want to open his Alzheimer's to Maddie's scorn. "But he gets around just fine. Eventually, Grandma Liv married again, and when Uncle Cyrus was ten years old, she and her second husband had a little girl, Alexandra. She's my Grandpa Gabe's grandmother."

"Sounds like there'll be somebody here from every generation since ... I don't know, when did they start naming generations? The Greatest Generation — that'd be your Grandma Liv— and the Baby Boomers, Millennials— all of them."

"Yeah, I guess. It's kind of a thing in our family to have children young. Not like fifteen or anything ridiculous like that, but not many of the older ones made it to twenty childless."

Avery was eighteen and she absolutely would be breaking that family tradition. She couldn't imagine having a baby *now*. How did all those women do it?

As they drew closer to the house, two things became more and more obvious — how big it was and how oddly it was shaped.

"That thing's … ginormous! How many rooms are there?"

"I don't know, never counted them all. But there are fourteen bedrooms on the second floor."

"Holy shit." She was surprised into momentary silence. "What's that little box thing on the roof?"

"The Crow's Nest, the Pigeon Roost, or just the Chicken House — depends on who you ask. Grandma Liv's husband built it. He liked to stand on the deck on the front and look out over the prairie from up there, said it made him feel like the captain of a sailing ship."

"Does your family … get along? From a hundred to … what? Who's the youngest?"

"Oh, nobody stays the youngest for very long. There's always a herd of little bitty ones — my cousin Cassidy's pregnant right now, and she has a four-year-old, Chapman. He's the youngest who can walk and talk. That's the Kavanaugh side of the family, Uncle Cyrus's kids and grandkids. I'm on the other side — Grandma Alex and the Harringtons."

"Your parents will be there, won't they?"

"They're divorced." She really didn't want to go there. "I live with my mom, and she's on a ski trip in Aspen. My father's a Harrington, and his sisters, Sydney and Brooke, have seven—"

"So your father will be there?"

"Not likely." She hadn't intended to let the hostility show, but there it was. Maddie instantly picked up on it.

"Why not?"

"He doesn't do a lot of traveling, what with being in prison and all."

Maddie waited a beat.

"What'd he do?"

Avery kept her eyes on the road.

"He was sentenced to ten years in prison for vehicular homicide."

"In a wreck where somebody got killed … and the wreck was his fault?"

"Something like that. I don't want to talk about it."

Avery wanted to tell Maddie the truth, to blurt out the hateful words that rose up into her mind like burning bile in her throat every time she thought about it. That would spark more questions, though, and talking about it always conjured up memories of that day, and the blood on the highway, the woman with just one shoe, and the mangled bicycle in the weeds.

The little boy's name was Nicolás Hernandez. He'd been ten years old and had gone to Shallowater Elementary School. She saw his school picture in the newspaper. He had black hair, cut short, and big brown eyes and was smiling that smile you hung on your face when the photographer says, "Smile now." The fake, phony smile. But she could tell just by looking into his eyes that when Nico really did smile, it would light up his whole face.

Maddie let that part go, but she was like a dog pulling on a dishrag, kept tugging at the rest of it.

"What was it like — visiting your father in prison?" She paused for a beat and then added in a strangely hollow voice, "I won't ever let anybody lock me up in a cage. I'll kill myself. I have to be free."

"You'll have to ask somebody else what it's like to visit a prison inmate. I never went."

"Never?"

"Nope."

"Why not? Why—"

She did turn to Maddie then and she let her feelings show.

"My mother divorced him after the sentencing so there was nobody to take me." Avery was pretty sure that was just the final straw, that her parents' marriage had been a goner even if that hadn't happened. "I could have gone with my grandparents, or other relatives visited him. I didn't go because I didn't want to. I haven't seen him in years, and that's just fine by me. I don't think my cousin, Jude, ever went to visit either, and he was riding in the car with my father when it happened."

Chapter Nine

"Hey, Jude, where you going, man?"

Jude's brother-law, Rick, his sister Dannie's husband, called out to him just as he reached to open his car door. He almost made it. And he didn't have to stay. Jude never should have come here, and he could still leave, drive away. Just let his mother pitch a fit that he didn't come to his own grandmother's funeral.

But Rick had seen him and that would be awkward. Jude hung a smile on his face that engaged the lone dimple on his right cheek. It was singular — there was no matching dimple on the left. When he was a kid, his sisters called him Uni-Dimp.

Jude turned and called back, "Just left something in the car."

Rick approached across the field behind the house where the family was parking and extended his hand.

"Where you been? Haven't seen you in a coon's age. You didn't get the memo that the pandemic's over, you don't have to" — he slathered his words with sarcasm — 'shelter in place' anymore."

"Been real busy is all," Jude said, shaking Rick's hand.

Rick felt in his pocket and pulled something out.

"They tell me I gotta wear a mask, I don't argue, I just put this on." Rick dangled a Lone Ranger eye mask from his finger. "Hey, it's a mask, isn't it."

Jude realized Rick was waiting for laughter, but the best he could manage was, "That's a good one." Then he started toward the house.

"I thought you left—"

"S'okay. I don't need it."

He actually had left something, his vape pipe, but he let it go — smoking would be frowned upon.

Striding beside Rick as his brother-in-law babbled, Jude considered that he did, indeed, know the lockdown was over, maybe better than anybody on the planet. He knew he could come out, re-connect, visit family, go to work … to his therapy sessions. And AA meetings. But by the time it was over, the damage had already been done. Now, it didn't matter.

Jude was surprised at how quickly it had happened. He'd never let it go that far before, had never allowed the process of tearing to continue for so long. That's what it felt like, too. Tearing. Ripping. The sound of fabric ripping that so resembled a woman's scream.

In the past, he'd always managed to stop it. Had gone to therapy, took his meds. Even went to "ninety meetings in ninety days," when his sponsor told him he had to.

But when all that vanished, he felt like one of those shells you see on the beach, a big one, just lying there after the tide has gone out. He'd lost his cell phone — can you believe that? — actually tripped and dropped it down into a storm drain. He'd had no way to communicate with the world, since the Apple Store hadn't been considered an "essential service." Left with a clunky old laptop and bad internet, he'd tried for a while. Struggled against it. But that was then and this was now, and now it seemed he could actually feel the sensation of letting go, of not trying to stop the inevitable tearing apart of his thinking processes and personality.

Jude Kavanaugh had first figured out he was different when he was ten years old. Oh, he had always stood on the sidelines, watching, didn't join into the activities around him because he had no desire to be a part of what was going on in the world. His parents said he was shy, standoffish, that he lacked social skills. And maybe all those things were true, but what he really lacked was motivation. A reason to want to participate, a reason to want to be liked, a reason to want his mother to hug him and his father to approve of him and his sisters to stop calling him names.

That day, a baby bird had fallen out of the nest in a tree into a puddle on the ground and was drowning there, scrambling and splashing, trying frantically to get out. Jude watched it, wondering what propelled the frenzy, what made the little creature fight so desperately to live. Why? What was there in a bird's life that mattered so much it would —

And that's when his little sister, Leanne, seven, had come along. She and the other neighborhood children had been playing ball and she was chasing it when she found Jude at the end of the driveway watching the bird.

The instant Leanne saw the baby bird in the puddle, she rushed over, picked it up, and began drying it with the tail of her shirt, cupping it tenderly in her hands and talking to it like it was a baby.

She'd shot him a disgusted look.

"What's wrong with you? Why didn't you help? The poor little thing was drowning. It would have died. Don't you care?"

No, he didn't care. But he understood, probably for the first time, that he *ought* to care. It ought to matter to him. He should want to help a creature in distress, ought to be kind and loving and giving, all those things.

He'd looked for that caring inside himself, looked for whatever it was that propelled Leanne to save the bird, as he'd looked for whatever it was that made the bird want to be saved — and he couldn't find either of them inside him anywhere. He looked into that place where such things ought to be and found an empty hollowness instead.

In that hollowness, it was cold, dim, and shadowy. He was utterly alone.

No. Not alone.

At that moment, he felt something else in the darkness, a presence. *It* was there. And the knowledge of its presence filled Jude with a mindless terror that was indescribable. He'd just stumbled upon the reality that there was within him a horrifying thing, an unknowable, immensely powerful being that had always been there but had never before that moment shown itself. This was not some terror lurking in the darkness of the world that would climb up out from under his bed or out of his closet. It wasn't in the world around him. It was inside Jude. He could never escape from it.

It owned him.

Jude learned by bitter experience that he had to hide the presence of the Other from the world. He told his sister Danni that a voice told him to throw a frog into the campfire to see what would happen to it, to watch it burn. She'd told their parents and that had ushered in the army of shrinks and institutions and therapists and counselors and uppers to perk him up and downers to calm him down, and all manner of other medications to somehow fix what was different about Jude. When he pushed the blind girl into the pool at the behest of the Other, stomped Danni's china tea set, rung the necks of half a dozen of Grandma Hannah's chickens and pulled up all the neighbor's tomato plants by the roots — saying the Other or "it" had told him to do it — only made matters infinitely worse.

And even if the army of mental health professionals over the years had believed in the existence of the Other, Jude would never have been able to make them understand that there was no "getting rid" of it.

It was a part of him. Sometimes the best part. Nothing out there in the world was as smart as the Other, or as utterly fearless. It propelled Jude forward in his life in a wild dash others called a carefree spirit. He played sports, always won, because he was willing to accidentally jab out an opponent's eye in a pile-up on the field. With the Other's prodding, with its help sometimes, or forced by it on other times, Jude's life became an extension of the wants of the Other.

When Ariana came along, Jude was unprepared for the struck-by-lightning feeling of his attraction to her. From the first moment he saw her, he wanted her, had to have her, and his swaggering courtship had enticed and impressed her. At first, she'd enjoyed his constant attention and over-the-top enthusiasm. But when she tired of his helicoptering her every movement, she tried to break up with him. He set her car on fire. He would have done worse, would have done *anything* to make her his, but he'd gotten a tick bite that gave him Lyme disease, was in bed for six months, and by the time he was on his feet again, she was engaged to Wes Durham, Jude's childhood friend. Before a weakened Jude could do anything to eliminate Wes, Ariana was marrying him, and Jude had to fake a sprained ankle to get out of being a groomsman at the wedding.

On her wedding day, and in the nightmare days afterward, the Other had taken over for Jude, propelled him forward when he was empty inside, kept him upright and functioning.

After that, Jude went into a sanitarium and silenced the Other. He never thought about it in those terms, but that's what he'd done. Doctors finally came up with the right cocktail of drugs to pack the Other in cotton in the hollow place, and for five years, probably the best of his life, Jude lived his own life — carefully, medicated, with therapy and AA meetings keeping him between the fence posts.

Then Covid. Lockdown. Days that became weeks that became months alone. Maybe that was it. Maybe that's why he'd tossed out the drugs and run up the white flag of surrender ... just to have somebody to talk to.

Chapter Ten

DURING THE CAB ride back to her hotel room after her diagnosis, Alex had Googled the word "die" on her phone and was surprised at all the ordinary, mundane things it meant.

Die was the singular form of dice.

Die meant absolutely straight.

And it was an event — the die is cast.

And there were all the phrases. Die hard, die on the vine, never say die, to die for. It even meant, and this had that little "archaic" symbol beside it— to have an orgasm.

Die meant to decay from the tip toward the root — that was for a plant. Die off meant there were only a few left. Died down was for storms and noise, and die out meant to become extinct.

It took up six inches of gray screen in the dictionary app on her iPad.

But right at the top, before all the other weasel words, was the only definition that mattered.

Die: stop living.

Alex Harrington was going to stop living. How do you get your head around such a thing? Stop living! Not be here. Everybody else smiling and laughing and planning, and you six feet under the dirt. (Not Alex. Like the old Bob Dylan song, her ashes would be "blowin' in the wind."")

Inoperable brain tumor.

Well, for starters, shouldn't it be *un*-operable? She'd been an English major in college — a lifetime, a literal lifetime ago — and she was always uncomfortable when someone played fast and loose with the sanctity of the English language. Alex had an *un*-operable brain tumor.

She didn't look up brain tumor, though. Who wants to see a drawing — or worse yet, a picture — of some bloody lump thing that was going to take away *everything*. The whole world. After her doctors at the Mayo Clinic confirmed the test results three times, she'd stayed drunk for something like thirty-six straight hours in a hotel room in Rochester, Minnesota, trying to cope, to figure it out. She'd told the family later that an on-the-blink cell phone was the reason she'd missed all their calls and messages. After that, she'd had trouble even thinking about it. Her thoughts were water spiders that skimmed across the surface of the reality, but never sank into it. She didn't like that analogy, though, because she was arachnophobic — not as arachnophobic as Leanne, but still, Alex would rather die than get killed by a spider. Ha ha.

Alex refused to remember the exact name of the growing *thing*, but it wasn't like some balloon getting bigger and bigger. It was more like the roots of a tree, stretching out farther and farther. That's the reason it was inoperable. *Un*-operable. She'd had a flash of an image when the doctor'd said that, the top of her head open on a hinge and some guy in a white lab coat pulling a weed up out of it. When the roots popped free, her whole brain came out with them.

She didn't know its name, but she gave it an AKA. She'd heard someone say once "a thing as important was what's going to kill you ought to have a name … but no sense wasting a good one on it." So she called it Thelma. Then changed it to Sylvester, because who knew if it was a girl tumor or a boy tumor. Alex had definitely picked the perfect moment in time to grow a gender-confused brain tumor — when the whole world was losing its collective shit about biological realities that'd been accepted by every person who had ever lived throughout the entire course of human history until about fifteen minutes ago. Shoot, there were couples who didn't name their children when they were born — sayonara to pink and blue booties — wanted to wait until the child selected their own gender. And if it required mutilating surgery to change the child's anatomy to match their choice, that's what surgeons were for, right? Why, those people actually—

She heard the siren wailing, saw the red lights blinking behind her, so she backed off. What did it matter, anyway? Alex wasn't going to be around to witness the ten-years-from-now horror of all those mutilated people coming to their senses. She wouldn't see that. She'd be dead.

So she named the un-operable thing growing in her head Persephone, the goddess of springtime, just because she liked saying the word.

Alex had told no one about the diagnosis. Though the lonely weight of the knowledge sometimes threatened to crush her, there were things she needed to do before anybody knew.

It had been a little like stepping out the back of the wardrobe into Narnia when Alex suddenly understood the absolute freedom of impending death. Think of all the things she could do! There were actions you could only contemplate, deeds you could only accomplish, if you weren't going to be around to face the consequences. Alex was all about consequences. Nobody'd given her a "participation trophy" just for showing up at a cross country race. If you worked hard, you won, sometimes. If you were lazy, you came in dead last. Those were the consequences that reality imposed on you. The whole millennial generation had been denied the privilege of learning that important lesson as children, but life was sure as hell teaching it to them now!

But what would you do if you knew that you wouldn't face any consequences whatsoever, if you'd be long gone before anybody ever even knew you were responsible? What could you do with no restraints of any kind on your behavior? As Nike so pithily put it — Just Do It.

And Alex had done it. The unthinkable. By the time "the chickens came home to roost in her henhouse," as Mama would say, Alex would be dust in the wind.

She wasn't finished, of course. It'd all come together unexpectedly quickly, with Monday as the sudden drop dead — pun intended — date, and she took pride in the fact that she never wavered. There was more to do to tie up all the loose ends. But committing premeditated murder was a good, strong step in the right direction.

Chapter Eleven

WHEN GABE SAW the first flash of light in his peripheral vision, he was not really surprised. What made him think that after a shock like finding his elderly aunt dead on the floor in her bedroom, the migraine machine in his head would pass up an opportunity to skewer him. Not surprised, just resigned. But maybe it wouldn't be so bad. He'd had his monthly injection of Vyepti, the newest whiz-bang treatment, on Monday, after all and …

That was just fooling himself. This would be a barnburner. Because it hadn't been seeing Aunt Hannah on the floor dead that had lit the fuse on this one. It had been Uncle Cyrus's screams. The sounds had unlocked that old terror. No, worse than that. The screaming had *unleashed* the terror to wander the dark hallways of his mind, and he wasn't at all certain that he could lay hands on the creature and wrestle it back into its cage.

Gabe had *seen* things when he awoke yesterday in the predawn darkness, and now in the light he couldn't un-see them, pieces of images, memories, *real* memories of the night he had experienced some kind of horrific psychotic break triggered by a high fever and an allergic reaction to a hallucinogenic narcotic that sent him running out into a storm. He almost died of hypothermia and pneumonia. The Gabriel Chandler who woke up in the hospital the morning afterward had opened his eyes to a new world where he only existed in broken pieces. It was up to him to put himself back together again. He couldn't, of course. He was just a little kid. It took the combined efforts of an army of shrinks and therapists over the years to fit all the pieces back in place. But the pieces never fit right after that, and there were pieces missing.

And so he suffered through debilitating migraine headaches. He slept very little — just three or four hours at a stretch. He was often awakened by night terrors — *still!* — that left him screaming and sweating, so incapacitated it drove two wives to divorce. They were all variations of one theme. He's a little boy running away from a monster more terrible than any AI generated special effect. The diagnosis: PTSD. Post-traumatic stress disorder. The first therapist who'd pronounced that verdict over him had been pleased as punch that she'd figured out the obvious. What shot that diagnosis in the foot was the fact that he didn't have flashbacks, because there had been no real identifiable stress. There was no *real* monster. Gabriel Chambers was a six-year-old child who had a *nightmare* about a monster. And that dream had altered the whole course of the rest of his life.

On his way to his bedroom to lie down, Gabe passed his nephew Paul, the fourteen-year-old son of Gabe's sister Brooke, in the hallway.

"Is Avery here yet?" he asked the boy. "She said she was going to cut her Friday classes and come home early." Gabe doted on his oldest granddaughter.

"Haven't seen her," the boy said, without lifting his eyes from his phone.

"I think I'll skip lunch, take a little nap." Paul probably didn't hear him, certainly didn't attend to what he said if he'd heard.

Gabe saw another bright flash of light. That was called an "aura," a classic sign of an impending headache. Sometimes he felt a pins-and-needles sensation in his arm or leg, sometimes his face went numb. He didn't feel nauseous — yet. But he would. Rarely did he survive a migraine without tossing his cookies. Often, he was able to head off the worst of a migraine by taking a drug called Ubrelvy, which also helped relieve the symptoms of nausea and sensitivity to light and sound. It'd give him dry mouth and make him sleepy, so maybe it'd make him drowsy enough to take a nap.

After popping a pill, he made sure the room-darkening drapes were drawn, not so much as a crack of light, and felt his way to the bed and carefully stretched out on top of the bedspread. Gabe closed his eyes and tried to empty his mind of all thought.

GABE DOESN'T KNOW where he is. There's no Star Wars poster on the wall across from his bed and the sheets smell like something sweet, lavender.

Then his spinning thoughts slow, allowing him to think — he and his mother are spending the night at the Harrington House, his Grandmother Olivia's house. Uncle Cyrus's three teenage boys, Sam, Lawson and Jordan, went with their mother to Houston for the weekend, so the huge, creepy old house is empty and quiet.

Gabe is sick. His head is pounding. Every heartbeat blurs his vision and stabs the throbbing pain in his left ear deep into his jaw. His chest is tight and when he coughs, he can feel the goo down there. His mother gave him medicine to make it not hurt so bad and to make him stop coughing, something called co-bean with cherry flavoring to make it taste better, but it still tasted nasty. It did make him stop coughing. It made him dizzy and sleepy, too, but he only dozed, woke up every time his mother came in and put her cool hand on his forehead. He heard her tell his grandmother that his fever was "spiking," a hundred and four, and if it didn't break soon, she'd have to take him to something called an E R. He was wondering what an E R was when he finally fell into a restless, fitful sleep, troubled by dreams of angry voices yelling until —

A horrible shrieking sound rips through his head. That's what woke him — screaming. He puts his hands over his ears to keep the sound out, but it pierces through like an ice pick.

Somebody screaming!

Somebody who's ... what?

What would it take, what would you have to do to somebody to make them scream like that? Chop them up with an ax? Feed them alive to a monster — like the picture in the National Geographic magazine of that fish with sharp teeth that curved back into its mouth so when it bit you couldn't get away.

Another scream starts low and gets louder and louder, becomes a wail. Through blurred vision, he sees that the room is unnaturally dark — the electricity has gone out again.

Or maybe the monster that's eating somebody downstairs made it dark so Gabe can't see it coming for him.

GABE LAY on the bed in the darkened room, too surprised to move. He'd emptied his mind in an effort to ward off the relentless pain that would slam hammer blows into his skull — and into the emptiness had ventured a *memory*. It wasn't a night terror, not a distortion of reality. What he remembered had really happened. He'd been sick. His mother had come into his room — here, in this house — and she'd given him some medicine and he'd dozed off. And then he'd heard screaming. *Real* screaming. That's what had awakened him. He hadn't imagined that part, hadn't conjured it up out of some drug-reaction hallucination. He'd sat in the bed, listening, trying to figure out who was screaming. His mind had been muddied by his fever, but he was still lucid. And then what? The electricity had gone out, the room fell dark. That's it, that's all he remembered.

But his mother had told him, had been telling him for

more than four decades now, that the *whole thing* had been a dream. It hadn't been, not all of it. Why had she lied to him? He'd been awakened that night from a fitful sleep by a *real scream.*

Gabe lay in the dark as the migraine ramped up its pressure in his skull, wondering now, as he had wondered all those years ago — who was screaming? And why?

Chapter Twelve

JULIANNA CHAMBERS, Casey Nelson, and Cassidy Schaeffer sat huddled together on the plank floor surrounded by boxes in the back of the Grandma Liv's attic, trying not to disturb the centuries of dust, it felt like centuries, or they'd all sneeze their heads off. Juliana and Casey were sisters and looked it — both had black hair like their grandmother, Alex, though Juliana wore it short and straight with the left side of her head shaved, and Casey's hung all the way down her back in curls. Cassidy was their cousin, or second cousin, and her hair was a strawberry shade of blonde. But then, Cassidy was a Kavanaugh. Juliana and Casey were Harringtons.

Each the three had a separate cardboard box — storage boxes which might or might not have pictures of Aunt Hannah in them, and they had been dispatched by aunt/cousin Leanne to find any such pictures and bring them downstairs so Brooke's husband, Steve, could scan them in. There were three or four screens — from the funeral home, Juliana supposed — set up in the parlor, and the photographs would be displayed on them in a continuous loop during visitation tomorrow.

None of them was having much luck finding photographs,

59

though they discovered all manner of other things Grandma Liv had saved — she called them keepsakes. Juliana thought that was a quaint name.

Cassidy held up a toy helicopter, GI Joe style. "I bet this was Uncle Jude's," she said. "Chapman calls them heck-loptifers."

"When Willie was little, he called them hopper-poppers," Casey said. She held up a finger-paint drawing — a hand-print, with the name Gabe scrawled in little-kid handwriting — and showed it to her sister. "Dad made this when he was …" She looked for a date on the paper, but there was none. "Looks like kindergarten, maybe first grade. It's adorable, but …"

"But why did Grandma Liv hang onto it," Cassidy finished for her. "I'm thinking the same thing about most of this stuff. Why'd she keep it? Some of it, yes, but …"

"Look at these," Juliana said. She'd found a handful of black-and-white pictures and the others leaned forward, trying to identify the people in the top one, searching for a face they recognized. "That's Uncle Samuel, don't you think, when he was a little boy?"

"No, Uncle Lawson," Casey said. "Remember him talking about that snowman he built in the backyard when he was a kid. He said—"

Cassidy took the disputed picture and dumped it and the others in the discarded box.

"It's a lead pipe cinch it's *not* Grandma Hannah and that's our mission—"

"Should we choose to accept it," finished Juliana. She'd been about to remind her sister Casey about the vintage tele-vision shows they'd watched as kids, how they'd change the channel to *Dancing with the Stars* whenever their father left the room.

She left the words dangling, though, didn't finish. The words brought back to her — and maybe to the others, too —

memories of the *Star Trek* binge some of the family'd gone on last Thanksgiving — the Thanksgiving where she, her sister, and all three of her cousins had been at each other's throats.

AVERY, Casey, and Juliana are crumbling up the dried bread for the dressing. Casey toasting it, Avery putting it on the cooling rocks, and then all of them tearing it into little pieces. Her cousins Leanne and Cassidy come into the kitchen, with Cassidy's three-year-old son, Chapman.

"Need help?" Leanne asks.

"You know what that got the Little Red Hen, don't you?" Juliana says.

"Who's the Little Red Hen?" Chapman asks his mother. That kid is always underfoot and so cute he could get away with murder. Casey's four-year-old, Tally, Juliana's niece, is far better behaved.

"She's a chicken in a story, she goes all around the barnyard asking for help to make bread, but none of the other animals will help her," Juliana says.

"I didn't know chickens made bread."

"It's a story, Chap, work with me here, buddy." Chapman snitches one of the pieces of toasted bread out of the bowl. "So she makes the bread all by herself, and when the other animals smell how good it smells, they come running, asking for a slice. And what do you think she told them?"

"To bring mustred for the samitches."

"It's mustard, hon, not mustred," his mother corrects.

"And no, that's not what she said. She told them that because they didn't help her make the bread when she asked, they couldn't have any bread now."

"Hey, we're here to help," Leanne says.

"When we're almost done," Juliana says.

"There's still plenty to do, potatoes to peel, and hardboiled eggs to shell and make the fruit salad," Casey says.

Daniella picks up a grape and holds it out to the others. "I swear, the ruby in Grandma Hannah's ring is this big."

"That's why I love it," says Leanne. "I put my dibs in on that ring a long time ago."

"Whoa, there, hold your horses," says Juliana. "Aunt Hannah told me I could have that ring when I was five years old."

It's friendly banter, at least on the surface. But there is hardness underneath that you didn't have to scratch very deep to find.

"Seriously," Leanne says, "I really did say that's the only thing I wanted — remember, it was two, three Christmases ago. Everybody wanted to go Christmas caroling but Grandma Hannah—"

"And I'm serious, too," says Juliana. "She really did promise it to me when I was five. It was my birthday and Uncle Cyrus heard her. She was wearing it and I said it was the prettiest thing I'd ever—"

"Then she must have forgot or changed her mind," Leanne says. "She told me I could have it."

Derrick and Damon, Aunt Brooke's two oldest sons, are getting uncomfortable. Nobody wanted to see a family cat fight. They were brutal.

"I'll tell you who doesn't want it," Damon says. "Me. It wouldn't go with a single pair of cufflinks I have."

"Cufflinks? You wear cufflinks?" Derrick counters.

"Sure I do. With a suit."

"And you wear a suit … when? When was the last time you—"

"Why don't you see if Grandma Hannah will give you that Christmas brooch, the one with emeralds and diamonds, set in gold," Leanne urges. "I'm sure—"

"I don't want the Christmas brooch. I was promised the—"

"Well, I do," says Daniella, Cassidy's mother, "if we're divvying up the spoils here. I would love to have that brooch."

"Or the sapphire earrings," says Julianna's sister, Casey. "Or the diamond bracelet that she had special made in the shape of a dragon. It never looked like one, but she thought it did. I have always—"

"I just want my ruby ring," Leanne says. "Ask Grandma Hannah. Just ask her. She'll tell you she promised it—"

"Now that's classy," Juliana says. "'Hi, Aunt Hannah. When you croak, can I have the—?'"

"Fine then, we can ask Grandpa Cyrus, he was there. He heard her promise it to me."

"Why are you all talking about that now? She's not going to give them to anybody until she dies, and she doesn't look sick to me," Derrick says.

Jude speaks for the first time. "Would that she did."

"Jude!"

"Oh, come on, you think there's anybody on the planet who'll shed an honest tear for the old crone."

Everybody knows that Jude has a particular bone to pick with his grandmother. She spent his whole childhood trying to get him committed, kept telling his parents he was crazy.

"Uncle Cyrus does," says Damon.

"Yep, you gotta give her that much," Casey says. "She's got that man tied around her little finger." They all shake their heads. "Anybody want to hazard a guess how she pulled that off?"

"A witch's potion," Avery says.

"Hypnotism," says Daniella.

"Seriously, though," Damon says. "Why do you think that is? Uncle Cyrus is a good-looking man——" He holds up his hand at the protests. "Was a good-looking man, and he still is in the eighty-to-a-hundred-year-old set. And she treats him like shit. Why does he take it?"

"He's just a nice guy," says Avery.

"And nice guy s——" says Casey.

"Finish last!" says Jude. "Well, he does. He finishes last in every discussion, in every decision, in every——"

"Because he chooses to," Casey points out.

"So why does he choose to?" Daniella asks.

"Would you like to go up against that Sherman tank in high heels?" Damon asks.

Juliana turns to Leanne. "Well, you're going to have to go up against her if you think you're getting that ruby ring. She promised it to me."

"No, she didn't! I'm tired of this. Ask Grandpa Cyrus."

Jude rolls his eyes. "Here we go again."

Derrick and Damon's father, Steve, has come into the room during the conversation and catches the gist of it. Holding up both hands in front of him, he says, "Now don't anybody shoot the messenger here ... but I don't think anybody's getting that jewelry." There is a general gasp. "At least not one of us. I heard she's just about decided to give it all to the museum."

"What for?" Casey is horrified. "I can see the Remington and Reynolds stuff. I think it's stupid — those things are worth a fortune— but at least it makes sense, western artists in the Museum of the South- west. Who'd go there to see a bunch of jewelry?"

"She's got some kind of plan is what I hear, wants to put mannequins in the place dressed in period costumes," Steve says. "Authentic ones, the best you can make them. And she's going to display the jewelry on the mannequins."

"Mannequin hookers?" Jude says.

"Why would they be—" Avery begins.

"How can you have a Museum of the Southwest without prostitutes? They were part of the wallpaper. And besides, they're the only ones in her little scenario who'd wear that kind of finery. You think Mrs. Jones out on Route Four would put that ring on her finger to feed the chickens? 'Here chick, chick, chick ... oh, shit, a chicken just ate my ring.'"

"This isn't funny," Juliana says. She's tired of all the bickering. Aunt Hannah did promise her the ring. It'd been on Juliana's fifth birth- day. She remembers it like it was yesterday, how she'd seen the ring when Aunt Hannah was cleaning cake icing off her shoe. Juliana'd said it was pretty — "all twinkly-sparkly" — and Aunt Hannah had thought that was so cute. "I'm going to put it in my will that when I die, you can have this ring." She'd said that! Uncle Cyrus was standing right there, heard the whole thing. Juliana'd dreamed of owning that beautiful ring her whole childhood. "That ring is mine. She promised it to me twenty-three years ago."

"No, she did not." Leanne had a temper, and clearly she was about to lose it. "And even if she did, she's changed her mind since then because she said I could have it a couple of years ago. She told me ..."

. . .

Juliana didn't remember how the argument had ended, only that it'd become a shouting match before it was done, with everybody yelling at everybody else. Of course, none of that mattered now, with all the jewelry going to the museum. Unless ... maybe Aunt Hannah hadn't settled that deal—she'd died so unexpectedly. And if they looked at her *old* will, it would say right there that the ring was Juliana's.

Hmmmm.

She would ask around.

Chapter Thirteen

MADDIE DIDN'T ASK any more questions about Avery's father and the wreck, contented herself with staring out the windshield at the Big Empty stretching to the horizon.

But Maddie'd picked at the scab covering the wound. Not a scar. Scars were for healed wounds, and this one wasn't healed. The flood of memories always started at the same spot.

Itching. And wind blowing through wheat.

AVERY IS careful not to let the screen door slam shut behind her as she steps out on the porch, then she gives her whole body a big wiggle — sooo glad to be out of that silly dress and into jeans and a tee shirt that don't itch. She'd told Mommy when all the flower girls were trying on their dresses that hers was scratchy, and Mommy'd said, "Oh, that's the netting that keeps the dress foofy."

Like knowing it had a name — netting— would make it not itch or something. She'd tried hard not to squirm around. She and the other two little girls were supposed to look straight ahead and not wave at anybody when they passed, and then she and Chloe had to stand still holding the bride's train while the bride did stuff. Avery'd wanted to be the one who scattered flower petals out on the floor — that would have been fun — but Deidra was only four and they wanted the smallest to do that part, said it was "cuter." Avery and Chloe were ten, and Avery was bigger than Chloe, so Avery never had a chance. She'd just had to stand still and not wiggle, wishing her mommy hadn't been the bride's college roommate.

Now that part was over, and Avery is on her way to get a second piece of wedding cake. She'll ask for a piece that has a rose on it this time, made out of icing. And another glass of punch from the bowl where there are big chunks of rainbow sherbet ice cream floating around in it. It's the punch for the kids and doesn't have any liquor in it, but the other one does.

The reception is happening under a big tent in the backyard of the bride's parents. Well, the food is under the awning and the live band and tables and chairs to sit and eat. But there are dressed-up people all over the house and yard — there are six bridesmaids and six groomsmen. Avery wonders if the bridesmaids' dresses itched like her dress did — and maybe Ariana's wedding dress, too. No, probably not, or they'd have changed into something comfortable as soon as the photographer finished taking their pictures like Avery did, wouldn't just be standing around itching. Avery has already decided that she's going to have a big wedding like this, bigger, even, when she gets married. She'll make sure the dresses don't itch, though.

From where she's standing on the top part of the multi-level deck, she can see how big the crowd of people is. She sees it when the commotion starts in the yard down by the road. Somebody … she doesn't know for sure, but it looks like Aunt Millie Kavanaugh, who was wearing a purple dress that was too tight and sat by the aisle on the bride's side in church, screams and starts crying. She's gesturing to her phone, and then other people look at her phone and get upset, too, and a crowd gathers. The people who can see the phone turn around and tell the people behind them what they see. And word about whatever awful thing has happened spreads out from the woman with the phone, one person to the next, looks like wind blowing through wheat.

And then Avery is behind the big hay roll in the field, peeking out around it. She was dressed for running, and when people started hearing sirens, and jumped in their cars to drive down the road, or just took out *running, she hopped over the fence and ran through the field where nobody can see her, because she's sure that her mother wouldn't let her go see whatever it is.*

There's a fire truck with its lights flashing and a Bailey County Rescue Squad truck, and sheriffs' cars, Texas Highway Patrol cars, and the wail of an ambulance stops with a gulping whoop as she crawls through small piles of hay toward the fence where she can see everything.

Everything's jumbled up. People are scrambling around, police officers and firemen, and there's paint spilled all down the center of the road, and the sheriff's department ...

Then she sees it, the mangled bicycle. At least she thinks it's a bicycle, a mashed-up one, like it'd been put in one of those things that compact old cars. It's lying in the weeds on the side of the road. And there's paint on it, too.

Red paint.

That's not paint in the road. That's blood.

What could leave that much blood? Mommy hit a deer one time and the impact messed up the whole front fender of the car, and they went back to see, Avery made her go back to see, and the deer was dead but there hadn't been this much blood. What could make that—

She sees the woman then. She comes running right down the middle of the road from the opposite direction that Avery came from. Frantic, wild. She's Hispanic, wearing sweatpants and a tee shirt, and one shoe, one flip-flop, but the other foot is bare. And she's making this sound, this high, keening sound, like some kind of animal might make if it were caught in a trap.

One of the policemen tries to stop her but she crashes through the yellow police tape they are stringing across the road. Still screaming, she shoves a second officer aside, and a third grabs her arm. Another officer says something but lets her go. She keeps running ... then she stops. Stops dead, looking at the paint, no, the blood on the asphalt, and her eye travels as Avery's did, follows the line of blood to the mangled bicycle in the weeds.

She screams a name.

"Nicolás!"

Screams it again and again as she drops to her knees, or collapses, looking at the bicycle, wailing the name, high and hysterical, and then some officers come to her and they lift her up, talking to her, and whatever they say, she doesn't want to hear, shakes her head frantically from side to side. They've taken her arms and are trying to move her away from the blood and the bicycle, but she breaks free and runs to the bicycle, stops and looks at it. Then she reaches down and picks up something Avery can't see out of the weeds. It's a baseball cap. Avery knows the team, the Shallowater Cardinals, red and black like the colors of Texas Tech. She saw them playing a game against the Muleshoe Mules in the park when she went there to swing on the swings once, remembers the team because of the red and black uniforms.

Was he there in the park that day, the little boy whose bicycle now lies mashed in the weeds?

The officers come for her again, but she still pulls away, looking around. Frantically she starts calling, "¿Dónde estás, Nicolás?"

Avery's best friend is Hispanic, and she knows enough Spanish to understand the desperate words: Where are you, Nicolas?

"Ven aquí ahora mismo!"

Come here right now!

The officers are at her side, gently pulling her away as she continues to call out, demanding that her little boy come. And then pleading for him to come.

"Nico, por favor … estas asustando."

Nicky, please … you're scaring Mommy.

They finally get her into a police cruiser, and pull out onto the road, with the lights flashing, a siren whoop every now and then, probably to make people get off the road and out of the way. Then she hears the siren begin to wail in a solid cry that goes on and on until she can't hear it anymore.

The officers mill around, almost like they're waiting for something, and maybe they are. Avery doesn't know what. They just keep everybody back behind the police tape, and then a Texas Highway Patrol car pulls up and an officer gets out. He has a clipboard and a measuring tape, and he walks around the trail of blood, measures things. She doesn't know what he's doing. And she can't keep her eyes on him. They keep going back to the mangled bicycle in the weeds. She sees the handgrip on the twisted handle bars sticking out above the weeds. It's a Spiderman hand grip, with red and white streamers. She saw it in the store when they bought the Disney Princess handgrips for her bicycle.

Then several officers approach the fence in front of where she's hiding in the hay, moving back to get out of the way of the man with the clipboard. They're talking softly but as they get closer, she can hear what they're saying.

"... not any skid marks to measure ..."

"... didn't even try to stop..."

"... over that kid, dragged him and the bike under the car and then just drove away. Just drove away."

"What kind of monster does a thing like that?"

Chapter Fourteen

JULIANNA MADE herself stop thinking about the jewelry and dug deeper into her box, unearthed report cards from thirty years ago — her father had talked too much in class, big surprise there. She found old pennants, a couple of pre-Barbie dolls, one was missing eyelids and its bare eyeballs stared at her until she dumped it on the discard pile and covered it with a green-haired troll doll, a pile of certificates of excellence in various subjects, curled-up Polaroid pictures with images too faded to recognize, and a handful of Matchbox cars.

Cassidy could have wiggled out of this assignment, played the "pregnant" card — she was due any day now. But she got her husband Andy to chase after Chapman. Andy was a fire fighter, in really good shape with way more energy than Cassidy. She said she'd rather sit in a dirty attic than try to keep the four-year-old from building a fort out of the couch cushions or shooting somebody with his Nerf gun.

Juliana loved the herd of small children downstairs that was growing bigger as different family members arrived — particularly her sister Casey's three, Willie, Tally, and Ethan. What she loved most about them was that when she was tired of them ... make that *when she finished enjoying them* — painting

Tally's fingernails or reading a story to little Ethan— she could hand them back to Casey and Will and walk away.

Happily single at twenty-eight, Juliana was glad she and Jamal had decided to move in together instead of getting married. Neither of them was ready for that, and they certainly weren't ready to have kids! Couldn't have afforded it if they had been with inflation eating up their pay checks. Both commuters, the price of gas — in Texas! — was maxing out their credit cards. Jamal was struggling to establish his law practice, and she'd taken a second job — used her master's degree in interior design to peddle draperies at Macy's during the day and worked as a motel desk clerk at night. Between them, they had over a hundred thousand dollars in student loans to pay back, and just like Grandma Alex predicted, the loan forgiveness plan that would have saved their asses had just been a ploy to get votes. As kids, they'd both been encouraged to aim for the stars, dream big, but so far, success had eluded them, and now, approaching thirty, they were more than a little disillusioned that all the happy talk about chasing your dreams and job fulfillment hadn't amounted to — Grandma Liv's phrase came to her — "a hill of beans."

"Check these out," Casey said. "Cassettes. If we had a cassette player, we could listen to" — she picked up one after another — "Chicago, Creedence Clearwater Revival, The Eagles."

Cassidy held up a handful of discs. "And if we had a compact disc player, we could watch ... okay, these aren't movies, they're computer backups." She dug around further. "But this one's for a DVD player. We could watch ..." She turned it so she could read the label. "Wayne's World."

"I'll pass," Juliana and Casey said in unison. They all laughed.

Cassidy waggled a flat, rectangular box. "I don't believe this. It's a movie rental. Dead Poet's Society. I guess I could watch that for ... what? Thirty years? Forty?"

"Late fee's gonna be a bitch," Casey said.

"This is like being on a cultural anthropology dig. As you go down through the boxes, the artifacts get older and older," Juliana said.

"Maybe we'll find Piltdown Man," Cassidy said.

"That was a hoax," Casey said.

Cassidy readjusted her position on the floor to get more comfortable. She was dressed in a sweatshirt and sweatpants, baggy enough, wasn't wearing the kind of tight, belly-showing top that was fashionable. Juliana thought she'd like to get pregnant just to strut her stuff in that kind of maternity outfit.

"You want this thing?" Casey asked, holding an old throw pillow. "Maybe put it behind your back and lean against the wall? That helped me when I was carrying Tally."

"I'm good." Pulling out the waistband of her leggings, she said, "Won't be long before I won't be able to get into these." She turned to Julianna. "I remember how Kim only wore sweatshirts. I was just a little kid, and she was the first pregnant woman I'd ever seen — dressed in nothing but Spencer's old sweatshirts the whole time she was pregnant with Avery."

"I'm sure that was all they could afford," Casey said.

"Is Avery coming?" Cassidy asked.

She didn't ask about Avery's father, Spencer, of course.

There was that kind of awkward pause then, like there always was when family members were tiptoeing around the gigantic hole Julianna and Casey's brother had blown in the family. She knew he'd been up for parole awhile back, but she wasn't sure how that'd come out. Casey would know. She kept track of it, wrote to Spencer and visited him, Dad and Grandma Alex did, too, of course, and maybe some of the cousins. Alex had gone a few times to Smith Prison in Lamesa. But it was so depressing to go there, to see her big brother and know he was going to be locked up there after she left — she'd think about him as she drove home, that he wouldn't be in a car going anywhere for years. When she sat down to dinner, she'd think of the prison cafeteria, which she'd never seen but had seen plenty of movie versions to paint in the details, sitting down to eat whatever somebody dished out for him, whether he liked it or not. And after a while, the whole thing got to her and she couldn't go back. She hadn't seen Spencer in — she didn't like to think about it.

"Yes, Avery's coming," Juliana said. "She's bringing somebody home with her from school."

"Who'd want to spend the weekend at a funeral in somebody else's family?" Casey asked. "You'd have to be pretty desperate to get away from campus to—"

"Look at this," Cassidy said thoughtfully, holding out a wrinkled envelope to Juliana and a piece of yellowed newsprint. "The envelope was sealed. Read the clipping that was in it."

It was like others they'd found — a clipping of Daniella's engagement announcement, Aunt Brooke in the school play, somebody's Little League team standing beside a trophy. None of them had been in sealed envelopes, though. This one was so old it was fragile.

"It's a news story, clipped out of the ... I don't know what paper."

Juliana turned the clipping over. The advertisement on the other side was for a dry cleaner in "Lubbo—." Had to be Lubbock.

Then she read the clipping aloud.

"Father Paul Daniels, the pastor of St. Augustus Catholic Church on 34th Street in Lubbock, found a surprise on the steps of the rectory on Tuesday morning when he was leaving to perform early Mass. Wrapped in towels in a cardboard box was a newborn baby."

Juliana looked again on the back of the clipping for a date. Besides the "Lubbo" ad for dry cleaning, there was a piece of the newspaper's header. Not the name, which she was sure would be "The Lubbock Avalanche-Journal," but a part of the date. "Just the letter 'y' at the end of the month, then the day, '26, 1976.'"

"So the baby was born … January 26, 1976," Casey said.

"Or February, it ends in -y," put in Cassidy.

"So do May and July," Casey added.

"Spring, summer or dead of winter, that narrows it down," Juliana said and she continued to read.

"The Lubbock County Sheriff's Department as well as the Texas State Police are investigating the incident, but at press time today, there was no further information about the child's identity. The little girl being called Baby Jane Doe was turned over to the Texas Department of Family and Protective Services."

"I've always wondered how the 'Doe' thing got started," Cassidy mused.

Juliana turned the envelope over to see if there were any markings on it and something fell out of it onto the floor. She picked it up. "It's a lock of hair."

It wasn't the first lock of hair they'd found among the boxes. They'd unearthed several — red hair, usually. Locks from all three of Cyrus's sons were there — old and dusty. Apparently, Grandma Liv had a thing for baby hair.

This one was different. The hair was black and curly. Kinky. Looked just like Jamal's hair.

"If this is a 'first lock of hair,'" Juliana said, "the baby was Black."

"So what's it doing in Grandma Liv's box of keepsakes?" Cassidy asked. "Who put it there? Who cut that clipping out of the newspaper?"

"And the mother of all questions …" Casey said. "Why?"

"Why what?" asked a voice from the doorway. They turned to see Grandma Alex standing there.

"Why?" Juliana echoed and got to her feet. "I'll give you a why. Why are we doing this? It's useless. We've been here an hour and haven't found a single picture of Aunt Hannah."

"That's what Mama sent me to tell you," Grandma Alex said. "The pictures are in boxes in the basement."

"Goody," Cassidy moaned. "All this has been for nothing."

Casey stood and held out her hand to Cassidy. Juliana slipped the envelope with the clipping and lock of hair into her shirt pocket.

Chapter Fifteen

WHEN ALEX OPENED the door to her bedroom, the hallway and room went suddenly dark. Electricity was out, blown breaker. In her Dallas condominium that she'd sublet almost two years ago, the electricity had never failed. But that was about the only saving grace of the condo, with its Home-owners Association the residents called Condo Nazis. The Texas High Plains had brought Alex home, and the Harrington House was the perfect place to write her book. It documented the birth of the oil industry in Texas and the oil barons, like her grandfather, Landon Harrington, and his rag-tag crew of rowdy cowboys. She told the story of the pioneers who'd chased their dreams, digging one dry hole after another looking for black gold. The book sold well — didn't hurt that the author's last name was Harrington — but it was an unqualified success in Alex's eyes because it proved to her that she could do it. She could write a book. Her second book was fiction. After a lifetime career as a journalist had disappointed and disillusioned her, she'd concluded that just making stuff up would be more fulfilling than telling a truth nobody wanted to hear. She'd never finish it now, of course, and she regretted that. She would dearly love to know if she had any talent.

Other people were closer than she was to the downstairs breaker box. Somebody'd fix it. The bedroom drapes were drawn, leaving the room in shadows. She patted her pockets for her cell phone and its flashlight app, but she'd left it in the pocket of the sweater that she'd taken off when she got hot helping her granddaughters, Tasha and Sierra — Sydney and Juan's girls— strip the sheets off all the beds in the house to put in the wash.

Feeling her way to the bed, she sat down to wait for the lights to come back on. Over the years, she'd stubbed too many toes, banged too many shins, and tripped too many times to wander around in the dark.

She'd gotten to the attic just as the girls were giving up on finding Hannah pictures in the storage boxes there, and if they'd come upon something else in the boxes that was earth-shattering, they hadn't mentioned it. What was in there that Mama was afraid they would find? It had something to do with that night, Mama had sent that message loud and clear.

The electricity had gone off that night, too. Twice.

ALEX LOOKS down and sees she has blood on her hands. Still. She'd washed them, hurriedly, watched the red water turn pink. She thought she got it all, but she'd had only the flickering candlelight before the electricity came back on. And she had been focused on checking on the children. She can do that one small thing, check on the children. She can do that and not think about what's just happened.

One thing at a time.

The girls are sleeping in one of the bedrooms in the back of the house. Four-year-old Sydney is in the big double bed, but Alex was afraid to put her sister Brooke in the bed with her, afraid the two-year-old would fall out of the big, tall bed. She'd put a protesting Brooke down in a playpen on the floor instead.

Opening the door a crack, Alex allows the light from the hallway to fall across the bed and the playpen. Both of her adorable babies are sound asleep.

She wasn't thinking about it at the time, but later ... afterwards ... the thought struck her that all the noise, the yelling and screaming, could have awakened them. Thank God it didn't! What would she have done if one of the children had wandered downstairs into ... that!

Gabe is sleeping in a room closer to the stairs, but Alex is sure that with his ear infection stopping up his ears, he couldn't have heard a thing.

She doesn't just peek through a half-closed door. She goes into the room to the bed. She needs to feel his forehead to see —

The bed's empty. She looks around.

"Gabe?"

She touches the sheets. They're not warm. The bathroom is dark.

Her heart suddenly in her throat, she flips all the light switches. The boy is gone.

After that, a jumble of flashed images, her terror elongating time, distorting reality.

The dark hallways, her calling, "Gabe! Gabe where are you?"

One bedroom after another.

Not there.

Not there.

Shouldn't have given him that narcotic cough syrup. Some people have bad reactions, hallucinations. Oh, dear God, where is Gabe?

"Gabriel, answer me, where are you?"

The electricity goes off in the house again. How will she find him in the dark if she can't find him with the lights on?

Where could he have gone?

A strobe of lightning flashes outside the window. Because the house is dark inside, there is no reflection on the windowpane, and she can see into the pouring rain in the backyard. Something white is out there beneath a bush.

His soaked body is cold, so very cold. Is he dead?

"Gab-ri-el!"

. . .

THE OVERHEAD LIGHT and the lamp on the bedside table blinked on and then off again. When they came on the second time, they stayed on and banished the awful memories — smoke from a dying campfire disappearing into the darkness.

Alex noticed it then. A piece of paper on the floor in front of the door. She went to it, picked it up and read it. The words were printed in all capital letters.

WE KNOW YOUR SECRET.

What in the world?

She barked out a burp of inappropriate laughter then. Which secret? The secret that somebody else'll have to wear my pink bunny suit and hide the Easter eggs next year, or the secret that I have committed first degree, premeditated, cold blooded, life-in-prison-or-needle-in-the-arm murder?

The paper that'd been shoved under the door was a plain sheet of typing paper, folded once, in half. She turned the paper over. Nothing. The page was totally blank except for the four words printed on the inside.

This was crazy. Nobody knew her secrets. She certainly had not confided in her family — *Oh, in case anybody was wondering — there's a tumor named Persephone eating up my brain and I'll be dead before Groundhog Day. And also, I offed one family member to save the life of another ...* so technically, that wasn't murder, was it? Well, except for the planning it all out part.

No, there was no way anybody knew what was private in Alex's life. So there was only one other explanation for the note — 3-D. Dumb, Dumber, and Dumbest — that's what the sane members of the family called them. Their doting parents actually believed they didn't put bubble bath in the Saint Francis fountain, or a smoke bomb in the Porta-Potty at the Little League park. Her brother Cyrus's three sons had produced a herd of children, grandchildren and great grandchildren that Hannah doted on and their parents never disciplined. His granddaughter, Leanne Giordano, had two sons — fifteen-year-old Peyton, who was Dumb, and thirteen-year-old Ryan, who was … well, even Dumber. Their fourteen-year-old cousin Douglas, the youngest child of Lawson and Cynthia Kavanaugh, rounded out the trio as the Dumbest of the lot. Leanne's boys alone were a force to be reckoned with, but add in Douglas — whose mother called him Dougie, the *Huggable Dougable* — and their combined capacity for mischief was way bigger than the sum of the parts. Leaving a WE KNOW YOUR SECRET note was right up their alley.

Covid Lockdown Arrested Development Syndrome— that would be Alex's diagnosis of their stupid little prank. She could not imagine being locked up in a house with Peyton and Ryan … trying to homeschool them, for crying out loud! — for a whole year. Alex tried really hard to find sympathy and compassion for the kids, hell for all the kids in the country victimized by Dr. Doom, purveyor of the Fauci ouchie. Stuck at home. No school. Remote learning. Never see their friends, deeper dependence on electronic devices — it'd take a decade, no, make that two decades, to undo the damage the deranged government — *not* the pandemic— had caused.

Peyton, Ryan, and Douglas were casualties, the walking wounded. And that was true as far as it went, but Alex was certain 3-D would have cooked up a scheme like this even if the Chinese hadn't infected the world with a virus funded by American tax dollars.

Those three boys were undisciplined little cretins who'd never been held accountable for their misbehavior. That was the long and the short of it. Maybe the poor mutants didn't even recognize what was and what was not acceptable behavior.

Well, she'd make sure they found out.

Chapter Sixteen

As Avery pulled off the highway and started up the long drive to the Harrington House, Maddie said in awe, "It's even weirder looking close up, like something built by Dr. Seuss."

"Wait'll you see the *inside.*"

Because the house had been added onto so many times in a totally haphazard fashion, there were all manner of architectural anomalies. Rooms that had no windows to the outside. Hallways leading from one part of the house to another that passed on the *back side* of rooms that opened into a hallway on the other side. None of the hallways had windows, of course, and were dark, gloomy, and shadowy even with bright Texas sunshine frying the world outside. During thunderstorms and sandstorms, the hallways were black tunnels. There were lights, of course — ceiling fixtures in some halls, recessed lighting in others, the track lighting in the upstairs hallways between the bedrooms illuminating the family portraits lining both sides like the paintings in a museum.

The trouble was, all those renovations and additions over the years had made electrical service in the house iffy at best. During storms, the electricity blinked out, then back on, then

82

off again all on its own — like a flickering Joe's Beer Joint sign. It was something about the wind whipping the wires leading to the house. And inside the house, breakers tripped with maddening regularity. Oh, you could blow your hair dry — this was 2022, after all. And you could use a curling iron to curl it. But if you plugged both of them in at the same time in the same outlet, all the lights might go off on that side of the house. Then you had to feel your way down the coal-mine dark hallways to the nearest breaker box to figure out which switch had tripped. It was just part of life in the Harrington House, accepted as normal because it had always been so.

"Pleeeease tell me it's air conditioned."

Avery read the temperature off the car dashboard. "It's only eighty-two degrees outside. Why would you need air conditioning?"

Maddie looked horrified.

"You Texans! Are you telling me—"

Holding up her hand, Avery laughed. "Joke." Then she hedged. "Some parts better than others, though." Maddie raised her eyebrows. "Be grateful it's not just the gulf stream."

"And that is?"

"Before they had air conditioning, they discovered that with all the other windows closed, they could open the windows on the back wall of the first-floor music room and in the hallway on the top floor, and it would form a chimney effect, sucking air in the bottom — hot air rises — and out the top. Gulf stream."

"How'd they figure that out?"

"Burning garbage caught the grass on fire outside the music room ... Grampa Gabe said you could see the trail of smoke traveling up the stairs and down the hall, floating along like Casper the Friendly Ghost."

"How'd that keep all those people cool?"

"Oh, it didn't. But it was better than nothing."

"How many kids did that hundred-year-old grandmother of yours have, anyway?"

"Only two — this house was built by her husband's family, and they'd had thirteen or fifteen … something like that. Every time they had another baby, they added another room, I guess."

"How'd they afford it? Rob banks?"

"One three-letter word: oil."

She saw Maddie make the connection: Texas oil money. Oh.

"Your family can afford to hire an army of electricians to fix the place, or bulldoze it and build something brand new — why don't they?"

"I think my grandmother likes it the way it is."

Avery had figured something out a long time ago. From the old woman's viewpoint, there was a time once — Avery wasn't exactly sure when that was, but there was a whole century full of years to pick from— when the world was the way it was "supposed to be," when everybody worked hard, sunup to sundown, and sweat and dirt were almost revered, or that's the way it sounded to Avery. When men's hair was properly short and women's skirts were properly long, when the family had dinner together every night— even though they all left the table hungry, and everybody went to church on Sunday morning, Sunday night, and Wednesdays for prayer meeting. Oh, that was a simplistic, glorified view of the way her great-great-grandmother's life had been, but it was more accurate than not. Which meant that Olivia Harrington now looked around her every day at a world so corrupted that it had become an unrecognizable parody of the world as it "should be." She must be horrified by it. Avery often felt sorry for her, living out beyond a normal lifespan into a reality that was not of her making or choosing.

Of course, Avery envied the life Grandma Liv had lived, too, sometimes. The safety and security of *home* and all that once had meant, the unchallenged family unit as the under-pinning that stabilized society. Grandma Liv had never had to worry about the viability of life itself — in a world where crazy presidents were entrusted with nuclear launch codes, on a planet that was slowly dying because mankind flatly refused to stop poisoning it. There'd been no terrorists blowing up innocent people in the world where Grandma Olivia lived her days, and the solution to most of life's problems had been hard work, determination, and grit.

Avery's world was far more dangerous and complex. Hard work might or might not get you where you wanted to go — but there were all kinds of other factors that you couldn't control. You could put in a sunup-to-sundown regimen of effort, could be the best there was at what you did, but it wouldn't matter if you were black and the people in charge were racists. The same had been true in Grandma Liv's day, only she'd been privileged and was unaware of it. The reverse, however, had not been true in Grandma Liv's day. Being the very best didn't mean jack if opportunities were apportioned on a DEI — Diversity, Equity, and Inclusion— basis and you were white instead of Black, Hispanic, or some other margin-alized people group. In the world where Avery had to build a life, all kinds of extraneous considerations trumped talent, skill, and hard work every time.

Not that Avery was opposed to the principles embodied by DEI. Whole segments of society had been disenfranchised for centuries, and they were entitled to special treatment now. She was totally on board with that. Still … she'd slammed into the reality of it the first summer semester when she'd had to have an emergency appendectomy at the teaching hospital. As they wheeled her into surgery, she'd seen the Pacific Islander one of the seniors in her dorm was dating among the med students in white lab coats. A lawsuit was pending against the university claiming that more than a dozen students who were more qualified had been passed over for the med school slot he'd been given — that he'd been selected because he ticked "diversity" boxes they didn't. Maybe that was true and maybe it wasn't. Avery didn't know. But she did know that he'd failed every class his first semester — his girlfriend said so — and his grades had been changed to passing after he protested that the school's "rigorous academic standards" were racist.

And Avery couldn't help it — she was *glad* that he wouldn't be the one cutting her open! But he would be cutting *somebody* open someday. What would happen to that person? It had been sobering to realize that the viewpoint she knew was *right* was flawed, too, in its own way, with bad outcomes that might be unintended but were very real.

"I think Grandma Liv told the family to fix it to suit themselves when she was dead." And, of course, nobody ever considered that she might live for a century, dooming her descendants to decade after decade of darkness, shadows, and feeling along the wall for the breaker box.

Avery parked just beyond the back fence, and the mingled aromas of more than a dozen different dishes filled her nostrils the minute she walked through the back door.

"Sure smells good in here," said Maddie, raising her voice a little to be heard above the hum of conversation.

"Tastes better than it smells. The whole county brings bussin' food."

Coming through the mudroom door that led to the hallway behind the kitchen, they encountered Aunt Cynthia and Aunt Marilou — who gushed over Avery appropriately, and gave welcoming, if confused, smiles when she introduced Maddie.

"All these people are related to you?" Maddie asked as they stood in the doorway looking into the crowded kitchen. "Seriously?"

She nodded, then pointed to Grandma Alex, who'd just come into the room through the parlor door.

"She's my great-grandmother."

"That woman doesn't look old enough to be anybody's great anything. What do you call each other?"

Avery didn't understand the question.

"Call each other?"

"You know, like Cousin Jane and Great-Great-Uncle Joe or ..."

"Oh, nobody says 'cousin' anything or 'great' anything. Then it depends on which branch of the family tree you descended from, Harrington or Kavanaugh."

"Which are you?"

"Harrington. And Alexandra *Harrington* — she took back her maiden name after her last divorce—is my hundred-year-old grandmother's only daughter. I call her *Grandma* Alex, not *Great-Grandma* Alex. But ..." — she looked around, then pointed to a forty-ish woman with strawberry blonde hair — "Daniella *Kavanaugh* Morgan calls her *Aunt* Alex, not *Great-Aunt* Alex. When you're a little kid, every female relative who isn't your mother or grandmother is automatically Aunt Somebody ... unless they're a cousin your age, of course, then you just call them by their first name."

She could tell Maddie was totally confused.

"Never mind." She made a sweeping gesture. "To everybody in this room, the woman who died was either Aunt Hannah or Grandma Hannah."

Two little boys careened off the bodies in the kitchen and blew past Avery and Maddie, one with a big plastic gun chasing the other through the crowd. "That's Chapman Schaeffer," Avery said. "He's Andy and Cassidy's little boy — and he's a handful! I told you about him, remember?" Maddie looked blank. "And the other one's my Aunt Casey's oldest — Willie." She thought about explaining that she didn't call her "Aunt" Casey because she was a Kavanaugh but because she was Avery's father's sister. But there was no point in explaining. You couldn't expect any outsider to keep it all straight.

"At supper tonight, or sometime when everybody's kinda

gathered, I'll introduce you to the whole family at once, so I don't have to drag you from one person to another."

Maddie didn't seem to want to be introduced at all. "Can't I just blend in? Some cousin they don't know?"

"There is no cousin we don't know. Everybody knows everybody. Tomorrow, though, the house will be packed with strangers."

"Strangers?"

"Well, strangers to me, at least. The viewing is tomorrow, and everybody in town — and I do mean *ev-ry-body* — will be here to pay their respects. They'll be lined up through the house and out onto the porches and into the yard."

"What if it rains?"

"It won't rain. It wouldn't dare."

Avery pointed to the back stairs that led to the small, decorated-in-pink bedroom on the second floor where she always stayed when she visited Grandma Liv, and she supposed it'd be hers and Maddie's tonight.

"Our room's up those stairs. It's a cute little bedroom in the back corner of the house right by the stairs. We'll go dump our stuff and then—"

They froze in place when Grandma Alex started banging on a pot.

Chapter Seventeen

AFTER GABE and Alex left her bedroom, Olivia got dressed and saddled up her walker. She moved slowly — she liked to think of it as "regally," which sounded a whole lot better than teetering or doddering — to the elevator only a few feet down the hall from her bedroom door. That'd been a big deal for her, deciding to put in the elevator. It was small and unobtrusive, of course, not much bigger than a phone booth — one of the old-fashioned kind. A cage-like box you could see into rose slowly up and down. On each floor, there was an ornate grill-work door that had to be closed before the elevator would move. She'd finally given in because it got to where wouldn't nobody let her go up and down the staircase without rushing out to hold onto her elbow. She'd told them that if she was to trip with somebody attached to her elbow like that it wouldn't stop her from falling, it'd just break her arm off at the shoulder. She'd finally given up. The elevator operated off a small generator in the basement, so she wouldn't get stuck in the thing when the electricity in the house went out.

Tonight they'd have dinner, all of them sitting down together as a family. But lunch would be catch as catch can ... well, not sandwiches and canned soup or anything like that.

There had, after all, been *a death in the family* and seemed like food had started arriving before Hannah's body'd even got cold. A glance into the kitchen revealed buckets of KFC, cakes sealed in plastic from the Save-A-Lot bakery, trays of cold cuts from the deli at Piggy Wiggly. Oh, sure, there were plenty of homemade dishes, too, but it wasn't the way it usta be when deaths were the occasions when every woman in the county showed off her cooking skills — almost like "covered dish" socials at the church. Wasn't ever enough room in the kitchen for all the casserole dishes, pie pans, cake plates, and pots of simmering vegetables. "Taking a dish to the house" when somebody died had been more than just a social obligation baked deep into the fabric of the community. It had been a source of pride among the women folk, where they displayed the best they could whip together on short notice. Kind of a mini state fair competition. Least that's the way it usta be. Olivia couldn't stifle a small, disappointed sigh. She wouldn't ask who'd brought Colonel Sanders to the party. She didn't want to know. It seemed disrespectful somehow.

THE DINING ROOM and kitchen were controlled chaos ... well, chaos, anyway, when Alex got there. Little kids were running around screaming, her daughters Brooke and Sydney were arguing about something, Avery and some girl Alex didn't know were standing outside the door on the other side of the room, and 3-D sat together huddled over an iPhone. She heard one of them mention Cyrus and another of them giggled and called out, "Whaddaya call a person who wanders around aimlessly ... a 'Meanderthal.'" Then the group collapsed in a gale of giggles.

Alex took a pot out of the cupboard and a wooden spoon.

Bang, bang, bang.

The surprised silence was equal parts rewarding and comical.

Holding aloft the piece of paper she'd found on the floor, she announced. "Two words, people: *Not. Funny.*"

She saw Peyton shoot Ryan a furtive glance that was instantly replaced by a look of pure-as-the-driven snow innocence.

"I'm not calling any names," she said, and then looked pointedly at Douglas, Ryan, and Peyton, "but it stops right here, right now. We clear?"

"What stops right here right now?" Casey's husband Will Nelson asked as he came into the room.

"This," Alex said. She held up the paper, which ignited several side conversations.

"What is it?"

"Where did you get that?"

"I found one of those this morning, too, and I thought …"

"Did you boys do that?" Leanne asked her two sons, who couldn't have looked more angelic if they'd been kneeling for the Pope to grant them sainthood.

Douglas's father, Lawson, took the paper from Will, then read it and burped out a laugh. Of course he did.

She banged the spoon on the pot again.

"So here's the TLDR," she said, talking over Leanne's beginning defense of her offspring. The teens were surprised she knew the term — Too Long, Didn't Read. "*Somebody* pulled a stupid prank. The kind of immature moron who'd do a childish thing like that wants to be noticed. This—" she held aloft the paper — "is a little kid on the diving board crying 'look at me, mommy!'" Ripping the pages in two, and then in two again, she tossed the pieces into the garbage can. "But we're not going to satisfy the pathetic little wuss by looking. Any more of these go *immediately* into the trash." She figured no actor stays on stage after the audience has left.

Chapter Eighteen

OLIVIA MOVED into the kitchen during the momentary hush Alex's words had produced. She didn't catch all of what Alex'd said, just enough to know that somebody'd pissed in her daughter's Cheerios and Alex was giving them what-for about it.

A little boy with curly blond hair came charging into the dining room before she got to her spot at the table, pointed his gun at Olivia, and shot her. A projectile from the barrel landed smack in the middle of her chest, hung there for a moment before the suction let go, then fell to the floor between the wheels of her walker.

"Good shot!" Olivia told the little boy. "I'd fall over dead like I used to when your Grandpa Cyrus shot me" — she made her thumb and finger into a gun to demonstrate — "but if I fell over dead right now it'd probably kill me."

Chapman was one of Cyrus's great-great-grandchildren — maybe another great, she'd lost track. Different generations of grandchildren ought to have their own collective nouns. Nothing standard seemed to fit. Herd of grandchildren? Flock of great-grandchildren. Pod of great-great-grandchildren ... was pod for porpoises or whales? Murder was for crows, of course, and she'd appropriate that one if she dared.

"Chapman Andrew Schaeffer, don't shoot your Grandma Liv!" his mother, Cassidy, cried, and hurried over to snatch the gun out of his hands.

"Where'd he get that gun?" Marilou Kavanaugh asked. "Why would you buy a child a gun and teach them to be violent?"

"Seriously?" said Chap's grandfather, Rick. "You looked outside lately? This is Texas."

"Andy got it for him," Cassidy told Olivia. "I don't like guns."

"I do!" Olivia said, "I was a pretty good shot back in the day. Couldn't go to sleep at night without a pistol in the nightstand."

"Well, the world's not the same anymore, you know," Marilou's sister-in-law Cynthia told her.

God, how Olivia hated condescension.

"Can I have my gun back, pleeeeease," Chap whined, trying to snatch it out of his mother's hands. "I promise I won't shoot anybody else."

Andy Schaeffer sailed into the room and swept the boy off his feet and into the air.

"How about I set you up a target in the pantry, big guy." A door on the back wall of the kitchen led to a pantry large enough to house a family of Haitians — shelves covered with enough food to feed every blond man in the Norwegian Army.

The boy squealed in delight, his mother gave her husband the fisheye, and Olivia made her way to a chair at the end of the table and sat down in it. When she glanced up, she caught sight of Jude Kavanaugh, standing in the doorway where Avery and that girl had been, musta missed Alex's fireworks display. That man hardly ever came around anymore, like he was avoiding the family and maybe he was. She knew he had "mental problems" but didn't nobody ever get specific about what they were, or if they did, she couldn't remember. She caught his eye and smiled at him, and he nodded, gave her a smile that looked like he'd learned how from a manual.

Olivia looked around for Cyrus but didn't see him anywhere. Probably didn't want to come down and eat with the rest of the family. Hannah's death had affected him in ways Olivia would not have predicted. He was devastated, of course. Olivia had been in the background yesterday when they found her, stayed out of the way when Cyrus's cries summoned Gabe to Hannah's room and wailing sirens announced the arrival of EMTs tromping into the house. Cyrus had been hysterical, pleading with the ambulance crew to save her, when even Olivia could see from twenty feet away that Hannah had long since departed this life. Olivia was worried about Cyrus. He was not a well man. She'd ought to send somebody to check on him, see if he was alright.

CYRUS STOOD in the big bathroom in Hannah's "suite." He had come into the room to … what? He couldn't remember. Wash his hands before he went down to lunch? No, they were wet. If he'd come in to wash them, he'd already done it, so why was he standing here? Seemed like there was something important that he was forgetting. Something he was supposed to do, or something that had happened, or was supposed to happen.

Then the fog lifted and he knew his precious Hannah was dead and it was his fault. He wasn't sure why it was his fault, but he was certain that it was. He had done something … some terrible something …

How could he go on without Hannah? She was his anchor. She'd promised to stand by him that day in the produce aisle at Higgins's Market.

· · · ·

HE HAS an orange in one hand and an apple in the other, just looking at them.

"Cyrus?" comes a voice from behind, and he turns to see Hannah standing beside Ralph Higgins. "Cyrus, are you alright? Ralph called and said I needed to come get you."

Why would Ralph do a thing like that? Cyrus's car was parked outside. He'd driven to the market. Or had he?

He doesn't know, and suddenly understands, maybe for the first time, how fundamentally wrong it is that he doesn't know. How can a man not know if he drove into town or not? He looks at Hannah in confusion and she can tell that he's afraid. Nobody but Cyrus ever sees this side of Hannah — the loving, compassionate side. She hid it from other people behind a wall of grumbling grouchiness, but he sees the real Hannah.

"You come on along now, Cyrus," she says brusquely, in charge like she always is. She takes his hand. "We're going down to the drugstore and get us a milkshake." And he follows along beside her like a child.

When they sit across from each other in the quaint little booth in the drugstore's soda fountain — where a sign proclaims, "Just like Happy Days!" — Hannah reaches out and takes both of his hands in hers.

"It's okay, Sweetheart," she says. "I'm here."

But it isn't okay, and he needs to say that. Shaking his head, he says simply, "No." He squeezes her hand as he lets himself feel a wave of fear and despair wash over him.

"I've lost ... me, Hannah," he says. "I can't find ... sometimes I ... it's like pieces of me are missing, things that just aren't there anymore and I don't know how to find them and put them back. Sometimes, I don't know where ..." His voice trails off because he can't seem to say what he means.

But Hannah understands without an explanation.

"Don't you be worryin' anymore about what you don't know. Because I do." She leans toward him and whispers urgently. "I do." There are tears in her eyes and her voice is thick. "I know who you are and where you are so you don't have to. I'll take care of you."

. . .

Cyrus looked at his reflection in the bathroom mirror, then stepped to the sink and turned on the tap. He needed to wash his hands before he went downstairs to lunch. He smoothed his hair down and was glad he'd shaved because they were having company. He could hear the hum of voices downstairs. He wondered which ones of the kids had come over today. He'd ask Hannah. She'd know.

Chapter Nineteen

"... ICED TEA?" her granddaughter Sydney was saying to her,
but Olivia missed the first part. The one — and so far, the
only — area in which Olivia didn't defy all the medical expec-
tations was in her declining hearing. She reached up and
punched the button on the side of her hearing aid to adjust
the volume. Which meant, of course, that the background
sounds of conversation, banging pots and pans, silverware
clattering, and some kind of music floating into the room were
also much louder. Least wasn't no dinging, donging, breaking
glass, dogs barking — whatever sound somebody picked as
their cellphone ring. Olivia's ironclad rule — no electronics at
the table — was inviolate. Course you could tell everybody'd
put 'em on "vibrate" when they'd sneak 'em out to look at the
screen or jump up to answer a call in another room. Olivia
believed cell phones were a way worse blight on humanity
than the bubonic plague, the Spanish flu, and Covid all put
together.

"What did you say?"

"I asked if you'd like some iced tea?" Sydney said. "No,
ice, of course."

Olivia nodded. Alex was in the kitchen fixing Olivia a

plate. Of course, everybody fussed over Olivia. Looked after her, always seemed to be tensed to catch her if she toppled off her walker — alright, that was probably her imagination, but it was reality that her family treated her like a delicate china doll that they must be oh so careful with or she'd break.

Well, she was ninety-nine years old, less than twenty-four hours away from a hundred, so she figured that entitled her to some deference. She didn't mind the china doll part. What really chapped her butt was the sense that everybody thought she was some kind of mindless twit. They never engaged her in complex conversations. Though she couldn't hear very well even with her hearing aids, she could think just fine, and she hated being treated like an intellectual two-year-old. At least by the younger ones. When no one ever listened to you, really listened, you could begin to lose the ability to tell whether or not you were making sense when you talked.

She shook her head slowly. When she dropped the bomb on them after the funeral on Sunday, they would *all* be questioning more than her thinking ability and wouldn't likely be treating her like a fragile china doll. She'd brought all her faculties to bear in considering what was best for the family, though, and had not come to her decision lightly. Oh, sure, it'd be easier just to let it all slide, not make waves, particularly right here at the end. But Olivia had never been one to let things slide.

"Grandma Liv," said her great-granddaughter Juliana, who was seated on the other side of the table with a plate of what looked like Kentucky Fried Chicken in front of her. "Do you know what this is?" She held an old envelope in front of her, then reached in and pulled out something even older and yellowed. A newspaper clipping.

"Does anybody know?"

The moment woulda passed on its own if Juliana hadn't noted the lack of curiosity around the table and got miffed by it. "If nobody knows, what's the clipping doing in the box of family papers?"

That didn't get much of a rise out of them, either, and Olivia thought maybe …

"You got that out of one of the boxes *in the attic?*" asked Millie, the plump little wife of Cyrus's oldest son Samuel. "How'd you stand it? The last time I was in that attic, the dust set off my allergies, my eyes swelled up, and I sneezed for something like an hour."

"Xyrtec," Juliana said. "A pill a day keeps the allergies away." She dangled the clipping in the air as she went to the coffee pot on the counter and started to select what kind of custom coffee she wanted.

Custom coffee. Coffee'd ought to taste like coffee. How hard was that? But noooo. Nothing was good enough the way it was. Everything had to be new and improved. Just once she'd like to see a product advertised: "New, but not near as good as it was before."

Laying the yellowed piece of paper on the countertop beside the pot, Juliana continued. "It's a clipping out of *The Lubbock Avalanche-Journal* — at least that's my guess — a news story about a baby abandoned on the steps of some church on Thirty-Fourth Street. It says a priest …" She picked up the paper and read from it. "… found a surprise on the steps of the rectory on Tuesday morning when he was leaving to perform early Mass. Wrapped in towels in a cardboard box was a newborn baby."

She put the paper back down and fit a little container of French vanilla or caramel or peppermint or mocha or whatever into the machine. "So what's the clipping doing in the box?"

"What's the date on the clipping?" Brooke asked her niece.

"Some month that ends in a y — that part's torn off. But the date is the 26th, 1976."

"That was four years before I was born," said Daniella. "That'd make the baby … what, forty-six?"

"That's not all that was in the envelope," Juliana continued. "There was a lock of hair." She held out her palm, but Olivia couldn't see what was in it. She didn't need to see to know what it was. "And the baby was African American."

"That ups the ante on interesting," said Juan Gutierrez, Sydney's husband. "A Black newborn abandoned in 1976, I'm surprised it even made the paper."

Juliana turned from Juan and looked directly at Olivia. "Did you put the clipping and the lock of hair in the box, Grandma Liv?"

Olivia looked into Juliana's eyes and proceeded to lie like a rug. She actually managed a smile. At least, she thought she was smiling. It was hard to tell for sure since her whole body had gone completely numb.

"I ain't got no idea how that clipping got into the box." She made a gesture to the others at the table. "How do you all think it coulda got there?"

She looked around for Gabe. He always had something to say, but he had never come downstairs to lunch. Probably had one of them headaches. His opinion wasn't missed, though. Everybody had a theory. Everybody except Alex. She just sat there, looking down at the food on her plate. Never said a single word.

Chapter Twenty

OLIVIA WAS grateful to be distracted from the discussion of the newspaper clipping by a vibration on her wrist. She looked down at her Apple Watch — which both her children, Cyrus and Alex, had joined forces to make her wear. It was either that or some kind of device on a lanyard around her neck so's she could summon help if she needed it — the proverbial "I've fallen and I can't get up" button. She'd argued vehemently that she hadn't fallen in decades, only used a walker because of a bad knee that'd got to where it sometimes collapsed out from under her with no warning. But the knee didn't have nothing to do with her being old. She'd messed up the knee in a riding accident twenty years ago — and even then she hadn't been the one that stumbled. It'd been the horse, fell right on her knee. No, come to think of it, it was more like forty years ago. No … actually it'd happened before she got pregnant with Alex … who just turned seventy-two. She shook her head. And she'd lived every minute of every day since then, heart pumping, bowels gurgling. The wonky knee was the only physical limitation she had. The only one. She was about as proud of that as she was her hair. Her joints worked, her plumbing worked — heart, liver, gall bladder and whatever — and her heart and lungs were in waaaay better shape than Cyrus's.

"Okay, so you haven't fallen in thirty years," Alex'd said. "But Mama, your bones are brittle now. A fall that thirty years ago wouldn't even have skinned your knee could break your arm or hip or worse."

She'd lost the battle in the end, picked the watch because it offended her dignity less than some stupid Help-Me! necklace. And the watch was useful for more than summoning the medics, had a weather app so she'd know if it was supposed to rain … and a telephone.

That phone was ringing now, well, vibrating on her wrist. She looked at the number and her heart leapt into her throat. It was Reginald Underwood. She was sure no one in his life ever called him Reggie. He was her lawyer. Was there some last-minute glitch?

She had an iPhone, too. The only thing she used it for was to listen to audiobooks because it sent the sound directly into her hearing aids. It did the same with telephone calls … but the phone was on her nightstand. The watch didn't send telephone calls into her hearing aids, so when she answered a phone call on her watch, anybody standing nearby would hear not just her side of the conversation but the other side, too.

She had to take the call, though. Had to.

She answered it and whispered into the watch face, "Hold on. I need to go somewhere I can talk."

The bathroom was too far. It'd take too long to maneuver her walker through the crowd to get there. But the door to the pantry was half a dozen steps away. Everybody was busy talking about what Juliana had found in that box in the attic. Nobody'd notice if she slipped into the pantry for a couple of minutes.

Olivia stood up slowly and had barely got her walker situated proper in front of her before Gabe's daughter Casey wanted to know what she needed and could she get it for her.

"I just got wondering if there's any of Hannah's sweet pickles left in the pantry, maybe in the back."

"Oh I don't think so, I'll look—"

"Don't trouble yourself, dear. I can look for myself, thank you." She put just the hint of indignation in her tone, enough to get Casey to back off. When Olivia opened the pantry door, she was shot in the chest, for the second time this morning."

"You gotted in front of my target!" Chap lamented. "You made me miss."

The boy stuck out his lower lip, as if hers was the gravest of transgressions. He might have been tuning up to a tantrum, she couldn't tell with the little ones anymore, didn't seem like it took nothing a'tall to set them off.

"You didn't miss. You got *me!*"

She told Reginald, "I just got shot."

"Did it kill you?"

"Not so far's I can tell."

She stepped the rest of the way into the pantry and closed the door behind her. Then she moved down between the shelves, past the oversized hot water heater to the window at the back of the room. Most folks didn't have a window in their pantry. The old house had been added onto and redecorated and "renovated" so many times over the years that there was even a door on the third-floor hallway that didn't open into nothing no more, just a wall.

"Who are you talking to?" Reginald asked.

Reginald Underwood was a round little man as broad as he was tall — looked like one of them Weebles. *Weebles wobble but they don't fall down.* Reckon kids still played with Weebles? Prob'ly not. They'd likely gone the way of pet rocks, troll dolls, Magic Eight Balls, hula hoops, and Appalachian apple dolls.

Over the years, the other members of the family had got attorneys of their own. For some of them, their personal affairs needed some kind of specialty lawyer, like Cyrus's oldest, Samuel, and his real estate. But mostly they didn't feel no more loyalty to Underwood, Armstrong, and Conklin — who'd served this family well for more'n sixty years! — than they did to where they got the oil changed in their cars.

Olivia had stuck, though. She understood loyalty, and since Reginald and his firm now represented only Olivia Rose Harrington, she could direct them to do whatever she wanted with her affairs. And not only would they do whatever she asked, they wouldn't tell nobody about it, couldn't tell anybody.

"Chap and I are in the pantry. He shot me in the chest but I'm recovering nicely."

"Oh."

"I had to come into the pantry to talk or the others would hear every word you said."

"Can't have that."

The little boy stood with his back to her now, launching one projectile after another at the bull's eye made of typing paper taped to the door. His father had colored crude concentric circles on it with Magic Markers.

"So what's wrong, Reginald?"

"Nothing's wrong, Mrs. Harrington." She'd given up trying to get him to call her Olivia three decades ago. "I just wanted to confirm your plans. What with Mrs. Kavanaugh's sudden passing—"

"Well, she sure coulda died at a more convenient time, I can tell you that." Then she thought how self-centered it was to be upset that somebody's death messed up your plans. And maybe it did, maybe it didn't. Olivia wasn't sure yet. She had planned to sign the papers Friday and then tell the family what she'd done on Sunday when they all showed up for the surprise one-hundredth birthday party they thought she didn't know about. She figured that was a good time because they'd be together in one spot then — certainly not *everybody* like had gathered here, but a fair number. Now, though … to announce a thing like that after a birthday party was one thing. To announce it after a *funeral* was something else alto-gether. "Shame Hannah won't be here to pitch a fit when I drop the bomb."

"Knowing your family, I'm sure there'll still be plenty of fit-pitching to go around without her." True that. She laughed out loud when Reginald told her she needed to be "buckled in, with your tray table up and your seatback in its upright and locked position."

"I ain't decided 'bout telling 'em. I hate to wait, though, 'cause I don't want them to get wind of something 'fore I get a chance to explain why." Not that any of them was likely to understand when she did.

They talked about the specifics of what she was planning for a minute or two, and she could tell he still wished she'd change her mind. But it was made up.

"All right then, let's just make sure everything's still in order."

How could it not be in order now if it was in order the last time he went over it with her and nothing'd changed since then? But she supposed he was just being thorough, so she tried to listen as Chap's bullets made *thwuck, thwuck, thwuck* sounds when they stuck to the target on the back of the door.

She gazed out the window as Reginald's voice droned on, going over the particulars. There wasn't no bird feeder outside this window like there was outside the other windows in the kitchen. Olivia had got her great-grandson Spencer to build it for her — he was always good with his hands — but it hadn't never attracted many birds. Wasn't a big bird population in West Texas what with there not being a whole lot of trees to nest in.

When Cyrus and Hannah'd moved in, Hannah'd took over, of course — like she done everything else. Hannah wanted to see birds — and not just any birds. She was deter-mined to see hummingbirds.

Never one to allow an unpleasant reality to get in the way

of whatever it was she'd decided to do, Hannah'd studied up on it, then hired a gardener to plant columbines, day lilies, and lupines under the windows, fox gloves and hollyhocks too. Every spring, she commissioned a planting of impatiens and petunias. Then she'd gone out and bought hummingbirds! Olivia didn't know where she'd gotten them, might have known at the time but couldn't remember anymore. She did remember Hannah'd had to keep replenishing the supply every year. She couldn't never get two of them to mate up and lay eggs and have babies.

Olivia was sure Hannah would end up having to do the same thing with that stupid koi pond in the backyard. She'd got that bee in her bonnet more'n a year ago and Cyrus had been horrified — absolutely did *not* want to dig up the whole backyard. But there was no talking Hannah out of a thing once she'd purposed in her mind to it. Even though Cyrus had got real upset, more worked up than Olivia'd ever seen him, Hannah'd ignored him, said in three days he wouldn't remember why he hadn't wanted the pond in the first place. Hannah'd scheduled a backhoe to show up Monday morning to start digging.

Olivia sighed. Now she supposed the backyard would remain undisturbed. And maybe all Hannah's jewelry and them art things would remain in the family, too. She'd been hellbent to donate it all to that Museum of the Southwest of hers, but Olivia didn't know if that'd all been all sewn up. Her dying so sudden and all, maybe she hadn't signed it all over yet.

She heard that word — "sign"— and tuned back in to what Reginald was saying.

"… Monday morning."

"Come again."

"I said I'll bring out the final papers to sign Monday morning so you don't have to come into the office."

Oscar was supposed to take Olivia and Hannah to what

Hannah believed was Olivia's medical checkup in Amarillo on Friday. She smiled when she pictured Oscar — grizzled old coot in a weathered Stetson and work-worn Tony Lama boots — looked like he'd just walked off the set of some Western movie, just needed a sidearm slung low on his hip. She'd told him if he'd dress up like one, she'd call him a chauffeur, since it was his job to drive her wherever she needed to go. He'd made some kind of grunting sound and spit in the dirt in reply. Once they got into the car, Olivia'd planned to tell Hannah that the real reason she was going to Amarillo was to finalize everything with Reginald Underwood. Yeah, Hannah dying sudden like she done did throw a monkey wrench into things alright. And come to think of it, the reason Hannah'd wanted to go with Olivia on Friday was that Hannah needed to pay a visit to her own attorney that day. Maybe all that jewelry was still up for grabs, too. Goody. What a kerfuffle *that* was gonna be.

Chapter Twenty-One

BESIDES ALWAYS FUSSING OVER HER, the family never would let Olivia do anything to help out when there was work to be done, made her just sit there while they dust and swept and cleaned the kitchen — scraping the remains of food off the plates into the sink. So *wasteful.* The way they heaped out vegetables and casseroles and pieces of ham and chicken onto their plates and then didn't eat more'n half of what they'd dished out! Olivia coulda told them they'd left on their plates enough food to feed a whole family, that there was lots of hungry people who'd take their leavings and be grateful for it, but she'd given up saying things like that decades ago. She hated the sound of the disposal, grinding up all that good food like some hungry monster. Least they coulda put it in a compost heap, but they didn't even have a compost heap.

"We need to use paper plates," her great-granddaughter Leanne said. "With everybody here there's two sinkfuls of dishes that won't fit into the dishwasher. I just chipped a fingernail and the dishwater's drying out my cuticles."

Washing dishes is drying out your cuticles? Well, bless your heart.

. . .

MAMA MUSTA GOT the littles in the house soon's she seen it coming, but Olivia is a long way from the house. Ten now, old enough to help with the farm work, she is out in the cotton patch, hoeing weeds. What was the use in doing that? Them pitiful little cotton plants wasn't never gonna grow big enough to produce flowers, let alone bowls with cotton in them. But you had to try. Had to keep at it. What else was there to do?

She'd have heard her mother calling her sooner if she hadn't been wool gathering, remembering what it used to be like when there was rain and everything was green and the cotton plants grew head high — her head. Daddy used to let her swim in the cattle trough at the base of the windmill when Mama wasn't looking. Mama said that water was nasty, them cows slobbering in it, that Olivia'd get some bad disease. But on a hot day, with the sun blazing down out of the blue bowl of sky that covered the plains from horizon to horizon, the water'd felt so deliciously cool it was worth getting sick for.

"Ohhhh-livvvv—iaaaa," she hears her mother calling, but the words are almost carried away by the wind that'd picked up some since Olivia took her hoe right after lunch and walked down one of the dry rows between the even rows of cotton plants, all the way to the end. She'd chop the weeds out of that whole row before sunset. Once that'd have been a job even Daddy couldn't complete in an afternoon. Now, the weeds was as starved for water as the cotton, sprouted up out of the dry dirt—

"Saaaandstorm!"

Olivia hears that word right enough and whirls around to see it bearing down on her from the ugly brown western sky. She drops the hoe, runs two steps, then turns back, picks it up and carries it with her. Leave it in the field and might not be able to find it after the wind rearranged the dirt there, leaving dunes sometimes tall as snowdrifts.

Running with the wind at her back, she strains to make it to the house before the heart of the storm reaches her. If it does, she won't be able to see more than a couple of feet in front of her. The wind will whip her hair into her face, rip at her skirt, blur her vision, fill the air all around her. She won't be able to find the house! And the terror in that thought gives her the strength to keep sprinting, ignoring the stitch in her side.

She drops the hoe. She can run faster without it.

Mama's on the front porch watching her approach, one hand tented over her squinting eyes, and making come-on gestures with the other, crying out something that Olivia can't hear.

The wind suddenly slaps her in the back and almost knocks her down, whirling around her, the sand scratching her skin. Mama and the porch vanish in the sea of swirling brown, but Olivia keeps running the direction she'd been running, can feel the slight indention of the space between the cotton rows with her bare feet, reaches out on both sides to feel the dancing cotton plants, using them as a fence to guide her to the porch.

She stumbles, falls into the row of cotton plants, tries to get up and can't tell which one of the rows she'd been running in. Suddenly, she's not even sure anymore what direction she was running. She gets to her feet terrified, confused. She can't just stand here, but if she runs off the wrong direction in the storm …

A figure materializes out of the swirling dirt in front of her. Daddy! He grabs her hand and drags her beside him back to the house, pulling himself along with a rope he'd tied to the porch railing. By the time they get to the house, Olivia can't see anything with the dirt and grit in her eyes, can't breathe. She staggers up the porch steps and Daddy opens the screen door. The wind instantly rips it out of his hands, yanks it free from the bottom hinge and bangs it into the side of the house. They stumble into the kitchen and Daddy slams the door behind them. It's mid-afternoon, but the kitchen is so dim Olivia can barely make out the forms of the furniture through her squinty eyes.

"Get on down here," her mother says from beneath the kitchen table and lifts up the sheet she has laid over it to form a tent. The littles are huddled together there — three stair-stepped boys, three, four, and six years old. They are all breathing through wet wash rags covering their mouths and noses.

"Why didn't you come when I called you?" Mama snaps as she pulls a damp washrag from the bowl with about an inch of water in it and hands it to Olivia. "Shouldn't never have got so far from the house."

The air is better inside the tent, easier to breathe than in the kitchen where Daddy is easing himself down on the floor. There isn't enough room for Daddy in the tent.

"This here's a bad 'un," he says as he leans back against a cabinet, sand raining down on him out of the ceiling.

They huddle together under the table while the wind attacks the house and it creaks and groans in response. Olivia is sure that this time the house won't hold, this time the wind is too strong. It will rip away the planks nailed together in the walls, tear the shingles off the roof, grab the whole structure and scatter its parts and the people in it across the prairie.

It eases off some, enough for Mama to crawl out into the kitchen and pump more water into the bowl she's using to wet the rags on their faces. The white rings of clean around the littles' mouths shine in the dim light. Jeff'd crawled into her lap as soon as she sat down. The sandstorms terrify him, and now the three-year-old is huddled so tight against her, Mama has to peel him off to replace his washcloth.

Hours drag by before the storm finally gives up and retreats. The wind is still sighing outside, but not strong enough to keep the big grains of sand aloft, and they settle into sculptured mini dunes that track in a line across the front and backyards.

The family emerges like rabbits out of a hole into the kitchen. Daddy stands up and hugs Mama. Olivia can see the outline of his body in the dirt that covers the floor, the table, and every other surface in the house.

Olivia shakes her head and sand flies out from it like drips of water off a wet dog. She is the filthiest, was out in the wind. Her mouth is gritty. There is sand in her shoes, in her everything — even her underwear. Mama pumps out just enough water to dampen the wash rags again, but this time she uses them to wash the children's faces and hands.

"Gate's gone, but most of the fence held," Daddy reports as he comes stomping back into the house. "Posts is buried on the west side. I'll dig them out at first light."

And then ... they do what they do every time a sandstorm tries to chew up their little farm and swallow it. What they've been doing for so long Olivia can't even conjure up in her mind the daydream she'd had as she hoed weeds in the cotton field, the images of green plants and cotton falling out of the bowls and cool water in a cattle trough. They light lanterns so they can see to clean. Everyone helps, even Jeffy. They dust the dirt off the surfaces, the countertops in the kitchen, and tables in the parlor onto the floor, and then carry it outside in dustpan loads until the floor's clean. While Olivia takes all the bedclothes, sheets, and blankets outside and shakes the dirt out of them, Mama makes dinner — a pot of beans and a small pan of cornbread. They eat what she's prepared with grit in their teeth and leave the table still hungry. Then Mama and Olivia do the dishes, using as little water as possible. Mama hands Olivia the glasses and she sets them in the cabinet — upside down, of course, to keep out the dirt.

OLIVIA ROSE SLOWLY to her feet, moved to the sink and stuck her own glass under the faucet and turned on the hot water, rinsed it out thoroughly, dried it and set it in the cabinet upside down. Before she even got settled back into her chair at the table, Leanne's younger sister Danni opened the cabinet and began depositing a handful of other glasses out of the dish drainer, setting them in a neat row — still dripping, didn't even take the time to dry them. When she got to the glass Olivia'd just put there, she flipped it right side up to match the others.

Olivia watched the rest of the kitchen cleanup in silence, feeling very tired and very old. They shooed her away, politely, from the table because they was gonna bring up them picture boxes from the basement and spread the contents out on the table to go through. There was nothing "incriminating" in those boxes, Olivia was sure. Nobody'd been taking pictures that night.

"I think I'll go lie down for a bit," she said to nobody in particular among the worker bees finishing up the kitchen. "Worked so hard, I'm plum wore out." Nobody caught the sarcasm either.

Then she brushed off offers to help her upstairs — how'd them people think she got in and out of the elevator when they wasn't around to help her do it? She rode in the little phone booth box to the third floor, started down the hallway, pausing to look out the window at the prairie spread out in front of the house all the way to the horizon.

Somebody got out of a car that'd just pulled up and parked out front. He looked familiar, but at this distance with her old eyes, she couldn't quite make out ... oh, my. She sucked in a breath. The young man was tall and slender. Not skinny, not like he'd been when he left. He'd filled out, shoulders broad, muscled arms showed out of the sleeves of his shirt. He had a beard, too, neatly trimmed — not scraggly like you'd expect from somebody'd just got out of prison.

Chapter Twenty-Two

WHILE THE REST of the family was downstairs at lunch, Gabe drifted, the migraine medicine he'd taken before he lay down engaged in a valiant battle to keep his debilitating pain at bay. The medicine was winning, at least for the moment, but it was merely a reprieve, not a victory. He'd gotten no sleep at all last night, and as he relaxed, he finally he drifted off.

Sleep vanquished the specter of the migraine and its agony. But it opened the door to the dark place where all the monsters waited. They came for him.

He tossed and turned.

Perhaps he willed himself not to wake up, because if he did, he'd be fully aware of the pain it would take the drug another hour to fully relieve. Or perhaps he remained asleep because he was held captive by the nightmare images playing like a video on the inside of his eyelids.

HE'S IN A DARK PLACE, where bright light flashes and then is gone. He is terrified, wants to cry out, to yell for help, but he's so scared he can barely draw in a breath. And he needs to be quiet! There's a monster here.

It's murdering people — tearing them to pieces and eating them. It will hear him if he cries out and will come and eat him.

Jaws clamping down, jagged teeth tearing him apart. It will rip his arms off first so he can't defend himself, then rip off his legs so he can't run. Then it will bite his head off in one great gulp and swallow it down its slimy gullet.

Hide!

Another scream tears at his ears.

He can't hide — it will find him because he's scared. Everybody knows monsters can smell fear. He has to run away, out into the darkness beyond light, into the bowels of the rumbling storm where the monster can't smell his fear.

He staggers, falls, gets up and falls again. His wobbly legs won't hold him. The world is spinning around him. He's dizzy and loses his balance, bounces off walls in the darkness, but his terror drives him forward. He can barely walk, but he has to do more than that. He has to run.

He stumbles into a dark tunnel that goes down, down, endlessly down. No light of any kind. He is falling into hell, where the demons will eat him alive for all eternity. The screaming echoes off the walls around him louder and louder until a final ear-splitting screech ... and then silence. The monster has caught his scent. He hears it lumbering toward him, but all he can do is curl into a tight ball and whimper.

BAM! Bam! Bam!

Gabe sat up at the sound. The monster was gone. The terror was gone. Reality returned with a vengeance, and he was instantly awash in a wave of nausea from the pain in his head. A shaft of blinding light fell into the room from the doorway where the door was open just enough for a little boy to put his head inside.

"I knocked as quiet as I could," the boy said. Which he hadn't. Gabe was certain he'd used one of those battering rams SWAT teams used to break down doors. "Mama said to wake you up, to tell you — there's somebody here you'll want to see!"

Having delivered his message, the kid turned on his heel and went running back down the hall.

"Who …?" Gabe launched the word out into the emptiness that'd been occupied by the little boy with a battering ram.

Groaning, he moved his feet off the bed and onto the floor. The room lurched and a wave of nausea washed over him, taking him all the way to the brink, then washed back out to sea.

This had better be worth getting up for.

Chapter Twenty-Three

Avery felt bloated, stuffed, as full as a tick! She'd texted Rye a selfie with a huge piece of chocolate pie. Rye'd texted back: "Bring me a piece on Sunday!" with a row of pleading-face emojis. She and Maddie had eaten some weed gummies after they took their bags upstairs, then went back downstairs with the munchies. Food hits different after a little weed. As they headed back toward their room, Avery considered that at this rate, she'd gain five pounds before she got back to Lubbock.

Maddie had been … what was the phrase? Socially awkward around the family — even mellowed out with weed — and clearly the family didn't know what to do with the big girl with blue hair.

"Let's do some more Elden Ring when we get back to the room," Maddie said.

Translate that: let's hole up by ourselves and play video games instead of hanging out with your family. Avery wasn't surprised. Maddie didn't know anybody here … but hey, she'd known what she was getting into when she signed on to go to a funeral for somebody she'd never met. Avery liked video games, particularly this one, but she wasn't near as good as Maddie. That girl must have invested serious time to master a game where it took Avery hours and dozens of repeated attempts to defeat a single boss — the monsters in the ruined medieval fantasy world of the game. Again, not surprising. It was becoming more and more clear to Avery that Maddie's people skills were every bit as limited as the other girls in the dorm had said.

"That game just kicked my ass!" Avery remembered the hulking giant that flew into the air and slammed both fists down on her knight in shimmering steel armor, crushing him into the ground. Then crimson letters faded into view on the screen. YOU DIED. "I lost my last rune arc."

Raising her hand to cut off Maddie's response, she added, "I *tried* summoning Melina, but she got flattened as soon as I got to phase two."

"Just keep moving so you don't get hit. I can show you how to get into Mohgwyn Palace. I just finished Mohg—"

"It's not as easy as …" Her voice trailed off. They had come out of the hall into the sitting room. Standing there was a man.

It couldn't be. He wasn't out of prison. If he'd been out of prison, somebody would have told her. It wasn't—

He turned and saw her, and his shock/surprise/wonder morphed into happy emotions that glowed on his face. Yep, it was her father alright.

She froze, would have turned around and gone back the way she'd come, but Maddie was behind her, blocking the doorway. Besides, why should she go running out of her grandmother's house where she had as much right to be as he did?

"Hello … Avery?" he said, taking a step toward her. "It is you, isn't it? Avery?"

He'd certainly changed, didn't look anything like the few pictures of him that still hung on the walls, the ones she couldn't avoid seeing even though she wanted to. He was older — duh, of course. She'd changed more in eight years. The last time he'd seen her, she was a little girl. No wonder he wasn't sure who she was.

She thought about the letters then. She'd read the first few. Maybe for a year, she opened them and read them. They were stilted and formal and … anonymous. They could have been addressed to Any Little Girl, Anywhere, USA.

How are you doing? Do you like school this year? Who's your teacher? What's your favorite subject? Stuff like that.

Sometimes, he'd put in personal things, when he had anything personal to talk about.

Your Aunt Casey told me she saw you at church and you had a cast on your arm. She said you fell off the monkey bars at school and broke your arm. Did it hurt?

Of course it hurt, moron. It was a broken arm, for crying out loud. She didn't say that, of course. Didn't say anything. Never wrote back a single time.

His letters kept coming, though. After all, he had a lot of time on his hands to write letters. Eventually, she tore them up and put them in the trash as soon as she got them, without reading them. He still wrote. Every couple of months, she'd get something. She'd gotten one back in May, as a matter of fact. Maybe he told her in that letter that he was getting out, so maybe he thought she knew. Well, she didn't, and it felt like such an intrusion, such an outrage that he should be here, rubbing elbows with the family like he belonged here, like he was still one of them.

He gave up his right to a family, his right to be a card-carrying member of the human race, when he left a mangled bicycle beside the road, when he put a little boy in the ground and never even looked back.

Why couldn't he just go away and stay away and never bother them again?

Her anger pried her tongue off the suddenly dry roof of her mouth and propelled words from her throat.

"I didn't know you'd be here. I thought you were still locked up."

Maddie stood behind her, still blocking a retreat. But Avery wasn't in retreat mode anymore.

"I got out—"

"Why did you come here? Do you think anybody here wants to see you?"

She might as well have landed a punch square into his gut. He responded visibly, as if he'd been hit. The color drained out of his face.

"I'm sorry if my presence upsets you—"

"It does!"

"—but I came to pay my respects to Uncle Cyrus's wife." A lot of people in the family referred to Aunt Hannah that way. Probably in an effort to remind themselves they had a reason to be civil to her.

"She's in the parlor. You can go tell her goodbye … and then leave."

"I'm not going anywhere, Avery. I—"

All the air whooshed out of her then. Her anger had carried her this far, but the fire of it had fizzled out. Now all she felt was … sad. And disgusted.

"Suit yourself. Just stay away from me!"

Grandma Alex appeared in the doorway then, stood staring at her great-grandson, and then her hands flew to her mouth.

"They said you … oh, *Spencer* … I thought I wouldn't ever get to see you again—"

Then she rushed across the room and flung her arms around him. Avery turned and headed down the hall in the other direction.

Chapter Twenty-Four

WITH THE KITCHEN table cleared off, Jude's sister Leanne directed traffic as he and his other sister Dannie, who was Cassidy's mother, along with Derrick, Damon, and Paul McDowell, Brooke's three sons, and their twin cousins Zoe and Daphne Kavanaugh, brought up boxes of pictures from the basement. Leanne was arachnophobic — you couldn't have dragged her into the basement with a team of Clydesdales and the Budweiser beer wagon. The basement door was always locked, not because there was anything valuable down there, but to keep children off the narrow, rickety stairs with no handrail and away from the population of what Grandma Liv believed were mice but the rest of the family was convinced were rats.

Leanne's husband Rick hauled up an armload of picture albums and set them on the table with the boxes where the family could go through them for pictures of Grandma Hannah.

When they all set their boxes down and began to scatter, Leanne called out, "Everybody hold your horses. No way am I going to get stuck doing this all by myself."

Rick managed to successfully rescue Derrick and Damon

from the task, telling his wife he needed them to help him assemble a crib for Casey and Will Nelson's ten-month-old son, Ethan.

But the others were stuck.

"I'll give everybody a pile," Leanne said, digging into the first cardboard box overflowing with pictures, grabbing double handfuls, and depositing piles on the table in front of everybody. "Find pictures that have Grandma Hannah in them. There must be tons of them."

There was grumbling all around, but Leanne plunged ahead. "When you've gone through your pile, put the Grandma Hannah pictures here" — she pointed to an open space on the table — "and dump the rest of them in this box," indicating a huge empty box on the floor between her and Jude.

"Here's one." Fourteen-year-old Paul McDowell held up one from his pile. It was a photo of a man standing beside a "Tasty Barbecue" sign in the shape of a pig. "She's the one on the left."

Grandma Hannah had gained at least fifty pounds since she and Grandpa Cyrus moved to the Harrington House with Grandma Liv. Jude had heard one of the men from the funeral home talking to the other, saying that Grandpa Cyrus gave them a blue dress for her to wear and they'd had to slit it up the back to get it on her.

But making fun of your recently dead grandmother was a bridge too far.

"When I tell your mother about that remark, you can lean over and kiss your cell phone goodbye for a week." Leanne growled the words. "I'll see if I can get her to ground you, too."

"Aw, I was only—"

"Out! Go help your brothers put that crib together."

"But I—"

"Now!"

The boy left in a huff.

Zoe held up a picture taken at one of the backyard pizza parties, but Grandma Hannah's eyes were closed. Dannie found one where she looked like she'd just swallowed a jalapeño.

"Come on, people, work with me here," Leanne moaned. She was tall and pudgy, had inherited Grandma Hannah's body type. Couple that with acne scars and thick glasses, and it was no surprise that her older sister Dannie always had boyfriends and the only boy Leanne had ever dated was Anthony Giodone, and she'd married him. "None of us wants to spend the whole afternoon doing this. If we all help, we can find what we're looking for and be done with it."

So they set to work in earnest then, sifting through boxes containing a staggering number of totally uncatalogued and unorganized photographs, from shots of Christmas 1998 to Aunt Alex's wedding — one of them. As they worked, they tried to catch each other up on their lives. The cousins didn't get together often. Oh, different ones of them cruised in and out of each other's orbits — at intermittent backyard barbecues for the whole clan when one of the far-flungs came home for a visit. But continental drift was evident, their lives growing more and more separate. Jude figured it was inevitable. He didn't care, but he thought the others might miss it once gone.

Even as a kid, it had been apparent that his cousins shared some kind of bond that he didn't, some sense of kinship, maybe genetic unity that somehow eluded him. He was just beginning to relax though, was actually enjoying the banter between Zoe and Daphne, who bled University of Texas orange, and Danni, an alumnus of Texas Tech, when Paul burst back into the room.

"Guess who's here!" he cried, not waiting for guesses. "Uncle Spencer."

Jude was sure his gasp was audible, but he couldn't control

it, and then couldn't manage to draw in another breath afterward.

"Spencer?" A single word from everyone's lips.

"How do you know?"

"Are you sure?"

"If this is a joke, it's not—"

"It's him. He's got a beard, doesn't look like the pictures anymore."

There was a shuffling of feet in the dining room outside the kitchen and then a man appeared in the doorway, a stranger, except he wasn't. Spencer. He looked surprised, like he hadn't expected to see so many people.

"Oh," escaped his mouth, and then he just stood there.

He had changed, was different in many other ways than just the beard. He was taller, bigger, more muscled, had filled out. He'd become a man.

"Hello everybody," he said. Even his voice had changed. It was deeper, a low baritone. "I didn't know … Grandma Alex just said there was pie in the kitchen, and I haven't had lunch, so …"

Zoe broke their communal trance.

"Spencer, it's so good to see you," she said, and leapt to her feet to go offer a hug. Daphne did, too, but Jude and his sisters were spared the awkward gesture by Aunt Alex's appearance in the doorway. She was radiant, obviously thrilled by the unexpected appearance of her black sheep grandson.

She pulled on his arm. "Come see Mama, Spence. She saw you from the upstairs window when you got out of the car but thought she must be imagining it. You can get pie later." She threw a glance into the room. "Don't you eat all the pecan pie. It's Spencer's favorite."

Then a wave of "we won't"s and "we'll save him some"s washed them out of the room and they were gone.

Silence washed into the room on the next wave.

"That was certainly a conversation stopper," Danni said, and a chuckle relieved some of the tension around the table. Then everybody drew a breath and began to talk at once."

"… know he was here …"

"… never dreamed he would show up …"

"… thought he wasn't due to be released until …"

"… with that beard and all …"

Jude had to get some air, had to get out of here, had to get away from all these people who would read the look of distress on his face and wonder what he was upset about.

"Whoa there, Bro, where do you think you're going?" Leanne asked when he got up from the table.

Somehow, he managed not to babble, actually did have somewhere to go.

"To get my suitcase out of the car. I need my allergy medicine." He heard himself keep talking. "Has Aunt Cynthia got the room roster put together yet? I'll take the bag to my room if she can tell me who's sleeping where."

"You're in one of the second-floor bedrooms — end of the hall on the right, by the stairs, I think," his sister Danni said. "But you'll need to check the sheet." She paused as a thought occurred to her. "We could put Spencer in with you."

"Bunk in with me" Jude was incredulous. "What is this, some kind of sick joke? You think I want to—"

"We'll have to put him somewhere. Who knew he'd show up? And that bedroom has twin beds." She looked around. "I don't hear anybody volunteering to sleep in a double bed with him."

"Yeah, he was in prison! And you know what they do in prison—"

"Put a sock in it, Paul!" Jude snapped. "You want Aunt Alex to hear you?"

But the boy was on a roll. "There's this video on YouTube that this guy made who'd just gotten out of prison and he described—"

"Want me to stuff that sock down your throat?"

Jude didn't mean to sound so harsh, but he was furious — at himself. If he'd had any idea Spencer would show up — shoot, he didn't even know he'd gotten out. His parole hearing wasn't scheduled until ... that didn't matter. He was out, period. If Jude'd known he'd have to face Spencer, you couldn't have gotten him here if you'd put a gun to his head. Let Mama pitch a conniption fit. When she'd called, he'd tried to weasel out of it and she'd said, "It's your grandmother. It's not like you have a broken leg or anything."

The words had drilled such a hole in his belly that he hadn't been able to talk. Yeah, that old broken-leg dodge had saved his ass. If it hadn't, he'd have been the one in a prison cell fighting off the cons who wanted a piece of fresh meat!

Stop it!

Leanne stepped in to keep him from decking his cousin. "Go get your pills or your inhaler or whatever and get your butt back here."

He glanced at the handful of pictures she was holding in her hand, and that's when he saw it. It was glowing, outlined in red light — at least that's how he saw it. The top picture on the stack in her hand was a picture of a kid, a little girl with blonde curls standing in front of some other little girls in pretty dresses, smiling at the camera. Nothing remarkable about it, nothing anybody else would notice.

But the sight nailed Jude to the spot.

In the background of the shot was a convertible, *his convertible!* The driver's face is turned away, but he has red hair, cut short, and he's wearing a bright red shirt.

His eyes shot up to Leanne's face, knowing she'd seen. How could she not have seen? It was right there, inches away. Like most of the other pictures, there was a date and time stamp. He couldn't see it from where he was standing but he didn't need to to know what it said. How could he possibly explain away a picture like that, taken only a few minutes before the horror that changed the whole family?

But obviously she hadn't seen, not yet anyway. He didn't dare reach for it. Grabbing it would call attention to it and she'd look at it then, actually see it. Examine it.

For a lifetime — three seconds — he stood frozen before Leanne dumped the handful of photos in the discarded photos box by her feet and said to him, "Go on." She shooed him out of the chair. "And don't take all afternoon." She gestured at the piles of photos in front of the others seated around the table. "Look what all we still have to go through."

He had to go. There was no way to retrieve that picture without drawing attention to it.

Chatter about Spencer started immediately as Jude left the kitchen and headed toward the front hallway. His head was spinning.

"Don't be gone long," Leanne called after him.

Chapter Twenty-Five

JUDE HURRIED out of the kitchen, down the hallway, and out the front door, weaving his way through his parents, Sam and Millie, who were talking to his Uncle Lawson. He didn't stop to talk to any of them, just headed for his car.

"Don't be gone long," Leanne had said.

"DON'T BE GONE LONG." Jude's mother's voice wafts out to them above the general din of the crowd on the patio. Jude doesn't bother to respond. He is so frantic to get out of the crowd, out of the reception, out of the whole scene, that he'd leapt at his mother's request to go get more ice, and he will drag the task out for as long as he can.

He is drunk, so unsteady as he crutches out to his car that he almost falls. Ought to chuck the things now, no need for the pretense anymore, but he can't very well show up at a wedding on crutches because of a severely sprained ankle — with ACE bandages wrapped around it to make it look swollen and a brace from a medical equipment store — and then as soon as the ceremony is over, suddenly be able to walk fine.

"Be healed!" he blurts out. Spencer looks at him. He'd had to recruit somebody to come with him because he can't drive with his right foot trussed up like a Christmas turkey, so he grabs the first likely candidate.

His cousin Spencer is standing by the punch bowl, looking bored. It isn't until later, way later, that he learns that Spencer was leaning against the punchbowl table because he was so drunk he might otherwise have fallen down.

Everybody's drinking. That's what you did at wedding receptions, right?

He catches a glimpse of Ariana as he crosses to his Firebird convertible, top down, parked under a tree by the mailbox. And the stab of pain that slices into his heart is so acute, it takes his breath away. Ariana in a beautiful wedding dress, with little pearls on the front and a veil that hangs down behind it so far that Avery and Chloe had to walk behind her to hold it up. Ariana, with her face radiant and her long blonde hair entwined with daisies. Ariana, the vision of a beautiful bride that he'd entertained for as long as he can remember. She is every bit as lovely as any fantasy could have made her. Only she isn't his bride. She has just become Mrs. Wesley Durham, the enchantingly beautiful bride of his childhood friend.

Jude had been asked to be a groomsman. No way. No way in hell. He would not stand there only a few feet away from her and look on while she married somebody else. So he'd faked the sprained ankle. Can't go hobbling down the aisle with a bridesmaid on your arm when you're on crutches.

He'd hung around in the sanctuary long enough to see her walk down the aisle on her father's arm, grabbed a seat on the aisle and watched her come toward him so he could entertain the fantasy one last time — that she's marrying him, the look of rapt adoration on her face is for him, not for the man in a tux standing on the dais behind him. When she walked past Jude, he stepped into the aisle behind her and her father and hobbled on his crutches out of the church.

And ever since that moment, he has been concentrating on wiping away that image, the one he'd angled to get. Now, the image has filled up his whole body. All he can do to blot it out is to get drunk. And so he does.

Turning away from the brief glimpse of Ariana, Jude concentrates on crutching frantically across the front yard toward his Firebird. It is, of course, the most expensive thing he's ever owned. He hadn't wanted to buy it, but it was a prop. Like his stylish clothes and the upscale apartment his job in his father's company has made possible. He's just trying to fit in, to be like everybody else, to silence the constant prodding of the Other to … do things, dark, ugly things.

Suddenly, he needs that car, the thrill of driving fast, careening around corners with the wind in his hair — away, away, away from his heartbreak. When he and Spencer reach the car, he leans against the trunk, reaches down, and begins unfastening the Velcro straps that hold the brace in place.

"Why are you—" Spencer asks.

"It was a joke, okay," Jude snaps, "a ruse, a gag." He tosses the brace into the back seat along with his crutches but doesn't take the time to unwind the ACE bandages off his ankle, just hobbles around the car toward the driver's side.

"Hey, I thought I was driving," Spencer says.

"I lied." He pulls open the door and slides in behind the wheel, then looks up at Spencer. "You comin' or not?"

"Can I drive on the way back?" That's what this is about. Spencer agreed to go with Jude to get the ice because he wants to drive the sports car.

"Maybe. Get in."

Spencer hurries around the car and leaps into the passenger side of the vehicle. Jude guns the engine and tears out onto the road, leaves a twin trail of rubber tracks where he peels out as he heads toward town.

Those rubber tracks … they become a big deal later on. They prove recklessness from the moment the car left the reception.

And nobody sees them drive away. Witnesses say later they saw the two of them leave the reception together — Jude on crutches and Spencer beside him. That becomes a very big deal later on, too.

As soon as Avery closed the bedroom door behind her, she said to Maddie, "Put your stuff down and then go get those magic mushrooms out of the car."

Maddie didn't say a word, just turned on her heel and left the room. Avery thought maybe the girl's people skills were better than everyone thought — she'd certainly picked up on the fact that Avery wanted to be alone.

She sat down on the bed and grabbed hold of her emotions. She would not cry! She had shed the last tear she ever would for that man a long time ago. Now she was angry, furious. How dare he show up here, come waltzing in like he owned the place — like he could hold up that silver thing in *Men in Black*, punch the button and they'd all forget what he did. Well, Avery wouldn't forget. She'd *seen*.

Nobody in the family knew that, though.

After the policemen walked away from the fence and she could make her way to the hay bale in the field unnoticed, she had run back to the house — ran the whole way, got there with pieces of hay in her hair and stickers stuck the bottom of her jeans. She got all the way to the backyard before she stopped running, and when she did, the horrible stitch in her side suddenly made her nauseous, or maybe it was thinking about what she'd seen. Either way, she threw up all the wedding cake and punch into a rainbow-colored pile of puke in the grass.

She didn't tell anybody what she had seen because she'd have gotten in trouble. And because she couldn't tell, she couldn't explain why she was so traumatized by what her father had done. Oh, everybody was upset. Her mother was a complete basket case, didn't know or care how Avery was handling the situation because she was too wrapped up in her own reaction. Mom didn't *stand by him* in his hour of need or anything like that. She bailed at the first opportunity, and Avery was absolutely fine with that. Avery didn't remember much about those first years before everything settled, just that she spent tons of time with her father's huge family — her mother only had a sister in Omaha — and after a while those family members stopped inviting her to go with them to visit her father in prison because they knew what her answer would be. A couple of times Grampa Gabe tried to get her to talk about it, but she shut him down.

So now, Avery was probably the only person in the family who couldn't stand to be in the room with the man! She balled her hands into fists and pounded them on the bed. Grandpa Gabe, Grandma Alex, Grandma Liv … they were probably over the moon happy that he was free. What was she supposed to do with that? Nothing! Absolutely nothing. If they wanted to welcome him back into the fold with open arms, that was their business, but not Avery. The image of the little boy with brown eyes who never got to play another game of baseball swam in the air in front of her.

Avery would never forget.

She had her emotional ducks in a row by the time Maddie returned.

"They're dried, not fresh," she said, holding out the baggie. "So they'll be bitter. We'll need some tea."

"We'll make some after supper and bring it up to the room."

Chapter Twenty-Six

GABE WAS in the junk room when the overhead light suddenly went out, plunging him into absolute darkness. The room had no windows and there wasn't much light shining through the doorway because it opened off a hallway, which was also dark. He'd come here looking for some kind of spray sealer to use on one of the flowerpots in the parlor, one of the big ones, that had a crack in it. He and Spencer had volunteered to try to fix it without having to take all the flowers out.

He *and Spencer.*

The joy that rippled through him made him want to laugh out loud. Spencer was out, he was free! Well, maybe not completely free, something about a halfway house. It was clear Spencer did *not* want to talk about it, just wanted to re-engage with his family and be normal again, so Gabe hadn't pressed. He'd find out when Spence was ready to talk about it. All that mattered was that he was here!

Reaching into his pocket, Gabe took out his cell phone but didn't turn it on immediately. The momentary darkness felt good on his pounding head. Bursts of light flashed in his peripheral vision. He called them 'graine lights. Not much in life would have gotten him out of his bed with a headache this bad, but his son released from prison — that'd do it every time.

THE WORLD AROUND HIM VANISHES, and he's a little boy, cowering in a ball on the floor of the back staircase that leads from the second floor to the kitchen. He's terrified. There's a spike of riveting pain deep inside his ear, and he can hear rumbling. Thunder.

Maybe he should just hide here, not go out into the rain.

Putting his good ear to the door, he listens, hears nothing. His heart and breathing slow. Maybe the monster left, got full eating all those other people … what people? Who did it eat? People, just people, just somebody, not anybody he knows, and it isn't hungry anymore. Then he hears sounds in the kitchen, footsteps maybe, but no light shines under the doorway because the electricity is out. Besides … monsters don't need light. They can see in the dark. There is a thump — something big fell — with a grunt. Then the sound of metal clunking to the floor, followed by an angry, growling murmur. Somebody is mad. Somebody or something.

GABE BLINKED and his eyes opened to the semi-darkness of the junk room, and for a moment he couldn't breathe. Then he grabbed a shelf and leaned his forehead against it, taking great heaving breaths.

A flashback. People with PTSD had those, soldiers suddenly transported back to the jungle or the desert fighting for their lives.

Gabe had never had a flashback, and clearly that's what this was. In fact, until a few hours ago, he'd never even had a real memory of the night he'd hallucinated a monster. And he hadn't had time or the emotional energy since then to process that memory. He hadn't imagined everything that'd happened that night. Some of it was real. He had been awakened by *real screaming*! Then Spencer's presence had shoved everything else in his mind to the back of the bus. The battering ram on his bedroom door had summoned him to the best news he'd had in ... eight years. Eight long years. His only son was finally home.

Of course, the battering ram had awakened Gabe out of a nightmare, not a memory. Slightly different, but always fundamentally the same, night terrors had stalked his sleep his whole life. Debilitating migraines were somehow tied to the night terrors, though he never figured out how. He couldn't do anything about them but suffer — as a youngster, teenager and young adult, the night terrors and subsequent migraines ruled his life. He missed so much as a boy — a sleepover at his cousins' house, Boy Scout camp, family vacations — things he either didn't do for fear he'd have a night terror, or did (bravely) do until a night terror and migraine completely spoiled everything. Until he'd finally stumbled upon the ... *release* (and the cure was definitely as bad as the disease), he had been destined to live the pale shadow of a life, in a permanent state of sleep deprivation from staying awake, fearing the night terrors or actually experiencing in a horrid, visceral way the vivid images of blood and monsters with teeth and tentacles. But this was not that. He was wide awake and not dreaming. What he'd experienced, the flashback, it was *real*. It had actually happened.

The scream he'd heard before dawn yesterday, Uncle Cyrus wailing when he found Aunt Hannah's body — that's what did it. That scream broke something inside Gabe because it was just like *something that'd really happened*. He'd *remembered* that earlier. First jogged-loose memories, and then flashbacks? Was he finally cracking up? Spencer, always blunt and to the point, had pointed out that Gabe did not look good. He didn't, of course. Others hadn't noticed — well, the observant ones did — because they saw him frequently, and the change, the deterioration, had been gradual.

Tapping the flashlight app, he continued to search the shelves and drawers for the spray can. Spencer looked good, tanned and healthy and strong. He remembered the first time he held the baby, his baby, in his arms (think wide-eyed innocent meets horny teenage boy who manages to perform without a migraine). He didn't know how to hold a baby, was terrified he was going to drop him. Amy didn't know a whole lot more about parenting than he did, just nineteen, children raising children. The marriage didn't last, of course, and his life became about seeing Spencer every other weekend and Thursday nights. And he never missed. He was determined not to be a workaholic like his mother — but fathering that way was an awkward, strained construct, not like real life at home, where you wandered around in your underwear on Saturday morning while your son ate Cheerios at the kitchen table. You had to *go* somewhere, *do* something, not just hang out and do life. Amy'd remarried and moved a hundred miles away, so he had nothing but a motel room to take his son to. But it was a construct that framed and defined father-son/daughter relationships for millions of fathers, just in case he decided to get all pouty about it. He had to admit it kept him active. That's when it started. That's when he'd stumbled upon what he later came to call "the release." He could go back in his mind and pinpoint the exact moment it had sunk its vicious teeth into his soul. Spencer had been there.

Chapter Twenty-Seven

JUDE HEADED FOR HIS CAR, parked in the field beside the house. He didn't drive a Firebird anymore. When he'd finally been released from the hospital almost a decade ago, he had used the insurance money on the totaled Firebird to purchase a black Jeep. And after that, a Honda.

He'd never really had a desire for a luxurious lifestyle, just knew he was supposed to, so he'd faked it. He was an astute observer of other people, watched those his age and learned to talk their talk, walk their walk. If his peers yearned for fancy things, success, a corner office as a CEO of some big corporation, then he appeared to yearn for them, too. He never asked himself what he really wanted because there was no point in it. He knew that when he looked into the black maw of his inner being, he would see hollow emptiness. And the Other.

Whatever the Other wanted, Jude wanted too.

His family kept him afloat financially — his mother pampering him because he was "fragile" and "different" and had "emotional issues." He never worried about the future because, well, he was a Kavanaugh. His family had money. His Grandma Olivia was sitting on a fortune — millions. And

Grandma Hannah'd had her own money, even before she married Grandpa Cyrus — but she'd been planning on giving all that, plus all her accumulated treasures, to the Museum of the Southwest she'd founded. Maybe she'd already done that, or maybe she died before she had the chance. It didn't matter. You only had to look at Grandma Liv — she'd be a hundred years old, for crying out loud, in a couple of days. And Grandpa Cyrus had all manner of other things wrong with him besides just being senile. The wealth would start sliding down the mountain to the younger generations pretty soon now.

But he wouldn't be enjoying the fruits of his ancestry. Would they lock him up when they saw that picture?

His heart slammed in his chest like a sperm whale in a fish tank. Taking the key fob out of his pocket, he tapped the button and the trunk opened to reveal his suitcases and the bag for his dress suit. He was one of the pallbearers. But he didn't get them out, just paced back and forth behind the car, trying to calm down and think.

Who'd taken that picture? It could have been anybody. What was in the background hadn't registered with whoever took the photo, or they'd have said something at the time. It's not like it was a secret what'd happened. The family had been in the middle of a media hurricane for months before the dust settled.

The headlines still haunted him.

Police Investigate Hit-and-Run Fatality

Ten-Year-Old Boy Dead, Hit-and-Run Driver Suspect in Custody

Son of the Prominent Harrington Family Charged with Vehicular Homicide

He shook his head. He didn't remember that part. Didn't remember any of it, and he was grateful for that. If he'd seen the kid go flying over the car and tumble off the trunk into the street …

He had seen the police recreations of the accident. How the boy had been in the street — and there was no "bike lane" but he had been close to the curb and was wearing a red Texas Tech tee shirt so it's not like he would have been hard to see.

He pushed the images out of his head. He had to think. If anybody saw that picture and put it together ... what would happen? It didn't *prove* anything ...

Yes, it did. Jude had been wearing a red shirt that day, had taken his suit coat off so you could see it. Spencer still had a dark suit on. And Spencer's hair was blond and curly, hung down over his collar in the back. Jude's was Kavanaugh red.

The picture proved a guy in a red shirt with red hair had been driving the Firebird when it pulled away from the reception. How could Spencer have been driving half a mile down the road where the kid was hit? Did they stop and change drivers? Why would they do that?

Since the facts of the case were never in dispute, how much investigating did the police really do? Probably not a lot. Was there some way, some forensic method they could use to determine who was behind the wheel of a car that was involved in an accident? Maybe. But it was too late for that now, wasn't it? All the evidence was gone. The car didn't exist. It'd been crushed into a cube and sold for scrap years ago. The road wasn't even the same. It'd been widened and repaved. Was that picture enough to convince the police they'd got the wrong guy?

Would they ... what? Arrest Jude? After all these years? Would they prosecute him? Surely, some pricey lawyer could get him off if the only evidence they had was that picture.

But the family would know.

Spencer would know.

Spencer would come after him, demanding an explanation. He wouldn't have one. Jude didn't know for sure what had happened, couldn't remember all of it, just snatches. The wind in his face, drying his tears. How hard it was to work the gas pedal and the brake with a foot the size of a bowling ball. Is that why he didn't stop? He doubted it. He didn't think he would have stopped for anything that day. He remembered the grass under his head and the sensation that he was spinning around in a circle.

HE OPENS HIS EYES, but the world doesn't right itself, so he closes them again. He is lying on his side in the grass, can smell the grass, feel it tickling his nose.

He smells dirt, too, freshly dug-up dirt. And gasoline.

And smoke. Something is burning, something plastic, because that it a particular kind of stench.

He opens his eyes again, can see nothing but the grass in front of his face. He rolls over onto his back so he can see — The motion sends lightning bolts of pain through his whole body. His arm, his right arm. His chest. On his back, he's having trouble breathing, like there's a weight on his chest. Without turning his head — he doesn't want to move anything again to awaken that pain— he can see a sight that doesn't make sense, the image isn't right, and it takes him a moment to figure out that it's a car upside down, he can see the wheels and smoke or steam or something wafting up in the air from it.

He blinks, but in the time it takes to blink, everything has changed. He is on his back, strapped down on something, people in blue uniforms leaning over him, their lips moving but he can't make out their words because of the great roaring sound in his head.

So he closes his eyes again, just blinks. And when he opens them, he is in a room with a white tiled ceiling.

"Jude?"

Someone speaks and he turns his head enough to see his mother leaning over him. He's in bed. A hospital — he can see those little bags handing on poles above his head. His whole right arm is bandaged. And he doesn't hurt, but the hurt is there. He can tell that there is great pain, but right now there is a veil of numbness between him and the pain and he is profoundly grateful for it because he senses that the pain, when it returns, will be torture.

His mother's voice seems to be coming from a great distance and he only catches phrases— "... be all right ... a wreck ... thrown out ..."

He wonders about Spencer, tries to ask, but discovers he can't speak, so he closes his eyes and goes away again.

WHEN REALITY finally did make its presence known, it was an uglier monster than the pain.

His sports car had run down a little boy on a bike and never even slowed down. Around the next bend, the car left the road, traveling at some ridiculous speed, and flew out into a field, and rolled three, maybe four times. He and Spencer had been thrown out. He never found out how. They'd been wearing seatbelts, hadn't they? But maybe they'd never buckled them. He couldn't remember. Spencer was in a coma, and when he finally came out of it almost a week after the wreck, he had no memory of it. He remembered standing beside the punch bowl table at the wedding reception ... and then waking up in the hospital.

Everyone assumed Spencer had been driving. After all, that's why Jude had taken him along in the first place, to drive because Jude *couldn't*, had a sprained ankle, was on crutches. Both of them were so drunk they should never have gone near an automobile. When Spencer was well enough to leave the hospital, he'd been arrested, charged with vehicular homicide, and eventually sentenced to ten years in prison on a plea bargain. Had to serve at least half the sentence before he'd be eligible for parole.

Jude remained silent, claimed he didn't remember any more than Spencer did. He only spoke to Spencer a time or two after that, both of them hollowed-out husks of the strapping young men they'd been when they climbed into that sports car on that sunny Saturday afternoon.

So Jude went to rehab to heal his mangled arm, then into a sanitarium to heal his mangled mind, and Spencer went to jail and then to prison.

Would anybody really be willing to pick at the scab that'd formed over that family wound, rip it off and set the blood flowing again, because of a photograph? If Leanne saw it, would she turn her own brother in? Would the others turn him in? What if *Spencer* saw it?

Jude had to get his hands on that picture, and any pictures like it — shoot, there could be half a dozen more buried somewhere in that box. Maybe there was just the one. It was damning enough. He had to get it ... which meant he needed to get back into the house right now and watch over that box, make sure nobody disturbed the pile of discarded pictures before he had a chance to go through them.

He didn't have time to go take his things up to his room. Would they really put him in the same room as Spencer? Oh, dear God, he hoped not. He had bigger fish to fry right now, though. Slamming the trunk lid firmly shut, Jude hurried back across the field to the house, almost collided with some girl he didn't know, tall, with blue hair, coming out as he was going in.

Chapter Twenty-Eight

Jude didn't think he'd been gone long, had left the kitchen to go to his car and then came right back in. But time had a way of getting away from him sometimes, and he must have spent longer pacing back and forth behind his car than he'd intended, because Leanne gave him a where-have-you-been look when he came in. There were several empty boxes on the table now. Apparently, they'd dumped all the remaining uninspected photos into a pile in the middle of the table and were grabbing handfuls off the pile to go through before tossing the discards into the big box on the floor — the box where a photograph lurked in the shadows, ready to pounce on Jude and destroy his life.

Picking up a handful of pictures off the pile in the middle of the table, Jude sat back down in his empty chair and started going through them — not looking for pictures of Grandma Hannah but checking each picture for a baby blue Firebird convertible.

Gratefully, Zoe and Daphne were arguing about Elon Musk's purchase of Twitter.

"You watch, he's going to give all the haters their accounts back," Zoe said. "Issue some kind of blanket amnesty."

"Not all the people who got cancelled were Looney Tunes trying to overthrow the government," Daphne said.

"No, some of them were spreading disinformation about Covid."

"The government was the one spreading disinformation about Covid. Those people were right all along, those jabs didn't …"

Jude tuned them out, concentrating on carefully scanning each picture for an image that could send him to prison.

Don't think about that. If he let himself consider what would happen if he didn't get his hands on that picture, he—

"Any of that pecan pie left?" asked a voice from behind him. He jerked around to see the new and improved, now-bearded Spencer in the doorway.

"We saved you some," Zoe said and started to rise.

"Just tell me where," Spencer said. "I can get it for myself."

The pie was among half a dozen crowded on the cabinet to Jude's left.

"Jude, get him a plate," Leanne said, pointing to the cabinet above the pies.

Jude wasn't really sure what happened after that.

Spencer stepped toward the cabinet, protesting that he could serve himself.

Jude scooted his chair back too quickly and leapt to his feet — bumped into Zoe, who was heading toward the pies, and knocked her off balance.

Spencer and Jude both reached out at the same time to steady her … and there was a three-car pileup.

Zoe fell backwards onto the table on top of the pile of pictures, knocking them every which way, mostly into the discarded picture box on the floor.

Leanne tried to grab the cascading pictures, cursing.

"I'm sorry, I—"

"I didn't mean to—"

"Look what you—"

"Oh shit!"

When the dust settled, it was obvious that most of the pile of uninspected pictures had just been dumped on top of the discarded ones.

"It's my fault," Spencer said. "I'll sort them all out again."

"Oh, never mind," Leanne said. She pointed to the considerable pile of Grandma Hannah pictures. "Those are enough."

"No, really, I'll do it. You guys have other things to do and I … I'm kinda at loose ends. Let me fix it."

"No, I'll do it," Jude blurted out, too forcefully. "I don't mind."

"You were hot to trot out of here a few minutes ago," Leanne said.

"Both of you do it," said Danni. "Help me gather them all up and you guys can go to work in the music room. We're going to need the kitchen table to make supper."

Jude had never known why the room down the hall from the dining room was called the music room. Rooms got named in that house according to their original intent, even if the room stopped serving the function for which it'd been constructed — nobody'd sewn in the sewing room upstairs for fifty years. There were no shelves full of books in the library, and the sunroom was on the north side of the house, its windows shaded by trees. He supposed that with a rabbit warren of a house like this one, you had to have some way to identify the rooms. Maybe the music room had had a piano in it once. Shoot, maybe that was where Uncle Gabe rehearsed with his heavy metal band. No, the vibrations would have disturbed the fish. The room should have been named for its most distinctive feature — a massive aquarium built into the wall across from the door — five feet wide, three tall, held two hundred twenty-five gallons of water. No fish, though — maybe a couple of guppies and a handful of little goldfish.

When he was a little kid, he used to beg Grandma Liv to put a dolphin in the tank. It would have fit.

Jude carried the huge box of discarded pictures, Spencer carried the two biggest empty boxes, one for the new discards and one for Grandma Hannah pictures. There was no table in the study, so they sat on the couch, one on each end.

"So, how ya been?"

What a stupid thing to say.

Spencer shrugged. "Can't complain."

Yeah, what's to complain about in a prison?

"Nobody knew you were out. Why didn't—"

"You don't go from prison to walking out the door a free man when you're on parole. You go to a halfway house first. It isn't anywhere you want your grandmother to visit."

"Want a beer? There's cold ones in the fridge in the basement."

"I'm good."

Now what could he say?

It's not like they'd ever been BFFs. He'd asked Spencer to go along that day because he happened to be standing there. That was the extent of their previous relationship. Spencer had "spared the boy's family the ordeal of a trial" by pleading guilty, so it's not like Jude had sat in the witness box and pointed a finger at him. Theirs wasn't an adversarial relation-ship. It just wasn't a relationship of any kind, and he was acting like he'd been the best man at Spencer's wedding.

Pasting a smile on his face, Jude said, "I hate for you to get stuck doing this, seeing as how I volunteered in the beginning to do the whole thing." He hadn't, of course, volunteered, had in fact been only a couple of steps from freedom when his sister was lassoed and required to do his part. But Spencer hadn't been there to see it. "Why don't you go on upstairs and get unpacked — Aunt Cynthia says we're bunking in together this weekend. I can handle this by myself."

There was a heartbeat of time in there where Jude

thought Spencer might take the bait, might thank him profoundly for his kindness and leave it all to Jude, who would have made short work of finding the offending picture and destroying it. But that's not what happened.

"No, I'll stick. Two of us can get it done in half the time."

Before Jude could say another word, Spencer dug his fingers into the pile of pictures in the box, drew out an overflowing handful, and held them out to Jude, who took them wordlessly.

"Pictures of Aunt Hannah — right? Does she have to be smiling? Because if she does …"

"No, not necessarily smiling, just there, obvious in the picture. There won't be very many. Remember, we've already been though almost all of these once."

Spencer nodded, unsmiling, and grabbed a second handful of pictures and dumped them in his own lap, then began hurriedly picking through them.

Jude had never felt so trapped in his life. Robotically, he began to lift picture after picture out of the pile in his lap, not even scanning them for Grandma Hannah. His eyes couldn't focus. There was a fifty-fifty chance that the offending photo would show up in Jude's pile, and he could just scoot it off to the side and into his pocket.

He had to concentrate — not only looking through the pictures in his pile, but watching Spencer out of the corner of his eye, expecting any second for him to stop, hold a picture up and stare at it, then slowly turn his unbelieving gaze to Jude.

No. It wouldn't happen. It *couldn't*.

But it did.

Chapter Twenty-Nine

ALEX'S PHONE rang as she was trying to find a spot on top of the sideboard to put the chicken casserole that'd just been delivered to the house. Maybe she should take it in the kitchen and put it with all the other chicken casseroles — the chicken and rice casserole Lucy Trujillo had brought, and the chicken and sausage one from Phyllis Pettis. Alex was pretty sure Phyllis had just used the tried-and-true breakfast casserole recipe — eggs, sausage, and cheddar cheese on top of a crust made by flattening out Pillsbury crescent rolls on the bottom of the dish — and added leftover chicken to it. Or the chicken and stuffing casserole from Bertha Simmons that used Stove Top instant stuffing mix and canned chicken and mushroom soup. Nobody had time to cook from scratch anymore.

"Hello."

There was nothing but mumbling on the other end.

"Hello." Alex got few spam calls because she had relentlessly hunted down the source and had her number removed from their list every time she got one.

She looked at the phone and the number swam in her vision, blurred so she couldn't read it.

"Final hello and then I'm hanging up."

No sound at all.

She punched the end call button and scooted the casserole dish up next to the bowl of cucumber salad, her mind occupied with images of Spencer. Spencer *free!* Spencer home with his family where he belonged! When she saw him, standing there talking to Avery, she'd genuinely thought she was imagining it. Too good to be true. And then she wouldn't let go of him, couldn't stop touching him —

The phone she still held in her hand vibrated but didn't ring. Had she turned the ringer off? Then she froze, realized how quiet the house had grown.

Turning slowly around, she watched one of Jordan's twin daughters — Daphne, she thought — close the china cabinet door soundlessly.

"Testing, testing ..." she said softly to herself. She barely heard it, like it'd come from the bottom of a drainpipe. She felt like she'd been hit in the chest with a wrecking ball, couldn't breathe or think, just stood with a single sound in her ears — the pounding thud, thud, thud of her heart.

Suddenly, the vibrating phone in her hand rang. She *heard* the ring, then all the ambient noise of the busy house returned, like turning up the dial on a chandelier dimmer switch. She sat down heavily on the closest chair, heard her phone ring, and felt it vibrate twice more, and then it fell still.

The hand holding the phone was shaking.

It's started.

The image from the *Lord of the Rings* movie filled her mind. King Théoden's grim words as he stood in the rain watching Saruman's army march on Helm's Deep — "And so it begins."

The phone rang again and she jumped, heard it plainly. The number was clear. Barney! She looked down at the beautiful blown-glass pendant that hung on a chain around her neck. She had to take the call. Hesitating as it rang again, it suddenly occurred to her that she'd better use her faculties while she still had them.

"Hello, Barney."

"I've been trying to reach—"

"Lousy cell coverage. Is anything wrong?"

"Just wanted to let you know I put the final payment in the box this morning. Got a good price for that last one."

When he told her how much, she whistled softly.

"You're a magician as well as an artist."

"I aim to please. It's all there now. If there'd been any more cash, we'd have had to get a bigger box. This one's full."

"So we're done. They're all … *gone.*"

"All gone. I … tell you … wanted to …"

Barney's voice sounded like it was breaking up, but Alex knew it wasn't his voice that was the problem.

"I'm sorry, I have to jump off, now. Thanks."

She punched the end call button and listened as the sounds around her ebbed and flowed, loud, then soft, then loud again. She had tried to erase her few memories of her time in Minneapolis, but some memories had stubbornly hung on a nail in her head.

Why do doctors find it necessary to use their diplomas as wallpaper? Do doctors think patients need evidence? If some guy's pointing out squiggly lines on some MRI image and spouting words as unpronounceable as the names of towns in Wales, that's proof enough.

"… listening, Ms. Harrington?"

"No, I'm sorry, what did you say?"

"I said we will schedule you for your next appointment—"

"Next appointment? Why do I need to come back?"

"So we can monitor your condition."

"Condition? The tumor, you mean? Why monitor it? You already said there's nothing you can do about it, no cure, no drug that'll slow it down, nothing … you did say that, right?"

"Yes, but we will need to observe—"

"You want to watch it grow?"

"*So we can keep you apprised of the progression—*"

"*Tell me how much longer I've got? No thanks! I'd rather not know.*"

"*But—*"

"*Tell me again what … will happen to me … at the end? You said I wouldn't … die in pain.*"

"*Every patient is unique, and the progression of every tumor is—*"

"*In general then, what can I expect?*"

"*It all depends on—*"

"*Don't you guys ever give a straight answer?*" She's close to tears, but she won't cry. She won't! When he doesn't say anything, she figures she'd stepped in it, had offended him, but when he does speak his voice is kinder, less clinical and more human.

"*I would tell you if I knew, but I don't. As the tumor grows, it invades the surrounding brain tissue, interfering with its function. So how it affects you depends on what part of your brain the tumor damages.*"

He did something unexpected then. He reached out and took her hand and spoke softly.

"*Best-case scenario based on the current location of your tumor — you're likely to experience hearing loss, blurred vision, double vision, or loss of peripheral vision. Maybe abnormal eye movements, seeing floating spots, an aura of light around objects. There could be drowsiness, headaches, cognitive changes—*"

"*I won't be able to think!*" Alex is horrified.

"*You may become confused and forgetful, won't know how to perform simple tasks—*"

"*Like?*"

"*Like how to brush your teeth or how to make toast.*"

Alex stopped breathing and she began to squeeze the doctor's hand tighter.

"*One side of your body, it'll likely be your right side, may become weak, so you stumble and become clumsy, maybe even paralyzed.*"

She realizes she's squeezing the doctor's hand so hard it must hurt, but she can't release it.

"*How long will these symptoms last?*"

"They'll probably come and go over the course of several weeks, but maybe just days."

"And ... at the end ... the very end?"

"This is just a guess. I would expect that you will lose your sight or hearing completely, become progressively drowsier until you drift into unconsciousness. You won't likely be aware of the final dying process as your organs shut down."

She draws a shaky breath.

"And worst-case scenario?"

He doesn't hesitate, she has to give him that.

"Seizures, delirium, vomiting, personality changes — violence and aggression, total paralysis."

Into the dark abyss of her thoughts, words drop, like out of the sky. The old Woody Allen line: "I don't mind dying, I just don't want to be there when it happens."

She actually smiles a little and releases the doctor's hand. Whereupon he begins to hedge his bets.

"You might experience all of what I've described or none of it. There's no way to know—"

"I get it. That's the bottom line. There's no way to know."

SHE WAS ENTERING that final phase they'd talked about, and she chose to believe that she would cruise through it in best-case scenario mode. Surely, the universe would grant her that one mercy ...

The universe? Where had that come from? She was parroting the culture's weasel words that she so loathed, the what-people-say that doesn't really mean anything at all. Word salad.

She backed up ... surely *God* would grant her that one mercy. God was in the granting mercies business. Galaxies of lifeless stars were not.

Chapter Thirty

JUDE WAS HOLDING IT TOGETHER. He was proud of himself. He was fine. Just fine.

He realized he'd been chucking pictures into the discard pile without even looking to see if Aunt Hannah was in any of them. Maybe she was, he didn't care. He just wanted had to find that picture of—

"You see much of Aunt Hannah recently," Spencer asked absently, just making conversation.

"Does anybody see Grandma Hannah if they can help it?" he popped off. He was instantly sorry. He ought to be sad his grandmother was dead. He needed to look like he cared, needed to look normal. "Just kidding, ha ha." He actually said that. "Ha ha." Who says "ha ha?" You write that in texts, but nobody talks out loud like they write texts.

The racing thoughts, he couldn't grab hold of them. Around and around in his head. He had to calm down. He had to look like he gave a rat's ass about his dead — he had to get that picture that showed he was driving the car, the one he'd caught a glimpse of earlier. He had to find it!

Calm down.

He wished he could grab his thoughts, like you'd grab a

merry-go-round that was spinning too fast. Just grab a bar and hold on, drag your feet in the dirt and it slows. Thoughts weren't like that, though.

Who had this many pictures? Nobody had print pictures. Just digital. There was Christmas 2013, and the lake trip, and the kids playing in the mud, and some kid's birthday party, and Uncle Jordan's new bass boat, and …

"Hey, that one's got Aunt Hannah in it," Spencer said, indicating the picture that Jude had just dealt out onto the discard pile.

He picked it back up and looked at it. He hadn't been looking at any of them. Shoot, half the pictures he'd gone through could have had Grandma Hannah in them and he just went right past.

"Oh yeah, there," Jude said and set the picture in the small but growing pile of Hannah pictures. This one was Paul's birthday party, and Grandma Hannah was standing right behind him as he blew out the candles. Hard to miss.

What other pictures of her had he missed? He thought maybe Spencer was wondering the same thing, because he saw Spencer glance at the discard pile, must be looking to see if Jude had missed more Grandma Hannah pictures.

Spencer glanced up at him.

He thinks I have. He thinks I've missed more pictures.

And what if he does. Racing thoughts, racing thoughts. Slow down. He kept himself from putting the heels of his hands to his temples and squeezing to stop the spinning.

They know.

The voice spoke into his head with such suddenness that he dropped the handful of photos he was holding into his lap in surprise.

Spencer looked at him with a quizzical look.

"Oops," he said stupidly, reached down and picked up the handful of pictures again and continued to go through them, dealing them like off a deck of cards.

They know.

Not now, the Other. How could Jude have … he'd hidden from the Other in a blur of booze and drugs for months.

Miss me?

He looked furtively around like maybe somebody had spoken. Spencer gave him a concerned look.

"You okay, Jude? You don't have to keep doing this if—"

"I'm fine." He almost shouted. Maybe he did shout. Too loud. Calm down. "I'm really fine. I just have … you know I have migraine headaches sometimes."

"If you have a headache, I'll—"

"No, I don't have a headache. But I did. I had one last night and didn't get much sleep. And those headaches will scramble your brains sometimes."

Spencer nodded sympathetically.

Jude ought to make conversation. That's what somebody would do. They'd make conversation, talk about nothing things. But what did you talk about to a guy who just got out of prison. *How'd you like prison? Food good? Like your roommate* —cell*mate?* Right.

That's where they'd put Jude if he didn't find that picture.

That's when Spencer stopped cold, holding up a picture. He looked at Jude and back at the picture.

What should Jude do? Should he grab the picture, snatch it out of Spencer's fingers and rip it up before he … or grab it and run away and burn it … or punch him, just slug him in the jaw and grab the picture, or …

All those thoughts blew through Jude's head so fast he was surprised their passage didn't set his hair on fire. He didn't have to do any of the things though, because Spencer held the photo out for him to see.

"That's you, isn't it? The chubby baby in Aunt Hanna's arms?"

It was a picture of his grandmother alright. He didn't know or care who the kid was.

"Yeah, that's me. Put that one in the keeper file."

As Spencer dropped it in the file, Jude saw that the next picture on Spencer's stack was the one! The picture that showed him in the background, driving the car. He was so shocked and horrified he couldn't move, watched in slow motion as Spencer looked down.

He picked it up and smiled.

"Look at that dress." For the first time, Jude focused on what was in the foreground of the picture, what the photographer had been aiming at. It was Avery — he supposed it was Avery — with blonde curls, standing in front of some other little girls, all in matching dresses, the flower girls at the wedding.

Before he could do anything, Spencer slid the picture into his shirt pocket, then saw the look on Jude's face.

"I … missed a lot, missed seeing … Halloween costumes, Christmas morning, things like that. I have a few pictures Brooke sent me. And Grandma Alex, she sent me … but I don't have many. I'm keeping this one."

He didn't see it.

Spencer didn't notice what was in the background. He was so enthralled with his little girl standing there in her flower girl dress that he didn't notice, oh by the way, that in the background is the sports car he supposedly used to run down a little boy … and Jude is driving it.

But eventually, Spencer would see that. He would take the photo out and look at it, gaze at it, and when he did, he'd see it. He'd notice. And then he'd come looking for Jude.

Kill him.

The Other spoke calmly in his head this time, not some booming voice like God speaking from the mountaintop. Just the voice of somebody he knew.

You don't have any choice, man. You have to do it while he's not on guard, before he has a chance to see that picture.

Kill him?

People fall out windows every day. And the room you're in is the one above the side porch. Wouldn't be the first time you crawled out the window there and up onto the roof.

Jude remembered. As a little boy, he and Spencer, Juliana, Dannie, and Casey would climb out the window of that room, right above the porch roof. It was one of half a dozen ways to get out onto the house roof, and they played there all the time. The slant wasn't steep, and all the odd roof angles made climbing it easy. They'd never thought about what'd happen if they fell off, because all children are invincible. But if they'd fallen from there, it was two floors down to the patio. Flagstones and concrete. A fall like that *might* have been survivable.

Not if you're already dead when you hit the rocks.

No, that's crazy.

You want them to lock you up?

The Other's words paralyzed him with fear.

Want them to put you behind bars? You want everybody to know it was you who ran over the kid, that you let Spencer rot in a prison cell for eight years for something you did. You want everybody to know that? Do you?

Jude couldn't breathe.

Then Spencer slid another picture into his pocket with the first. He saw that Jude had noticed.

"It's a group shot of all the flower girls. Nobody wants these things. They've been in a box in the basement for decades. Nobody will care if I pick out some to keep." He got a sad, resigned look on his face. "It's going to be a long, long time before I can make new pictures with her. Maybe I never will."

Jude could do nothing but nod. Couldn't have done anything to get that picture now even if he'd wanted to, because his feet were nailed to the floor and he was doing well to keep breathing with the hole torn right through his belly.

They continued to work, sort. Spencer found a couple of other Avery pictures, swimming in a pool, playing with a dog, in a group of kids at a birthday party. And he was right, with two of them working diligently it didn't take long at all to go through the box of photos. They had a decent stack of pictures of Grandma Hannah, too.

"I'll take these to Dusty so he can scan them in with the others and put them on a loop in those monitors," Spencer said, then barked out a laugh. "He knows how to operate all the tech. I sure don't, missed that boat. You techie?"

"Naaa, whenever I have a problem with my phone, I go find a ten-year-old."

He hadn't meant it as a joke, but it'd come off as one, and it was a pleasant thing … making a joke, hearing Spencer laugh. That's what people did. They made jokes.

His Aunt Marilou breezed into the room.

"Here you are," she said. "Give me those." She indicated the pictures Spencer had of Grandma Hannah. "I'll take them to Dusty." She was gruff with Spencer, barely civil, and snatched the photos out of his hands. It occurred to Jude then that the response to Spencer's sudden appearance wasn't going to be uniformly positive. On the Harrington side of the family, maybe, but not on his side, the Kavanaughs. Some of them probably had no use for him anymore. "Alex wants you guys to come eat now."

Spencer followed after her. And Jude followed Spencer. That's all he could do, stay glued to Spencer, not let him have a second alone — even to take a leak — to look at those pictures. Then when he pulled them out tonight … he wouldn't get much of a look before Jude sent him flying.

Chapter Thirty-One

JUDE DIDN'T LIKE the way his father Samuel was looking at him.

He sees it.

How could he see it?

He *sees it*.

And maybe he did. Maybe they all did. Maybe they could see what he thought only he could see — the visage of the dead boy, standing in the corner. Objectively, Jude understood it was a hallucination. God knows he'd been forced to recognize and acknowledge the existence of such things during his involuntary stays in various psychiatric facilities. He could define the term: "perception of a physical phenomenon that does not exist in the physical world."

But knowing the image he could see didn't exist in any real sense didn't matter, and he'd never been able to convey that understanding to the shrinks who poked and prodded him. No, it wasn't really there. But it was *real* nonetheless because it was real to Jude. He could see the child's face — which was never marred whenever the boy had paid him a visit. His face looked just like the kid's school picture published with his obituary in the newspaper.

. . .

Nicolás Hernandez, ten, the son of Juanita and Luís Hernandez, died on June 15, 2015 as a result of injuries he sustained when he was struck by a car on Tyler Road. He is survived by his parents, two older sisters, Lia, fifteen, and Guadalupe ten, and a brother, Carlos, sixteen months.

His face never changed. It was a mask the dead boy was looking out through. Jude could tell. He could see the hatred and violence in those innocent eyes. And everything below his neck was the ruin from the roadside that he hadn't seen but must have seen because if he didn't, how did he know exactly what it looked like?

None of his limbs was attached properly to his body. His arms hung at odd angles to his torso, and his left leg was bent sideways at the knee. He might have been wearing jeans and a tee shirt like the accident report said, but the tee shirt was not visible. There was nothing but gore from his chin down to where his chest had been ripped open and his guts smeared all over the road.

Somebody told him one of the troopers had seen the boy's body and vomited. A trooper who saw wrecks every day.

"… the green beans."

A voice penetrated his fixation on the image in the corner that wasn't real.

"Knock knock, Jude. You in there, Buddy?" Danni's husband Rick asked. "Aunt Marilou wants the green beans."

"Sorry, I was daydreaming."

He was astonished by how normal his voice sounded, not like it was coming from the throat of a man who saw dead children in the corner and who responded to the directions of a voice in his head. He picked up the bowl of green beans and passed it Rick's direction.

"You didn't like the chicken corn chowder?" Danni asked, and when he looked down, he realized he hadn't touched a bite of what had been heaped onto his plate. It'd been like eating in a cafeteria, except instead of going through the line and selecting what he wanted, his sisters and cousins had merely dolloped food onto his plate as they passed dishes down from one end of the table to the other.

"It's a little … too salty for my taste," he said, though he hadn't had a bite of it. "But I like the" — he looked down at his plate — "ham." Then he realized that it was obvious he hadn't taken a bite yet because the piece of meat hadn't been cut. "I snitched a piece off the plate earlier." He hastily speared the piece of meat with his fork and sliced off a big bite. Stuffing it in his mouth, he said, "I like the honey-glazed ham we have at Thanksgiving better. Who makes that?"

As he chewed the tasteless piece of meat, Aunt Cynthia told him how her sister-in-law Millie always brought the ham and her other sister-in-law Marylou the chicken. She, on the other hand, had carved out her own niche with "dark meat" turkey, baking thighs and legs in a dish with cornbread dressing.

Jude washed the dry piece of — what was it? ham? yeah, ham — down with iced tea. It was sweet tea and he hated sweet tea, but he didn't complain, tried to concentrate on forcing some of the food on his plate down so the others wouldn't notice he wasn't eating.

A group of teenagers all laughed at something Peyton had said. Jude laughed, too, though he hadn't heard the remark.

His mind had gone all jerky-jerky on him, like the movement of a bird on a tree limb. He had trouble putting thoughts together. He tried to calm himself, tried to remember the words and the melody to his favorite song. But at that moment he couldn't even recall what his favorite song had been. Or his favorite food. Or what the girl he'd slept with two nights last week looked like. Couldn't even recall how the sun felt on the back of his neck, or the paint horse, Taco, he'd had as a boy, the power of it beneath him as he rode out across the prairie.

He looked at Spencer, sitting opposite him, eating quietly, not participating in the general hum of conversation around him, but not totally outside it as Jude was. Jude didn't belong here among these people. They were as foreign to him as Martians. But Spencer did. Even though he had committed such a heinous act, killed a child and went to prison — he was still one of them. He was *family* in a way Jude had never been, because Jude didn't belong to anything but himself.

And his terror of being locked in a cage had burned away all the chaff, reduced him to his essential self. There was nothing in the world he wouldn't do, no act too vile to prevent that. And not just the locked-up part, but the rest of it, the horror that dragged along behind the act. The revulsion in the eyes of all these people. He'd seen it on their faces eight years ago, heard the disgust in their voices when they talked about what Spencer had done. Jude had been right there with them, contributing to conversations at the time — "… can't believe he could just drive off and leave the boy lying there" and "what kind of person runs down a kid on a bike?" And "how could you do a thing like that and still sleep at night?" Of course, Jude slept soundly, his slumber not disturbed either by the images he'd seen or guilt over what he'd done. But over the years, it wore him down.

When Spencer had arrived, Jude'd kicked himself for showing up here at all, never should have come. But what if he hadn't? What if somebody else had happened upon that picture and Jude wasn't here to do anything about it?

He quickly set his glass of icky sweet tea down because thinking about it had sent a chill through his body that termi-nated in a literal shudder. His whole body shook for a moment, then he grabbed hold of his emotions, gritted his teeth, and willed himself to stay calm. The picture ... he'd take care of the picture.

Now, with fear nipping at his heels like an angry dog, he understood that he couldn't wait. He would not be able to keep his wits about him sufficiently now to keep up the charade. No, he would have to kill Spencer *the moment he got the chance.* He couldn't just go up to the room with him, hang out, hope he'd get a chance to get the picture out of his pocket before he really looked at it. His terror had grown so big it was about to burst out of him, and it was an effort to simply sit here waiting. He would hit Spencer over the head with something as soon as the door closed behind them, then toss him out the window.

With his mind so distracted, Jude had been unaware of the scene going on around him, until Avery's words penetrated. She was seated at the far end of the table next to that strange girl with the wild eyes and the nose ring.

"... why should I make nice?"

Apparently, someone had said something to her about Spencer, maybe that it must be good to have him home. Avery did not agree.

"Why would I want him home? It's a little late for him to be a father, don't cha think? My bike's fixed, don't need help repairing it. Homecoming's over, don't need anybody to walk me out onto the field. I'm good." She cast a scathing look Spencer's way. "I don't need a father anymore."

There was a moment of shocked silence, then the table erupted with indignation from half the family and agreement from the other half.

Spencer got to his feet, leaving behind a half-eaten plate of food.

"I'll see you all in the morning," he said to everybody in general but to nobody in particular. Then he turned and left the room. Jude stood and followed him. Shoot, after that little scene, maybe everybody'd think Spencer jumped.

Chapter Thirty-Two

As ALL THE males in the family cleaned up the kitchen after supper — the women had done lunch — Avery put a tea kettle on the stove. This was a bad idea, a phenomenally bad idea. She'd only suggested it because she was so upset about seeing her father. She was over that now. She'd brooded about it all afternoon, then lost it and jumped in the middle of him with both feet at supper. *That* had been a mistake. Of course, she knew not everybody in the family shared her disgust for her father, but knowing it intellectually and seeing their horrified faces was another thing entirely. She had hurt Grandma Liv, Grandma Alex, and Grampa Gabe in particular, and she never intended such a thing. And the disappointment in Grampa Gabe's eyes when he looked at her! It broke her heart. That was the worst part — Avery's response had made her the bad guy and her father the victim, and damned if she was going to let *that* happen. Her own fault. She should have taken the high road, and from now on she would.

Clearly, he was going to be in her life now and *she* would set the parameters of that relationship. She would not be hostile, she'd be civil and polite. She'd never again let him get the emotional upper hand on her. She'd begin mending

164

fences with her grandparents tomorrow. As for tonight ...
after supper, different groups of people had gone off to
different parts of the house —to hang out, play Charades or
board games or blackjack — and to drink and do some weed,
of course. Oh, how she wanted to join them. But that, too,
was her own fault — Maddie. Nobody'd put a gun to her
head and forced her to bring the girl home with her from
college, so she'd just have to suck it up and suffer the consequences. Avery had signed on for magic mushrooms and
she'd see it through. Maddie was upstairs, doing ... well,
whatever you had to do to mushrooms to make them palat-
able in tea.

When Avery took the tea pot, cups, and tea on a tray into
the room, Maddie was zipping up that huge duffel bag of hers
and had a bag of something in her hand. She held it out to
Avery.

"Brownies."

"I thought you only brought—"

"I almost forgot I had these, stuffed them in at the last
minute. Got them from a girl ... who didn't need them
anymore."

Didn't *need* them anymore?

Avery set the teapot tray on her dresser.

"I thought we agreed to do the—"

"Let's save those for later," Maddie said.

Avery breathed a silent sigh of relief. If she played her
cards right, kept Maddie occupied, maybe she could push *later*
all the way into never.

They settled in to enjoy the brownies. Avery tried to get to
know Maddie, but it was a lost cause. She wouldn't talk about
herself, her past, her family — or lack thereof — or even
school.

Finally, Avery gave up and just enjoyed the weed.

"This weed really slaps," she mumbled to Maddie as she
relaxed. She hadn't had any weed as good as this in a long

time, and it took all the tension out of her and gave her a warm inner glow.

"Maybe she was murdered," Maddie said.

Avery turned to her, totally confused. It seemed to take a long time to say anything, and the rest of the conversation felt like it was in slow motion, too.

"Who?"

"Who do you think? The corpse that's laying in the parlor downstairs, your Aunt What's Her Name. Like that's the most normal thing in the world — a dead body on one of those black-draped funeral home gurneys just—"

"Hannah. Her name's Hannah."

"— just plopped out there right in middle of everything, so you have to close the door to the dining room or you'd have to" — Maddie shivered — "*look at it while you eat!*"

"She's just dead. She's not roadkill."

Avery felt like she was watching some vintage movie where the sound was off and the character's lips didn't sync with what they were saying. She couldn't seem to keep up.

"What do you mean, murdered?"

"How many things can murdered mean? Killed. Executed. Offed. Wiped out. Wasted—"

"Is your thesaurus app in your favorites so you can get to it quick when you need it?"

Avery burst out laughing at her own humor, doubled over. That was a good one, a reeeeally good one. It took her awhile to settle enough to notice that Maddie didn't seem to think it was particularly funny.

"You said they didn't know the cause of death."

"What I said was that there hadn't been an autopsy, so there was no *official* cause of death. We know how she died — she overdosed on insulin."

"Doesn't that strike you as odd? She's been taking that stuff her whole life, right? You'd think she would have figured out by now how much to take."

"This isn't the first time she's overdosed. I was at the house the other time and it was awful. Aunt Hannah was late for breakfast and Uncle Cyrus went to her room and found her—"

"Her room? They don't have to same one?"

"Don't all old people stop sleeping in the same bed when they're too old for sex?"

That wasn't the reason, though. The real reason was complicated, and it seemed at that moment it would take a very long time to tell it.

Aunt Hannah had knocked out walls and made her own suite when Uncle Cyrus started having nightmares. It sounded like PTSD to Avery, but he'd been too young to be in World War II, and by the time he was old enough for military service, he was excused because his eyesight was so bad. Seemed like every year, the lenses of his glasses got thicker and thicker.

She thought about her uncle's glasses, how they sometimes sat crooked on his face.

But she'd been thinking something else, hadn't she? Oh, yeah, she'd been thinking about Uncle Cyrus's violent nightmares. It'd started after Aunt Hannah announced some kind of new project, so maybe he'd finally got tired of carpenters and sawdust. Whatever the reason, his nightmares were so awful he was all over the bed, flinging out his arms, hitting and kicking. Aunt Hannah got a black eye and that was the end of it. She went for a separate room, knocked out a wall and added on a balcony. Easier to just move in double beds, but she had always wanted a king size, while Uncle Cyrus had remained adamantly devoted to a double bed.

Why would you want to sleep in something so big? he'd asked. *I didn't get married to sleep by myself.*

That struck Avery as funny, and she started laughing.

"What? What's so funny?"

Avery wasn't completely sure.

"I thought you said it was awful when your uncle found her."

"It was. She was lying semi-conscious on the floor beside the bed. She kept a candy bar on the nightstand and managed to get a bite of it — that's what saved her. He called an ambulance, but it was a near thing, apparently. They said she'd taken too much insulin."

"What'd it do to her?"

"Nothing you could see at the time — it's not like she turned blue or broke out in spots or anything like that. When you get too much insulin, it gets rid of too much glucose, which depletes the glycogen in the brain. The brain shuts down, you go to sleep and never wake up. Same thing happened early Thursday morning. Uncle Cyrus found her on the floor beside her bed in a puddle of spilled orange juice. Maybe she was reaching for the glass, but she was dead. The EMTs tried to revive her but she was pronounced DOA at the hospital."

Maddie looked thoughtful.

"Maybe it was suicide."

Chapter Thirty-Three

WE KNOW YOUR SECRET.

The words paralyzed Jude, froze his breath, turned him into a statue.

He'd been trying to work himself up to action, tensing his muscles to strike as soon as they walked into the room. There was a paperweight on the desk there, he'd use that to ...

Then the note on the floor.

He looked around, stepped out into the hallway and looked up and down it. Nobody was there. But somebody had slipped this piece of typing paper under the door of his room.

Who?

How could anybody ...?

Spencer hadn't even noticed the piece of paper on the floor when he opened the door, maybe even stepped on it when he crossed the threshold.

They know!

The voice in his head sounded positively triumphant. I told you. I told you everyone knew, that they get together and whisper about it when you're not in the room. I know. I listen. They say you're a murderer, that you need to be locked away in a cage so you can't hurt anybody else. They say—

"Shut up!" he cried and dug the heels of his hands into his temples.

Spencer turned around, surprised.

"What?"

Careful. Be very careful here. You're walking on the edge of a razor. If you let Spencer know there's something wrong with you, he might … what? At the very least he'd be watching, on his guard. Jude would lose the element of surprise. If he got the chance, Spencer would say something to Mom and Dad, and they'd come poking their noses into Jude's business, demanding to know if he was taking his meds. Like taking meds was the equivalent of popping an aspirin for a headache. Let them take those meds for a month and see how they feel — dizzy and wrapped in cotton all the time. Nauseous. And … can't get it up. The proper term was erectile dysfunction. Or impotence.

Racing thoughts, traveling through his brain with the speed of a meteor on its way to earth.

Don't let Spencer see!

He managed a laugh that sounded, to his own ears at least, genuine.

"Damned ear buds." He was, indeed wearing earbuds, but wasn't actually listening to anything. They needed charging. "Must be busted. It gets into some kind of warped fast-forward and whatever you're listening to suddenly sounds like the vocalist is Alvin the Chipmunk."

That was *good!* Jude even impressed himself with how easily and effortlessly he squirmed out of that one.

"Wouldn't know," Spencer said, turning back to taking a few things out of a small suitcase. Might even be everything he owned in there. "Never used them. I never cared that much for music anyway."

Then he noticed the piece of paper in Jude's hands.

"What's that?"

"Some kind of stupid joke." He spoke the first thought

that came into his head. And heard the ring of truth in the words as he spoke them. Some dumb joke, that's all it was. A joke. Yeah, 3-D, probably. This was about their level of maturity.

"We know your secret … riiiiight."

He wadded up the piece of paper before Spencer could ask to see it, spotted the empty trash basket in the corner.

"… he dribbles, he shoots, a Hail Mary …" He launched the wad toward the can where it plopped in. "Three points! Nothing but net." He made a whoosh sound along and an exaggerated wrist cock.

Spencer stood, pulled out his shirt tail, and began unbuttoning his shirt.

"Care if I take a shower first?"

Jude was staring at the photographs in the pocket of Spencer's shirt as he took it off and tossed it on the bed and headed for the bathroom. "Hope there's hot water," he called out to Jude from the bathroom. "There've been times I would have sold my soul for a hot shower. And given the Devil change."

Then he pulled the door shut behind him. Jude stood staring at the shirt Spencer'd tossed on the bed, then literally leapt across the room and grabbed it. He fumbled at the pocket, dumping several photos out on the chenille bedspread. He picked through, looking for …

There it was! Now, that he got a good look at it, he understood why Spencer had been so mesmerized by the image. It was a really adorable shot of Avery. She'd have been … what? Ten, eleven years old. The flower girl dress had lace on the top and shoulders and a satin pink satin bow on the front at the waist. She wasn't wearing a "smile-for-the-camera smile." It was genuine. She looked like a merry little elf, full of joy. She looked just like her father.

In the background behind Avery was Jude's blue Firebird

convertible. Jude was driving — the red hair, the red shirt. Spencer was in the passenger seat.

In a flash of terror fueled fury, he ripped the picture in two, then ripped the halves in two, and attempted to rip … but the pieces were too small. He took two steps toward the trash can where he had just nailed an impossible three-point shot but stopped short. He couldn't let Spencer find the pieces of the picture in the trash can. He'd flush it down the toilet, except Spencer was in the bathroom.

What could he …?

He heard Spencer make a squawking sound from the bathroom and then the shower shut off abruptly. Hot water ran out. He wouldn't stay in there now, luxuriating in a hot shower, steaming up the mirrors. He could step out any second. Jude stuffed the remaining pictures back into Spencer's shirt pocket and then spun slowly around, looking for somewhere to deposit … then a sound at the bathroom door panicked him and instinctively popped the pieces into his mouth and began chewing frantically. Spencer didn't actually open the bathroom door, just bumped it, but Jude was committed now, chewed as fast as he could, wondering if there was anything in a photograph that was poisonous. Mushing the pieces of paper up the best he could, he finally managed to choke them down his gullet.

Problem solved!

His knees suddenly weak, Jude sat down heavily on the twin bed on the far side of the room from the window that led out onto the roof above the front porch roof. He'd gotten it, snagged the hateful photograph and destroyed it before Spencer had a chance to see the damaging background image. Air whooshed out of him as he considered how close he'd come to disaster, then he leaned back against the pillows piled high at the head of the bed and put his feet up. Yeah, on Grandma Hannah's bedspread — who cared.

A few minutes later, Spencer stepped into the doorway

with a towel tied round his waist. There was a jagged scar over half the length of his abdomen. He'd been cut — bad.

"Hot water to cold in a nanosecond. I'd forgotten that part."

Then he went immediately to the shirt, removed the pictures from the pocket and began to go through the one at a time. When he got to the end, he looked around on the bed, then checked the pocket again.

"That picture of Avery at the wedding, the first one I found, it's not here."

"Must have left it in the box."

"No, I was sure I had it." He searched the floor and bedspread around him. "That was the best of all of them."

"Maybe you dropped it somewhere."

"Couldn't have," Spencer said, "I never took the pictures out of my pocket." He continued to search for the picture where he'd already looked until he was convinced it wasn't to be found. Then he plopped down on the bed and picked up the other pictures. "I'm not going to give up. They put the boxes back in the basement. Soon as I get a chance after the funeral, I'm going down there and go through the pictures again." He rolled his eyes. "*All* of them. There were a couple of sleeves of negatives in there, too. Maybe I'll get lucky."

He tried a smile of confidence.

"Don't know what they were paying that wedding photographer, but he must have taken half a dozen pictures of those flower girls."

And who knew what might be in the background of *those* other pictures!

Fear and dread sank vicious fangs into Jude's soul. He'd have to beat Spencer to the boxes. Get the basement key, go down there tomorrow and check the pictures before Spencer had a chance. All those pictures, hundreds, maybe thousands of them. He'd have to check every one. Out of the frying pan …

Chapter Thirty-Four

"Suicide?" Surely, Avery hadn't heard Maddie right.

"Why not?"

"You didn't know my Aunt Hannah. She was right in the middle of … all kinds of stuff."

"Like?"

"She was going to build a koi pond in the backyard for one thing. She had backhoes scheduled to show up on Monday."

Aunt Hannah had been talking about it for years but got serious right before she took a detour to renovate her bedroom. She had the pond all drawn out on paper, had shown it to Avery, how she was going to dig up the entire backyard and turn it into an Oriental garden.

"I'm not sure building a koi pond constitutes a reason to keep on living."

Avery thought that was funny. Not as funny as what Avery'd said a little while ago. She tried to remember what it was but couldn't. Still, this was funny, and she laughed.

When Avery stopped laughing, Maddie picked up where she'd left off.

"Maybe she wanted to but couldn't afford it."

"Oh, she could afford it alright."

Avery didn't often think about how rich her family was. She knew that when Grandma Olivia's husband was killed in an oil field accident at age seventy-one, Grandma Olivia had inherited the Harrington fortune — Harrington Oil Company, plus real estate holdings, hotel and restaurant chains, shopping centers. Avery had no idea what all. In the normal course of things, Grandma Olivia would have died herself soon after and the wealth would have passed down to the next generation. She'd heard Grampa Gabe say the fortune would be broken up then to divide among the heirs, each of whom would become multi-millionaires.

Well, that'd been thirty years ago, and the Energizer Bunny was still going and the fortune was still socked away. Avery knew the children and grandchildren had individual "trust funds" of some kind, enough money to ensure that nobody in the family ever wanted for anything — a stake to start a business, a college education, a down payment on a house — but the rest was Grandma Olivia's. And she was ... Grandma Alex called it "thrifty." The rest of the family made jokes about it. "Grandma Liv's so cheap she eats cereal with a fork to save milk," or "she looks under the bed in the morning to make sure she didn't lose any sleep." Things like that. Grandpa Gabe had rolled his eyes when Grandma Liv made him take the toaster apart and try to repair it instead of just going out and buying a new one.

But Aunt Hannah had ... Mother called it "come from money" in her own right. She'd been rich when Uncle Cyrus married her. She had expensive tastes, and over the years she just about wiped out her parents' whole estate indulging her two passions — art and jewelry. But not just any art. And not just any jewelry.

Hannah Kavanaugh was obsessed with the work of the great western painters/sculptors Frederic Remington and Charles Russell. She'd inherited a couple of pieces when her mother died, and she was constantly expanding the collection, paying exorbitant prices for any bit of their art that came on the market. She claimed to have the largest private collection of it in the world, and she probably did. Her other obsession was bright shiny things. She loved rocks … okay, jewels — the stones themselves— emeralds and diamonds and sapphires. Big ones. She'd purchase stones, and then have them hand-crafted into the gaudiest jewelry Avery'd ever seen. The girls in the family always drooled over her collection and Aunt Hannah liked to flaunt it, would wear a rock so big she could barely lift her hand just to go into town to the post office. Everything she owned was one-of-a-kind and therefore priceless.

Grandma Liv always said Aunt Hannah was never content for long without a project, and for decades the project was that old house. She had done all kinds of work on the old place, renovated the parts of it Grandma Liv would let her change — which were few — and adding on rooms to suit her own fancy. She'd made the multi-floored old house even more eccentric, a collection of the old and the new — rooms with exotic rugs on Moroccan tile floors beside rooms wallpapered with ugly purple flowers. Almost all the rooms had eighteen-foot ceilings and dormer windows above the doors.

"When I was a senior in high school, Aunt Hannah decided to become philanthropic, and she built a museum in Muleshoe."

"In Muleshoe? A museum of what?"

"It was about ranches and cowboys and cattle drives — Texas stuff. But she also put in it her Remington and Russell collection and *that* was worth the price of admission."

"*The* Remington and—"

"The same. She also had hand-designed and antique jewelry worth … I don't know, it was priceless. All the women in the family have been salivating over it for years. Then she told Mama she was planning to donate it all to the museum, too. Grandma Liv said she'd probably decided to give it up because her vision had got so bad she could barely see it."

"I bet there was no joy in Mudville when the family found *that* out. So there you go. There's motive."

"Motive?"

"For murder."

"How'd we get here? You leapt right over natural causes. Knock, knock … she accidentally overdosed."

"You said yourself it was odd that a lifelong diabetic would screw up an insulin dose so bad it killed her."

"I didn't say that, you did."

Avery's head was spinning.

"You said there was no autopsy, so—"

Avery held up her hands, her right palm over her left fingertips in the universal sign for time out. She was coming down off her high and she didn't want to, looked around and saw another brownie, picked it up and took a bite.

"About that autopsy …?"

She chewed and swallowed.

"There was a partial autopsy. Before Grandma Liv freaked out and demanded they stop at the eleventh hour — she has this thing about not cutting up dead bodies — they'd already conducted the outside part of an autopsy and were just about to—"

"What's the outside part?"

"Outside! Skin, you know. External." Maybe Avery should consult a thesaurus. She almost giggled at that, but Maddie didn't seem to be in the mood for chuckles. Fine. She didn't care what mood Maddie was in, as long as she didn't decide it was time to do the shrooms.

"There was no reason to suspect foul play, no bruises like she'd been strangled, no head wound where somebody whacked her over the head. Nothing like that. There was a bruise on her right ankle where she probably bumped into something in the dark." She paused. "It's dark in this house a lot."

The electricity had gone out twice, no, three times since Avery and Maddie arrived. Not surprising with so many people—

"Somebody could have given her an additional shot—"

"No recent puncture wounds. Just the one place where she gave herself a shot before she went to bed. So she loaded up too much insulin in that shot — or maybe she doubled up sometime during the day and didn't remember — either way, what was in that one shot was enough insulin to kill her."

"They checked her body, all over?"

"Everywhere — just the one needle mark."

Maddie had no comeback for that, seemed deflated.

Avery relaxed back against her pillow and munched on the brownie.

"Everywhere, huh … even between her toes?"

"Yes, even between …"

And that's when Avery remembered Aunt Hannah's toenail.

"My Aunt Hannah had a fake toenail."

Avery just blurted it out and was instantly sorry. She should have kept her mouth shut.

"A fake toenail?"

"It doesn't mean anything."

Maddie said nothing, just looked at her.

"Okay … when I was a little girl, I loved fingernail polish. I painted the nails of every girl in my first-grade class, and I went around begging my family to let me paint their fingernails and toenails."

She looked down at her fingernails now — ragged and bit off. That was a childhood habit she should have kept.

"Aunt Hannah didn't have a full complement of toenails, though. She dropped something heavy, I think it was one of those black iron skillets, on the big toe of her right foot when she was in her twenties. The nail turned black and fell off and nothing else ever grew there. So I'd paint the other nine toenails."

She remembered how Aunt Hannah would examine her foot, hold it out in front of her to see the toenail job. Avery was only a little girl, but she had gotten quite good. Her aunt would shake her head sometimes and point to her toenail-less toe. "That messes up the set."

"Then one day when I was nine, she actually asked me to paint her toenails. She'd never done that before. She only let me paint them because I begged her. She took her shoes off and held out her foot and said, 'Look, I finally grew a toenail.'"

Avery'd been astonished and Aunt Hannah had laughed, then reached down and hooked a fingernail under the end of the new nail and popped it off into her hand.

"She'd gotten an acrylic nail? Why hadn't she ever done that before?"

"No, that's not it. Not acrylic. Something else. Remember, she didn't have a nail to put an acrylic one on top of — just skin. It was stuck down with some special kind of adhesive, I think. Anyway, she had to stick it back on before I could paint it."

"That was ten years ago. Surely she's gotten something more permanent like, I don't know, a toenail transplant. I bet there is such a thing and she could have afforded—"

"I went into her bathroom to get some aspirin right before I left for school and I saw this little container on a shelf and it had toenails in it, so she must swap them out, or maybe they get old and she has to replace—"

"So the toenail still comes off, and you're suggesting …"

"I'm not suggesting anything."

"Yes you are. You're suggesting that somebody could have popped that fake toenail off, given her a shot in the toe under it, then put the toenail back on to hide the needle mark."

"Why would she let somebody—"

"The bruise on her right ankle! Maybe she fought back and—"

"This is crazy."

"Or they held a gun on her or a knife or—"

"Wouldn't take much to subdue Aunt Hannah at night. She loved wine. Sometimes she was three sheets to the wind before she went to bed. But she wasn't murdered. That's certifiable."

"You don't know that. There was motive."

"What … her next-door-neighbor ten miles away didn't want her to put in that koi pond?"

"Not the koi pond, the *jewelry*. Somebody might have wanted to keep her from donating it all to the museum. You said your aunts and cousins always wanted—"

"Far as I know, my aunts and cousins are not assassins."

"Right. As far as you know. You'd be amazed at what some people will do when they're desperate."

There was a haunted quality to Maddie's voice when she said that, and Avery suspected she was speaking from some kind of personal experience. Avery had never been *desperate* about anything.

Chapter Thirty-Five

AVERY WAS THINKING about the leftovers from supper. And the desserts — chocolate and pecan pies and some kind of cobbler.

"I got the munchies," she said. "Let's go raid the refrigerator. I want some—"

"Later, maybe. I'm not hungry."

Not hungry! How could she not be hungry? Avery looked at the diminished contents of the bag of brownies. There was one with a bite out of it on the bed beside Maddie. Avery studied it. Was that the same brownie she'd bitten into when she set the bag on the bed between them? If it was ... had Avery eaten the rest? Wouldn't be surprising. They were delicious. But why hadn't Maddie eaten more?

"How come you're not eating—"

Maddie blew by her question, intent on a piece of paper where she'd been writing things down as Avery babbled.

"So this is a list of the possible suspects," Maddie said, studying the names on the list, tapping the end of the pencil on her nose ring as she thought. Nose ring. Avery wasn't fond of the nose ring, but Maddie's tats, *yes!* Those were impressive. There was definitely a tattoo in Avery Chambers' future —

more than one. First, she had to decide — a tattoo of what? She'd tried to study Maddie's for ideas but hadn't gotten a very good look. Sitting on the bed in a baggie old tee, her right leg and thigh were awash in the light on Avery's nightstand now, though. She concentrated on it. A woman's face. Glancing around, most of her tattoos were faces. Avery turned her attention back to the one on her right thigh. The woman might have been pretty. There was no way to tell with her face contorted in a rictus of terror. Avery'd never seen a look of fear like that.

"You're really good."

Maddie stopped in mid-sentence. "Good at what?"

Avery pointed to the tattoo. "You drew that, didn't you? The design, I mean."

Maddie followed her gaze and the look on her face shifted. She reached down and stroked the tattoo, the way you'd pet a puppy. Her voice seemed unnaturally deep when she spoke.

"… just the right moment. You capture it, freeze it so it never changes."

"I want a tattoo. Nothing dark and brooding or anything." She looked down at her own right hand, turned it over, palm up. "A rose, maybe. On my palm. But I've heard it's really hard to tattoo on the palm and it hurts—"

"What do you think of the suspects?" Maddie asked.

"Suspects?"

"Murder suspects."

Avery looked up and saw that Maddie was again studying the notes she'd taken.

"Top of the list is her husband, Cyrus. He certainly had opportunity, but I don't have a motive for him. The spouse or lover is always the primary suspect."

"Uncle Cyrus has Alzheimer's. I doubt he could pull off something as complicated as a murder."

"Your aunts have motive — getting their hands on the jewelry they always wanted—"

"Reason enough to kill their grandmother? Listen to your-self, Maddie. You're suggesting they committed murder."

"What's wrong with murder?"

"Are you serious?"

"Wrong, right, what's the difference? What's wrong for you may not be wrong for me. It's all relative, and you have to find your own way, that's part of being faithful to your essential self."

Word salad. That's what Grandma Alex called it. Random wise-sounding phrases strung together to form a totally mean-ingless concept.

"Suicide's not wrong." Maddie had a thousand-yard stare in her eyes. "Not for anybody! Life bestows the inherent right to decide not to, to decide to die." Then she slowly turned toward Avery and the left-the-building look had taken over her face. "You just have to practice, that's all. No matter how many tries it takes."

That was sick. Not word salad, sick. Yet again she kicked herself in the metaphorical ass for getting sucked into this.

Avery pointed to the paper in Maddie's hand.

"You can't assign a "motive to kill" to every member of my family who ever got crossways with Aunt Hannah. That's everybody. Grandma Alex has been mad at her for sixty years! She hated the way she treated Uncle Cyrus. My cousin Jude can't stand to be in the room with the woman, and she's his grandmother. She spent his whole childhood telling his parents he was a psychopath — said she could tell just by looking in his eyes. My grandfather Gabe swears he's seen Aunt Hannah's face on the harpies on the walls of castles in Scotland. Her granddaughters Leanne and Dani—"

"We already have them on the jewelry motive list. Who else?"

This was all moving about twenty miles faster than Avery's synapses were firing. Her thinking was too muddled to form any coherent arguments … but that was okay. Every minute

Maddie was obsessing over murder suspects was a minute she wasn't brewing up tea with magic mushrooms.

"So what's your plan to narrow down the lists?"

"We're going to lure the fly to the spiderweb."

"How?"

"The way your cousins did, the ones your grandmother was yelling at when we came in."

"Three-D?" Maddie didn't get it. "Dumb, Dumber and Dumbest."

Maddie roared. And it wasn't that funny. Well, maybe the first time you heard it.

"They went around sticking stupid notes under—"

"And when we do the same thing, who's everybody going to blame? Your dumb cousins. But the person who's guilty can't take a chance that it's only a joke. They will *have to* find out if we really do know something."

You could tell Maddie thought her idea was brilliant.

"What will we say on the note?"

"Something general, then tell them to meet us somewhere and we'll see who shows up. Or maybe something more vague — 'I know you're a killer, meet me somewhere or I'll tell.'"

"You're suggesting we give notes to all my family members saying we know they're killers! They're here for a funeral and we're not going to play some stupid game—"

"This is a game to you? It's more than a game. Killers never stop at one, you know. There's always another … and another."

Avery felt her skin grow cold.

"If you're suggesting we give my father a note that says, 'I know you're a killer,' *that* is extra." Her voice was icy. "You wanna do some shrooms, fine, or go blow up some bosses in Mohgwyn Palace. But *this* game is over."

Maddie was silent for a few moments

"That hit a nerve. I'm sorry, Aves." She did sound sorry, contrite.

"I forgot you don't know. Everybody else does. My father *is* a killer. He wasn't just in a wreck where somebody died. He was sentenced to ten years in prison for running down a kid on a bicycle."

Maddie got up and crossed the room and put her arm around Avery's shoulder. It should have been an awkward gesture, but somehow it wasn't. It came off as kind and compassionate.

"I made that up about not knowing who my father is," Maddie said. "I know. He didn't live with us. When I was a little kid, he'd come to the apartment. My mother was always out of it, didn't know what was going on. And he …"

Avery looked up, shocked, and saw tears in Madeline's eyes. Their gazes locked, and Maddie slowly nodded.

Avery squeezed her hand, heard Maddie mumble, "When I couldn't take it anymore, he came and I threatened to kill myself if he touched me. I meant it, too. I would have killed myself, should have jumped out a window or slit my wrists or … Everything that happened after that was my fault because I didn't. I was to blame every time I felt his breath on my neck. It was *my fault.* I should have died."

"Maddie, don't say that."

"I should have—"

"Maddie." Avery was beginning to be frightened for her. "You didn't do anything—"

"Wrong?" Maddie's voice was cold and hollow. "I told you, suicide isn't wrong. It's never, ever wrong. And you have to kill yourself over and over until you stop coming back from the dead."

Maddie put down her list of suspects and went to the pot of now-tepid water for the tea. Avery scrambled.

"Okay, fine. Look, I don't believe it for a minute, but if somebody in my family was murdered then, yeah, I'd want to know. So let's assume my aunt was murdered. What do you propose we do with that assumption?"

Maddie reengaged immediately.

"We find out. We get proof."

"Proof."

"Yeah, evidence."

"Where?"

"Isn't that obvious?"

It took Avery a moment to realize what Maddie meant.

"No. You can't mean … *that*."

"Why not?"

"*Why not?* You're the one freaked out by just being in the same house with a dead body. Now you're suggesting we … what?"

"I'm not suggesting we mutilate a corpse."

"Then what are you suggesting?"

"We sneak into the parlor when nobody's around, pop the fake toenail off your aunt's toe, and see what's under it."

"You can't mean that."

"Oh yes, I can."

Chapter Thirty-Six

GABE COULDN'T SLEEP. Of course, he couldn't sleep.

He could not recall ever being able to just lie down, close his eyes, and drift off like other people did. It was always a chore. When you know every time you go to sleep that you might wake up screaming ... as Grandma Liv would say, "It kinda puts a hitch in your get-along."

At least, he had a lot to think about as he stared wide-eyed at the ceiling. First, there was Spencer. And then, of course, there was Spencer. And, well, *Spencer.*

Thinking of his son's face put a smile on Gabe's. He had lots of memories of time he had spent with the boy, and he'd about worn those memories out thinking of them all the long years Spencer was locked away.

He'd taken the boy to baseball games and football games and soccer games. To plays and concerts ... even to the Home-A-Rama, where they wandered from displays of gutters to window units, laminated decking to ceiling fans, HVAC systems to driveway sealant — though, of course, Gabe didn't own a house.

And then one day, he took the boy to a horse race. It was a spur of the moment thing. The matinee movie they'd intended

187

to see was sold out because they were late, and driving down the street, Spencer had pointed to the sign advertising horse races at Palo Duro Downs near Canyon, Texas. It wasn't far, and Gabe had never seen a horse race. Rodeos, of course, he was a Texan after all. But not a race. Sounded like a good time — there would at least be a concession stand where he could feed the kid all the junk food his mother wouldn't let him eat.

He paused the memory movie that was about to roll in his head.

If only he'd *lost* that first time, lost his shirt. Things would have been different then. They would, wouldn't they? Maybe, but then it might have been something worse. Addiction of some type had always stalked Gabriel Chambers, and it would have found him somewhere eventually. Still, if he'd lost that first time ... But he didn't. He won big. Really big.

GABE PICKS up the big sheet of paper that has all manner of information on it, and unrecognizable symbols and abbreviations, front and back sides, and hands it to Spencer.

"That's the instructions."

"How to build a racehorse from left over parts in your garage?"

Gabe laughs out loud. Spencer is one quick kid, sharp and funny. He watched people, seemed to understand them, and was always coming up with some random remark that put everybody on the floor.

"Nobody likes a smart-ass twelve-year-old, you know that, don't you." He takes the paper back and examines it. "This is a racing form. And if this game is played the way I think it is, this gives you all the information you need about a horse to decide which one you're going to bet on."

"We're gonna bet?"

"Sure we are. Makes it more exciting. I'll spot you the first two dollars — that's the smallest bet you can make. I'm going to go big time — five dollars."

"Can you read this thing?"

"You mean you can't?"

"You're bluffing. You can't really read this."

"That right there — the 116 pounds — that's how much the jockey weighs." Gabe looks for anything else obvious. "And there, the purse is fourteen thousand dollars. That's what the winner gets."

"So what does 7-4 or 6-1 mean?"

"Those are the odds."

"But what does it mean?"

Spencer has him, and Gabe runs up the white flag.

"Okay, I give up. I have no idea what any of this stuff means."

"It means that for every four dollars you bet, you get seven dollars in return," says a voice from behind Gabe. He turns to see a grizzled old man who might or might not be homeless — it's a toss-up—with a stub of a pencil clutched in his grubby fingers, making marks all over a rumpled racing form of his own.

"Well, unless its pari-mutuel betting where the pay-outs come from separate pools. So for a two-dollar bet, you divide the first number in the odds by the second number and multiply by two. So for a horse at 7-4, you divide 7 by 4, 1.75, multiply by two, 3.5, and add two ... the amount you bet. Pay-out's five-fifty."

Gabriel Chambers is seldom at a loss for words, but he can think of nothing more erudite to say than, "Oh."

Spencer turns to him.

"I take it back. All that whining about memorizing the multiplication tables."

Gabe needn't have worried about making conversation. The gentleman wasn't interested in anything but the racing form.

"This here one," he points to the list of horses' names on the form, "that's the one. Tinder Box in the seventh. Bet the farm."

Gabe must not have looked sufficiently convinced, because the man hurried on. "Honest to God, I talked to the stable hands, they're the ones know everything. The favorite's got a sore hamstring but nobody's noticed it. Sucker Punch'll pull up, won't make a furlong. The number two, Easy

Money, he's got the willy-wams bad, but they don't have a hood on him. Tinder Box is stoked, he's itching, he's ready."

Spencer points to the other names on the list. "What about all of these other horses?"

The man smiles with the too-perfect teeth of denture-wearers.

"Ever heard about the two men in the woods that come up on a grizzly bear. One says to the other, 'Can you outrun a grizzly?' and the other fella says, 'I don't have to outrun the bear. I just have to outrun you.'" He chuckles merrily at his own funny. "If Tinder Box can outrun the first two ..." He shakes his head and wanders away, chewing on the stub of a pencil and continuing to make marks on the sheet.

Gabe and Spencer look at each other. "Tinderbox in the seventh ... that horse has eighty to one odds," Spencer says.

"Sounds like our kinda horse. I'm going to bet my mad money, all of it." In an effort to teach Spencer to think ahead, be prepared, Gabe had taken to carrying a fifty-dollar bill in his shoe.

By the seventh race, he and Spencer have won almost a hundred dollars on $5 and $10 wagers on the previous six races. Feeling reeeeally lucky, they "bet the farm" on Tinder Box, all their winnings plus Gabe's mad money. By race time, Tinder Box was coming in at a hundred to one odds.

For their $150 wager, they walk out of the track with $15,150.

GABE PUT ALL THE WINNINGS — except fifty dollars in mad money — in an account for Spencer that he couldn't touch until his eighteenth birthday.

On that day, Spencer had withdrawn it all and bought himself a custom Harley Davidson motorcycle *and* a vintage Pontiac Grand Prix, black over silver. Gabe suspected Avery was likely conceived in the backseat of that car. (He could afford a car but not a box of condoms?) Spencer and Emily were walking down the aisle before the boy turned nineteen. Like father, like son.

What gambling became in Gabe's life was as psychologically tangled as strands of spaghetti in a bowl. Over the years, he'd spent way more money than Spencer'd spent on that car paying shrinks to help him unravel it. None of them ever did. Closest anybody got was the analogy that gambling somehow became for Gabe what cutting was to disturbed teenage girls. Gabe's gambling addiction was industrial strength cutting — cutting on steroids. The excitement, anticipation, endorphin-releasing rush — whether he won or lost — relieved the pressure in his head, at least temporarily. When he gambled, the migraines eased off, their vice grip fading away. He slept without night terrors. It made no sense to him or to anybody else, there was nothing rational about it — it was just reality as Gabe experienced it. In the years after he and the boy bet the farm on Tinder Box, Gabe had won and lost hundreds of thousands of dollars, almost bankrupted his lucrative real estate business — twice— and broke up two marriages. He bet on football games, baseball games, basketball games, bet the ponies, went to Vegas every time he had a chance …

Then came Covid lockdown. He lived in front of his computer, got so deeply entangled in online betting that he didn't even know who was bankrolling it all. By the time he realized who he'd been betting against, it was too late. Since then, he had been desperately trying to dig himself out of the hole. Too little, too late. In the past eight months, he hadn't gambled a single time. Didn't miss it much — quitting smoking had been way harder. But the night terrors and migraines returned with a vengeance. Oh, he'd quit gambling several times in the past, so he knew what was coming, and it had eventually driven him back to the *release*. Not this time, though. This time there was more on the line than headaches and nightmares. It wouldn't take much for Gabe to lose it all — not only his money, but his life.

Chapter Thirty-Seven

JUST WHEN YOU thought it was safe to go back in the water. Avery couldn't have imagined anything worse than putting I-Know-You're-a-Killer notes under her family's bedroom doors. But now she was entering a whole new world of batshit crazy. Magic mushrooms would be better than … wait a minute. She paused, then smiled.

"Bet!" she said with fake enthusiasm. "But first things first. Put your magical fungi friends away and let's finish off these brownies."

"Fine by me." Maddie had been unconsciously picking off her fingernail polish. "You got any nail polish remover?"

"Saw some under the sink in the bathroom." Avery got up, then returned with what looked like a quart bottle and held it out, grinning. "Think this'll be enough? Grandma Liv's cheap. She shops at Costco."

Fifteen minutes later, Maddie's nails were polish free and Avery was feeling *good*. This was some of the best weed she'd ever done.

"Where did you say you got this?" She held up a half-eaten brownie.

Maddie smiled, recalling a memory. "A friend. I thought there was no sense wasting it."

Avery almost asked what that meant. Didn't matter. She stayed tuned in enough to make sure that this time, Maddie was eating brownies, too. The mellower Avery got, the more anxious she was to indulge their raging cases of the munchies in a midnight raid of the refrigerator after their little plot bombed.

And it would bomb. Avery knew what Maddie didn't — that they'd never have an opportunity to put the plan into action because Aunt Hannah's body would *never* be left alone. Maybe it was a family thing or maybe a southern thing. Either way, Maddie didn't know that custom required that somebody "sit up with the body." There'd be shifts through the night, and during the day, the parlor would never be empty. Avery was glad to agree to Maddie's plan because she knew she'd never have to go through with it.

Except not.

When they went tiptoeing down the stairs at three o'clock that morning, the parlor was dark and deserted.

Aunt Hannah was laid out beneath the huge windows that looked out on the garden she'd planted on the south side of the house to attract birds to her bird feeders. In the springtime, she left the parlor windows open in the morning before it got too hot so the fragrance could waft into the room on the morning breeze.

She was going to be cremated, so there was no casket. She was lying on some kind of funeral home gurney thing artfully disguised to look like a small bed, with midnight blue velvet fabric stretching from the table to the floor to cover up the frame and the wheels. The upper part of her body was propped up slightly on silk pillows, with beautiful needlework on the edge. An ugly quilt that'd been in the family for like centuries covered her from the waist down, and her hands were clasped delicately on top of it.

When Avery had first seen the body soon after she arrived, she was surprised that her aunt was wearing the blue silk dress she'd worn to Cassidy's wedding. It'd been tight then, and that was forty or fifty pounds ago. She couldn't imagine how they'd managed to stuff her into it. It fit like the skin on a sausage. But Avery hadn't been surprised that Aunt Hannah was decked out in jewelry that'd sparkled even in the dim, dignified lighting they set up all around her. On her left hand, beside the wedding ring with its huge solitaire diamond amid half a dozen smaller diamonds, was a sapphire ring surrounded by emeralds. On her right hand was a ruby ring with a stone as big as a grape and other colorful stones around it. She wore emerald earrings beneath her stylishly short gray hair, with a matching necklace and bracelets. The jewelry didn't go with her dress. It looked like somebody'd just picked out the gaudiest things she had. Probably Uncle Cyrus.

There were three entrances to the parlor. It opened into the great foyer at the front of the house where the twin staircases rounded down from the second floor like the staircase where Scarlett O'Hara had stood in *Gone With the Wind*. Except the one in the movie looked elegant, while these stairs looked like it'd been added as an afterthought, which they probably had. There was a door in the right back corner of the room that led to the south side hallway, and another door that opened into the dining room — the door that would have to be closed to keep those eating lunch from having to look at the body.

Maddie had laid the operation out like it was some Navy Seal attack on a terrorist stronghold. They would come down the circular staircase that went down from the second-floor hall into the parlor. If they came upon anyone, Avery's job was to engage the person in some kind of inane conversation — what do you talk about at three in the morning outside a room with a dead body? — while Maddie excused herself to go to the bathroom, whereupon she would sneak into the parlor and do the deed.

If they ran into nobody, Avery would stand outside the archway into the foyer while Maddie sneaked into the parlor. Avery had insisted that she'd be willing to be a lookout but nothing beyond that. If Maddie wanted to check for a puncture wound beneath the toenail of Avery's dead great aunt, well, she was welcome to take a peek.

Avery had hoped that her refusal to be any more than an observer, leaving the dirty work to Maddie, would queer the deal immediately. When they'd arrived here, Maddie refused to even go into the parlor where Aunt Hannah was laid out. She never dreamed Maddie would be willing to actually *touch* the corpse. More than touch it. Take a shoe off and then pry off a toenail! Maddie couldn't possibly manage such an act.

But Avery'd been dead wrong — pun intended.

Maybe if Avery had had her wits about her, she could have figured out a way to put an end to the madness before it got this far. But with her mind fuzzy — comfortably fuzzy, but fuzzy nonetheless — she couldn't manage anything more complicated than following Maddie's instructions.

"It shouldn't take but a couple of minutes," Maddie said as they stood in the second-floor hallway in front of the staircase. She'd pocketed a pair of cuticle scissors to remove the fake nail and her cellphone to photograph whatever she discovered beneath it.

Then they inched their way down the steps.

This can't be happening. It's all a dream. It's the weed, something in the weed. I'll wake up in the morning with a funny story to tell Maddie.

Avery didn't actually acknowledge the reality of it all until she stood with her back to the wall outside the archway, her eyes frantically flitting from the stairs to the parlor, to the doors leading off the foyer and back to the stairs, trying to see everything at once, and consequently not seeing anything at all.

She wished she'd looked at her watch, so she'd know how

long Maddie had been gone. Time was as elongated as her sense of proportion. The staircase in the foyer looked like it was a hundred yards away. And surely Maddie had left her side at least half an hour ago.

She needed to pee.

And cough.

Oh, she *really* needed to cough. She tried to swallow rapidly to keep the cough from exploding out into the silent foyer. If it did, that single sound would awaken the whole household and summon them immediately. But her mouth was so dry, there was no spit to swallow, so she had to hold her breath to keep the cough inside.

That was hard, holding her breath, because now she *really* needed to pee.

And cough.

What was she thinking? This was lunacy, plucking off her dead aunt's toenail in the middle of the night.

She thought she spotted movement on the second-floor balcony overlooking the foyer. No, it was nothing. Just a shadow. Then the dark shape of somebody began to descend the stairs on the other side of the room. Slowly. Ponderously. It was Uncle Cyrus. He was coming down to be near his beloved Hannah.

Chapter Thirty-Eight

ALEX COULDN'T SLEEP. Of course, she couldn't sleep.

She was losing her hearing! Hard to hide a thing like that. Surely, somebody'd notice eventually. She really should just come clean, tell the family about Persephone and be done with it. But every time she contemplated the prospect, it made her want to puke. Who knew how long she'd hang on — and in what condition! — with everybody hovering ... no, not happenin'. Of course, maybe she'd grab the brass ring, just go to sleep one night and never wake up. That would be so much easier on everybody, particularly Cyrus. He had become so *fragile* in the past few months. It broke her heart to think about the bereft look that would be on his face. How could she leave him behind when he'd been there for her every day of her whole life? He had *saved* her.

Not just from the buck-toothed kid on the bus who blew his nose in her hair. Her big brother had moved that nose to the other side of the kid's face. Cyrus was the father she didn't have, after Landon Harrington fell into the gigantic crater of his business enterprises and never crawled back out. Cyrus had come home from his job in Oklahoma City to walk her out onto the football field when she was one of the homecoming queen candidates. The other girls were on their fathers' arms, but she didn't even know where her father was — Mexico, maybe, or Honduras, somewhere there was lots of oil and nobody to drill a hole in the ground to get it.

Cyrus was her hero.

He had kept the Boogie Man away.

There should have been lots of people within yelling distance that day, farmhands and migrant workers, but no one saw the man grab her by her ponytail and yank her off her feet, clamping his hand over her mouth before carrying her into the dirty shed where the yard equipment — a mower, clippers, shears, weed whacker — were stored.

Maybe the years had darkened Alex's memories of him, but she didn't think so. He really had been that ugly, that mean looking, that perverted.

He keeps his hand over her mouth so she can't scream, mumbles awful things about how she'd been asking for it all summer, running around in that itty bitty bathing suit, and now he's gonna give it to her. He paws at her with one hand, ripping at her shirt, tearing it open and fondling where she is as flat-chested as every other eight-year-old girl.

She wiggles and squirms to get away until he produces the knife and holds it up to her cheek. His breath smells of whiskey, tobacco, and rotted teeth.

"You lie still, Little Missy, and I'm gonna do you like you been wanting me to. You make any noise, I'm gonna slit your throat."

Alex freezes, stops struggling.

"That's better. Now get them shorts and panties off. Go on, get them off." She is so sick and terrified she can't breathe, can't imagine taking her clothes off.

He pricks the skin of her neck with the knife and she begins to pull her shorts off. He fumbles with her free hand at his own crotch, then pulls a thing out of his fly that Alex doesn't even know exists. She's never seen a boy or a man naked. She'd seen the bull, though, and that's what it looked like. And then she understands what he means to do with it, and she can't breathe.

No!

She clamps her knees together as tight as she can and he slaps her face, hard, snaps her head to the side, yanks her legs apart and starts moving toward her with that thing—

Then he's gone. Above her, leering down, then only empty air and the sound of grunting. And she sees that Cyrus has grabbed the back of his shirt and pulled him off her into the dirt.

Cyrus is slight of build, smaller than other boys his age. Even at eighteen, he probably doesn't weigh more than a hundred and thirty pounds. But he goes after the handy man like he's ten feet tall. Kicks the knife out of his hand, then with a vicious uppercut with his boot, he catches the man in the chin and propels him backward onto his back, then starts hitting him and kicking him, making wordless grunts, angry, like growling. It's a while before he realizes the man is unconscious, but when he does, he keeps hitting and kicking him anyway, can't seem to stop.

Then he comes back to himself and turns to her. She has her pants back on by then, but all the buttons are torn off the front of her shirt and she can't close it.

She isn't crying — she's too scared and shocked to cry.

Cyrus takes her by the shoulders and asks with a tenderness she can't imagine he could summon after the wild fury she has seen, "Are you all right?"

She can't speak, just nods her head.

"Go get Duley," he says, then takes her chin in his hand and makes her look him in the eye. "Tell him that Bill attacked you, had a knife, and that he and I were fighting, and you ran away. Can you get all that? Can you say it just like that?"

She bobs her head up and down dumbly and runs. Slams the door open and takes great gulps of fresh air to get her breath back, then sees Mr. Hawthorne and runs to him. That's not who Cyrus had said to tell, but he's the first man she saw, so she tells him — just the way Cyrus had told her.

When she and Mr. Hawthorne, and soon after that all the

farmhands, arrive at the storage shed, they stand in the doorway, not saying anything. The handyman lies on his back on the dirty floor, his fly still unzipped and the thing still visible between the metal teeth of his zipper. A knife is sticking out of his belly. Cyrus is leaned up against the work bench, his head down, his shoulders shaking. She runs to him and he hugs her hard, doesn't seem to want to let her go.

She never finds out what actually happened. She can guess, but Cyrus never says. He tells the others that he'd pulled the man off her and they were fighting over the knife and it ended up in the handyman's belly.

THE SHERIFF ASKED FEW QUESTIONS. Her swelling-shut eye and torn clothing told the story. And the sheriff would have been disinclined to contradict Cyrus Kavanaugh, the son of Olivia and Landon Harrington, even if there had been any doubt.

Only once did Alex glance at Cyrus. She caught his eye, their gazes locked. That's all it took for her to know what'd happened. She had run out of the shed to get help, and Cyrus had stabbed Bill in his belly while he was lying there unconscious.

They never spoke of it.

Cyrus had already been her hero, her protector — even before that happened. She would have done anything for him. Then afterward ... the years of watching Hannah chip away at him, humiliate him, berate him. But the harpy never managed to damage who Cyrus was, and Alex could never understand how Cyrus was able to take the abuse with no apparent need to retaliate. Of course, who knew why Cyrus had fallen in love with Hannah in the first place, why he had married her. She had been an altogether unpleasant human being her whole life. But Cyrus loved her. The heart keeps its own counsel and there was no denying he loved her, and somehow it just didn't seem to matter to him how she behaved. His love was unconditional.

And Alex was not about to let Hannah *destroy* him now.

Cyrus had killed for Alex, and she was more than willing to return the favor. She only feared getting caught because the explosion it would cause in the family would do irreparable harm. As for her own well-being — it didn't matter. Only as she was grinding up the pile of sleeping pills to dissolve in Hannah's orange juice had she considered the moral implications of the act. If there were consequences for what she'd done, either in this life or the next, she would accept responsibility for them.

If they could just get the body "lying in state" in the parlor to the crematorium without any suspicion, there'd be nothing left of her to point any fingers, figuratively speaking or otherwise. Alex had gotten lucky — Hannah had fallen out of bed. Maybe after she finished the orange juice, she'd felt the effects of the pills, got dizzy and knew something was wrong, tried to get help. Finding her lying like that beside the bed — déjà vu — poor Cyrus. Alex had so hated to hurt him that way she couldn't bear to look at him. She'd hung back, didn't go into the bedroom when he yelled. Gabe had gone running and found Hannah on the floor beside her bed just like she had looked the other time she'd taken too much insulin. That told the story, so insulin overdose was the assumed cause of death. Unless somebody questioned that between now and Sunday, that would be official.

The rest of what Alex'd done to tidy up her life had been … well, most of it'd been legal. Some of it had. Selling off every share of stock she owned was certainly not a *wise* financial decision— as her attorney had pointed out numerous times — not with the stock market tanked and the economy shot to hell thanks to a president suffering from advanced dementia and a Congress suffering from full-bore, bull goose stupid. And she'd liquified every other asset she could — turned it into cash to put into that box alongside the ill-gotten gains derived from the part of it that hadn't been legal. She'd give every dime of it to Gabe. She knew the name for what she was doing. It was called "enabling." But she couldn't help herself, couldn't help clinging to the totally irrational belief that his addiction to gambling was in some way her fault, that it was all tangled up with *that night,* the migraines and the night terrors — and every one of *those* chickens had long ago come home to roost in *her* henhouse.

This time was different from the other times he'd lost his shirt, though. This was far worse than previous financial holes he'd dug himself into. Something had gone terribly wrong several months ago. She'd never seen him look so lost and desperate. She *had* to help him. And with impending death granting her ultimate freedom, she had decided not just to think outside the box, but to think outside the box the first box came in. And her plan, if she did say so herself, had been masterfully conceived and executed. Maybe giving him his life back would in some way atone for stealing it from him when he was just six years old.

She had saved Cyrus, though he must never know what she'd done. She would save Gabe, too, but he would have to know. Now, it would appear, the countdown on her death had started. With her own time running out, she couldn't wait for an opportune time to tell him what she'd done. If she didn't tell him soon, she might not get to tell him at all.

Chapter Thirty-Nine

AVERY'S JOB was to make sure nobody interrupted Maddie until she'd finished what she went into the parlor to do. She was supposed to start some inane conversation to delay them and divert their attention. But Avery couldn't make herself approach her uncle. What would she say? *Oh, hi Uncle Cyrus, I just got up to go to the bathroom ...*

Although she really did need to pee.

There were two light switches at the foot of the stairs, and he would flip them both on as soon as he got to them. The switch on the right would light the gigantic chandelier that hung in the ceiling high above the foyer floor. The switch on the left would turn on the three table lamps artfully arranged around the room. He was almost there. As soon as he turned the lights on, he'd see her, hunkering in the shadows ... and how would she explain that?

She couldn't do this!

In one quick movement, she stepped around the archway doorframe into the darkened parlor and flattened herself against the wall where there were deep puddles of shadow. But all the shadows would disappear as soon as he came into the parlor and turned on the lights there. And when he did, he'd see Maddie prying up his dead wife's toenail.

Avery froze with dread.

His house shoes flopped on the tile floor of the foyer. She squeezed her eyes shut. He didn't turn on the lights!

Run!

Where? He'd see her if she moved. She looked toward the body, expecting to see the ugly quilt in a heap on the floor and Maddie digging around with her cuticle scissors at Avery's dead aunt's foot. What she saw was Aunt Hannah lying peacefully on the gurney bed. The quilt was in place, covering her from the waist down. Maddie stood at the foot of the table, as frozen in place as Avery.

Avery only had time to make a frantic hand motion — *get down!* Maddie dropped instantly to the floor behind a spray of flowers with the inscription "In Loving Memory." Avery crouched down behind the wall of flower arrangements sitting on the floor and on flower stands of varying height, praying the foliage was sufficient to conceal her presence. Uncle Cyrus couldn't see very well, couldn't hear very well either, so maybe he'd miss the sound of her heart banging away like a sperm whale in a fish tank beneath her tee shirt.

Uncle Cyrus shambled in house-shoed feet into the parlor.

He didn't flip on the light! He just walked slowly through the shadows to the not-a-coffin table against the far wall. He stopped about three feet from where Maddie was hidden behind the magnolias. He reached out his hand and put it on Aunt Hannah's cold hands folded on the quilt that covered her feet where she might or might not still have ten toenails.

Then he leaned closer and began to speak softly. Avery couldn't hear what he was saying, just the urgent tone of his voice. Just a few words at first. He kept talking.

She needed to pee. But he kept talking. On and on. In a single stream of mumbled words that was interrupted now and then by stifled sobs. Hours passed. Days. Weeks. Months. Geologic epochs.

Okay, minutes, but a lot of them. If she'd looked at her watch when Maddie went into the parlor, she'd know how long. Now, she didn't dare move her arm to look at it.

Then she heard voices on the other side of the foyer, coming from the kitchen. Women's voices. Cynthia and Marilou— two of Aunt Hannah's three daughters-in-law. They were speaking quietly, but not whispering, coming this way. They would definitely turn the lights on when they got to the parlor. In the very best possible scenario, they wouldn't see her or Maddie, in which case they'd be trapped in their hiding place. Worst case, one of the women would spot them instantly.

Avery acted before she had time to consider whether or not it was a good idea. Didn't matter. It was the only idea she had.

She stood up, edged out past the flowerpots, then walked boldly out into the dark foyer that her aunts were about to enter.

Chapter Forty

"Oh," Avery gasped, feigning surprise. "You scared the bejesus out of me!"

Aunt Marilou let out a squeak. Aunt Millie only gasped and stepped back. "Look what you made me do!" she cried. Avery saw the cup of coffee in her hand. "All down the front of my robe!"

"We scared *you?*" Aunt Marilou said when she caught her breath. "Where'd you come from?"

"I was in the parlor. Well, sort of." She turned and gestured toward the dark room. "I came down to … well, you know. I kinda wanted to say a private goodbye." She tried to make her voice sound thick with emotion, but only managed to sound hoarse. "But then I saw Uncle Cyrus just standing there in the dark, and I didn't want to disturb him."

"Papa Cyrus's in there?" Marilou asked. "He shouldn't be out of bed. That Xanax Alex gave him should have knocked him out cold."

"And coming down the stairs by himself all drugged up," Millie cried.

Both women rushed past Avery into the room and switched on the lights. Avery followed behind, her eyes scanning the "In Loving Memory" spray of flowers near the foot of the table. Gratefully, the flowers were stuck to it tight enough for a Rose Parade float. It was an impenetrable wall of petals.

Uncle Cyrus blinked like an owl in the sudden illumination.

"Papa Cyrus, what are you—"

"All by yourself—"

"Should have gotten Gabe to—"

"Could have tripped on the stairs—"

"Need to go back to—"

They sounded like a flock of twittering birds.

"We just got up to get coffee," Aunt Millie said, gesturing with the cup that'd splashed a brown stain down the front of her pink robe. Avery looked at the nearby table, where a cup sat on an empty coaster. On the sofa, a pillow was stuffed down the cushion for Aunt Marilou's bad back. They *had* been down here "sitting up with the body," she realized, and grasped how lucky she and Maddie had been that they hadn't walked right in on them. No, *unlucky.* If anybody'd been here, they'd have abandoned their stupid little plan and gone after the leftover pies in the kitchen. Avery was hungry enough to eat a whole one all by herself. But first, she had to figure out a way to get Maddie out of hiding without being seen.

Again, she spoke before she thought, and her voice was only a little squeaky, didn't reveal that she was high as a kite and scared shitless.

To Aunt Millie she said, "Why don't you go in the kitchen and get some water on that stain before it sets?"

Then to Aunt Marilou, "You can help Uncle Cyrus back to bed. I'll stay here until you get back." She paused for a beat and couldn't help adding, "Take your time."

That was it, her only shot. If it didn't work …

After a beat of agonizing silence that lasted at least half an hour, both women bought the crock she was selling. Aunt

Marilou took her father-in-law's arm and guided him to the archway, then flipped on the foyer lights and started up the stairs. Aunt Millie hurried across the foyer to the kitchen door.

"Can I come out yet?" The urgent whisper came from behind the Rose Parade flower arrangement.

"Not yet! Aunt Marilou and Uncle Cyrus are still on the stairs." They were moving so slow. Any second, Aunt Millie could pop out of the kitchen with the front of her robe wet and they'd be stuck.

Uncle Cyrus and Aunt Marilou were almost at the top of the stairs when Maddie stood up. Uncle Cyrus turned their way and stumbled, then he and her aunt passed out of sight.

"That way!" Avery pointed to the door leading into the dining room. It took too long to climb the spiral stairs. "If you run into anybody, act like you belong there. Say you came downstairs with me to see Aunt—" The door Aunt Millie had gone out opened. "Now, go *now!*"

Maddie hopped behind the flower arrangements like a baby rabbit and hurried to the dining room door. She closed it behind her about half a second before Aunt Millie came into the room, complaining that the coffee'd soaked through to her nightgown and the stain was probably permanent, that it was really hard to get coffee out of satin — making it clear that she held Avery responsible for the ruination that had befallen her. Just like she'd blamed Avery the time her cousin Leanne left the cookies in the oven and they burned, and the time when she was real little that Leanne's sister Danni had been running through the house and knocked over a lamp and said Avery did it. And the time Avery had accidentally dropped her biscuit into the gravy bowl and it splashed everywhere —okay, that time, it had been her fault, but not the other times.

Avery stood there, listening to her bitch, offering profuse apologies like she'd wrecked her aunt's car or run over her aunt's dog or something. Babbling was Avery's relief bubbling up out of her that Maddie'd been stopped before she did the deed that had been growing more and more heinous in Avery's mind since the moment she'd agreed to it.

Then her bladder reminded her that she had less than thirty seconds to get to a bathroom, or it would rebel and release its contents.

"I gotta pee," she said abruptly, then hurried to the powder room off the foyer in that peculiar walk/waddle all women adopt when they are trying to not wet their pants.

When she finally made it back to her bedroom, she flung the door open, stepped inside, shoved it shut, then leaned against it, panting.

Maddie was seated on her bed eating potato chips.

"Holy. Shit!" She lost it then and dissolved into hysterical giggles. Maddie joined her and they laughed until their sides ached and tears were running down their cheeks.

"Thank God, you hadn't started yet," Avery gasped when she finally wound down. "What if you'd been poking away with those scissors—"

The remark threatened to send them both back into a gale of giggles.

"Hadn't started?" Maddie looked confused. "I was finished." She held out her hand and Avery discovered to her horror that what lay in her palm wasn't a potato chip. It was a toenail.

All the humor drained out of the moment in a heartbeat.

"You kept it!" Avery was horrified.

"What was I supposed to do with it? It wouldn't have stuck if I'd tried to put it back on. Nobody'll notice the missing toenail."

Avery supposed not, and why would they take off her shoes?

"But the hole I had to cut in her hose — that's hard to miss."

"You cut a hole ..."

"Who knew old ladies still wore those things? It wasn't like her shoes would rub a blister or anything if she went bare legged."

Avery was stuck in a loop.

"You cut a *hole*?"

"It was either that or take her hose off." She paused, then blurted out, "Can you imagine trying to get pantyhose on a dead fat woman in the first place?" She roared with laughter, doubled over, but it didn't strike Avery funny at all.

Avery plopped onto her bed and wrinkled her nose.

"Can you put that *thing* … somewhere?" She pointed to the nail Maddie'd dropped on the bed when she burst out laughing. Maddie looked at it and tossed it over onto the nightstand dismissively.

"I had in mind out of sight—"

"Forget the toenail, we have bigger fish to fry."

Avery felt a sudden weight descend on her chest and she couldn't catch her breath.

"Bigger fish?"

Avery held out her cellphone.

"It's not a very good picture. I took a couple, but I didn't dare stand there snapping away."

Avery had no idea what she was looking at. A blob of pinkish … something … with blue …

"The second one's better."

It wasn't. Still showed nothing but —

"See, right there." Maddie pointed to a black spot in the middle of the blue area surrounded by pasty pale pink. "That's a hole, a needle mark. Has to be. It's bruised around it."

What Avery saw was not definitively a needle mark. It could have been, she supposed. But it wasn't clear enough. It could have been any number of things.

"You can't tell from that picture that there's a puncture wound—"

"Yes, you can. Are you looking?" Maddie shoved the phone closer to Avery's face. "Look at it."

Avery looked again, saw basically what she'd seen the first time. A black mark that could have been a hole and the purple around it … that did look like a bruise. And once you knew what you were looking at, the pink was skin. Looked like skin anyway.

But it wasn't definitive.

"This doesn't prove anything."

"Of course it doesn't. A medical examiner would have to look at the actual mark." She paused for only a beat. "And that body's going to be cremated on Sunday."

Avery could only look at Maddie in dumb silence.

"There's more," Maddie said.

Avery didn't like the ominous way she spoke the words. "What more?"

"The guy who came in and stood by her, holding her hand …"

"Uncle Cyrus. What about Uncle Cyrus?"

"He was talking to her, and I heard what he said."

At that moment, Avery absolutely, one hundred percent did not want to know what Uncle Cyrus had said. If she could have, she'd have leapt up and clapped her hand over Maddie's mouth. She knew without having any idea how she knew that Maddie's words would open a door into … somewhere dark and ugly. And the darkness would spill through the doorway and out into the room around Avery, the way light spills through a doorway into a dark room. And the darkness would spread out, ink in a blotter, until all the light in Avery's world was diminished. Once Maddie opened that door, Avery's world would never again be as bright.

Chapter Forty-One

CYRUS COULDN'T SLEEP. Of course, he couldn't sleep.

How would he ever sleep again, reaching across the bed to feel the warmth of Hannah when she wasn't there? When the bring-a-dish food was all gone and the relatives had departed to go home and take up their lives where they'd left off, he would be alone. He had no life to pick back up. Hannah was gone.

Suddenly, he had to see Hannah, had to, couldn't wait another minute, knew where to find her, too. She was lying on a bed in the middle of the parlor downstairs. He couldn't remember why exactly that was, but it didn't matter. As long as he could find her, as long as she wasn't ... *gone.*

The red letters on the bedside clock said it was five minutes after three o'clock, but it didn't matter what time it was, he wanted go see her right now and he was her husband so they couldn't keep him away. Cynthia and Marilou and maybe Millie would be sitting up with her, of course, maybe others, too, but he'd get them all to leave so he could have time alone with her. He had to talk to her, had to explain.

Cyrus had concealed the pill Alex had given him under his tongue so she would think he had taken it. That was easier than trying to talk her out of giving it to him. Nobody talked Alex out of something if she was determined to do it. Even when they were children, he'd seen that trait in her, admired it, was envious of it. He was a teenager and she just a child, but she had an authority he never had. He'd spent only a small amount of time on a therapist's couch, back when he and Hannah were having trouble and she demanded they get marriage counseling. The counselor conducted some of the sessions with each of them individually, and he had gotten more insights about himself from those sessions than he'd ever gotten about their marriage.

Cyrus's father, Benjamin, was killed in the war, so Cyrus had grown up with only a mother who had to work hard to keep a roof over their heads. But they weren't the only families like that. Lots of little boys' daddies got killed in the war. Since it wasn't uncommon, the effects had been pretty well documented. The kind of little-boy confidence bestowed on a kid through daily interaction with a father, a strong man, was not available to Cyrus and other fatherless little boys. So he grew up quiet, reserved, and shy, suffering from the lack of guidance a strong father figure would have provided to mold his character.

When he married Hannah, she was the strong-willed one, while he was … oh, people had the wrong idea about their relationship. He knew they thought she'd led him around by the nose, but it wasn't like that. In all the ways that mattered, Hannah did respect and admire Cyrus, gave in to his wishes, it was just that when other people were around that she needed to be in charge. So he'd let her. What was the harm?

He would go to her now, hold her hand and confess it all, explaining that what he'd done was the only thing he could do to make it all right.

Leaving his bedroom in the dark, he got to the top of the stairs and couldn't remember where it was he was going. Oh, yes, downstairs. Why? He wasn't sure, only knew it was tangled up in the terrible thing he had done to Hannah, his beloved Hannah.

His daughters-in-law were nowhere to be seen, so he could be alone with Hannah. He went to her, took her hand, it was so cold, and told her he was sorry, so very very sorry. Repeated it over and over again.

What else could he do? He'd had no choice.

"Please, please forgive me. I love you. I've always loved you. But I was in such a dark, bad place. Please don't hate me. I am so sorry." He burped out a little sob and then was afraid he would start crying and not be able to stop.

"Sorry … so sorry…"

Then he wasn't sure what it was he was sorry for, only knew that he felt such great sorrow and such profound regret, it was like a vicious sword stabbing into his heart.

Suddenly, the parlor lights came on and Millie and Marilou were all over him, clucking like hens.

"Papa Cyrus, what are you—"

"All by yourself—"

"Should have gotten Gabe to—"

"Could have tripped on the stairs—"

"Need to go back to—"

Then Jordan's wife, Marilou, was leading him across the foyer to the stairs. Practically dragging him. They went slowly up the steps and Cyrus looked back into the parlor where his precious Hannah …

Avery was there, standing beside Hannah.

And then …

It couldn't be, but it was. Someone magically appeared beside Avery — not there and then there. No, not some*one* … some*thing*. It rose up out of the floor. From below, from the *depths*. A blue-haired demon suddenly appeared right next to his precious Hannah!

He stumbled, tried to turn and go back, was too shocked and horrified to cry out, his voice and speech stolen from him by the monstrosity. But Marilou was steamrolling him ahead, propelling him down the hallway, then the parlor vanished from view.

The demon had come for Hannah! Had risen up from hell to snatch her eternal soul. No, oh God no, he wouldn't let that happen! He would protect her. He would never let the blue-haired demon have her — never!

Chapter Forty-Two

AVERY WAS self-aware enough to admit that the adventures she and Maddie had gone on tonight had in large part been her effort to distract herself from thinking about her father. He was, after all, her father. And he was out, free, in her life now. She had memories about what the world had been like *before.* Her parents didn't get along. Her father wasn't home much, worked hard at two jobs, and used work as an excuse to stay away from her mother. Trouble was, that meant he was away from Avery, too, and she'd felt a growing sense of resentment for his absence. In some ways what she'd seen that awful day had granted her a Get Out of Jail Free card. She didn't have to deal with her ambivalent feelings about a father who was ignoring her. She could simply hate him.

But seeing him today, it had kicked a hole in her gut that she would have to figure out a way to mend. Right now, she was filling that hole with food. She and Maddie sat leaned against the headboard of the bed with a feast of leftovers they'd snatched out of the kitchen laid out on the bed in front of them. Avery had piled a plate high with ham and turkey slices, dished out several helpings of the casseroles that didn't need to be heated, and topped it all off with a piece of chocolate pie and a couple of kitchen sink cookies. Maddie had piled a couple of plates high with Mexican dishes. When Avery'd warned they would be spicy, Maddie'd said simply, "I like it hot."

Neither of them was still high, and the brownies and edibles were all gone. Avery'd have to talk to her Aunt Juliana tomorrow and see what she'd brought. She'd just about gotten over the shakes at the close call they'd had in the parlor when Maddie brought the whole thing up again.

"Your Uncle Cyrus did it, you know he did," she said.

"I don't know anything of the kind. He has Alzheimer's!"

"He seemed pretty lucid to me at supper."

"Uncle Cyrus is with it sometimes, his old self. Then he just sort of fades away."

"Maybe he's selectively lucid, more aware of what's going on than everybody thinks."

Maddie held out the cell phone with the picture she had taken of Aunt Hannah's toe. Even in good light, you couldn't really tell anything. You had to look at it just right to know it was even a toe. And the puncture wound. That wasn't clear. It might not have been a hole. It might have been a speck of dirt on the camera lens.

"If he didn't kill her, what was he so sorry about, begging her forgiveness? Did he forget to pick up the dry cleaning or something?"

Maddie was stuffing enchiladas in her mouth, dripping the sauce down the front of her tee shirt. Her blue hair had somehow acquired a bedhead look, and her eyes ... There was something off about her eyes. Avery'd thought it was just that she was high, but she could see it now, too. They were blue, but not robins' egg blue like Avery's. They were a deep blue, and in dim light, their depths made it appear you were looking into her soul. And it was very dark there.

"Okay, if you're convinced your kindly old uncle didn't kill her, fine. But *somebody* did."

"You keep saying that, but you don't know it's true." Avery bit into a sandwich she'd made from a croissant and a chunk of ham and chewed while she talked. "You don't know that's even a puncture wound. Only a doctor could tell something like that."

Maddie stopped and looked coldly at Avery. "This is just you and me. We're not telling anybody. No doctors. No police. Are we clear on that?"

So let it be written, so let it be done.

Exactly when was it that Maddie pushed Avery aside — in her own home, mind you — and assumed control of their activities?

"Who died and left you in charge?" Avery said, her tone cold.

There was a moment of silent tension between them. Maddie started to say something, stopped, and when she did speak, her tone was conciliatory. Avery was relatively sure what she'd started to say hadn't been.

"I didn't mean to sound bossy. Don't *you* think we need to keep this private?"

An image flashed through Avery's mind of a lion tamer. The lion didn't balance on the ball or jump through the hoop of fire because it *wanted* to. It was *forced* to. And if it ever had a chance, it would rip the lion tamer to pieces.

"Of course I do. What do we have to tell anybody? That you cut a hole in my dead aunt's pantyhose, pulled her toenail off, and—"

"If your aunt was murdered, don't you want to catch the person who did it?"

No, actually, she didn't. If the only suspects were members of her family, then no, she did not want to know who did it. She'd prefer to drop the whole thing … but would she really? If her aunt had been murdered, could Avery live the rest of her life knowing that but never telling anybody? How could

she behave normally to Uncle Cyrus if she knew he'd killed —
but they didn't even know for sure she'd been murdered.

"So if not Cyrus, who else? Juliana and Leanne —
Juliana's the one with the side of her head shaved and
Leanne's the dumpy one with acne scars, right? You said those
two were at each other's throats over that jewelry."

"They weren't the only ones." Avery recalled the blowup
last Thanksgiving. "There was a big fight about it, and by the
time it was over, everybody was … Casey and Dannie and
Cassidy. But none of them would have committed murder."

Maddie tapped the cellphone with her knuckle, couldn't
pick it up because her fingers had taco sauce all over them.

"Well, somebody did."

Chapter Forty-Three

SATURDAY

Rowan Douglas leaned back against her car, tented her hand over her eyes to shade them from the glare, and stared across the empty prairie at … holy crap! What was that place? Way out here like a desert oasis — so *green*. Huge trees, a wide expanse of lawn, bushes and splashes of multi-hued color that must be flower beds —with nothing around it but empty prairie. The Harrington House, that's what the fellow in town had told her, on Circle H Ranch. There was a big metal archway with the letter H inside a circle — looked like a cattle brand — that cars were passing beneath as they drove up to the house. When she'd asked directions, he'd smiled and told her to drive out Farwell Road and she couldn't miss it. He got that right! Now, why would somebody build something that huge … though you could see from here it hadn't all happened at once, the original structure had newer additions. There was no single style of architecture. It was a hodgepodge of boxes, each of which she would bet had been added on to the rest one at a time — rooms here and there — with a little box on top, like a cherry on a sundae. It didn't quite seem to fit together, had odd angles and misaligned roofs— a house built by Dr. Seuss.

Rowan had pulled over to the side of the road, just looking, in part because the half-mile lane leading from the highway to the house had cars three deep parked on both sides of it. And there was a side field where she could see somebody directing the cars to park.

Getting back into her car, Rowan didn't start the engine, just sat there staring at the building, wondering about the kinds of people who would build and live in such a structure. She was overwhelmed and unsure, so she just sat where she was, trying to get her emotional and mental ducks beak to tail feathers.

Cars turned into the lane steadily. Almost every car that came down Farwell Road was bound for there. They were coming to the viewing of Hannah Kavanaugh, who, Rowan assumed, either owned the house or was related to whoever did. She'd stopped in the little town of Muleshoe to eat breakfast because she was hungry — wrong! Her Lying to Myself alarm began clanging. Rowan Douglas was not reluctant to lie to other people, though she'd learned over the years that it was easier to tell the truth. Then you didn't have to remember what you said last time. But she had a hard and fast rule that she never lied to herself. Never *knowingly* lied to herself, because that would get you into a world of trouble.

Correction: she had *not* stopped to get breakfast in Muleshoe because she was hungry. She had stopped there to put off going where she had driven more than five hundred miles to get to. She'd parked across the street from a little cafe and noticed an impressive building on the right, a single story — brand new when every other building on the street was thirty, maybe fifty years old. Maybe older. The building had the white stucco walls and red tile roof common to the Southwest.

"Museum of the Southwest," said the tasteful sign beside a flagstone walk leading from the sidewalk to the door. "The art of Charles Russell and Frederic Remington, the largest private collection in the world." In smaller letters, though still prominent, beneath were the words "Donated by Hannah Kavanaugh."

A man was passing by on the street, looked friendly enough. But this was Texas, after all, and even though it was 2022, in the older people she often saw a tightening-around-the-eyes reaction — nothing more pronounced, they'd learned to conceal it, when they got a good look at her and saw that she was of mixed race.

You couldn't miss a thing like that about Rowan Douglas. Her facial features showed her Black heritage, but they were small and delicate — warm caramel-colored eyes, and the full lips — thank you, Jesus! — that men went all stupid over. Her skin was a tawny brown … with *freckles* — not really as gross looking as it could have been, as she'd thought it was as a teenager, when the juxtaposition of the two elements of her heritage seemed more than interesting. Call it jarring. Call it off-putting. She called it freak-show time. Over the years, though, she had finally owned it — life and death combat had a way of putting everything else in perspective. Now, she felt comfortable in her own skin. On her better days, she liked to think of her look as exotic. Of course, she could, and *did*, do something about the most off-putting of her natural features. But the most prominent feature of all couldn't be hidden — an eight-inch, puckered scar that ran across her right cheek from her eye to her chin, and then down her neck.

"Excuse me, sir," she said to the gentleman passing on the street. He stopped and smiled at her, and it was real. Rowan could tell about those things.

"What can I help you with, Missy?" he asked.

"That museum …"

"It's a pure D shame Hannah didn't live to see the grand opening. I hear it's right nice inside." He indicated the sign. "Guess they ought to change that sign to read, 'In Memory of Hannah Kavanaugh,' though."

"She died?" Rowan asked, though she knew the answer.

"She did, indeed, couple of days ago, Thursday." He gestured toward the building. "And now ... don't know if they'll hold the grand opening next Friday or not. Maybe there'll never be one. It was her idea to build it here and put her Russell and Remington collection in it. Hannah was always the engine driving that train — and by that I mean she was definitely pulling all the other cars along behind her on the track."

And the famed Hannah Kavanaugh was Rowan's ... what? Oh, yes, what? Therein lay the mystery, the challenge ... the quest. Yes, you could call it that. It was Rowan Douglas's quest to answer the question: Hannah Kavanaugh what? Her aunt/cousin/second cousin/grandmother, great aunt ... the list was long. The quest had led her here to the vast Texas high plains in search of answers.

She squinted as sunlight glinted off the chrome on a car turning into the lane leading to the Harrington House. Rowan was related in some way to the woman lying in ... what? In state? Surely, they weren't that self-absorbed. She knew she was related to the woman because Ancestry.com said so. Someone named Avery Chambers had done genealogical research on the site a few years before, and when Rowan sent off for her own results, they were a match. Not that Rowan had gone to the site looking for relatives *up* the family tree. All that had mattered to Rowan at the time was the younger generation — finding her son. Sterling ... that's what she had always called him in her head, thought it the moment the doctor laid him in her arms — so she could tell him goodbye. Sterling was far too ostentatious a name for the fatherless son of a worn-out, used-up combat veteran. But it had hung on a nail in Rowan's head all these years. That's who he would always be in her mind.

She had spent half her life trying to find Sterling, and that disastrous endeavor was in large part the reason she was here.

The name Sterling was one of a couple of things that had hung on a nail in her head during that nightmare time. So had the horrifying sign on the side of some clinic, counseling clinic, she couldn't see the name they sped by it so fast. She saw the sign, though. "Abortion doesn't make you un-pregnant. It just makes you the mother of a dead baby." The horror of that thought sliced into her soul and she never forgot it. But over the years, the sentiment had morphed into a description of herself. "Giving your baby up for adoption doesn't make you childless. It just makes you the mother of a missing child."

Sterling was "missing." And the whole saga of finding him had sent her here, to the viewing of a woman she'd never met — because Rowan Douglas was a card-carrying member of the Harrington/Kavanaugh sprawling brood. A DNA card. Somewhere among all those people who would be gathered here to mourn the passing of one of their own could be Rowan's mother. Her father, maybe, though she knew way more people who'd never met their fathers than those who had a functioning one. A father can deny you. Not a mother, though, not after you grew inside her. Nobody can completely sever that bond.

Rowan had come because the funeral of Hannah Kavanaugh meant the clan would all be in one spot, most of them anyway, maybe even all of them. And those people were her family — her parents, perhaps, or siblings, and certainly aunts, uncles, cousins. It was finally time to open the closet on that Boogie Man and drag it kicking and screaming out into the light.

She rolled her eyes at how trite it sounded, even in her own head, but it was true. Rowan Douglas had come "home" to find her roots.

Chapter Forty-Four

"WE'RE SO sorry for your loss," said Bob Gillespie, the pharmacist at Dalton's Drug Store in Muleshoe, as Alex turned sideways to allow him, his wife, Carmen, and their daughter, Chenille, to edge between her and the other people in the crowded hallway that led to the parlor.

"Thank you, we appreciate it that you came," Alex parroted for the umpteen billionth time. Variations included: *How sweet/kind/nice/thoughtful of you to come,* and *we appreciate your kindness/thoughtfulness/condolences.* And the ever popular *we are warmed by your presence* and *we are uplifted by your prayers.* It was probably about time to switch lines.

Alex looked beautiful, with her long hair swept up into a dignified bun — because it had started falling out and it was harder to tell how thin it was in a bun —and dainty diamond stud earrings. She did wear black well, and she had worked hard with her makeup this morning, was wearing much more than usual to hide the dark circles under her eyes and her pale complexion. She'd noticed in the mirror that her eyebrows were thin. Why would a brain tumor make your eyebrow hairs fall off?

"We're right sorry 'bout Mrs. Hannah," said Herbert

Beddingfield, then his tiny little bird wife tweeted something similarly appropriate as she took Alex's hand and squeezed.

"How sweet of you to come," Alex replied and gestured toward the parlor, not that anybody needed to be directed there, because the line into the room stretched all the way out the front door.

She had to be careful or she'd be swept away in the sea of people, a flooding river carrying her along into the parlor where Hannah lay "in state." That's how Mama thought of it. Alex wouldn't let that happen. She wasn't going in there. She could manage the funeral —that was a public event, where you put on your public persona and soldiered through. But this — Hannah lying dead in there, in the next room — that wasn't public. No matter how many people showed up, it was still personal in a way standing around in a funeral home would never be. The glut of people kept the family from noticing that she hadn't been in the parlor to "pay her respects" or whatever inane phrase they gave it.

Well, Alex certainly didn't have any respects to pay because she hadn't respected Hannah in … fifty years, maybe. She thought about it, wondered when it was exactly that she'd shifted from dislike to hatred. There ought to have been something she could point to, a place, a time, an event she could gesture to and say, that's when it was. Maybe it had been that time at the lake when the kids were little.

ALEX IS BUSY CORRALLING GABE, Sydney and Brooke. There is, of course, a lake out there. That's why they'd come. But just its presence adds a whole new layer of stress to being a mother. She's always counting noses, making sure nobody's drowned. Right now, she has to find Gabe. Brooke put gum in Sydney's hair, or so Sydney'd said. Brooke said Sydney'd done it accidentally and made up the tale to get Brooke in trouble. Apparently, Gabe had been there at the time. She needs to find him, get him to testify as a disinterested party, shed some light on who was the victim and who was the villain.

When she passes by on the walkway out front, she hears Hannah and Cyrus in their rented cabin arguing. Hannah's voice carries out of the little kitchen/dining room.

"You're stupid."

"Honey, don't get—"

"You're a complete moron. Don't you know everybody is aware of that? Do you think people look at Cyrus Kavanaugh and see a smart man, with drive and purpose, a strong leader, a—"

She breaks off and the acid returns to her voice.

"Do you, Cyrus? Do you?" Then, as if she's just reached that conclusion, she adds, "Why, I guess you do. You're so stupid you don't even know that the rest of the world knows how dumb you are. You're pathetic."

Somehow Cyrus stays above it all.

Alex always wonders how he does that. He responds in an even tone, "If you're done, Hannah, I need to go talk to the man who leased us this cabin, tell him that—"

"Oh, don't bother. I already did. I told him if he didn't get the toilet unclogged, we would be moving out this evening, and we would not pay him a dime for the three days we've stayed."

"You didn't really tell him—"

"Of course, I did. You were too stupid to demand a rental contract, so it's not like we have any ..."

AND SO IT HAD GONE. Hannah berating Cyrus. Had it been then? Had Alex started hating her then?

You really should be able to identify the moment, the bell-wether moment, the point after which everything changed and you conducted your affairs and your internal life differently.

It might have been then, all those years ago, over that trivial stopped-up toilet that Alex felt the seismic shift in her soul, recognized the reality — she genuinely wanted to kill her sister-in-law Hannah Kavanaugh. She promised herself that if she ever got the chance, she would.

And she had.

"Pretty good turnout, wouldn't you say?" said Gabe into her ear, then shook hands with somebody and replied to the man's condolences, "You coming here today makes it easier."

Alex would have to remember that one.

She turned toward her son and was surprised at how wrung-out he looked. He looked way worse than she did, and she was dying.

"You look awful," she said, surveying his gaunt face and hollowed-out eyes that looked like two cigarette burns in his face.

"Grief."

"Bullshit."

Clearly, he wasn't sleeping again — might not even have gone to bed since Cyrus's scream had awakened them all on Thursday morning. That was what, forty-eight hours? Seventy-two? She wasn't good at math. And he was having those night terrors again. She silently cursed herself for giving him the codeine cough syrup that'd caused the devastating allergic reaction and subsequent hallucinations — as she had done a couple hundred thousand times in the years since, so often it'd become a litany, a Hail Mary. All she needed were rosary beads.

"You seen Spencer?" he asked, and a genuine smile lit his face that hers instantly mirrored.

"He left early this morning — went back to that halfway house, I think. He'll be here by supper, said he didn't want today's visitation to become about him being released from prison instead of Hannah." He was right, of course. One Spencer sighting and word would sweep through the whole house like a grassfire. "And besides, he's not ready to face all these people yet." Over the years, Alex had come to believe that shame was the single most debilitating human emotion. Gabe smiled sadly.

"Oh, if you see Claudia Hanson, tell her I want to talk to her," Alex said. "Spencer mentioned this morning he's looking for pictures of Avery when she was a flower girl in her daughter's wedding."

There was a heartbeat pause. That had been the day…

"Will do. I'm sure she'll be here. The whole county's here."

Gabe melted back into the crowd.

"I was so sorry to hear about Hannah's passing," said Rosanne Phelps.

Alex turned to her and said, "You coming here today makes it easier."

Then the spot beside her that'd been occupied by Gabe was filled by his granddaughter.

"Wipe that smile off your face, young lady," Alex scolded. "Don't you know there's been a death in the family?"

Avery made a show of putting on a sad face. "This better?"

"Infinitely. What were you smiling about?"

The smile returned.

"Well, actually it's as inappropriate as smiling because somebody died. I was smiling because somebody's sick. Maddie woke up this morning with a raging case of Montezuma's Revenge. Something in one of those Mexican casseroles she ate in the middle of the night did *not* agree with her."

"And that makes you smile because?"

"Because I don't have to keep her out of trouble."

"She's a handful?"

"You have no idea, Grandma Alex. Seriously, you have absolutely no idea."

Avery was washed away by the current of people, then Alex turned to greet the next person with an outstretched hand. It was Claudia Hansford.

"I want to offer my condolences," Claudia said.

For a moment, Alex forgot her line.

"You coming here today makes it easier," she stammered when it came to her. Claudia beamed and Alex kept holding her hand. "How is Ariana doing?"

"Just chasing those two little ones. I babysat last week, and by the time I got home I was so worn out I had to take a nap."

"Avery was one of the flower girls in Ariana's wedding, and I was looking for a picture of her in the cute little dress she wore, but I can't find it. Do you have—"

"Honey, I've got three albums full of pictures of that wedding. That photographer shot everything that moved."

"Could I—"

"I'll put the albums in the trunk of my car soon's I get home. Herb can put them in your car at the funeral tomorrow. You're welcome to any picture that strikes your fancy."

"That's very kind of you, Claudia."

Claudia turned away and Big Buford Collins stepped forward and took Alex's hand. The man looked like a Coke machine with a beard. His hand was the size of a catcher's mitt.

"… heard Hannah had …" *whum, whum, whum,* silence "… told Mildred we … here today …." *whum, whum, whum, whum* "… family doing?"

Alex caught her breath and realized she was squeezing Buford's hand in a vice grip. She let it go.

"Good," Alex managed to say. Or thought she did. She didn't hear herself say it — which was horrifying. "We're … holding up." Alex didn't hear that either. Alex heard nothing, absolutely nothing. She was completely deaf.

She let go of Buford's hand, said, "Please excuse me," or tried to, and made her way to the bathroom off the foyer. She stood inside the small locked room, feeling her heart exploding in her chest. She heard a wave of sound, like a song carried to you on the wind and then it was gone. Another wave flowed over her, then washed back out to sea. What would she ... how could she ... *deaf?*

When sound returned again, it was more subtle, like a faint whisper that grows louder and louder. It didn't turn off again instantly but remained constant.

Somebody tried the doorknob, then knocked.

"Just a minute," she said. She heard herself say it. She turned on the tap and ran cold water over her wrists, looked at her face in the mirror. She looked awful.

Then she squared her shoulders and went back out into the crowd. Someone spoke to her. She heard the words, still so rattled she could merely function on auto pilot.

"Thank you," she said. "You coming here today makes it easier."

Chapter Forty-Five

GABE SHOOK his head in disgust when Mitchell Kavanaugh —
everyone called him Doodle for reasons Gabe could no longer
remember — swaggered in the front door of the Harrington
House like the lord of the manor. He was no doubt as high as
the Goodyear Blimp on something. He always was.

Doodle's father, Jordan, was Uncle Cyrus and Aunt
Hannah's youngest son. Jordan and his wife Marilou had five
children. They should have stopped at four. If you asked
Gabe, Jordan should have had a vasectomy after Becky was
born. It would have saved him, his wife, and the rest of the
family a lot of misery. But he didn't, and a surprise package
arrived a decade later when the other children were almost
grown. Maybe they spoiled Doodle, gave him too much and
expected too little. Who knew? Whatever the reason, the boy
had caused Jordan and Marilou nothing but heartbreak his
whole life. A one-word description of him as a boy — *mean.*
He was a bully, delighted in hurting smaller children.
Constantly in trouble at school for fighting, he was expelled
at sixteen for selling drugs and never went back. Eighteen
now, he yo-yoed in and out of the family's lives, around just
long enough to convince his gullible parents he had turned

over a new leaf before he bailed and crawled back under a rock.

Doodle spotted Gabe and made his way through the crowd. He was more than thin. He was gaunt. His freckled complexion had a gray cast to it. Even his red hair looked faded. A crack addiction will do that to you.

"Long time no see," he said, holding out his hand. Gabe took it — the palm was wet with sweat. "How ya been?" Doodle's gregarious facade disguised a limitless capacity for treachery. He didn't look at Gabe when he spoke — his gaze flitting around like a dragonfly. "I think Grandma Hannah looks good, don't you? Real natural."

In truth, Gabe thought she looked awful. Her hair had been gummed up with orange juice, looked like a whole glass spilled. The morticians had obviously tried to get it out, with only moderate success, so her white hair had an orange cast to it and sat on her head as rigid as a pith helmet.

Besides, Gabe had seen Doodle come into the house and he hadn't yet been in the parlor.

"Uh huh."

The boy made eye contact briefly. His pupils were dilated so wide his blue eyes had become black eyes outlined in blue Magic Marker.

"You seen my dad? Hard on him, you know, her being his mother and all."

"Uh huh."

"I just came home to offer my support." Eyes flitting, seeing everything and nothing. "Wanna be there for him, ya know."

That was it. Doodle was here because he knew this was his father Jordan's year for a share in the disbursement. The federal government had devised a way to get its greedy hands on retirement accounts by requiring that every investor take a mandatory disbursement from what they'd socked away — and pay taxes on it. Grandma Liv withdrew the required money every year and spread out the disbursements among her adult children and grandchildren, had worked out a rotation so that every fourth year, it was your turn. She called it an "advance on your inheritance." Doodle knew that in order to beg/borrow/steal most of what his father would soon receive, he had to at least pretend he gave a rat's ass that his grandmother was dead. For Doodle, even the facade of being a decent human being was an accomplishment of some note all by itself.

This was Gabe's year, too. And without the disbursement, Gabe would be dead.

Literally.

You saw things like what'd happened to Gabriel Chambers on television cop shows that featured gritty detectives paired with way-too pretty-to-be-a-cop babes who chased pimps and drug dealers down back alleys wearing stylish heels.

GABE IS LATE FOR A SHOWING, and he hated to be late. It isn't his time compulsiveness that fuels his desire to be on time tonight, though. He needs to make this sale — a quarter million-dollar house on a one-acre lot with city water. No, he has to make this sale, has to have that commission.

He steps out the door of his office onto the sidewalk.

He never even sees the men who grab him. They must have been standing on either side of the door and leapt at him as soon as it closed behind him. He only remembers feeling hands on him in a steel grip, a black hood forced down over his head, and then he is chucked into some kind of vehicle, a van or truck.

It couldn't have taken ten seconds from the moment the men touched him until he could hear the squeal of tires as the vehicle pulls quickly away from the curb.

His hands are pulled behind his back and bound there with zip ties, the new restraint of choice for today's upwardly mobile kidnappers.

What's going on?

Who?

Why?

And then his heart takes up the rhythm of a lunatic woodpecker and he understands what is going on, who's doing it and why.

No.

Oh, please no.

The ride to wherever seems to take an eternity, must have taken that long because he died a thousand times during it. He feels the familiar tightening of the iron band around his head and knows he's about to have the mother of all migraines. And that's certainly not the worst of his problems.

The vehicle stops. He hears grunts, a couple of words spoken in Spanish, then he is hauled to his feet and thrust out of the vehicle into the arms of two other men who drag him into a building.

He smells the musty smell of an unused space and something nastier, an animal long decayed.

He can hear the sound of a train whistle in the distance.

Where have they taken him?

What does that matter? It's not like he's going to escape and needs to know which way to run. The only way out is the way he came in.

He is flung down into a chair, loses his balance and tumbles to the floor. Without his hands to break his fall he face-plants painfully on a hard surface, probably concrete, and smashes his lip and nose.

Someone clips off the zip ties around his wrist.

Someone else removes the black hood from his head.

He is seated in a chair in a windowless room so anonymous he could literally be anywhere.

There is a desk in the room and the man seated there says nothing as Gabe takes a swipe with the back of his hand at the blood seeping down his lip from his smashed nose. His split lip is bleeding, too, dripping a drool of red down his chin and onto the front of his shirt. A white shirt. He always dresses professionally when he's showing a house.

He won't be showing a house today.

"Gabriel Chambers." The man speaks in a soft, almost gentle voice that somehow manages to sound cold and sinister at the same time. Just

his name. Not as a question, or even as an affirmation. Just his name. Gabriel Chambers.

He'd tried to think what he should say as he lay with the zip ties cutting into his wrists in the back of that van. He'd believed he should sound confident, that he should not appear to be afraid that he should ...

All a useless effort. Once he was finally confronted with the reality off the situation, he can't attempt to be anything. All he can do is gasp for breath and look with eyes he hopes are not pleading at the man seated behind the desk.

"Yes, I'm Gabriel Chambers." He is surprised his voice is firm, not shaking. How can it be firm when his insides are quivering — no, vibrating — with terror? "Who are you?"

"You do not need to know my name." The man smiles just a little bit. "I could give you any name. How would you know?" His words are blurred a little with an accent. Eastern European? No, more likely Russian. "My name is not important, my words are not important. What matters here right now is that you listen and you believe."

Gabe said nothing, just stared. Then he thought perhaps he was supposed to nod, so he did.

"Mr. Chambers, you owe my employer a large sum of money." When he stated the amount, Gabe was thunderstruck.

"What? Wait a minute, I only owe—"

"Shut up. You have nothing to say that is of any consequence. You owe money and the account is past due."

The amount of money he'd lost was less than half what the man said he owed. There had to be some mistake.

As if he had read Gabe's mind, the man says a single word.

"Interest."

"But I—"

Suddenly his cheek is aflame with pain.

He doesn't see the blow coming and would have been knocked out of the chair to the floor if the man behind the chair hadn't grabbed him and held him there.

"We are civilized people and this is a business arrangement. My

employer wants his money, nothing else. He does not want to harm you in any way"— the barest of pauses —"or your family."

My family? Dear holy mother of God —

"So let us behave like civilized men. This is the arrangement he has instructed me to convey to you. You are to repay one third of what you owe by June first, another third by August first, and the remaining balance by October first."

There is no way in God's earth Gabe can scrape together enough money to make the first installment, let alone the second and the third.

"You understand that payment schedule, correct?"

He is terrified to open his moth, but what's the use in playing along, as if he could somehow magically come up with the money.

"I can't even make the first payment. And the other payments—"

"Mr. Chambers, this is not an offer I am making that you can decide to accept or refuse. It is a statement of the way this account will be closed out."

"I can't—"

"Mr. Chambers, do you think my employer is unaware of who you are, what kind of money your family has?"

"My family, sure. But I don't have access to—"

"Failure to make a payment is not an option. We will, of course, accept only cash."

Gabriel almost loses it, cries out, "But I—"

"Mr. Chambers, you have no choice. You will make these payments."

He can't stop himself. "Or?"

"Or we will kill you."

IT WAS THE OFFHANDED WAY, the cold, indifference in the tone of voice, that so chilled Gabriel. This man absolutely would have slit his throat on the spot. This was not a bluff, an effort to goad him into coughing up money he had but didn't want to part with. This had been the simplest of syllogistic logic: if this, then this. If you pay, you live. If you don't pay, you die. Pretty straightforward proposition. And since he could not fulfill the first part of the arrangement, he had no doubt that the man with the dead, marble eyes of a shark would kill him.

In the months since his hooded ride in the back of a van, Gabriel Chambers had managed a miracle. There was no way he could make the first two payments. No way! But he'd done it. Sold everything — *everything* he owned — his rare book collection, a classic car he'd been restoring, his house, his bass boat, his ski cabin in Colorado, everything. Now, he was looking the final payment in the eye, and to make it he had cobbled together income streams from half a dozen different sources. It wasn't quite enough. It was achingly close, though, and he had lines in the water, pending real estate deals that if even one came through would put him over the top.

He'd been living in the constant tension of scraping up that last little bit, and the constant fear that one of the income streams he was counting on would suddenly dry up. He was down to the end of it now. Everything had to come together by next Friday. That was the deadline.

"... seeing you, Gabe."

Gabe didn't know what Doodle had just said, but the fake smile on Doodle's face was beginning to twitch at the corners.

"Right back atcha," Gabe said.

Chapter Forty-Six

CHAPMAN COULDN'T WAIT to be a grown-up. Grown-up *tall!*
The parlor was crowded with all kinds of people he didn't
know, and he and the other kids had to thread their way
through them. From Chapman's height, he was always looking
right up close to some fat old man's belly, or a fat lady's, or
anybody's really. Who wants to look at bellies? But this was
better than being on a crowded beach, he figured, because if
you was at the beach, everybody would be dressed in swim-
suits and then you'd be looking at some fat old man's hairy
navel.

He didn't need to worry that Mommy or Daddy was going
to see him. The only people who could see him were the
grownups standing right on top of him. He was small enough
to hide in all the people, so that was a good thing.

He couldn't keep his eyes off the ring. It was so shiny, so
sparkling, he couldn't stop thinking about it. Then he heard
Daddy say that they were going to put Grandma Hannah in
some big oven and bake her until she was just ashes, which
meant they'd be destroying that beautiful ring on her finger.
Chapman couldn't stand the idea of that!

He would save it. He would rescue it from the fire.

Then he saw this lady in a flowered dress that looked like the cover on the couch in his basement. They'd put a box of Kleenex right there on the table beside Grandma Hannah because all the women needed it. They'd cry and sniff, wipe their eyes and sometimes even blow their noses — gross! — on the tissues and drop them in the trashcan in the corner. He bet it was just about full of snotty tissues now.

But the lady in the flowered dress did more than just sniffle and cry. She reached down and took Grandma Hannah's hand and held it while she talked to her. And nobody thought that was weird! A few minutes later, another lady did the same thing. This one was wearing a hat — in the house. He wasn't allowed to wear his baseball cap in the house, but rules were always harder on children than they were on adults.

Chapman kind of edged his way into the line of grownups going past Aunt Hannah's body, and saying stuff to her and crying, and then shaking hands with whatever family members happened to be standing at the head of the bed thing at the time. Grampa Cecil was there just about non-stop. His daughters-in-law would drag him away into the kitchen and force him to eat a sandwich, but then he'd be right back there beside Grandma Hannah.

When it was Chapman's turn to look at the body and say something, cry, and then blow his nose, he did what the two ladies had done, the one in the couch dress and the one in the hat. He reached out his hand and took Grandma Hannah's. It was gross, like it was the hand of a rubber doll, cold like a store mannequin.

He was just standing there, holding her hand, trying to think how to get the ring off her finger without anybody seeing him, when the next lady in line said to the lady behind her, "Why look at that." She pointed to Chapman and for a second he thought they could read his mind and knew what he was about to do. She didn't, though. "Isn't that sweet. Hannah's grandson is holding her hand." And the lady behind her said she thought it was sweet, too, and they asked the lady behind them and she said she thought so, too, so they all chirped about it over Chapman's head.

And all the while Chapman had his back to them, blocking what he was doing from sight, trying as hard as he could to get the ring off Grandma Hannah's finger. It was stuck! Wouldn't budge. He'd have to put soap on it or something, maybe spit on it. Her finger was fat and the ring was on there tight as a rubber band.

"You sure did love your Granny Hannah, didn't you, son," said the first old lady, the one in the dress like a couch, and she patted his head. He hated it when people patted him on the head, just ducked his chin down. "Awww, it's okay, darlin'. She's in a better place. Your Granny Hannah's with Jesus now."

She thought Chap was crying. And he would cry, too, if that would help. He couldn't spit on Grandma Hanna's finger to get it wet so he could get the ring off, but he supposed it wouldn't be disrespectful to cry on it. Except he wasn't sad or scared. He could cry if he was sad, like when his parakeet flew away, or was scared he was about to get a spanking. So he tried thinking about that, about the lost bird and the spanking he'd get if anybody caught him, but it didn't work. So he just kept his head down and made his shoulders shake like he was sobbing and tried to get some tears to come —

It came off! He'd been pulling on it the whole time he was making his shoulders shake and it popped off, slid off her finger into his hand so easy he almost dropped it.

The couch lady was leaning over him now. He could smell the soap they made all old ladies use, saying stuff about palaces in the sky. She must play a Wizard of Legend on her PlayStation. He didn't ask how far she got in the game, though, just kept his shoulders shaking as he let go of Grandma Hannah's doll hand and dropped the ring he'd gotten off her finger into his pocket.

He stood there for a little while, acting sad and sniffly, blew his nose on a tissue to put in the gross trash basket because that lady expected him to, and he wasn't dumb enough to just take the ring and run. Then people would notice and he'd get caught. He was smarter than that! When the couch lady started talking to some other lady, he moved away from the bed thingy and out into the middle of the jammed-together grownups. He kept his hand in his pocket, though, gripping the ring tight, didn't want to drop it now.

Then he thought that he couldn't just keep the ring in his pocket all day. But where could he put it? Where would it be safe until Mommy and Daddy took them home? Which wouldn't be tonight. Mommy had said the whole family was going to stay in Grandma Olivia's house for a couple of days so they could all be together. Tomorrow, they'd get in black cars and drive real slow behind a big black car that had Grandma Hannah in it to the church, where the preacher would get up and say some stuff … and he didn't know what happened after that. If they was gonna cream-ate you, where did they put you while you waited for the fire to be hot enough to burn you up?

He didn't know the answer to that question, but he did know where he could put the ring where it'd be safe! Just the right place, where nobody'd ever look for it. He left the parlor, put the ring safely away, and then started playing hide-and-seek with his cousins Willie and Tally Nelson, Star Kavanaugh, and Mateo Hernandez. But after Grandma Dannie opened the cabinet under the sink to get some dish soap and found Tally jammed in there with the cleaning stuff, the grownups said they couldn't play the game in the house anymore. So they went outside, which wasn't as good as in the house where there were a bajillion hiding places, but you could still hide behind bushes and up in trees. Star wasn't allowed to climb trees, so if she saw you there, she didn't have to tag you for you to be *it*. Then his bigger cousins started playing dodgeball, but they wouldn't let him or the other littles play. He sat down on the porch and pouted for a long time, but when that didn't make them change their minds, he went back into the kitchen to ask for a piece of pie. All the people who'd come to visit were gone now. He was just about to ask Mommy for the pie when Aunt Juliana suddenly came rushing into the kitchen and went right to his Aunt Leanne.

"What'd you do with it?" she said, and she was mad.

"Do with what?" Aunt Leanne answered.

"You know what I'm talking about. Aunt Hannah's ring. How could you do a thing like that?"

Uh oh.

"What about Grandma Hannah's ring?"

"It's missing, that's what. It was on her finger not five minutes ago!" Chapman thought, no it wasn't, but he kept his mouth shut. "So you can't claim some random stranger at the viewing made off with it. Those people were already gone, the ring was there — I saw it! — and now it's not. What'd you do with it?"

Chapman didn't hear what his Aunt Leanne said. He didn't want a piece of pie anymore and he ran out of the kitchen, bumped into his Uncle Gabe on his way to look at the red shiny thing he'd hidden in his room.

Chapter Forty-Seven

PEOPLE FILED from one room into another toward the parlor, the column snaking down the hallways where there used to be Russell and Remington art to look at to pass the time, 'til Hannah got rid of it all. The line wound all the way through the house and out the front door into the yard. Good thing it wasn't raining.

Olivia liked this part of the ritual society had set up as a transition from this life to the next. Most folks didn't. Oh, they came anyway! She looked at the horde of mourners and knew wasn't a one of them liked Hannah. But that wasn't the whole point. Sure, you came to "the viewing" to say your final goodbye to somebody'd passed over. But that wasn't the only reason. You came to offer your support to them as was left behind, to say, "I care that you're hurting" to family members who were. That was one of only a handful of traditions from her childhood that'd held. She figured it'd last another couple of years, a generation maybe, before it disappeared, too. Then folks would just send a text: *We're sorry for your loss.*

Olivia's knee got to aching, so she maneuvered her walker — needed a horn, maybe red flashing lights — through the crowd and into the kitchen. She sat down on one of the bar stools near the table where Leanne's oldest, Peyton, fifteen, was hunched over a screen with his cousin, fourteen-year-old Douglas, Lawson and Cynthia's only son. Huggie Dougie, the huggable dougable. She wondered where the other D was and chided herself for thinking such a mean thought. She could see over their shoulders and leaned forward to have a look at the Pied Piper that'd stolen all the world's children.

Why, it was just a cartoon — well, more realistic than one — and it appeared the boys were somehow controlling the characters on the screen. Now, wasn't that clever! A fella dressed like he might be some kinda wizard was standing on a rocky cliff face above a place where there musta been a forest fire, cause wasn't nothing left but charred and burnt-up things.

Then the wizard jumped all the way down to the ground, got on a horse, and started riding toward a castle that Peyton said was something that sounded like Starscourge Radahn. The wizard went inside the castle, but wasn't nobody there, just some skeletons with skin on them laying around on the floor. He wandered around the castle, went downstairs, and finally come to this shiny blue ring. When he touched it — poof. He wasn't in the castle no more. He was standing on a beach facing a huge warrior in golden armor that started throwing purple lightning bolts at him.

"This is like my ten thousandth try," Douglas said.

"How long have you been stuck?" Peyton asked.

"Two weeks."

"Bro, you need to learn how to play the game."

Gabe came into the kitchen and started to speak to her, but she pointed at the screen and put a finger to her lips.

"Grandma Liv, you don't have to be quiet. You could march the Marine Corps Band and bugle corps through here and they wouldn't notice."

Peyton took the controller thing from Douglas, pushed a couple of buttons, and a screen appeared that showed cloth-ing, swords and armor. "Why are you playing a wizard with only fifty intelligence? Do you know how intelligence works? And why do you have fifty arcane?"

"I thought arcane gave you spellcasting power," Douglas said, "and intelligence boosted incantations and—"

"Intelligence boosts spellcasting. Arcane boosts loot discovery. You have wasted forty levels in arcane. No wonder you're getting your ass handed to you."

Olivia turned to Gabe. "Do you have any idea what they just said?"

"Not a clue." He patted her on the arm. "Don't watch this too long or your brain will turn to mush. I'll be right back." He left and she was sure neither of the boys even knew he'd been there. They were … hypnotized, all thoughts of going out into the parlor to greet the people who'd come to pay their respects to their grandmother forgotten.

Olivia ought to say something. But … no. If she said something, they'd just nod respectfully — her grandchildren, by and large, were at least polite and respectful, their parents had painted that veneer of civility on them. They wouldn't really look at her, though. Okay, they'd look, but they wouldn't see her. Her words would sound like Charlie Brown's teacher in their ears. She yearned, just once, to have a real conversation with one of Jordan's kids — Zoe or Daphne or Ramsey — or one of Brooke's boys, Derrick or Damon or Paul. There were more than two dozen of them, after all, and surely there was at least one among them who could still think — about *anything* — and wanted to hear what she thought about it, too. Did they at least talk to each other sometimes? She doubted it.

"No! No! No!" Douglas cried. On the screen, the golden warrior jumped into the air and landed on the wizard, smashing him flat. In a moment, words appeared: YOU DIED.

Sighing, Olivia turned away. Not my circus, not my monkeys.

Douglas's mother, Cynthia, steamrolled into the kitchen

and did everything but grab the two young men by the ears and drag them back to the parlor, not before Peyton slid his iPhone into his pocket, of course. You know, so it'd be there for him to touch if he got anxious. Them kids was more addicted to their phones than a two-year-old to a security blanket — a beedle-a-bop was what Cyrus had called his blankie when he was wagging it around the house. She paused. That'd been eighty years ago.

Gabe came back in as they were leaving. "I see you survived Elden Ring." He saw her confusion. "That's the name of the game they were playing."

"I came through without any fatal wounds, but Douglas's little wizard got squashed."

"How you holding up, Grandma Liv?"

"Fair to middlin'. Something's wrong with your mama, though. She won't tell me what it is. Has she told you?"

Gabe looked momentarily stunned, then shook his head. "Sorry, I got whiplash from that change of subject. How do you know something's wrong with her?"

Sometimes Olivia wondered why her family didn't run into telephone poles, they had such blinders on.

"You can see it, that's how! Or you could if you really looked." He winced at that.

"Mom's out there greeting people and she seems fine."

"She ain't eating. You can see how much weight she's lost. Ain't sleeping neither, looks like, 'cause she's got steamer trunks under her eyes. She tries to hide 'em, wearing so much makeup looks like she put it on with a trowel. She's like a little bird, flitting here and there but never lighting anywhere, don't appear to me she's aware of what's going on around her half the time. You ain't noticed?"

"No, she seems fine to me."

Olivia shook her head. "Next time you need to take a dump, I got a flashlight you can borrow."

"Huh?" It took a moment, then he got it.

"I asked what was bothering her 'bout a week ago, and you'd have thought I'd poked her with a cattle prod. For just a couple of seconds, she looked so forlorn it'd break your heart. Then she climbed back into her Superman suit and flew away."

It's been Gabe's sister Sydney who'd come up with the Superman suit description and it was so appropriate nobody ever forgot it. It was like when Alex left the house to go to work, she was invincible. She was smooth, in charge, took everything in stride, smiled and made nice … and worked for the next eighteen hours to make sure whatever it was she'd told her staff to do got done. Then she'd come back into the house and the demeanor would fall away and she'd just be this exhausted woman, who barely had the strength to get supper on the table and never had the time to watch her children grow up.

"And she won't go in the parlor. I been watching. She hangs around the door but always finds something else to do so she don't have to go in there. Why you reckon that is?"

"She's okay, Grandma Liv. You worry too much."

"Stop patronizing me. Am I the only person in this whole family who notices anything?" She looked Gabe up and down. "And you look almost worse than your mother does. What you got your panties in a wad about?"

He didn't answer, just got a queer look on his face, then did a right slick bob-and-weave.

"You're going to be a hundred years old tomorrow, Grandma Liv. Did you ever think you'd live that long?"

"Everybody thinks they're going to live forever, so really old people like me ain't surprised when we do." She sighed, made a kind of encompassing gesture to include everything. "It's done, though. Whatever it was I's s'posed to do in this life, surely to goodness I already done it. I'm just sitting here at the station with my bags packed, waiting for the train to show up."

"You're not afraid to die?"

"Oh, Lord no, son. When you look something in the eye every day for a hundred years, you get comfortable with it, like a ratty old bathrobe. Ain't nothing to be scared about, just stepping from this life into the next."

He looked surprised, but his attention was riveted on her.

"Truth be told, I yearn for the peace, to go to sleep one night and just not wake up. I've been praying for that for about a quarter of a century now and God ain't seen fit to say yes yet. Keeps giving me one more day and one more day and one more day. My first words when I get to heaven are gonna be, 'Whew! Glad I got *that* over with.'"

She chuckled, thought that was pretty funny, but Gabe didn't even smile.

Chapter Forty-Eight

FOR ONE WILD MOMENT, Rowan feared that as soon as she crossed the threshold of the house, someone would immediately step forward and demand to know who she was and what she was doing here. Paranoia. She resolutely plastered a pleasant look on her face — not a smile, as there had, after all, been "a death in the family" — and feigned confidence as she climbed the wide front porch steps. There was no way in hell every one of the people here knew every one of the other people. As she'd crossed the field turned into a parking lot, she'd seen other license plates mixed in with the Lone Star State ones. Not just New Mexico and Oklahoma, either. There was Alabama, Kentucky, Kansas.

Gathered here were friends or relatives from different seasons of the deceased woman's life, and it wasn't reasonable to expect that anybody would know everyone present. Well, except for the dead woman.

Act like you belong and people will ignore you.

That was one of the many lessons in how to get along in life that Oscar, the old Black janitor in her elementary school, had taught her, along with *never explain, your friends don't need it and your enemies won't believe it anyway* and, of course, the proverbial *always wear clean underwear in case you're in a traffic accident* that other people's mothers told them. Rowan didn't have a mother.

She cut around the line that had formed out the front door of the house and was getting longer and longer as the people getting out of their cars in the field joined it. She didn't want to get into the receiving line. She just wanted to wander around, to look at people, study their features— without letting them know that's what she was doing, of course. She wasn't looking for anything specific, just somebody who bore some resemblance to the face she'd been looking at in the mirror for more than four decades.

There were Black people at the visitation, a respectable number, but far more Hispanics than Blacks and none of the Black men seemed quite right, somehow — too young or too old. Perhaps her father'd never been a part of her mother's life, but surely her mother's family members were scattered among the crowd of people.

That was another of Oscar's admonitions. *Always look like you're on your way somewhere. You want to look like a ship under full sail, not a becalmed schooner in the bay.* She should have brought a dish — that'd buy you unquestioned entrance to the home of any bereaved family anywhere.

She caught snatches of conversations as she snaked through the crowd.

"… *so natural, better than she ever looked alive …*"

"*…Cyrus is devastated. He loved her. I don't know why. Nobody else in the family did.*"

"… *just faking the whole dead thing so she can keep track of who shows up at her funeral.*"

"… *board meetings will be like without Hannah going off like a ballistic missile every time …*"

"… *hear Cyrus is gutted. Bless his heart. How he put up with her for…*"

Rowan wondered, if these people were Hannah

Kavanaugh's friends, what would her enemies have to say about her?

Searching the faces of the people around her, she was too freaked out to process anything. True fact: when you try to see everything, you don't see anything. The whole circumstance was so overwhelming, all her nerve endings were tingling and bright little sparkles of light formed in the air …

She'd seen sparkles like that when she woke up in the hospital after the IAD went off under the Humvee. Woke up with a permanent "tattoo" on her face, a going-away present from the Taliban. At least she woke up. None of the other soldiers in the Humvee did.

Maybe she ought to sit down. If she was going to pass out, she needed to put her head between her knees. Of course, sitting with her head between her knees was only slightly less of a spectacle than face-planting on the floor. She looked around the crowded room, searching for a seat not taken — an old leather couch was squeezed awkwardly between two chairs, where it clearly didn't fit. It'd probably been moved there when the furniture was rearranged to accommodate the bier.

Rowan sat down on it, grateful to be off her feet. She never got "dressed up" for anything. Wore her blue paramedic uniform every day, and had observed that the "uniform" for everybody under age thirty in the offices where somebody'd dialed 911 was a tee shirt and jeans. But she figured a funeral had social protocols that crossed generational lines, meaning even those in the crowd who never dressed up would have to dress up to suit those in the crowd who did. So she'd hauled out an old pair of heels and jammed them on her feet. She'd realized halfway across the field/parking lot that she had made a serious fashion blunder.

"Why'd you take your shoes off?" asked a voice right by her ear. When she jerked around, she saw a little boy had climbed up onto the back of the couch and was leaning over her. He was adorable — an elfish face and bright blue eyes beneath a brow knitted in confusion.

"My mommy would get mad if I took-ted my shoes off."

"Well, my mommy's not here, so…" She stopped. Because maybe she was wrong. Maybe her mommy *was*, indeed, right in this very house. Her heart took up a timpani drum rhythm in her chest.

The child slid off the back of the couch and plunked down beside her.

"I wanted to wear my Spiderman slip-slops, but Mommy said no."

"Slip slops?"

"You know, the shoes that have the thing that fits between your big toe and all the little ones."

"Flip flops."

"Yeah, those. You can only wear slip slops in the summer, though, not in the winter in the snow because your toes would turn blue and fall off."

The little boy was speaking softly, obviously trying not to be noticed.

"I shot the funeral home man and hadda go to time-out."

"You *shot*—"

"Wiff my Nerf gun. It didn't hurted him. And I did it on accident. I was aiming at the calendar on the wall and I missed."

"So you got in trouble."

He nodded, bobbing the full head of butter-colored curls she was sure would delight the girls in his life someday.

"What's your name?" he asked.

"Rowan Douglas.

"Rowing? Like wiff a paddle in a boat?"

"Yeah, kinda. What's your name?"

"Chapman Andrew Schaeffer. The dead lady's my grand-mother, but you hafta say 'great' a bunch of times in front of it. "

He leaned close and said conspiratorially, "I didn't think she was great and neither did Mommy, but then she gotted dead, so now you hafta say nice stuff. Is the dead lady your grandmother, too?"

The question hit Rowan like a wrecking ball in the chest.

Maybe she was.

Maybe the "dead lady" *was* Rowan's grandmother.

Which meant that maybe this angelic little creature was her nephew or cousin. Rowan's throat was suddenly so tight she couldn't say a word.

Chapter Forty-Nine

G‌ABE WAS DISTRACTED, had too many thoughts swirling around in his head, and his mind was foggy from lack of sleep. He'd slept maybe four hours on Wednesday night but hadn't even bothered to go to bed Thursday night. And last night, there'd been enough drama — what with the visitation from Christmas Past and all — to keep him wide awake, but exhaustion had hit and he did sleep for a little while. Still, he knew what sleep deprivation could do, had experienced it often, knew he had to sleep tonight to make it through the funeral tomorrow. And Grandma Liv's "bomb."

Dear God, what would Gabe do if she really …

If he hadn't been so caught up in the turmoil inside his head, he would have seen what was coming, recognized the impending disaster the way Pacific Islanders know what it means when the tide water begins to pull back away from the shore. But Gabe was caught off guard by the tsunami that crashed down into the kitchen when his daughter Juliana marched up to their cousin Leanne, who was peeling eggs to make deviled eggs, and unloaded on her.

"What'd you do with it?"

Her hostility — bottled rage — was unmistakable, and

Gabe wondered if Chapman had gone running out of the kitchen when she came in because he somehow sensed disaster in the making. Do little kids have some kind of sense like birds do about storms, so they can take to their roosts and ride it out? Maybe. Gabe wished he could have gotten up and bolted out of the room with Chap.

"Do with what?" Leanne asked.

"You know what I'm talking about. Aunt Hannah's ring. How could you do a thing like that?"

"What about Grandma Hannah's ring?"

"It's missing, that's what. It was on her finger not five minutes ago, so you can't claim some random stranger at the viewing made off with it. Those people were already gone, the ring was there — I saw it! — and now it's not. What'd you do with it?"

All right, time to turn the volume down on what was clearly about to be a major blow.

"Sit down, Jules," Gabe said. He knew better than to say "calm down." Telling either of his two daughters to "calm down" was at the very least counterproductive and usually resulted in a flashfire that singed your eyebrows. "What's up with Aunt Hannah's ring?"

Juliana remained standing. "It's missing, that's what," Juliana spit the words out.

"What do you mean, missing?" asked Leanne's sister, Daniella, who was peeling potatoes.

"How many things can missing mean? It's gone, not there." She turned back to Leanne. "You took it! Now give it back."

"Mama's ring's gone?" Jordan Kavanaugh asked, just coming into the room with his wife, Marilou, and catching the gist of the conversation. "Where'd it go?"

"Somebody took it, and we all know who that somebody is."

"Are you talking about the garnet one, with the sapphires around the stone?" asked Marilou.

"No, they're talking about the ruby one," Jordan told her.

"Oh, that one," she said. "That's the one Papa Cyrus picked out for her to wear. I was standing there when he handed the blue dress and things to Calvin Whittiker, and I thought right then that the ruby ring did *not* go with that blue dress. But Papa Cyrus said she'd want to wear that ring, said it was her favorite."

Jordan's brother Lawson's wife, Cynthia, joined the fray. "Papa Cyrus didn't have any more idea than a goose which ring was Mama Hannah's favorite. She always told me the one she liked best was the emerald one she had made—"

"Stop changing the subject," Juliana said. "The ring the funeral director put on her finger — the ruby ring that was there a few minutes ago — is gone now. Couldn't you even wait until your grandmother was cold?"

"Hold on just a minute here," Leanne said. She had a lot higher boiling point than Juliana, but she was clearly nearing it. "Are you suggesting that I *stole* the ring?"

"No, I'm not suggesting anything. It's not a suggestion. You wanted it. You've always wanted it. You knew she promised it to me when I was five and it pissed you off. With all the jewelry going to that museum now—"

"I don't know about that," Jordan put in. "I don't think that part was final, and we may have to get out her will."

Gabe shook his head. Talk about pouring gasoline on a fire!

"And in her will, she left that ring to me!" Juliana was triumphant. "You knew this was your last shot."

If you asked Gabe, and nobody had, he was certain that Aunt Hannah had promised the same piece of jewelry to two or three different cousins over the years for just such an occasion as this. If there was anything Aunt Hannah enjoyed, it was a good catfight.

He also suspected that's why she'd decided at the eleventh hour to give the lot of it to the museum — that way she could piss them all off and not have to make good on any of her conflicting promises.

"What my grandmother decided to do with her own jewelry was her own business," Leanne said.

"Unless she planned to give the ring you wanted to me, in which case you just snatched it off her finger."

"Off her finger!" Cynthia said. "You're saying the ring's gone? It's really *gone?*"

"Knock, knock. Earth to Cynthia. The ring is gone and Leanne took it."

Indignation finally landed with both feet in the middle of Leanne's soul.

"I did no such thing! How dare you suggest—"

"There's that word again. Suggest. I'm not *suggesting* anything. Just hand it over."

Everyone in the room picked up on the threat of violence in the words.

Leanne shoved her chair back and got her feet. She was a big woman, had five inches and sixty pounds on Juliana, but nobody who'd ever underestimated Juliana Chambers was still alive to tell the tale.

"Stop it *now!*" Gabe's mother roared from the doorway. Nobody had noticed her come in the room. "Both of you. *Stop!*"

His mother's tone brooked no interference. She gave her granddaughter, Juliana, and her brother Cyrus's granddaughter, Leanne, looks that would eviscerate internal organs. "Sit down and shut up. Both of you." She glared at Leanne, who sat down reluctantly. She turned her gaze on Juliana, who lifted her chin defiantly and said, "I think I'll stand."

Alex ground out through clenched teeth, "I think you'll *sit* ... if you intend to live to see another sunrise. Don't push me. Not now. Not today!"

Gabe's mother had always had the strongest will of

anybody in the family and commanded — *de*-manded — the respect of them all. But there was a difference today, and he wasn't the only one who noticed it. There was a wildness to it, a throw-caution-to-the-wind quality that made it possible to believe that if Juliana Chambers did not sit, Alexandra Harrington would grab her by the hair and slam her into the chair.

Juliana sat.

"How about we discuss this before somebody starts throwing punches," Gabe said. "When did you last see the ring on Aunt Hannah's finger?" he asked Juliana.

"It has been on her finger ever since Mr. Whittiker put it there until *she*—"

"*When* did you see it?" He put steel in his voice. "Five minutes ago? Two hours? Last month?"

"I saw it right before the Montgomerys left. Stella commented on the brooch."

"The brooch, not the ring?"

"Not the ring. Then I spoke to the Putmans and Joe Willis and Mrs. Pinkerton, then went back into the parlor and the ring was gone!"

"So … what? Half an hour ago? It went missing sometime in the last half hour?"

"Yes, more like fifteen minutes."

"Well, that eliminates Leanne as a suspect," her sister Dannie said. "I came in here to help at least an hour ago and Leanne was here. She has never left the room since. She's been shelling those eggs for the past twenty, thirty minutes."

"Oh, she left alright. You just didn't notice."

"Listen to me, Jules," Gabe said. "I came through here forty-five minutes ago and Leanne was sitting right where she's sitting now. You're going to have to find somebody else to blame this on, because that dog won't hunt."

"Sydney wasn't in here," Dannie offered, "and I know

Grandma Hanna promised her something — a ring, a brooch, something."

"How do we know you didn't take it, Juliana?" Leanne asked with acid in her voice. "Marching in here to accuse me would draw attention away from the real culprit."

"Mama told Brooke she could have the sapphire earrings," Marilou plowed ahead. "There was a ring that went with them, and those matched the blue dress." She looked around. "Where is Brooke?"

Everybody began talking at once then, accusing everybody else of taking the ring. Gabe noticed then that his mother wasn't there and he hadn't noticed her leave. Grandma Liv was right. His mother didn't look good.

Chapter Fifty

LEANNE WAS *NOT* GOING to get away with stealing Juliana's ring — and it *was* Juliana's ring because Aunt Hannah had promised it to her when Juliana was five years old.

Leanne might have had all the others fooled with her pleas of innocence, but Juliana didn't fall off a hay truck yesterday. Leanne found a way to do it … she got up and went to get a drink of water or something and nobody noticed. It wouldn't have taken a minute to slip into the parlor and pull that ring off Aunt Hannah's finger.

Well, Leanne would be sorry. Juliana would see to that.

She had texted Jamal and told him what she was planning to do and he'd told her not to, said it would only escalate the tensions. Fine. Escalate! Bring it. Juliana didn't care. Leanne had taken the ring Juliana had waited her whole life for and Juliana would never see it again, she was sure of that much. Leanne would never wear it when she came home to visit, of course, she'd just flaunt it among her friends in San Antonio when Juliana wasn't there to see.

Well, if she was going to get the ring, Juliana was by God going to make her pay for the privilege. And not just once. This was the first of many, many payments Leanne would be making — every time the family got together until Leanne died of old age.

Rounding the corner from the back hallway, she caught sight of Jude.

"Wait up," she called out. He turned to her and for a moment it was like it'd been when they were kids. The other cousins would be playing some kind of game — without Jude, of course, because he never joined in — and when he wasn't aware you were watching him, he'd get the funniest look on his face. Almost a scary look. Then Jude would smile and the moment would pass, except his smiles never seemed to reach his eyes.

"You need something?" he asked.

"Yeah, the basement key. Uncle Lawson said you had it."

She approached as he dug around in his pocket, and when she got closer, she could see his clothes were dusty.

"What were you doing in the basement?" she asked.

"I … wanted to go through some of those pictures again, the ones we looked at for those photos of Grandma Hannah."

"Why?"

He held out the key to her. "Spencer saw a picture of Avery that he wanted and I thought I'd go find it for him." She put it together then. She hadn't seen Jude all day.

"Did you spend *the whole day* down there?"

He shrugged. "Lots of pictures."

For Spencer. That touched her, that Jude would go to all that trouble for her older brother. But it felt off somehow, too. Most of the Kavanaughs wouldn't give Spencer the time of day anymore, let alone spend …

"I gotta get cleaned up for supper," he said, then walked away. He didn't ask her what she wanted the key for, but she had a story all planned out if anybody did ask, about the Christmas ornaments that were stored down there, too. If he knew what the real reason was, that it was all about his sister,

Leanne ... actually, it was the kind of thing Jude would appreciate.

She didn't turn the basement lights on, just inched down the steps holding out her cell phone with the flashlight app on. In her other hand, she held a paper sack containing an empty mason jar. She shown the beam along the ceiling rafters, searching, and down behind the furnace, she saw a couple, but she wanted just the right — there it was. Perfect. It was huge. It took some maneuvering to get it into the mason jar, but she managed. Bugs didn't bother her, but *snakes* ... get me outta here!

Once it was sealed tight in the jar, she closed the jar up in the sack and went back upstairs. She'd do the deed when everybody was at supper. She smiled, would have whistled as she walked down the hallway but didn't. There had, after all, been a death in the family.

Chapter Fifty-One

OLIVIA SAT at the table as family members wandered in and out. Supper wasn't no sit-down meal, but everybody kinda showed up in the kitchen about the same time so's leftovers was heated up and passed around and they ate together.

They looked rode hard and put up wet. A thing like this was draining on everybody, as was being jammed in here all together. It was to be expected that tempers had flared. She'd heard about a couple of the rows. Seems one of Hannah's rings was missing, the one she was wearing. Somebody took it — duh — and there was a considerable amount of finger-pointing. Leanne accused Juliana of doing it, or maybe it was the other way around. The way she'd heard it, they'd about come to blows.

Olivia saw Alex standing in the doorway deciding whether she wanted anything to eat or not. She looked like death on a cracker, had been eating like a bird lately, and she had a kind of awful, haunted look in her eyes Olivia had never seen there before. And half the time she ignored you when you spoke to her, acted like she didn't hear.

The only one who looked as bad as Alex was Gabe. Had he slept at all? He'd been awake Thursday night when Cyrus found Hannah, and never did go to bed then. Maybe got a couple of hours of sleep Friday night. Or not. How long could a body go without sleep before they .... what? Died?

Jude looked wore out. Spencer was reserved. And that friend who'd come home with Avery didn't have no color at all in her face. Avery said she'd got sick on the Mexican casseroles. They'd do a number on you if you wasn't used to the jalapeños.

Juliana's live-in boyfriend Jamal had driven in from Amarillo to go to the funeral with her tomorrow. Olivia didn't know if they's ever gonna get married, but if they did, she sure hoped that young man was full of piss and vinegar. He was gonna need it. Juliana was growing more like her grandmother Alex every day.

Avery was at the opposite end of the table, as far as it was possible to get from her father. Olivia shook her head, couldn't for the life of her figure out why Avery'd taken what had happened eight years ago so personally.

"How come that sweet girl from Laredo didn't come down with you, Aves?" Olivia asked her. "Mariah, isn't it? Ain't she your roommate?"

"She said to tell everybody hey. She wanted to come, but she had to go home to help her family move out of their house."

"They sell it, did they? Sell the ranch, too? I thought that'd been in the Alvarez family since ..." The thought that a family'd do that, just take the money and run, put a lonely ache deep in Olivia's belly. Would hers sell out when she was gone? "They had a good-sized spread, didn't they?"

"Oh, her father'd never sell! They're just closing it up. Her parents and little sisters are moving in with her grandmother in San Antonio. After Lupe found the dead body—"

"Dead body?" Cassidy said.

"A woman. Don't know how she died. Maybe she was murdered, or maybe just couldn't keep up. There's a twenty-mile stretch of *nothing* between their ranch and the river. Lupe saw the buzzards circling, rode over to see if it was one of their cows. You couldn't tell much after the coyotes …"

"Do we have to talk about this at supper?" Cassidy looked a little green.

"It's the second one. Last summer when there was that caravan thing — and the man wasn't too …" Avery looked at Cassidy and didn't finish. "Rye found him and he hadn't been very …" She stopped again. "But *Lupe*. She *totally lost it.*"

"She's what?"

"Nine."

"Fun and games at our" — Avery made air quotes — "'secure southern border.' Rye's parents don't even know anymore what all's been stolen."

"Like?"

"Anything. They're on the run, living on whatever they can find, so the livestock … Rye's dad says most of them are just hungry, looking for food, but how are you supposed to know which ones are smuggling heroin or cocaine or fentanyl, or trafficking—"

Aunt Casey cleared her throat loudly and nodded at Willie and Tally, who were listening intently.

"Anyway, it's not safe for Rye's little sisters to get off the bus after school at the road and walk down to the house anymore."

"Not safe to walk from the road to the house," Grandma Liv said quietly, shaking her head. "So they're leaving."

It wasn't a question, but Avery answered anyway.

"What else can they do? Shoot somebody for stealing a chicken? Call the sheriff? The State Police? The Border Patrol? With *hundreds of thousands* of … those guys have bigger fish to fry than a dozen stolen chickens."

❧

Avery didn't want to talk about it anymore. That's all anybody did, just talk. Nobody did anything to help. She sat down at the table beside a pale, shaky Maddie, as far away from her father as she could get. She couldn't help noticing he was stealing looks at her and it made her feel … what?

Sad. Tired. Confused. Angry. Add water and stir.

Juliana was introducing Jamal to the family members who'd never met him.

Maddie stuck out her hand. "I'm Madeline Shepherd — she, her."

Grandma Liv looked confused.

"Come again?"

Maddie looked confused.

"*Come again?*"

Avery jumped in to translate. To Maddie, she said, "Grandma Liv means 'what did you say?'"

To Grandma Liv, Avery said, "*She and her* are Maddie's preferred pronouns."

Maddie didn't know what else to say, merely shrugged. "I don't identify non-binary."

Grandma Liv shook her head. "Well, I wouldn't be too sure of that if I's you. Just 'cause you can't identify it, don't mean that 'non-binary' stuff ain't gonna come back on you … takes a while to get over the squirts like you had 'em last night."

There was a beat of complete silence, into which Maddie dropped two words: "Come again?"

That brought the house down. Grandma Liv chuckled merrily with everybody else. She knew they were laughing at her, but she was a good sport and joined right in, though she had no idea what they'd all found so humorous.

Buoyed by the family's accepting laughter, Maddie relaxed. As she ate, color returned to her cheeks.

Grandma Alex stepped out of the doorway and sat in an

empty chair and caught the end of what Maddie was saying to Aunt Brooke.

"… gender is about what's inside, not about whatever body parts you might or might not have on the outside. It's the authentic you, without having to 'play nice' for other people."

"Gender is fluid, then?" Grandma Alex asked innocently.

Uh oh. Maddie had no idea she'd just stepped on a land mine. It was no secret Grandma Alex was transphobic — she crowed it from the top of the henhouse. If you got her going — and Maddie would if she argued with her — Grandma Alex could literally go on for hours.

"Of course. Particularly in children."

"Ahh … *children.*" Worst possible thing Maddie could have said. "So a ten-year-old boy who plays with dolls should be given hormone blockers? Have surgery?"

"If he's really a little girl, sure."

The table had grown quiet as conversations died in mid-sentence. You could feel the barometric pressure in the room drop like it does before a tornado comes rumbling at you across the prairie.

"Hope his parents have got good health insurance," Grandma Alex said. "They're going to need it when all the complications hit him."

"Oh, there won't be complications. It's all perfectly safe."

"And you know that how? Research? Clinical trials?"

"Of course there's been … research … and trials."

"Who did them? Mayo Clinic? Boston Children's Hospital? Johns Hopkins? Cleveland Clinic? If they did, the results are a secret because not a single study on the long-term effects of using hormone blockers on children has been published in any legitimate medical journal in the world … duh, because the drugs were never intended to be used on kids."

"Well, they wouldn't let them keep doing it, gender affirming care, if it was harmful."

Grandma Alex froze, and then said slowly, quietly, "You

didn't just say that, did you? That 'they' — the mysterious somebody/organization/God out there who's in charge of everything — would actually stop the practice? Have you noticed what happens to anybody who even asks a question about it? Doctors sure won't be the ones to raise an alarm, not with the millions they're raking in cutting perfectly normal breasts off healthy teenager girls."

Maddie didn't know that Grandma Alex's career in journalism had granted her a command of the language that would eviscerate all comers. But she was finding out.

"If you don't, you know, the suicide rate is … I mean, it's high for … there's proof … would you rather have a live little girl or a dead little boy?"

"Live girl, dead boy — so those are the *only two* possible outcomes? How about an emotionally healthy boy who's been to therapy and worked through dysphoria? Ten years down the road when the trendiness has worn off, and enough horror stories have finally come to light, what you'll have then is a young adult whose life *you* ruined because he never really wanted to be a woman." She paused for emphasis. "And he can never be a man now because you cut his dick off."

The table literally exploded in response, like a bomb had gone off in the mashed potatoes. Avery was thrilled that almost nobody agreed with Grandma Alex — how could you? — but they'd never before dared risk her wrath by speaking up. Everybody was shouting, nobody was listening. It was quickly getting ugly. This was why Grandma Olivia had forbidden all talk of politics under her roof. Trouble was, what could you talk about these days that wasn't political?

It was Grandma Alex who spotted him, and the look on her face grabbed the family's attention and focused it on the old man with bedhead in rumpled pajamas standing in the doorway, looking forlorn and confused.

"What's everybody yelling about?" Uncle Cyrus asked, sounding so pitiful and forlorn that shamed silence washed over the family. "Hannah doesn't like shouting. But I can't find her." He looked at Juliana, who appeared poised to leap across the table to rip off her cousin Daniella's face. "Have you seen her, Jules?"

"Uh … no, I …" Juliana stammered.

Turning to his oldest son, Samuel, who was trying to separate his wife Millie and his brother's wife, Cynthia. "Sammy, where's your mother?"

He looked at the whole group and pleaded, "Somebody please … *help me find Hannah.*"

Before anyone else could move, Grandma Alex leapt up and put her arm around her older brother's shoulder.

"I know where she is, Cy," she said, tenderly. "I'll take you to her." She cast a look over her shoulder at the others. "Don't worry … there'll be *no more yelling.* We were just having a little civil discourse on the subject of gender fluidity, that's all." She paused, looked at Maddie. "She and I … *disagree.*"

Maddie gave her a patronizing, you-poor-old-lady-what-do-you-know? look and beamed a triumphant smile.

Before anyone else could speak, there was a sudden, ear-splitting scream from upstairs — then the cries of a hysterical woman. "Get it, Tony. Kill it! *How did a spider get in the bed?*"

Another shriek and the sound of furniture falling. "It's over there behind the dresser — Peyton, get it. Ryan, stomp it!" Another shriek.

"Sounds like Leanne saw a spider," Juliana said, with no expression of any kind on her face.

"Sounds like," said Grandma Liv.

"I hope it wasn't a wolf spider like the ones in the basement," Juliana continued. "They're *huge.*" She made a shape with her hands the size of a saucer. "Gray and hairy. Meanest looking spiders I ever saw."

Avery saw Jamal shoot Juliana a disapproving look but didn't have time to wonder about it because two things happened at once. Grampa Cyrus suddenly threw off

Grandma Alex's arm and moved with amazing speed from the doorway to the stove, where he grabbed a huge iron skillet. Lifting it over his head, he advanced on Maddie with murderous intent. Grampa Gabe, who'd been washing his hands, spun around and bolted out the kitchen door into the backyard— left the hot water running in the sink.

Everyone else sat frozen in place, looked like the painting of the Last Supper.

Chapter Fifty-Two

GABE WAS at the sink washing his hands, his back turned to the table where his mother was ramping up in a specular blow. Not now. Not tonight. *Please!*

His head was pounding, felt like it was in a vice. And he was exhausted. All he wanted to do was grab a bite to eat and go to bed. He did not want to deal with —

There was a scream, high and shrill and terrified.

THE KITCHEN full of people and voices and smells vanishes, and it is night. A storm is rumbling outside the windows. The electricity is out and it's coal-mine dark until flashes of lightning strobe the windows and illuminate everything in harsh black-and-white relief, leaving an afterimage in his eyes when the light is gone.

Gabe is hiding in the stairwell. Whatever was in the kitchen has left and the room is empty. Gabe has to cross the kitchen now, while he has the chance, before the monster returns. Make a break for it — the back door is on the other side of the room.

It's his only chance!

Bursting out the stairwell door into the kitchen, he races into the dark room, dizzy, the world spinning. He can see nothing but empty darkness until a flash of lightning makes the room bright for an instant. By then, it's too late. There's something on the floor between him and the back door, big and metal, but he's moving too fast to stop. Trying to dodge around it, his bare feet hit something wet and he slips, loses his footing and stumbles, crashing into the metal thing, knocking it sideways, tipping it over.

The floor is wet, stinks of copper or wet pennies. Blood! It's black, not red.

Flashes of sheet lightning light up the room, blinking on and off, turning reality into the herky-jerky motion of a convenience store surveillance video.

Whatever was in the metal thing slid out onto the floor when Gabe tripped over it. Gooey. Sticky. Smells awful. It lies there now, writhing, its blueish-purple tentacles reaching out for Gabe. It finds him, grips him. The others of its kind come then, with their sharp teeth, wriggling out of the shadows and down the walls.

Crying, wailing soundlessly, he wrenches his body free, then scuttles across the kitchen floor toward the door. On his knees, he lifts his upper body up and claws at the door, his fingernails scraping over the wood until his hand finally grasps the doorknob.

As soon as he turns it, the door is yanked out of his hands and the wind roars into the room. Cold rain comes at him horizontally. He stands, slips and falls, gets up and staggers across the porch to the steps. His body is soaked in cold water.

He can barely see with the rainwater in his eyes, but it doesn't matter. He would run if he were blind. Down the porch steps, he stumbles and crashes the final few, landing in a puddle at the base of the final step. Then he gets up and runs out into the muddy yard. The sky is a fireworks display of lightning. He slides in the mud by the fence. His shirt hangs on something but he rips free and keeps running—

"Dad! Dad, stop!"

The cold, hammering rain vanished, was replaced by warm air, the sounds of crickets and frogs and the mild fragrance of roses and crepe myrtle blossoms.

Gabe was in the backyard, with Spencer gripping his arm, shaking him.

"Dad? What's wrong?"

All the air whooshed out of Gabe and his knees buckled, collapsing him like an accordion into the grass. Spencer went to his knees beside him.

"Are you all right? Dad … say something."

"Something." Gabe gasped out the word, then couldn't speak again, just reveled in taking in deep lungfuls of the fresh night air.

"What's wrong? Why did you go running out—"

Then a woman's voice called from the porch. It was his mother.

"Gabe, what is it? What—"

Gabe staggered to his feet and stumbled across the yard to where his mother was standing on the back porch.

"Why did you lie to me?" He hadn't meant the words to come out harsh, but that's the way they spilled from his mouth.

"Lie to you?"

"Why did you tell me it was all a dream, a nightmare?"

His mother looked like he had slapped her.

"There was real screaming. I heard it. I didn't imagine it, *I heard it*. And in the kitchen there was …"

There was … what?

What was the thing on the floor that slithered toward him? The thing covered in blood? The horror that fastened its tentacles on him, choked him, strangled him. And not just one, but dozens, slithering down the walls, crawling over each other on the floor, a writhing mass … That *couldn't* be real. He'd imagined it. So had he just imagined all the rest of it, too?

No, it was real.

Couldn't be.

It *was!*

"Grandma Alex — Grandma Liv wants you," Gabe's daughter Sydney said from the back door. "She's trying to calm Uncle Cyrus, but—"

Gabe's mother's face wore a look he had never seen before. It was fear. Terror. His mother was scared to death.

"I can't now, Gabe … Cyrus thinks Avery's friend is some kind of demon and he tried to …" She stopped, said the rest louder. "I have to help him." She turned as if to go back into the house and then turned back to Gabe.

"I'm sorry!" Her voice was a harsh stage whisper, and she was near tears. "I never dreamed you'd be hurt by …." She stopped again and then spoke in an odd voice, devoid of intonation or inflection, like an automated attendant. "I fixed everything. You're safe, now. You don't need to worry. I'll tell you … *all of it.* Just not right now."

Alex turned and rushed into the house, leaving Spencer and Gabe in the backyard alone.

"What's going on, Dad? Why'd you come running out here?"

"Flashback. PTSD."

Spencer's face hardened. "Been there, done that. What happened to you that'd cause flashbacks?"

"I don't know. I've thought my whole life it was a dream. But now … I know something real happened. I just don't know what."

Gabe had to figure it out, though. If he didn't, he would lose his mind. He really would. If he couldn't reconcile reality and fantasy, Gabriel Chambers would go insane.

Chapter Fifty-Three

SUNDAY

THE FUNERAL DIDN'T START until eleven thirty and it was only nine o'clock, but Chapman was already in time-out. He was standing with his nose in the corner of the living room, and he had to stay there until Mommy said he could go play. He thought about crying but didn't. That worked sometimes. It always worked on Grandma Dani, who never put him in time-out and sometimes let him out before Mommy wanted him and then Mommy would give Grandma Dani a mean look.

He turned his head a little to see if Mommy was still talking to Aunt Casey. Just a little, because he was supposed to look at the wall during time-out, and if he moved or turned around, he'd have to stay longer.

This time-out wasn't one he could get out of by saying "sorry," like when he took away his cousin Ethan's toy and Mommy made him give it back and tell Ethan he was sorry. Chap always did it, so he wouldn't have to go to time-out, but he usually wasn't sorry. And he thought it was dumb that Mommy made him say sorry when he wasn't, and Ethan didn't care that Chap said it because he was only ten months old and he didn't even know what sorry meant.

Chap was in time-out this time for hitting Aunt Leanne in

the back with a bullet from his Nerf gun. If there hadn't been so many people around, Chap was sure Mommy would have yanked the gun out of his hand and spanked his butt. But she didn't usually spank him when people were around, except that time in the grocery store when he stuck his tongue out at her and she'd swatted him three or four times right then and it *hurt*.

This time, she just took the gun away from him and put it up on the mantel where he couldn't reach it and took him by the hand to the corner and said in her mean voice, "Time-out, young man."

He needed to go to the bathroom — just to pee, not to poop. And if he wet his pants, Mommy would really get mad, so she'd better let him out of time-out soon!

He heard Daddy's voice and he turned around and saw him talking to Mommy and then Daddy came over to him and got down on one knee in front of him. When he did that, Chap knew he was going to say a good thing because he said angry things standing up.

"Did you shoot your Aunt Leanne with your Nerf gun?"

Chap nodded his head and didn't look at his father.

"Are you sorry you shot her?"

Maybe Daddy was going to make him tell Aunt Leanne he was sorry, which he would do to get out of time-out. Uncle Gabe and Uncle Will came and sat down in the chairs nearby, but they stopped talking to let Daddy finish making Chap be sorry.

"I didn't meant to shot her," he said. "I was aiming at the rose in the ugly wallpaper and missed."

"The ugly wallpaper?"

"You know, in the dining room. Aunt Avery says she'd rather get stuck in an elevator with Kim Kar-Mashon than have to look at it."

Daddy tried not to smile and Uncle Gabe and Uncle Will both started coughing.

"Who's Kim Kar—"

"It doesn't matter who she is. It does matter that you shot your aunt with your Nerf gun. Nobody likes to get shot."

"Grandma Liv doesn't mind. She said she didn't."

"You shot Grandma Olivia?"

Uh oh. He probably shouldn't have said that. Now he might have to stay in time-out for shooting Grandma Liv.

He nodded.

"When did you shoot Grandma Olivia?"

"When she comed into the pantry to talk on her watch. I didn't mean to shoot her, but she was in front of the target you put on the door."

"Grandma Olivia talked on the phone in the pantry? When?"

"At lunch on Friday and I shot her on accident because she was in front of the target. But she didn't mind. She told the man named Regg-inold that she'd got shot and he laughed and asked if it had killed her and she'd said not as far as she could tell and she was smiling."

His father looked at his uncles, then said, "You mean Reginald?"

Chapman nodded.

"How do you know the man she was talking to said that?"

"I heard him. She was talking on her watch."

Daddy looked at Uncle Gabe.

"I guess she went into the pantry to talk because she couldn't hear him with all the noise in the kitchen," Daddy said.

Chap shook his head.

"No, that's not why."

"How do you know it's not?"

"'Cause she told Mr. Regg-nold that she was in the pantry because she was on her watch and she didn't want everybody else to hear *what he said.*"

Uncle Will spoke then, in his nice voice, but Chap was

sure he was still mad at Chap for pushing his little girl, Tally, into the swimming pool last summer.

"Chap, do you remember what Mr. Reginald said to Grandma Liv?"

"Will!" his Uncle Gabe said. "It's none of your business what he said. That was a private conversation."

"Reginald Underwood is her attorney." Uncle Will paused. "Don't *you* want to know what he said that she didn't want anybody to hear?"

Uncle Gabe didn't say anything, so Chap said, "He mostly used big words I didn't understand, asked Grandma Liv if she was still going to drop a bomb on Sunday."

All three of the men looked at him.

"What's a bomb?" Chap asked.

"It's … a thing that explodes," Uncle Will said. "Soldiers drop bombs out of airplanes and they explode."

"What's explodes?"

"Blows up," Uncle Gabe said. He was leaning forward now, listening to what Daddy was saying to Chapman. "You know. Like on the Fourth of July when Ramsey put those firecrackers in that cardboard box that'd been the Christmas piñata and there was a loud noise and pieces of the piñata flew everywhere. That's explodes."

Chapman didn't know what a piñata was but didn't ask because he was already too confused. Grandma Liv hadn't said anything about soldiers or airplanes or piñatas.

"You said Mr. Reginald used big words," Uncle Will said. "Do you remember any of them?"

Chap tried. But he didn't know what Mr. Regg-inold's words meant so he couldn't remember them. And he hadn't really been listening, he'd been loading the shells back into his Nerf gun.

"They were just big words."

"Big words like …"

Chap didn't like all the questions. They sounded angry. He

looked at his father and asked, "Are you mad at me? I'll say sorry to Aunt Leanne if you want me to."

Daddy gave the other two men a look and made a gesture with his head, and they turned back around in their chairs like they weren't listening anymore, but they still were.

Daddy put his hand on Chap's shoulder. "You're not in trouble, son. Your uncles were just curious about what that man said, that's all." He smiled a big smile and swatted Chap easy on the butt.

"Go on and play now. Time-out's over."

He leapt out of the corner and ran across the room to the mantel, where his mother had put his Nerf gun. He couldn't reach it up there. Somebody would have to get it down for him, and he knew Mommy wouldn't because she was mad at him for shooting Aunt Leanne with it. But Daddy didn't seem mad about it. Maybe Daddy would get it down for him.

Looking back at the corner of the room, he saw that Daddy and Uncle Will were gone. Uncle Gabe was going toward the back door that led to the yard. Then Chap remembered something Grandma Liv had said and he ran to Uncle Gabe to tell him.

Chapter Fifty-Four

GABE WENT OUT into the backyard where he'd stood with Spencer the night before, to the spot where he'd been compelled to go by the images of a flashback. He was dizzy from sleep deprivation, and exhausted — physically, psychologically, and spiritually wrung out. He couldn't shake the growing awareness that he was coming apart. As reality collided with dreams, fantasies, and nightmares, his hold on sanity, on who he was, felt more and more tenuous with every passing hour. The images from Gabe's childhood hallucination jarred loose by Cyrus's scream had stalked the dark corridors of Gabe's mind ever since, and he knew now what he'd never known before — that he'd been awakened as a child by *real* screams, that he'd run away in fear down the back staircase to the kitchen and ... if last night's flashback was to be believed, when he crossed the kitchen to the back door, he had encountered ... what? *Something* real, he thought. But maybe not. He had no idea anymore how to tell real from illusion, but as soon as the whole funeral ordeal was over, he would confront his mother and demand to know what had really happened that night. He would find out why had she lied to him then and why had she continued to lie to him for four decades. As soon as the dust finally settled and life returned to normal … Of course, "normal" might just be a whole new thing if Grandma Liv was planning to drop some kind of "bomb" on the family today. If she had been talking to her attorney about —

Not watching where he was going, Gabe stumbled into somebody half hidden in the crepe myrtle bush, smelled him before he saw him.

Vape smoke. Or vapor. Or whatever they called it. It wafted out from among the blossoms where Doodle stood out of sight.

"I come out for a smoke," Doodle said, his eyes bright. Was he already high on something? More likely, he was *still* high on something. "Want a drag?"

Doodle extended the vape pipe and Gabe barely disguised his disgust as he recoiled.

"I'll pass."

"If you wanna smoke — cigarettes, vape, weed, it don't matter —you gotta do it out here 'cause Grandma Liv'll slap a world of hurt on you for smoking in the house."

Gabe nodded and started to walk away when Chapman Schaeffer came out the back door, spotted Gabe, and came running at him so fast he almost bowled Gabe over when he collided with Gabe's legs.

"I 'member now!" the excited little boy said, panting. "The man on the phone and Grandma Liv were talking about a parrot."

CHAPMAN WAS proud as punch of himself for remembering what the voice talking out of Grandma Liv's watch had said to her in the pantry day before yesterday!

"Are you sure?" Uncle Gabe asked. "A *parrot?*"

Chap bobbed his head up and down.

"Uh huh. And Grandma Liv said nobody would like it."

"Nobody would like the parrot?"

Chap nodded again.

"Somebody was talking to Grandma Liv about pirates?" asked the man standing beside Uncle Gabe. Chapman had only seen him a few times, thought his name was Doodle, but that couldn't be right, could it?

"No, not about pirates, just about a parrot. It was a different kind of parrot, though —that was one of the big words. It was a parrot that … I think it hissed, like a snake, maybe."

Uncle Gabe got that look grownups get when they think you're making stuff up.

"What man?" Doodle asked.

"The man on Grandma Liv's watch." Chap wasn't making anything up. That's what the man had said. Well, kinda what the man'd said. It wasn't a hissing parrot, it was a *dissing* parrot.

"The parrot wasn't hissing. It was *dissing*, but I don't know what dissing means."

Uncle Gabe just looked at him. He must not know either. "Dissing?" he said, trying to puzzle it out.

"A dissing parrot?" Doodle asked, then put a pipe thing in his mouth, sucked on it and blew smoke out of his nose.

Uncle Gabe repeated the words slowly, one at a time. "Dissing. Parrot." Then he suddenly got a really funny look on his face. Like he was surprised and then he got upset, but maybe not mad. It was hard to tell.

He put his hands on Chap's shoulders and spoke slowly.

"Is that what the man and Grandma Liv said — dissing parrot?" He leaned over and looked Chap in the eye before he said the rest of it. "Or did he say … *dis-in-herit?*"

That was it!

"Yes, that's the word. The man asked if Grandma Liv was still going to drop the bomb on Sunday and she said maybe and the man said she needed to put a belt on because somebody was going to pitch a fit and nobody in the whole family would like the … parrot, the desin … the big word, what you said, and he said he'd bring Grandma Liv some paper signs on Monday morning."

"Paper signs … you mean papers *to sign?*"

"Yeah, that."

Uncle Gabe said nothing. Doodle looked from Uncle Gabe to Chapman and back to Uncle Gabe.

"Did I hear him right? Did he say Grandma Liv was talking to somebody about disinheriting … who?"

Uncle Gabe didn't answer him, just stood, not looking at anything.

"Uncle Gabe, would you get my Nerf gun off the mantel, please?"

Uncle Gabe looked like he hadn't even heard Chap.

"Mommy put my Nerf gun on the mantle and—"

"That's where it belongs," he said, gruff, like maybe he was mad. "You can't go around shooting people with it."

Then he turned and walked away from Chapman and Doodle.

ON FRIDAY, Gabe had told himself over and over, *Just get past the viewing tomorrow.* He'd clung to that piece of mental driftwood and held on tight. His thinking foggy from lack of sleep, his mind bludgeoned by terrors at night and migraines and flashbacks during the day, he thought he might really be losing his mind.

Yesterday, he'd told himself, *Just get past the funeral tomorrow and then this awful weekend will be over.*

Except, maybe it wouldn't.

Apparently, Grandma Liv intended to drop a bomb on everybody today, probably when they were all gathered together at supper.

"Hey, what was he talking about?" asked a voice behind him. Doodle. "Did he hear Grandma Liv say she was going to disinherit—"

"He's four years old and has an overactive imagination," Gabe said.

Doodle blew by him. "Somebody's going to bring her papers to sign Monday. The kid ain't imagining *that*. A new will, I bet."

Gabe turned on him, venom in his voice.

"Let it go, Doodle! Do you hear what I'm saying— *let it go!* If you tell anybody what you just heard, you'll answer to me. I will wipe the floor with your sorry ass. We clear?"

Doodle put his hands up palms out and backed away. All bullies are cowards. "Ain't sayin' a word to nobody." He made a zipper motion over his mouth, and as soon as he was outside grabbing range, he turned and hurried into the house.

Left alone in the yard at last, Gabe found the solitude he'd been looking for to clear his head. As the sun heated up the day, Gabe heard the word banging around in his head like a bowling ball in an empty oil drum.

Disinherit.

Disinherit.

Disinherit!

She couldn't. She wouldn't.

In actual point of fact, though, Grandma Liv could indeed write anybody or everybody out of her will. It was, after all, her money. But would she? And *why* would she? He stopped under a cottonwood tree and forced himself to remain still, to breathe regularly, not to panic.

Being disinherited … that was a blow, but that wasn't what had Gabe's heart in his throat. This year was his year to get a share of the disbursement. That money was one of the income streams he was counting on to make the final payment. If that money wasn't coming, Gabe's goose was cooked.

Chapter Fifty-Five

WHILE MOMMY WAS SHOVING his arms into the jacket of his suit and straightening Chapman's clip-on tie, he was pretending he was Spiderman putting on his spidey suit. He'd seen a big black car pull down the lane and around the front of the house and he was pretending it was the mothership of an invading army of aliens. He was going to sneak on board the mothership when nobody was looking, and capture the—

"Have you seen my shoe?" Mommy asked Daddy. She was limping around, wearing only one high heeled shoe. "Would you dig around in the suitcase and find it?"

Daddy was in the little bathroom, scrunched up between the toilet and the sink, trying to shave in the little medicine cabinet mirror.

"Can't right now, hon, I—"

Then he said some bad words which meant he had cut himself.

Mommy hopped over to the suitcase to look for herself.

"Is there a stip-dick pencil in the overnight case?"

"I didn't pack one."

"Why not? I look like I just went three rounds with an ax murderer."

"Why would you expect *me* to pack it?"

"For me."

"If *you're* the one who uses it, why didn't you—"

"Never mind."

The room got that sticky quiet where his parents were thinking thoughts they didn't want to say. He could tell by the scrunched looks on their faces. That's when Chapman stepped in it.

"Is the fum-eral when they put the dead lady in a oven and cook her?" he asked.

"Chapman!" his father hissed from the bathroom.

"Chapman Andrew Schaeffer!" his mother said. Never in his life had she used his whole name when he wasn't in trouble.

"You said they were going to burn her up until she was ashes."

'For one thing, I've told you to stop calling Grandma Hannah 'that dead lady,'" Mommy said. "And nobody ever said anything about cooking."

"I'm sorry." He didn't know why what he'd said had upset everybody, but clearly it had, so he really was sorry. And when his lip began to tremble, it was real.

Daddy looked at his watch and said another bad word.

"We're going to be late."

He was still holding a bloody piece of toilet paper to his chin, searching on the floor for Mommy's missing shoe. This bedroom, where his mommy and daddy were sleeping in the bed and Chapman was sleeping on the little couch under the window, was so small that there was no place to walk without stepping in their suitcases.

"Chapman, get down on your knees and look under the bed, see if it's there," Mommy said. She was too pregnant big to get on her hands and knees.

"Here it is," Daddy said, holding the missing shoe out to Mommy. "Let's go."

Chapman would need his gun to take over the mothership. He didn't have time to strap on the scabbard, so he shoved the gun and scabbard down into the back of his pants and pulled his suit coat down over them so they'd be right there when the time came and he could start blasting away.

As Mommy was hurrying him out of the room, he remembered what *else* was in the ammo clip on the scabbard! He couldn't take *that* to church for the fumeral. But it was too late to pull it out of his pants and leave it here. It'd be okay. Nobody would notice.

When he stepped out into the October sunshine, Chapman saw there was more than one black car. There were a whole bunch of them. A fleet of enemy spaceships! But he would save the galaxy when he jumped out of hiding and mowed down the captain. While Mommy and Daddy stood talking, he crouched down toward the ground and sneaked along the edge of the spaceship. He would board the mother-ship and hide away until—

"Chapman! where are you?"

He poked his head around the back of the car.

"I'm right here."

"Give me your hand and don't go wandering off again."

ALEX WONDERED what planet Chapman Schaeffer was on. Clearly, it wasn't this one. She watched him creep around the back side of the car in front of her, low to the ground, clearly trying to sneak up on … no telling what. Cassidy called out, came around the car and snatched his hand and pulled him along beside her to the next car in line, where the funeral home director and his assistant — looking like stuffed turkeys in suits — held the door open for them to get in.

She marveled at how the funeral directors had got the whole thing down to a choreographed sequence where each car pulled up to the front of the house and a family was deposited in it, then the car pulled away and another car and another family took its place.

She wondered how she could abort the parade of black elephants, hooked nose to tail, for her own service, absolutely did not want ... but what difference did the line of elephants make? She'd be the one family member absent from the circus?

Not here.

Alex literally stopped in her tracks, looked suddenly around her at the family being herded into cars, and it struck her that when that happened again, she wouldn't be here. They all would be. They all *better* be, or she'd come back as some kind of malignant spirit and Amityville-Horror them all!

Her mind still couldn't process the reality of it. She would not be here. There'd be a hole in the space in the family that she was supposed to occupy but didn't. Her mother'd always pointed out when Alex had lost something that "everything's got to be somewhere." So if she wouldn't be here, she'd have to be some other place. And what other place might that be? She knew what she was supposed to believe, what her mother believed, and it was a convenient story that tied up all the loose ends of life all tidy with a bow. But was it *true?*

"Mama," Gabe said, taking her arm, and she could tell by his manner that it wasn't the first time he spoken. She'd zoned out again. Or maybe gone deaf for a minute or two? Was Persephone dancing a jig in her skull? Perhaps, but it was more likely her own emotional response to the reality that ... she was dying. T.S. Eliot notwithstanding, Alex honestly wanted to go out with a whimper instead of a bang. No, not a whimper, a sigh. A relaxed breath that said she'd completed the tasks that'd presented themselves, and now she could let it all go.

The world.

Let it all —

"Mama, are you listening to a thing I'm saying?"

"Of course, I'm listening."

"Then why are you just standing there?"

"Because I ... wasn't really listening. Okay, what'd you say? Make it quick, there appears to be a hitch in the get-along of this elephant train and—"

"The hitch is *you*. You're supposed to be up there." He pointed to a long black vehicle several cars up. "You're supposed to ride with Grandma Liv and Uncle Cyrus."

"On it." She paused for just a beat, locked eyes with her son. He'd wanted her to tell him last night why she'd lied to him all those years ago and she'd put him off. Cyrus had needed her. But Gabe couldn't be stalled for long. Soon, she'd have to tell him — *what?* What could she tell him? What *should* she tell him? Did she dare open up that Pandora's box after all these years? What else might be lurking inside that would destroy the people she loved most?

Unhooking her eyes from his, she hurried as no seventy-two-year-old woman ought to be able to hop around, to the car where she was supposed to ride.

She got into the back seat beside Cyrus, who wore an uncomprehending thousand-yard stare. Mama was on the other side of him.

"Mama ... Gabe *knows*."

"Knows what?"

"He's having flashbacks or something — he *remembers* the screams."

Alex knew this probably wasn't the best time to bring up the subject, but she found herself just blurting it out. Probably Persephone was messing with her impulse control. Certainly was convenient to have something to blame for all your bad behavior.

The color drained out of her mother's face so fast the veins at her temples suddenly stood out like stripes from a blue Magic Marker.

"That why he went running out of the kitchen last night like his pants was on fire?"

"After the service, we need to talk. I have to tell him *something.*"

Cyrus looked around, confused.

"Where's Hannah?"

Just then, Alex's phone dinged with an incoming email. Who emails anymore? But before she could consign the offender to junk mail, she glanced at the sender — Bailey County Sheriff Ralph Hastings. Shifting her eyes down, she read the subject line — "Toxicology results."

Her heart leapt into her throat. The results weren't supposed to be available until next week — when Hannah would be dust and there'd be no way to confirm the report or do more tests. Would they be forced to postpone the cremation so the sheriff could investigate? No, no, no! Not now, not so close.

Holding up one finger to her mother in a "wait" motion, Alex opened the email and read it.

"I've attached the test results from the blood Dr. Carpenter drew from Hannah Kavanaugh."

Alex couldn't breathe, couldn't make her eyes focus, but certain words seemed to stand out in bold face — "official cause of death" and then "insulin overdose."

What?

Insulin overdose?

What about all those sleeping pills Alex had ground up and put into Hannah's orange juice?

"What's wrong?" her mother asked. "You look like somebody done walked over your grave."

Alex barely kept herself from blurting out what she was thinking: does this mean I *didn't* murder Hannah?

Chapter Fifty-Six

THE SANCTUARY OF ST. Anne's Church was full and Rowan was glad to snag the last seat on the aisle on the back pew. The service started almost immediately. As the organist began to play a hymn with a hauntingly familiar melody, the funeral directors performed their ceremonial walk down the center aisle of the church. The congregation stood. Gravely dignified, the two men in black suits stopped at the first row of empty pews at the front of the church. They turned and gestured for the family to file down the aisle and into the designated pew. When a pew was filled, the funeral director stepped backwards down the aisle to indicate the next pew for seating.

There was a protocol to the seating order. The more distant family members were at the head of the line, so they were seated in the rows behind those who came in after them. Gradually the pews were filled, one after another, leaving only the front pew that was reserved for the "immediate family."

When Rowan had been at the visitation the day before, she'd wandered from room to room, examining the faces of everyone she saw — dozens, maybe hundreds of people. But she didn't know then which of them were family members and which ones were merely close friends or neighbors, an old college roommate or somebody's first grade teacher. Now, the funeral ceremony seined from the sea of mourners only "family" — Hannah Kavanaugh's family.

And somewhere among the people entering the sanctuary together would be Rowan's mother. She was sure of it. The certainty had grown in her heart at the visitation yesterday after the little blue-eyed munchkin had told her the "dead lady" was his grandmother and asked if she were Rowan's grandmother, too. Realization had landed with both feet square in Rowan's chest then — maybe she was!

As Rowan lay awake in her motel room, tossing and turning, a scenario formed in her head and solidified into fact as the hours ticked away toward sunrise. Sitting in a lounge chair on the patio outside her room, wrapped up in the tacky floral bedspread off the bed, she'd watched in awe and wonder as the sun plowed brilliant ripples of red, gold, and pink ahead of it into the day. When the bright orange ball finally crested the horizon, Rowan was convinced that this special dawn was ushering in the day when her forty-five-year wait would be over. Today, Rowan Douglas would meet her mother.

It wasn't hard to figure out what must have happened. Hannah Kavanaugh's daughter had gotten pregnant. By a *Black* man — in 1976. A prominent white family would have closed ranks around her, forced her to give the baby up, and afterward they'd have pretended it never happened. They'd sweep the scandal under the rug to preserve the honor of the family name. Her mother hadn't wanted to give her up. Of course, she hadn't. But she'd had no choice. And ever afterward, her mother looked for Rowan's face in every crowd of children — as Rowan had looked for Sterling's for all those years. Her mother never got over the loss — life, a marriage, other children had not diminished the ache in her soul that only her lost child could fill.

Rowan would recognize her mother when she saw her.

There would be no doubt. And then … what? There would be no "what" today. Rowan's mother was grieving the death of her own mother and now was not the time, and here was certainly not the place, for Rowan to step forward. But she would, sometime soon. Her mind didn't travel far enough down that road to envision how that would happen, but it would. Rowan had waited a lifetime, so she could hang on another few days. And she was content today with the miracle that was about to unfold. Rowan was about to lay eyes on her mother for the first time.

As the crowd of people entered the sanctuary and made their way in single file down the aisle toward the spot at the front of the sanctuary where Hannah Kavanaugh's body lay, Rowan's heart began to hammer so hard in her chest that each individual beat shook her. Her hands trembled. Her knees felt weak.

And surprise at what she instantly noticed about the crowd brought such a smile to her lips she could have laughed out loud. But why was she surprised? It made perfect sense that Hannah Kavanaugh's was a family of *redheads*.

With them all moving together to the front of the sanctuary, she could pick out different hues of red — carrot-red, strawberry blonde, auburn, reddish brown. As they passed her aisle seat, she studied their profiles and could see that each did, indeed, bear a stamp of familial resemblance. Many of them had freckles to complement their red hair. Red freckles, just like Rowan's.

As the number of people dwindled to only a few, fear stole into her heart. Perhaps her mother wasn't here. Why not? Maybe she was dead. Maybe she'd even died years ago — killed in a car wreck or a skiing accident. Maybe she'd never married, never borne other children who would be Rowan's siblings. She desperately sought a resemblance to her own features among the last of the people but could find none in their profiles as they filed past her.

When all the family had entered, the congregation took their seats, and as an off-key soprano version of "When the Roll is Called Up Yonder" filled the sanctuary, Rowan suffered bitter disappointment. She began to cry, couldn't help it. But it was, after all, a funeral, so those seated near her understood. Through the whole service, Rowan sat crying softly, struggling to get her mind around the stark reality that her mother was not here in this room today. She finally grabbed hold of her emotions and told herself sternly that all was not lost. Okay, maybe her mother wasn't here. But there were other people here who shared a common DNA with Rowan. Ancestry.com said so! There were aunts, uncles, cousins — family. More family than she'd ever had in her life. Family members who could tell her about her mother.

By the end of the service, she had her emotional ducks in a row, was no longer engaged in a desperate examination of all the family members. That's probably why she saw it — because she wasn't looking for it. Like those pictures that have an image other than the primary one, an image you can only see when you stop trying.

The immediate family on the front row was the first to leave the sanctuary. Walking slowly down the aisle toward Rowan — she could see their faces full on, not in profile. An old man with a cane was at the head of the line, with a younger man on each side walking along with him. Though old and bent, his hair was still a deep burgundy color. It was a distinctive, not-often-seen shade of red, and Rowan instantly recognized it. It was, after all, the color of Rowan's own hair that she had gone to great pains to conceal with black hair color ever since she was a teenager.

She turned and whispered to the stranger seated next to her.

"The man with a cane — who is he?"

The woman gave her an expected if-you-don't-know-who-he-is-why-are-you-here? look but whispered back, "Cyrus

Kavanaugh. Hannah's husband." The woman offered more explanation then, telling her that the men walking with him were two of his three sons, Samuel and Lawson, and that the elderly woman at the end was his mother, Olivia Harrington, who was a hundred years old.

Rowan didn't care about them. Her eyes bored into the old man's face.

Time stopped then, froze. The world unhooked from the engine spinning the planets. Everything was still. And in that stillness, she recognized an undeniable reality. She could not have put into words the specific facial characteristics of the old man that somehow matched her own. She only knew, with absolute certainty, that if she'd overlaid a photo of her face on a photo of his, they'd have fit perfectly. Even factoring in how much older he was, their faces fit.

As the old man moved ponderously up the aisle toward her, she stared at him in wonder, gawked. The others around him — tall men with red hair, a striking woman with black hair, and an ancient old crone on a walker — were shadows passing through the world beside him. They had little form or color, just occupied space as he traveled in slow motion among them, his features in bright detail, every aspect of his face drawn in perfect clarity.

That man — *Cyrus Kavanaugh* — was Rowan Douglas's father. There was no possible way to know a thing like that, but she was certain, as certain as she was that she had spent her whole life picturing reality the wrong way. She had always believed that her *white* mother had borne a *Black* man's daughter. But it was the other way around. Her mother hadn't been white, a member of the Harrington/Kavanaugh family who'd gotten pregnant by a Black man. Her *father* had been white. He had gotten a Black woman pregnant and then … yeah, and then what?

What had the wealthy white man done? He certainly hadn't welcomed the child and her mother into his house …

duh, because he was already married to Hannah Kavanaugh! And the two of them already had three children — all boys. Rowan was Cyrus Kavanaugh's only daughter.

And that's when the unanticipated emotion slammed down around her like the bars of a prison cell. *Anger.* The emotion swelled up inside her chest like she'd pulled the cord on a Navy dinghy. Her fury grew exponentially with every heartbeat. The nearer Cyrus Kavanaugh got to her, the angrier she became. When he was beside her, so close she could have reached out and touched him, she was in such a rage, she could barely contain herself.

This man, her *father,* was grief-stricken over the loss of his wife, and he had his whole family around him to offer support and comfort in his time of sorrow. And where was Rowan in this little scenario? Where she had always been — on the outside looking in, her nose pressed up against the window glass as life as it should have been passed by just outside her grasp.

Her father was … what? In his *eighties*? So he'd been in his forties when Rowan was conceived. He had been *married* to Hannah Kavanaugh at the time, had three teenage boys — sons who grew up knowing who they were, participating in all the benefits of their heritage. While Cyrus's daughter, Rowan, grew up with no parents, no heritage, no family, shunted from one orphanage to another, then set adrift in the sea of the foster care system, blown from one placement to another, always unanchored. No harbor. No moorings. Nothing permanent to shelter her from the brutality of the world.

Rowan had been entitled to a family, a name, a home, a heritage. She had been denied it, and she knew the old man leaning on his sons' arms for support had been responsible. Cyrus Kavanaugh had abandoned Rowan, pretended she didn't exist.

Well, playtime was over. She would make him stop pretending.

Chapter Fifty-Seven

HE SHOULDN'T HAVE BROUGHT it with him. Chapman knew that now, but it was too late. The Nerf gun and holster made a lump so big that eventually somebody would notice it.

The somebody who noticed was Daddy.

"What's that lump in your pants?" he whispered. They were jammed together in one of the pews reserved for the family at church. Daddy hadn't seen the lump. He'd felt it. "Something's poking me. What is it?"

"Nothing."

"'Nothing' doesn't jab you in the ribs. Hand it over."

Chapman looked up with the most pleading look he could muster, but he knew it would do no good. Not here and definitely not with his father right now. Daddy was still mad that Chapman had called the dead lady ... had called *Grandma Hannah* ... the dead lady. Of course, Chapman could pitch a fit about it. This was such a quiet, grown-up place that Chap was sure his parents would cave completely rather than suffer the embarrassment of one of his tantrums. But he was just as sure that if he did throw a tantrum, he would pay for it later, pay big time.

Reaching under his jacket, he pulled the Nerf gun out of

his waist band where he'd stuck it. He didn't give Daddy the gun, just held it out to show what it was, hoping maybe Daddy wouldn't take it away. Not a chance. Daddy looked at it and his eyes grew wide.

"You brought your Nerf gun to a funeral?"

The way he said it, bringing a Nerf gun to a funeral was a really, really bad thing.

"Give it to me."

Chap reluctantly laid the pistol in Daddy's outstretched hand, wondering as he did what Daddy was going to do with it. He didn't stuff it down his pants as Chap had done, just reached under the pew and laid it there on the floor.

"And the rest of it."

The ammunition! Oh no, he couldn't let anybody look in the ammunition clip.

"It's just the bullets. I can't use them without the pistol."

"Hand it over."

There was no arguing.

Wordlessly, Chap held out the clip of bullets and placed it in Daddy's palm. Surely Daddy wouldn't take the bullets out of it right here in church.

He didn't. But he did look down into the cartridge case. And he saw it.

"What is that, stuck down in there?"

Chapman didn't know what else to do so he just shrugged, like he didn't have any idea what could possibly be jammed down between the rows of bullets in his ammunition clip.

Some music started then. Some lady in a black dress that was too tight stood up and started singing a song about a roll being called "up yonder" — how she'd be there. Chap didn't see what that had to do with the dead lady — with *Grandma Hannah*. Everybody looked at the lady who was singing — everybody except Chapman, whose eyes were fixed on the ammunition cartridge. Daddy dropped the cartridge down into his suit coat pocket, put a single finger to his lips, and gave Chapman a stern look.

Eventually, Daddy would take the time to examine the ammunition cartridge and he would see what was jammed down in there. And when he did, Chapman would really be in trouble, probably in more trouble than he'd ever been in his whole life. He couldn't even imagine what the punishment would be. Put him in time out for a whole day? Or spank him first and then put him in time-out? Maybe spank him before time-out and then again after? Two spankings. He'd only gotten a few spankings in his whole life, so two in one day would be a lot. Maybe take his Nerf gun and all his toys away from him. Or maybe something even worse, though he couldn't imagine what that might be. What punishment was bad enough for a little boy who took a shiny thing off a dead lady's hand and hid it in his Nerf gun ammunition cartridge? He would soon find out.

Chap didn't like being in big groups of grownups because he got swallowed up in them. He wasn't even on eye level with the belt buckles of some of the men there and being jammed up against the bellies and backsides of strangers was gross.

He stood up when the adults stood up and sat down when they sat. He pretended to sing when they sang and bowed his head when they prayed. Then the preacher started talking about Grandma Hannah, what a fine lady she'd been, which she hadn't. As he kept talking, Chapman began to hope that Daddy had completely forgotten about the Nerf pistol and the ammunition cartridge. But he hadn't.

When they all got up to leave together, Daddy reached down under the pew, grabbed the pistol, and shoved it at Chapman.

"Put that back where you had it, push it down farther so it doesn't show."

It occurred to Chapman then that Daddy couldn't very well file out of the pew with all the other unsmiling people while carrying a Nerf pistol. Apparently, Daddy did forget about the gun after that, because when they got back to the house and everybody stopped looking like they wanted to cry and started putting food on their plates, Chapman was able to go to the bathroom and pull the pistol out of his pants and stick it between towels in the linen closet.

Maybe he'd forget about the ammunition cartridge, too.

Not.

Daddy was talking to Grampa Gabe when something reminded him, and he stuck his hand down into his pocket and felt the ammunition clip. Maybe Daddy would just give it back to Chapman. Or put it on the mantel where Chapman couldn't reach it. Maybe he wouldn't look into —

Daddy held the ammunition clip so he could look down into it. You could tell he saw something in there but didn't know what it was. So he just turned the cartridge case upside down and shook it ... and Grandma Hannah's shiny red ring fell out of it onto the table. It didn't stay on the table, though. It rolled across it, between the plate of deviled eggs and the macaroni salad, then dropped off the table onto the tile floor.

Only he, Daddy, and Grampa Gabe even noticed. The three of them followed the ring's progress, saw the shiny stone hit the tile before the ring spun away under the table.

What if the ring was broken? If it was, Chapman would spend the rest of his life in time-out.

Chapter Fifty-Eight

GABE WATCHED in surprise as Andy Schaeffer turned the ammo case of Chapman's Nerf gun upside down and shook it and a ring came tumbling out. The ring clunked down on the table, rolled past the macaroni salad that tasted like library paste with pasta in it, took a header off the table to the tile floor, and disappeared in the shadow of a cabinet.

Leaning over, Gabe lifted the edge of the white tablecloth his mother had set out along with monogrammed placemats and napkins and peered around in the gloom. He couldn't locate the ring in the forest of table and chair legs. Then he spotted it, up against the baseboard beneath the cabinet where pots and pans were stacked. He stretched out his arm, could barely reach it, then straightened up to examine what he'd found.

"Whatcha got there?" Juliana asked, indicating the ring. Then she did a double take that would have made the Three Stooges proud and fairly launched herself across the table, trying to snatch the ring out of his hand.

"There it is!" she cried. "Grandma Hannah's ring. Where did you—"

Leanne glanced that way and rushed to join the fray.

"See," Leanne was triumphant. "I *told* you I didn't take it."

"What is that?" Marilou wandered into the conversation and asked.

"It's Aunt Hannah's ruby ring that went missing yesterday," Juliana said.

"And *you* accused *me* of taking it!" Leanne said. "Clearly, I did not. Where did you find it?

"In the ammo case for Chapman's Nerf pistol," Gabe said.

All the grownups turned toward the little boy and Chapman looked like he wanted to drop through a hole in the floor into the basement — even if it were full of crocodiles.

"Chapman took it?" Marilou marveled.

Juliana was incredulous. Leanne was triumphant. Only Gabe was in possession of his wits enough to want to get a better look at the purloined ring.

Juliana tried to take it from him again, but he held it above his daughter's head.

"Don't be so grabby. The ring's ... the thing's sticky. Chap must have hidden it in his peanut butter and jelly sandwich before he put it in the ammo case."

"No, I didn't. I put it in the ammo case right after I ..."

"... *stole* it," his father finished for him, his tone severe.

"I didn't stoled it. I just ... borrowed it."

Several grownups at the table turned their faces and stifled laughs.

"You come with me, young man." Andy Schaeffer reached out, took Chapman's hand, and began hauling the boy to the door. "We need to talk."

"I was gonna gived it back," the little boy bleated in weak protest.

"I'll wash the goo off," Gabe said, and before anybody could protest, he headed down the hall to the bathroom. He closed the door behind him, snapped on the overhead light, and turned on the tap water in the sink. He didn't put the ring in the water, though, because it wasn't sticky. That had just been the first ruse he could think of to buy him enough time to examine it.

Lifting it toward the three wall lamps with glass shades above the mirror, he looked at it closely. Then he put the ring down into the sink and let the water run over it, wiped the ring on his shirt and looked again.

He saw clearly now what he'd glimpsed when he picked the ring up off the floor. There was a scratch running the whole length of the stone. Probably happened when it hit the tile in the kitchen, but maybe the wound had been inflicted when Chapman jammed the ring down into the ammo case of his Nerf gun. Gabe let out a breath and thought. He was certainly no expert on gemstones, but he did know you couldn't scratch a ruby with floor tile or a plastic gun casing. He didn't know what the big red stone inset in the beautiful gold ring was, but he did know what it wasn't.

Chapter Fifty-Nine

THE WHOLE FAMILY was gathered around the supper table when Alex tapped her fork against her glass to get everyone's attention, then announced grandly, "Mama, we've got a *big* surprise for you."

Olivia thought, *Not as big as the surprise I've got for you.*

Then Gabriel started everybody singing as Leanne came through the doors from the kitchen bearing a gigantic birthday cake with four candles shaped like the numbers: One. Zero. Zero.

Wise choice. A hundred of them little bitty candles woulda brought out the fire department.

"Haaaaaaaapy birthday to you," everyone sang. "Happy birthday to you. Happy birthday dear Grandma Liv-i-a. Happy birthday to you!"

"I'll blow the candles out for you, Grandma Liv," offered Chapman Shaeffer. "Mommy said a hundred is so old you might not have enough air to——"

Cassidy jabbed him in the ribs and gave him a look the surely caused internal hemorrhaging.

"You come right over here, Sugar, and do that very thing.

I's planning on pourin' a glass of water on 'em but blown' 'em out's probably a better idea."

The boy's father, Andy, lifted him out over the candles and Chap extinguished them with a mighty *whoof.*

"One hundred years ago today," Gabe intoned in the hush that followed, "in a little house in Tahoka, Texas, a baby girl named Olivia Anne Henderson—"

"This ain't gonna be no Gettysburg Address, is it?" she asked. "I can't hold my water that long."

The interruption didn't faze him.

"And every person seated at this table is here because of that birth."

He kept on talking, but Olivia stopped listening. When you've been nigh onto deaf for twenty years, you've perfected the art of looking like you know what somebody's saying.

A full century of living. That was something, she had to admit. And Olivia Harrington didn't feel a day older than … oh, ninety-nine, maybe.

Truth was, Olivia was certain she wouldn't be seated at this table a year from today. She'd lately become aware of it all startin' to feel … tenuous. Like all her pieces-parts had suddenly got real delicate, and the balance of them all working together day in and day out like they'd been doing for a hundred winters and a hundred springs … seemed like now it wouldn't take much at all to upset that balance, and all them delicate parts would throw up their hands and say, *I'm done.*

She'd figured out what she wanted the family to do with her ashes. She wanted them to wait until a spring storm, one of them where the clouds start building in the western sky about nine o'clock in the morning, getting meaner and darker and uglier as the day wears on, the tops of some of 'em stretching up forty or fifty thousand feet — eight miles tall! — the bottoms boiling cauldrons of baby-puke green or the dark purple of a day-old bruise. Then they'd come charging across the prairie like a herd of stampeding buffalo, the wind whipping through the willow tree out back like a Roman soldier flicking his cat o' nine tails. She wanted the family to go out then and stand with the wind lashing 'em, then throw her ashes out of the jar into the wind, watch the gray dust disappear with the rest of the blowing dirt.

Dust thou art, and to dust thou shalt return.

She realized Gabe'd stopped talking and everybody was looking at her.

"That was right nice, son." What else was there to say? "Y'all go on ahead and eat 'fore the food gets cold."

So everybody fell to stabbing pieces of ham off the tray and slathering their baked potatoes in butter. She allowed Alex to fill her plate up for her, but the disposal monster would get most of it. She wasn't hungry.

Conversation ebbed and flowed around her as she sat quiet, listening, letting them fill their bellies. Wasn't likely they was gonna be hungry after she said her piece.

Finally, she couldn't put it off any longer.

"'Scuse me," she said, reluctance to do the deed taking the force and volume from her words. The gentle hubbub around the table didn't diminish, so she picked up her fork and tapped her glass with it like Alex had done. Hard not to notice a thing like that and conversation trailed off, all heads turned her way.

She thought about standing but decided against it. If her bad knee was to go out while she was talking, she'd face plant into the potato salad.

"I got something to say to y'all," she said and the room grew instantly quiet. Even the little kids quit squirming and listened. Probably more impressive was the attention she got from 3-D and the other teenagers. They had the attention spans of hyperactive gnats, so she'd best keep it short, but it wouldn't take long to say what she had to say.

"You gonna tell us what you learned in a hundred years of living?"

Avery had asked the question. The blue-haired girl with

the nose ring seated beside her was totally tuned out, looked like a car somebody'd left at the curb with the keys in the ignition, hoping somebody'd steal it.

What Olivia'd figured out in a century was that the world was way more complicated, mysterious, and incomprehensible than she'd understood when she was young. But they wouldn't understand that any better'n she had at their ages, so wasn't no sense in telling them.

She cleared her throat.

"When I was twelve years old, our horse died, dropped over dead, didn't make no sound, no cry — nothing. Just collapsed into the dirt where she was standin'."

Chapter Sixty

I⒯'s a little after sunrise and they're halfway to town — Mama, Papa, and all four of the kids in the wagon, bundled up in blankets against the cold, their breath coming' out in little white puffs in front of their mouths.

Then Ole Nan drops dead.

Her falling pulls on the reins of the wagon so's it almost flips over on its side.

Olivia is the first to her side, drops to her knees in the dirt. Ole Nan's eyes are open and staring, glassy. She ain't breathing, but there's blood in her nostrils and on her lip. She'd been bleeding inside, had blood in her lungs.

"She's gone," Papa says, and the little 'uns tune up and start crying — all except Nathan, who's going on seven and has lately been trying to act more like a man. Olivia don't cry, but it ain't 'cause she's trying to be strong. It hurts too bad to cry.

Ole Nan has been a part of every moment of Olivia's life. Back when things was good, she was a beautiful animal. Tall and strong, with a chestnut coat you could brush to make it shine and a soft pink nose that felt like velvet. She'd use them teeth big as piano keys to lift a little piece of apple off your palm, delicate, like she was using tweezers.

"What are we gonna to do?" Mama asks.

But, of course, there ain't nothing to do. It ain't like they don't know *what killed her. Ole Nan hadn't had enough to eat in years, but she had to work every day anyway. And after they couldn't afford to buy gasoline for the truck no more, she'd pulled the wagon back and forth to town. They'd a'been stranded on the farm without her. Now, they'd just have to walk the five miles there and back, carry whatever they needed on their backs.*

"How we gonna dig a hole big enough to bury her?" Olivia doesn't even realize she's talking out loud until she hears the words.

"We ain't gonna bury her," Papa says.

"We can't just leave her here lying in the road for the coyotes and buzzards!"

"We're gonna take her home."

Olivia doesn't understand. They ain't no way they can get Ole Nan home — even skinny as she is, the old draft horse probably weights eight or nine hundred pounds.

"What for?"

"Cause we ain't gonna leave her to the scavengers." He pauses for a beat, and in that moment of silence Olivia understands.

No, Papa can't mean that.

"We need the meat."

"Eat Ole Nan?" Little Jeffy cries.

Olivia screams NO at the top of her lungs, yells it so loud it rips her throat as the word passes. She is so horrified and offended she can't find any other words to reject the reality of it. She will not eat …

"She died 'cause we didn't have enough feed for her. She starved — to death."

The implication is clear.

Her mother takes a deep, shuddery breath.

"Like your Pa says … we need the meat."

Though her whole mind, her body, even her soul is repelled and horrified by her parents' words, she can't deny the truth of them.

"So Pa sent me back to the farm for ropes and we tied 'em around her hooves. Then we dragged her."

One of Ramsey and Mia's little girls — River, maybe, or

Star, Olivia couldn't keep 'em straight — made a face and whispered something to the other. Olivia couldn't hear the words, of course, but she didn't need to hear to understand.

"That's right, Sugar, it was *gross*. Lotsa times, you gotta do gross things, ain't no way around them. It was January, freezing outside, and that kept the meat from spoiling."

A foot at a time as the winter chill seeps into their bones. Every step impossible. Hands and shoulders raw from rope burns. Their backs breaking from the strain. Mama and Olivia pulled on the rope tied to the horse's front feet. Papa and the other kids pulled on the one tied to her back feet. It'd been early morning when Ole Nan died. The black velvet sky was peppered with stars as big and cold as chunks of ice before they got her body back to the farm.

"We lived on that meat for six months. We *survived* because of it. And at the time, that experience was so awful I wanted to wipe it out of my mind, never think about it again." She paused. "It was years, decades, before I figured out how doing that hard thing changed who I was. From then on, whenever life brought something awful my way … well, I'd already done awful and made it through."

She paused again and cast her gaze across all the attentive faces.

"My money protected all of you from that kind of awful, and I ain't saying that's a bad thing, 'cause don't nobody want those they love to suffer."

She shook her head. "Trouble is, you can't keep out all the awful 'thout keeping out all the good that comes from it."

A wave of emotion washed over her, and her voice was suddenly thick and tear clotted.

"I love ever one you more'n you know, and I want the best life can give you."

Had to be her imagination, but it felt to Olivia like everybody at the table was holding their breath.

"But the truth in long johns with the butt flap down is that life don't never *give* you nuthin' that's worth having. You got to earn that part. It was set up that way 'cause the good Lord knew that what you get out of the earnin' of a thing is a whole lot more important in the long run than the thing itself."

For a moment, she lost the will go to on. She swallowed hard once. Twice. And she found it again. "Most of you ain't never gonna know that, though."

Tapping her forehead with an arthritis-gnarled finger, she said, "Up here, maybe some of you's thinking Ole Grandma Liv just might be right." She tapped her chest. "But not here. You can't know a thing like that in your heart 'thout learning it your own self. You can't teach it to your kids if you don't know it, nor them to theirs. So the heart understanding of what brings real satisfaction in life … all that stopped with me."

Most of them looked bewildered. But the sharpest knives in the drawer had figured out where this was going.

"So I made me a decision — been considering on it for a long time, for months. Shoot, maybe even for years — and it affects all of you."

Yeah, she shoulda stood up, but it was too late to do it now without it looking like she was about to deliver a speech and she wasn't. No speech, just keep it brief. Say what she had to say and shut up.

"I don't rightly know what all this" — she waved her hand in an all-encompassing gesture — "is worth. The house and the ranch, the company, the subsidiaries and oil leases. Reginald calculated it, added in the real estate and stocks and the like, and the number he tacked on it was ridiculous — going on a billion dollars.

"A *billion?*" Douglas Kavanaugh liked to choked.

"Hush, Dougie," his mama said. "Let Grandma Liv finish."

"All this become mine when Landon died, and it'd be natural to assume it's going to pass down to Alex and Cyrus when I'm gone."

"Aw, Grandma Liv," Julianna said, "you're gonna live forever."

"The good Lord willing, that part's gonna work out just like everybody expects it to. But the rest of it ain't. What I got, all of this — it ain't going to pass down to Cyrus and Alex when I'm gone … and then on down to the rest of you."

She glanced at Alex, who showed no response at all, and then at Cyrus, who had no idea what she'd just said.

"In other words, you's all set up to be millionaires when I croak, but that ain't going to be the way of it. I got Reginald to draw up a brand new will and it says that when I die, each one of you — individually, adults and children alike — will receive a hundred thousand dollars and a thousand shares in Harrington Oil." She took a breath. "And that's *all*. The rest of it will be used to fund a foundation named after Landon, a nonprofit that'll oversee charitable donations to all kinda charities."

Questions/comments/cries of disappointment, disbelief, the beginnings of anger — all that was poised before Olivia, hanging there in the air like a wave at its tallest point the instant before it crashes down on the sand.

"I ain't expecting none of you to burst into applause, or maybe give me the keys to the city or something. I do hope, though, that you'll … that *some of you* will understand the why of it. And maybe … maybe someday, you'll come to believe I done the right thing."

If she'd known she was gonna make a speech like that, she woulda stood up, but all them words just come to her and she said them when they did. In the instant before the wave of chaotic response crashed down on the shore, she looked at Gabe. And she was shocked that he didn't seem one bit surprised.

Then the hollering started.

Chapter Sixty-One

GABE HURRIED down the hallway to the double doors that opened into the foyer, hoping nobody had noticed that he'd left the kitchen. He was halfway across the foyer when he saw Andy Schaeffer beside the bottom step of the stairs. Chapman Schaeffer stood in the front corner of the big room, facing the wall.

When he spotted Gabe, Andy cocked his thumb toward the boy. "I'm thinking about leaving him in time-out until he graduates from high school, or his twenty-first birthday, whichever happens sooner."

Gabe smiled. "I know you don't think so now, but someday you will think this whole episode is funny." He held up his hand to ward off Andy's protest. "But probably not before he graduates from high school or turns twenty-one — whichever happens first."

"So what'd you think of Grandma Liv's grand announcement? Cass and I will be fine, but I'd wager it was a staggering blow to a lot of the family. "

Gabe knew Andy didn't make a whole lot of money as a firefighter, but he hadn't married Cassidy for her money, though if marrying into the Kavanaugh/Harrington family had been an Olympic sport, there'd have been medal winners over the years. Gabe could have handed out a couple of gold ones in the past decade. Take the little twit who'd married Jordan Kavanaugh's oldest son a couple of years ago. Greed radiated off that gold digger like radiation off a nuclear waste dump. Of course, she'd been surprised to discover, as had all the gold diggers over the years, that while there was great wealth in Harrington Oil, the vast real estate holdings, the oil and gas leases, and the stocks and bonds and miscellaneous property, the family's liquid assets were in short supply, thanks to Grandma Liv's penny-pinching frugality and Reginald Underwood's vigilant oversight.

Gabe understood that probably better than any other family member, because he'd been desperately trying for six months to find a way to pry free some of those assets. But laying hands on any great sum of Harrington/Kavanaugh money was impossible as long as Grandma Liv was the hen sitting on those golden eggs.

When Olivia Harrington died, the family would rethink all its financial options, and would likely chart out a course in an entirely different direction.

But as long as Grandma Liv was alive …

"You're not afraid to die?"

"Oh, Lord no, son. When you look something in the eye every day for a hundred years, you get as comfortable with it as a ratty old bathrobe. Ain't nothing scary 'bout a bathrobe. Whatever it was I's supposed to do in this life, surely I already done it. I'm just sitting here at the station with my bags packed, waiting for the bus to show up."

"… tell you what she was going to say?" Andy was asking when Gabe tuned back in to his words.

"No, no, nothing like that. But after Chap shot her on Friday—"

"*Shot* her?"

"Long story. Chap told me he heard Grandma Liv talking to Reginald Underwood on the phone about 'dissing parrots' ... which I ran through the Chapman Schaeffer Mispronunciation Translator and it came out 'disinherit.'"

"Disinherit! So you *knew* she was going to—"

"Not for certain, but yeah, I knew something like that was locked and loaded."

"It's certainly going to throw gasoline on the Jewelry Wars."

"Right ... that's why I haven't said anything yet."

"About what?"

Instead of answering the question, Gabe turned toward the stairs and made a come-on gesture.

"I'm going to put Aunt Hannah's ring back in the safe. Maybe you can help me figure something out."

As Andy started up the stairs with Gabe, he pointed a finger at the little boy facing the wall.

"You stay right there."

"But ... I gotta pee."

"Hold it or wet your pants, your choice."

Only Aunt Hannah and Uncle Cyrus knew the combination to the safe in Aunt Hannah's closet. He hoped Uncle Cyrus could remember the combination if they found the safe locked. It'd be a shame to have to dynamite the door. But perhaps Uncle Cyrus had left it unlocked when he got out the jewelry for her to wear at the viewing.

The safe sat in the back left corner of the closet, and from the doorway, it appeared to be made of some dark wood, cherry maybe, six feet wide and three tall. The door with its faux wood veneer had a single gold handle in the middle, and above it was a dial you could turn to any one of a hundred numbers, and to a full alphabet of letters.

"You know the combination, right?" Andy asked.

"Nope. This is a Hail Mary."

Gabe took hold of the door handle, lifted up on it, and heard a click, then the door swung out easily on thick metal hinges and he let out a sigh of relief.

"It wasn't locked?" Andy was incredulous.

"If you spin the dial to engage the lock, you have to enter the combination to open the door. Mama told me once that after Aunt Hannah's vision got so bad, she had trouble seeing the numbers and letters on the dial, so she'd close it but not lock it."

Gabe noticed a flashlight on the top of the safe. Though the room, particularly right there around the safe, was well lit, Aunt Hannah probably used it to illuminate the interior of the safe or the combination dial. He picked it up, flipped it on, and shone it into the box.

A dozen shallow drawers occupied the center of the safe, the ones on top only a couple of inches deep, the two on the bottom six inches or more. Above the drawers on a shelf was a cashbox and a pile of ledger books. Below the drawers was a two-foot area where his aunt had stored briefcases, a jewel-transport case, and three purses — that were likely there because they had cost a ridiculous amount of money.

He pulled open the top drawer, which was about at eye level. It was divided into two-inch velvet-lined squares. All the squares were filled with earrings — some loops of gold or silver, what Gabe's first wife had always called "danglers," and others she called studs. Closing that drawer, he pulled open the one beneath it — more earrings. The third drawer was full of earrings, too, but the fourth had rows of padded slots for rings.

"No wonder all the women have been salivating over this jewelry," Andy said. "Seeing it all in one spot like this, it looks like a pirate's treasure."

There was no obvious empty space where the ruby ring

had come from, so he closed the drawer and opened the next drawer of rings.

"Are you looking for something in particular?"

"No, but I'll know it when I see it."

He found what he'd been looking for in the next drawer. That drawer was filled with pins and brooches — each a unique design. He picked up a bracelet with a huge center stone — a sapphire as big as his thumbnail. If he was remembering his physical geology course in college from thirty-plus years ago, emeralds, rubies, and sapphires were essentially the same rock, but with slightly different chemical compositions that made their colors different.

Handing the flashlight to Andy, he pulled the ring out of his pocket and held it up into the light beside the brooch. He nodded his head toward the ring. "Take a good look, what do you—"

"The stone is scratched. How'd that happen?" Then he looked horrified. "You don't think Chapman is responsible for—"

"Oh, he might have scratched it, but he's not responsible for the damage to the stone."

Reaching into his pocket, Gabe pulled out his pocketknife, flipped the blade open, and held it up to the sapphire stone in the brooch.

"You're not going to—"

Gabe put the point of the blade down in the center of the sapphire, then dragged it slowly to the edge, leaving a ragged crater behind it in the stone.

"Why'd you—"

"This isn't a real sapphire. And the stone in the ring isn't a real ruby, either. When I saw the scratch on the stone in the ring, I googled it. On Mohs Hardness Scale, only a diamond is a ten, but rubies and sapphires are both nine. I don't know what a piece of tile flooring is, or maybe a piece of plastic from Chapman's ammo case. But the blade on a pocketknife is only 5.5." He held up the ring and scraped the blade down the stone. The trough was even deeper than the original scratch. "A knife blade is not hard enough to scratch either a ruby or a sapphire."

"What are you saying … the stones aren't real? Then what are they?"

"Glass, maybe. I don't know. I don't know what mineral or material looks like a gemstone."

Andy looked back at the drawers in the safe.

"You think they're all like this, that none of the stones here are real?"

"I'm not going to stand here and scratch them all with my knife to find out, but obviously it's possible they're all fakes."

"But why … I thought Aunt Hannah could afford to buy—"

"Oh, she could afford to buy the real thing. She *did* buy the real thing, paid a fortune — literally, her parents' whole estate— over the years to buy jewelry and Remington and Russell art. The stones in the rings and brooches and earrings were real when she bought them." He suddenly had a thought. "And they were real last summer when she announced she was going to donate them to the museum — an insurance adjuster came out here and verified their value."

"So sometime between last summer and now, Grandma Hannah … what? Took the real stones out and replaced them with fakes?"

"Hannah … *or somebody else.*"

Andy's eyes grew huge.

"You don't think—"

"I don't know what to think, but I do know what to *do.*" Gabe took the ring and the brooch and replaced them in the drawers. He closed the safe door and spun the combination dial all the way around. When he pulled on the door handle, the door didn't budge. "What we do is *tell nobody.* After Grandma Liv's announcement tonight—"

"It would set off an atom bomb."

"Followed by a nuclear winter! I'll call Sheriff Hastings in the morning."

"And what will he do?"

"I have absolutely no idea."

Chapter Sixty-Two

THIS TIME, Rowan didn't park on the road across from the lane leading to the Harrington House. She switched off her headlights, turned into the lane, and pulled off to the side beneath a low-hanging tree limb that partially hid her car. And just like before, she sat in her car looking at the house. Studying it. It seemed like an altogether different place in the moonlight, with little beacons of golden light shining out some of the windows. It wasn't the darkness, though, or the silvery moon glow that transformed the house. It had morphed over time in her mind since yesterday when she first stepped over the threshold, and now it seemed to be lit up like a city on a hill.

She thought of Motel 6 commercials … "we'll leave the light on for you." This house was that, a welcoming refuge to the family members who had come here to bury Hannah Kavanaugh.

It wasn't just a sanctuary for a sad event, though. It was a lived-in house, a comfortable-old-slipper house, a place where the scattered Harringtons and Kavanaughs regrouped, gathered as a family — for all those life circumstances where they functioned as one.

Did somebody put lights on the exterior of the house at Christmas? Of course they did. One of the older red-headed men in charge, directing the younger ones where to hang them, and how to configure the spaghetti tangle of extension cords to make them glow. Closing her eyes, she could see it — lights along all the eaves of the house — jutting out at odd angles to follow the undulating contour of the roof. The trees and bushes in the front yard, too, of course. White lights only on the house, but colored lights in the yard, and blinking lights wrapped like concertina wire around the railing of the front yard fence. Maybe there was Christmas lawn art. Nothing that blew up, no bulbous floating Frosty the Snowman or ugly green Grinch. Nothing comic bookish. The great old lady she'd seen walking stoically up the church aisle with her arm tucked firmly into the crook of the arm of the young man beside her — she was the matriarch, the woman the stranger in the pew had said was a hundred years old. Olivia Harrington. The Olivia Harringtons of this world didn't decorate their yards with blown-up Santas.

The display would be tasteful, Rowan decided, but casual and relaxed — with blank spots on the bushes where there were not enough lights or where one set went out. It'd be obvious that the family had done the decorating, that they hadn't hired professionals to make it look just so. There'd be a Nativity scene — yes, certainly. Life-sized figures of Mary and Joseph and the baby, the wise men and shepherds. Maybe they even staked out live animals to make it authentic. There would be a glowing white angel perched on the top of the manger scene. Perhaps even a bright star hung high in one of the cottonwood trees — a star you could see for miles across the prairie.

She envisioned it at other times, too. Not just filled with the smell of turkey and bubbling apple cider and children running around squealing at Christmas. But on Easter Sunday. She could barely make out the yard now, as clouds had rushed in to cover the moon. She could see it clearly in her mind's eye, though, the lush vegetation concealing Easter eggs. She could imagine children with Easter baskets hurrying around, looking under bushes and behind flowers in the garden … and children huddled together to ooh and aah at the bright lights of fireworks in the sky on the Fourth of July. The family would come together to make hot dogs and brats on Labor Day weekend and …

With a force of will, she banished the fantasy. Those occasions had passed, one year after another, with various family members present — but always *without* one member of the family. Rowan Douglas had not been present for any of it. And she should have been. She'd had *a right* to be.

Conjuring up the images had drilled two conflicting emotions into Rowan's heart. One was sadness, a deep longing for all that she had missed by not being a part of her birth family. The other feeling was rage.

Kindled from a single spark at the funeral, her anger had grown into a roaring blaze in the hours since. It had finally become so hot it melted away all her inhibitions and she knew she couldn't just leave. She could not get into her car and drive back to Galveston without engaging. She couldn't walk away as empty as she'd been when she arrived. She had a *right* to … so many things. What mattered most to her now, though, was her right to *know*.

Cyrus Kavanaugh had gotten some Black woman pregnant, and she had abandoned the baby — either because she'd wanted to or he had forced her. Rowan didn't know which, but she would, by God, find out!

That's why she was sitting in her darkened car, looking at the brightly lit house as rumbling thunder drew closer. A storm was coming — *inside* the house as well as outside. Cyrus Kavanaugh was about to become the eye of that tempest. He was inside the rambling structure, and she knew where, had heard people at the viewing talk about the renovated bedroom

Hannah'd built on the third floor with a big balcony overlooking the backyard. Rowan would find him now, tonight, confront him, demand to know what'd happened. Where was her mother? Why had she given Rowan away? Had he forced her to do it?

Yeah, it would be a much more sensible plan to go to see the man in the daylight. Call and make an appointment or something, like a reasonable adult. But right now, Rowan Douglas had no interest in being reasonable.

She wanted answers — and she wanted them *now*.

And if Cyrus Kavanaugh refused, well, then ... she reached into the glove box and pulled out her .38 caliber Smith & Wesson Model 642 — a sweet little pistol, made of titanium so it was light, with a concealed hammer so it couldn't hang on anything when you pulled it. She'd only fired it on the range, where she could land three chest shots in a three-inch circle at twenty-five yards. She planned to be a whole lot closer than that this time.

Chapter Sixty-Three

As soon as the family recovered from the initial shock and began to weigh in on Grandma Liv's announcement, Avery noticed that Maddie was no longer seated beside her at the table. She didn't know when she'd left. Maybe she didn't even hear what Grandma Liv had said, the story of the dead horse and dragging it back to the house ... and the rest of it, of course.

Disinherit.

That was a hostile, aggressive word, had a sense of violence to it. You couldn't attack others with that kind of antagonistic language and expect anything less than a hostile response. Of course, poor Grandma Liv didn't understand such complex concepts, was pitifully unsophisticated in non-linear thinking. Avery felt sorry for her.

As Avery left the heating-up discussions in the kitchen, she texted Rye, told her what Grandma Liv had said, and Rye'd wanted to know if that meant Avery would have to drop out of school. Or maybe get a part-time job. Avery hadn't processed it that far, wasn't sure what all the implications of being "disinherited" might be. Of course, she'd get a job if she needed to. In fact, she sort of liked the idea. But a job doing what? Well, she would want to do something that mattered, that's for sure. Not some "would you like fries with that order" job. Avery wanted her life to make a difference.

She found Maddie in their room, so engrossed in a video game she didn't even look up when Avery made a beeline for the shower, feeling a twinge of guilt that she hadn't warned Maddie about the first-man-to-the-hot-water-wins principle of staying in the Harrington House.

Turning the faucet dial all the way to H, Avery allowed the stabbing hot water to assault her skin as she considered the impact that Grandma Liv's announcement would have on the family. She didn't like the uneasiness of where those thoughts took her, so she focused her attention on a different conundrum — the enigma of her friend, Madeline Shepherd. Friend? No, actually Maddie wasn't Avery's friend. Not even a close acquaintance. If she hadn't been so friggin' weird, Avery would likely be forming a friendship with her now. Spending all this time together, surely she and any other normal human being would have developed some kind of bond.

But Maddie remained a stranger, emphasis on the first syllable. Even when she wasn't making some bizarre statement, like "You have to kill yourself over and over until you stop coming back from the dead," her eyes were … off. Different. They were a far paler blue than Avery's — a color so washed out that in bright light they looked translucent. And Maddie was often notably absent from those eyes. You'd say something to her and see that she wasn't tracking. Then she'd see you noticed, and she'd engage, but it was all hat and no cattle. Maddie would play whatever song you'd paid a quarter to hear — did she think school should abolish the grading system? Certainly, it was weighted toward privileged people. Did she think fossil fuels should be banned? Of course. And minimum wage raised to twenty dollars an hour? Absolutely. How about gay rights, reproductive rights, critical race theory? For 'em all! But none of it really *mattered* to Maddie.

Maybe nothing did. So Avery still felt sorry for her tall, tattooed house guest, but it was guarded sympathy. It was like seeing an injured dog on the side of the road and wanting to help, while also knowing that if you got too close, it might bite your hand off.

Avery could hear the sounds of the video game when she turned the shower off and hoped there'd still be hot water left for Maddie. If not ... well, she'd either have to take a cold shower, or just PTA (pits, tits, and ass) in the sink and dig out a change of clothes from her duffel bag.

Avery put on the tee and sweatpants she slept in and stepped barefoot into the bedroom, gesturing toward the steamed-up bathroom as she started to towel her hair dry. "Next — best get after it while there's still hot."

She was talking to herself. Maddie wasn't in the room. But she'd left her computer on the desk with the game pulled up and the sound still playing. Where'd she go? She'd get lost in five minutes wandering the dark rabbit warren of hallways in Grandma Liv's house. And why'd she leave the game playing with the volume not just on but turned all the way up? It was almost like she had wanted it to appear she was still in the room.

Then the door opened quietly and Maddie stepped inside.

"Where have you been?" Avery asked and Maddie jumped like she'd been stuck with a taser.

"Don't *do* that! I hate to be startled."

"Where were you?" Avery was merely curious, but the question came out as an accusation.

Maddie cocked her head to the side. "I saw your father in the hall."

The words kicked a hole in Avery's belly and Avery couldn't seem to catch her breath.

"My *father*?"

Her father's face burst into her consciousness a second

before the haunting image of the mangled bicycle on the side of the road, the tire still revolving slowly.

"You say you hate him, but you don't."

How did we get here?

"And he loves you."

"What are you … why are you telling me?"

"You can tell by the way he looks at you that he loves his baby girl. He called you that when you were little, didn't he?"

"How did you know?" Of course, half the fathers on the planet called their daughters Baby Girl. It was just a guess.

"He thinks it's the right thing to do. He agrees with me."

Avery didn't know what Maddie was talking about, but she did understand that mentioning her father had been calculated. Maddie'd intended to rattle her. And it had worked.

"He thinks *what* is the right thing?"

Maddie crossed the room to the laptop where she'd left the game running and picked up the controller.

"You need to get your hair dry. Hope the electricity holds out. It'd be a bitch for the lights to go out right in the middle of all this."

"All *what?*" Avery was pissed! "Stop talking in riddles. What?"

"Everybody's supposed to be in the kitchen in"— Maddie looked at her watch — "ten minutes."

Understanding dawned slowly, reluctantly.

"What have you done?" Avery's voice was weak and airless.

"Nothing more than we planned to do before you got cold feet." A fleeting smile danced at the corners of Maddie's lips. "I knew you didn't really want to give up."

Setting the controller down, she looked into Avery's eyes. Somehow, Maddie's eyes were the pure blue you only saw when she was in bright light. Even in the dim glow of the lamp, they were cold, lifeless blue marbles.

"I settled on: 'I've got proof. Want to see? Meet me in the kitchen at midnight.'"

If Avery's face displayed the bomb of emotion Maddie's words ignited, Maddie ignored it.

"Just to the ones who have the best motive. Let's see what they have to say when they show up."

Maddie picked up the controller and turned her attention to the video game. Avery bolted out into the hall, intent on getting to the kitchen to intercept the "suspects" to apologize profusely for Maddie's outrageous behavior.

Then the lights went out.

Chapter Sixty-Four

ALEX WASN'T SURPRISED by her mother's announcement. She'd suspected for a long time that her mother planned to disinherit the family. There'd been hints for months. Seemingly random conversations about "the important things" in life, as Mama put it. The list was short. God and family ... patriotism and love ... hard work and responsibility. Her mother was bouncing her observations off Alex. And as time went by, it wasn't hard to see where it all was going.

"The grandkids — the younger ones — you think any one of them ever got dirt under their fingernails?" Mama would ask. "I don't b'lieve I ever seen your girls sweat, neither one of them."

She had been surprised, though, that Mama had dumped the load on the family at supper tonight. True, they were all gathered in one place and that didn't happen often. And perhaps Mama'd got wind of the one-hundredth birthday "surprise" party and had been planning to make the announcement then. Still, right after a funeral was a little severe. Of course, in truth, Cyrus was the only person in the family who was really suffering because of Hannah's death — a death caused by an *insulin overdose*. How could that be?

Alex had gone immediately to her room after the funeral — read and re-read the toxicology results the sheriff had emailed to her. There was no sedative mentioned in the report — so either they missed it or Hannah never drank the sleeping-pill-laced orange juice Alex had placed on her bedside table while Hannah was in the bathroom. Hannah's blood alcohol level was .15. Blow more than .08 on a breathalyzer when you get pulled over in Texas and you go to jail for driving under the influence. So Hannah got plastered and took way too much insulin — a double dose.

Alex shook her head. Somehow that didn't pass the sniff test — at least not to someone who knew all that Alex knew. It was just too damned convenient.

Hannah had been giving herself injections of insulin three or four times a day for forty years ... and suddenly gives herself a lethal overdose *three days before* backhoes were scheduled to start digging up the backyard! Less than a week before Hannah was to deliver her one-of-a-kind jewelry collection to the museum and sign over her priceless Remington and Russell art collection.

Alex ticked off the possibilities on her fingers.

One — the toxicology report was wrong. Hannah had been killed by Alex's lethal cocktail of sleeping-pill laced orange juice, and whoever did the blood test botched the job.

Two— Hannah really did give herself too much insulin.

Or three ... somebody other than Alex had given Hannah another shot of insulin.

Merely considering that option took Alex's breath away. It was crazy. Of course it was. There were family members pissed off about her decision to donate the jewelry to the museum, but they wouldn't have *killed* her to stop her. Would they? (Be honest now, Alex. Hannah had been a loathsome human being. Alex'd been willing to murder her. Maybe somebody else had been, too.)

Of course, Alex knew what nobody else did. That the

"priceless" jewels weren't worth a buck. One of the many reasons she'd killed — *tried* to kill — Hannah was to put off that discovery for as long as possible. Alex had paid a fortune to that guy in New Orleans to re-create each stone from the custom jewelry and to place the fake stones back in the settings from which she'd taken them.

Maybe she'd get lucky now and nobody would notice for a while. It wouldn't take long, a couple of months at best, and after that Alex would be dust. And if they found out sooner? Well, it'd get ugly, but the authorities would have to track down all those transactions, one or two jewels at a time. The jewelry itself had, of course, been priceless — every piece an original. The stones, on the other hand, you could get rid of those if you knew a guy who knew a guy. Cut them into smaller stones, ship them out of the country.

Of course they'd find out eventually what'd happened, but by then it wouldn't matter.

And with the backhoes permanently canceled, no one would ever discover the other secret only Alex knew.

She paused. No, she wasn't the *only* person who knew. Cyrus did, and it was his life that would be ruined if anybody found out. Cyrus might not know much of anything anymore, but he did know that.

Cyrus?

The world suddenly became unnaturally quiet. Absolutely silent. Alex snapped her fingers, but she heard no sound.

Whum, whum, whum. Her ears spoke into the silent void with their own voices. *Whum, whum, whum, whum.*

Then it was over. As quickly as the deafness had appeared, it disappeared. She'd been upset about Cyrus. And apparently Persephone was … sensitive.

Alex couldn't put off much longer telling her family about Piffy. Her mother'd been asking probing questions, and it was getting harder and harder to pretend she was in perfect health when she kept losing weight, even though she stuffed as much food as possible into her mouth without the motivation of hunger. Her hair was getting thin — brittle. She wouldn't be able to hide it for much longer.

But first things first. She had to tell Gabe that he was off the hook. That whatever the psychopaths to whom he owned money were after, he could pay up. Of course, he had no idea she knew how much hot water he was in. When you'd spent most of your life as a journalist, you could find out just about anything if you tried hard enough. With this, her last act, Alex would save her only son, and that wasn't a bad way to go out.

But when she went to talk to him, he'd ask her about the screams.

What could she say?

Oh, she knew what she'd say about the money. Still, she mentally rehearsed a little speech as she wrapped her snuggly old robe over her nightgown, then left her room and headed toward his. She'd keep it short and sweet, no questions. She'd give him the key to the safe deposit box where she'd been stashing the cash. She would tell him the money was a stake she'd been saving, cash she'd been squirreling away "for a rainy day." Certainly, when it finally did come out about the jewelry, he'd put it together and know she'd been the one who took it. But by then …

She stopped in front of the door to the bedroom where Gabe was sleeping, rapped her knuckles quietly — loud enough to wake him but not loud enough to wake all the others sleeping in nearby bedrooms. How many and where? She wasn't sure, thought maybe her nephew Samuel and his wife Millie had left after supper and perhaps some of the other's had, too. Lawson was still here, though. She could hear him snoring in the small bedroom two doors down. She'd waited until late to seek Gabe out so they wouldn't likely be interrupted.

"Gabe, we need to talk." There was no response from inside. She rapped again. "I hope you're not in your underwear because this is important." She pushed the door open. "Gabe? You here?"

The room was empty.

When she turned to go, she stepped on a folded piece of paper on the floor just inside the room. She picked it up and opened it, read the words. "I've got proof. Want to see? Meet me in the kitchen at midnight."

Alex's temper burst into flame like a road flare.

The little shits were still at it! And if they'd stuffed one of these under Gabe's door, who else were they terrorizing? Why … Cyrus might think they knew about what'd happened all those years ago.

"Dammit!" she muttered under her breath, then marched out of the room and headed to the kitchen to find Dumb, Dumber, and Dumbest … and wring their fool necks.

Chapter Sixty-Five

JUDE WAS JUST FINISHING up his packing — if throwing the various bits of dirty clothing he'd worn over the weekend into a laundry bag could rightly be called packing — when he heard the grumble of nearby thunder and smelled the scent of rain on the breeze coming in the open window. Spencer came into the room, but Jude didn't turn around, just spoke over his shoulder.

"I'll be saying goodbye now, Bro. I'm cutting out. All that ..." He made a gesture toward downstairs. "... everybody all upset ... I'm not okay with that. Don't need the drama."

Which was true as far as it went, but it didn't go far enough. He didn't need to be around all that emotional turmoil. It took considerable effort to keep himself on an even keel psychologically, and that kind of turbulent atmosphere could set him off. Mostly, he just wanted out of this house and away from Spencer and the roller coaster of terror he'd been riding ever since he'd spotted the photo from Ariana's wedding of Avery-the-flower-girl ... with his sports car in the background.

The kerfuffle over Grandma Liv's announcement just gave him a convenient excuse to leave.

Jude didn't give a rat fart whether or not his grandmother disinherited him and all his various cousins. In fact, he actually kinda got a kick out of watching them all squirm. It was kind of a one-two punch. Grandma Liv cuts them all off from her millions … mirroring what Grandma Hannah had done with the jewelry she'd been telling them their whole lives they'd get. He recalled Sunday afternoons drinking lemonade on the front porch, trying to block out Grandma Hannah's shrill voice bitching about something, and listening to his sisters and cousins sucking up to the old cow. Leanne had wanted her ruby ring and Jude was certain he remembered Grandma Hannah promising the ring to her. But he remembered her promising it to Julianna, too, on her fifth birthday. Even at the time, and he was just a little kid, he'd figured out she couldn't give the ring to both of them and that one day there would be a reckoning. He'd vowed then not to be anywhere near Ground Zero when that bomb went off. Maybe the old bat had croaked before she signed the jewelry over to the museum … in which case somebody would have to be the mediator among all the cousins who all believed they were entitled to some piece of it.

"I got an interview in Odessa on Wednesday, applying for a job working on an oil rig," he lied. He hadn't held a steady job in … well, certainly not since the Covid lockdowns, and he managed to get by selling weed and harder drugs when he could get them while living rent-free in an apartment in a building owned by his uncle Lawson. Pulling the drawstrings on the laundry bag tight, he turned to face Spencer. "I need a couple of days at home …"

Spencer's face was made of stone. The bottom fell out of Jude's belly and he couldn't manage to do anything but stare at his cousin.

He knows, the Other shrieked into his head. Look at his face— he knows.

But how could he?

"Something wrong, man?" he heard himself ask, but the knowledge that passed between them when his gaze met Spencer's answered the question. Spencer's piercing blue eyes grabbed Jude's and wouldn't let go.

"I told Grandma Alex yesterday morning that I'd like to have some of the pictures of Avery in that flower-girl dress. She mentioned it to Mrs. Hansford at the visitation — who, of course, has albums full of wedding pictures. She told Grandma Alex she could have any that struck her fancy."

He spoke without any intonation at all in his voice, sounded like the AI voice that told you to press one for billing, two for medical records, three for...

"These two *struck my fancy.*" Spencer had two photographs in his hand, held them out toward Jude. One was a copy of the picture Jude had swallowed. The second was even more damning. Taken a few seconds before the other picture, the background image was Jude getting into the car on the driver's side, standing on his "injured" foot, his crutches sticking up out of the back seat. Jude didn't move to take them.

"Avery's cute as a button in that flower girl dress. But you remember that, don't you Jude. You saw her in the other picture, the one I kept, and then couldn't find. You thought she was cute, didn't you?"

He took a step forward.

Jude took a step back.

"You know what happens to baby killers in prison?" Spencer's eyes held Jude's in an unbreakable grip. Jude didn't reply. He couldn't speak.

"They rip you a new one, if you know what I mean— *literally.*"

Jude's head filled with the rumble of two words that somehow managed to sound like thunder, or the roar of a bowling alley when you get a strike, the pins banging, the crack of wood against wood: *Kill him.*

The Other screamed the words and it was like letting go

of a rubber band that you'd pulled all the way out past the point when it should have snapped. All Jude's pent-up rage and terror spent its energy in one lightning movement. He slammed his fist into Spencer's face. He had three inches and fifty pounds on his slender cousin, and his fear channeled every ounce of his greater strength and girth into that one blow.

Spencer's head snapped sideways, blood squirting out his nose and smashed mouth as he flew backward toward the wall beside the window above the porch roof. Jude paused then, before the act. For a single heartbeat he considered the implications of what his muscles were tensing to do.

Murder.

Not an accident … hitting a kid who shouldn't have been riding down the road on a bicycle in the first place. Not that. Murder. In cold blood.

Before Jude could consider further, a door banged shut in his soul, as a man might slam a door in the face of an intruder on his porch, some monster come to kill him and his family in their sleep. Only it was wrong side out. The intruder was *inside* the house. It was *reason* that stood outside knocking. But it was too late now. The Other had taken control and it would never willingly step back out of the driver's seat of Jude's life. The Other was in charge now and Jude was just along for the ride.

Spencer landed on his back and slid across the hardwood floor. Jude was already grabbing hold of him before he even stopped moving. The adrenaline rush of terror had given Jude a strength far beyond what he actually possessed. He grabbed Spencer by the front of his shirt and hauled him in one lurching motion toward the open window, preparing to hurl him out onto the slanted roof.

But Spencer didn't allow himself to be chucked out the window. He grabbed the frame and yanked himself out of Jude's grip. The look on Spencer's face— his mouth and nose a bloody ruin but his eyes as cold as a cougar's — was heart-stopping terrible.

And then the lights went out and the room was plunged into absolute darkness.

Chapter Sixty-Six

GRANDMA ALEX often claimed to be so mad "she couldn't see straight." Avery understood that phrase now. She absolutely was that mad. Reaching out her left hand and feeling empty air, she took small steps forward until her hand touched the wall, then she turned and started carefully toward the back of the house to the stairs that would lead to the kitchen, inching her way past the doorways of her sleeping relatives. How many of them would wake in the morning to find Maddie's idiot note, if they hadn't found it already?

She had dropped the towel she'd been using to dry her hair and now it was dripping rivulets of water down her back. All the lights in the room, including the three lamps, had been on before the electricity blipped off, so it would take Avery's eyes several minutes to adjust to the dark hallway. Anger had jacked up Avery's heartbeat so that it was pounding so loud in her ears she couldn't hear. As she calmed, the pounding slowed and she thought there was a sound from somewhere in the hallway behind her.

"Maddie, go back into the bedroom and stay there before you fall down the stairs."

Nobody answered.

Avery'd imagined the sound.

Moving carefully and slowly forward sobered her, began to drain away the intensity of the anger/embarrassment/remorse she was feeling about what Maddie'd done. Of course, she still wanted to apologize to whoever showed up in the kitchen. But … why would you show up after a note like that unless you had something to hide? Avery one hundred percent did not like herself for even entertaining the thought, but it had stepped out into the spotlight of her mind, hot and stinking, demanding attention. Something, or some*body*, had poked some kind of hole in Aunt Hannah's big toe. Of course, that didn't prove anything at all. Still …

There was no hurry now. Everybody would freeze in place until somebody put a fuse in a breaker box somewhere and the lights came back on. Negotiating the kitchen stairs would be tricky, but she could feel her way, traverse the steep, narrow stairwell with both hands on the walls to keep from falling. Of course, she could always resort to the technique she'd developed as a kid — sit down on the top step and bump your butt down one step after another until you hit the bottom. If the door at the bottom of the stairwell was open, there would be ambient light from the pole outside, which wasn't wired with the house lights. It was storming outside, though, and rain would dim that light.

She'd made it about halfway down the hall when she heard a sound. A footstep.

"Maddie," she hissed in a stage whisper. "You're going to break your damn fool neck! Get back in the bedroom." She paused. Silence. "What are you doing? If you think you can find your way—"

A shuffling sound, then silence.

And for absolutely no reason at all, Avery's anger was replaced by unease. Apprehension. Avery stood stock still and listened. Nothing. Or was there nothing? She thought … *imagined* she could hear breathing in the darkness behind her.

This was crazy. She'd been plunged into darkness in this old house dozens of times as a child, in just about every room in it. And never before had she been frightened. But it was, after all, a "dark and stormy night" — that hour when all bad things are possible, when the Boogie Man comes out of the closet and brings all his nasty friends. That hour when everyone you love is in imminent danger of drunk drivers, brain aneurisms, and stray bullets. And death seems as near and cold as the darkness, and as certain as the coming dawn.

She couldn't stand the sense of something coming up behind her, so she turned around and faced the direction from which the sound had come. Trailing her hand along the wall, she walked slowly *backwards*. Her fingers glazed the edge of the huge hall mirror and she dragged them slowly across it. A space of bare wall, then the painting of a stagecoach at night, a black storm in the background and lightning flashing in the darkness. It wasn't a Remington or Russell, which was why it was still there, and she traced her fingers from one edge of the frame to another. A door frame — the bedroom where Uncle Lawson and Aunt Cynthia were sleeping. No, she'd passed that one already. This was Uncle Jordan and Aunt Marilou, with a queen-sized bed to accommodate Aunt Marilou's ever-increasing girth.

Every step moved her away from the sounds — what sounds, Avery? You're a nutcase — but she didn't turn her back until she got to the door at the top of the stairs. Then she opened the door and stepped out of the hallway onto the top step.

Suddenly, she heard a sound behind her — breathing, but not slow and steady. This breathing was ragged and unstable. Was she imagining it? She sensed somebody behind her, could almost feel …

Then she did feel something. A hand on her back. The hand shoved her and she fell into the dark well of the stairs, tumbling head over heels all the way to the bottom.

Chapter Sixty-Seven

WHEN THE STORM STRUCK, it didn't ramp up into a downpour from a few spattering raindrops on the top and hood of Rowan's car. Ushered in by rumbling thunder and wild displays of lightning, it landed on the Harrington House with both feet. If it'd been daylight, Rowan was sure she could have watched its approach across the prairie, dark gray clouds eating up the blue sky and a wall of rainfall approaching like a curtain hanging down to earth.

Hammering rain instantly obscured the house, turning the lights shining from windows into blurs that became gold worms crawling down Rowan's windshield. The storm added to her sense of isolation, of being "out here" while the rest of the family was snug "in there." She didn't have a plan beyond getting into the house and finding her way to that big bedroom on the back on the third floor, the one with a balcony. She didn't know which ones of the people who'd been delineated as "family" at the funeral would actually be sleeping in the house tonight, though she knew a whole bunch of them must be staying because there were cars parked along the lane and out on the road. She hoped they'd all be exhausted after doing visitation and a funeral and had decided to go to bed early.

She had wandered around the house the day of the visitation, marveled at the tangle of rooms — not exactly what a real estate agent would call a wide-open floorplan. The warren of rooms would present a challenge to anybody who didn't know their way, and all she knew was where she was going … not how to get there. And in the dark …

It occurred to her then that there might be people still awake in the house in rooms that didn't have windows with lights she could see from the front, maybe a good number of people. Maybe others slept with the light on. There was no sense in waiting until all the lights were out, so she stepped out of her car into the deluge, slipping into her camo rain slicker, and then approached the house in soldier mode. Though the rain had rendered her invisible, she still darted from one tree to the next in the front yard until she got to the stand of crepe myrtle bushes by the front door. Peeking in the windows through the cracks of draperies, she could see that the light was on in that front room — whatever it was — but she could see no movement and could hear no sounds.

In her haste, she hadn't considered how she'd get into the house, just assumed that a place with so many windows — surely one of them would be unlocked where she could climb in. If not, she'd go around to the back and break out a glass pane in a door. As it turned out, she didn't have to do either. Circling the house around the south side, she tried the knobs on every door she passed, and she found one beneath a small porch roof in the back left corner unlocked, though what room it might lead to in there, she didn't know.

She looked at her watch. It was getting on toward midnight. Surely most of the occupants of the house were asleep. She turned the doorknob carefully, making no sound, then pushed the door slowly inward and stepped into the house, closing the door quietly behind her. She was somewhere near the kitchen, could smell the enticing aroma of food.

Then she summoned the discipline of combat and stood in place, still, with her eyes closed for four full minutes, allowing time for her eyes to adjust to the darkness and for most of the water to slide down off her slicker into a puddle at her feet.

When she opened her eyes, she could see very little — the ambient light from the fixture in the porch ceiling outside cast only a bilious glow through the small windowpanes on the door, but it was enough for her to make her way slowly around the walls of the room to a door. She cracked it open and peered into a room that was the utter, pitch-black dark of a closet — or a photography studio. She closed the door carefully and felt along the wall until she came to an archway leading out into another room that was just as dark as the one she was in, but she could see a big door on the other side of the room with a warm glow of light shining through the crack beneath it. She was sure the light came from the chandelier in the ceiling of the big foyer, where two huge staircases wound up from it to the floors above.

Then the glow vanished, the foyer plunged into darkness, and she could see absolutely nothing. Someone had turned off the light, which meant somebody was nearby and might come her way.

She turned back the direction she'd come and found utter darkness all around. No ambient light shone from the porch through the door's panes. That light was out, too.

Voices!

She froze.

Angry voices, not from the direction of the foyer.

And they were moving, coming her way. With only seconds to decide, she slipped back along the wall to the dark room, the one that might be a closet, stepped inside and pulled the door shut behind her.

There was a rumble of footsteps. Someone, more than one person, was running. She peeked out through the slit between the door and the jamb and could see absolutely nothing.

The argument/fight was getting louder, though, still coming her way ... clearly the combatants were stumbling around in the darkness.

What had happened to the lights?

Chapter Sixty-Eight

GABE GOT ALMOST to the end of the hallway before the lights
went out. He stood still, fumbling in his pocket for his cell
phone and its flashlight app. With it lighting his way, he
turned around and retraced his steps past the door to his room
toward the breaker box on the wall inside the utility closet at
the other end of the hall.

Flipping a switch there would restore the electricity ... if
the problem was a blown breaker. But if it was the storm
whipping the power lines outside ... the electricity wouldn't
come back on until it felt like it.

He was sure his mother wasn't asleep yet, but he'd like to
be able to check for a light shining beneath her bedroom door
before he knocked. If the electricity stayed out, he'd knock
anyway. Might not be the best time to have a conversation, but
the chaos that had resulted from his grandmother's announcement had kept his attention elsewhere earlier in the evening.
And he didn't want to wait until morning — if his mother was
still awake, they needed to talk!

There was a pattering sound, then a small form came
barreling toward him out of the darkness.

"Grampa Gabe!"

Chapman Schaeffer plowed into Gabe, grabbing him around the legs and almost knocking him off his feet.

"The lights went out!" the little boy cried. "And I gotted lost!"

He was struggling not to cry, but it was clear he was frightened. Gabe dropped to one knee in front of the four-year-old.

"S'okay pal, I got a flashlight. See?"

"Mommy was inna bathroom and I needed to go real bad so I went to the bathroom in the hall. But on the way back to the room the lights went out … and then that Doodle man comed down the hall … and I hided."

Gabe wondered what Doodle was doing out wandering the halls in the dark.

"You hid from Doodle — why?"

"He was talking on his phone and he was *mad,* saying bad words. And he doesn't like little kids."

Gabe suspected Doddle didn't like much of anything except getting high.

Standing up, Gabe took Chap's hand. "I'll take you back to your room, then I'll go see if I can get the lights back on."

They started down the hall.

"How come the Doodle man can call the lady in church a fat lady, but I get in trouble when I call Grandma Hannah a dead lady?"

Gabe smiled. "I didn't think the lady in church could sing very well — did you?"

"The Doodle man said she didn't sing at all."

"Didn't sing?"

"Uh, huh. He was talking on his phone and said Grandma Liv had dissing … that big word you said."

"Disinherit?"

"Uh huh, that."

Who was Doodle talking to in the middle of the night about Grandma Liv's announcement?

"Then the Doodle man said, 'But don't worry ... the fat lady hasn't sung yet!'"

Gabe felt a sudden chill.

~

OLIVIA HARRINGTON never had been one to second guess herself. Most times, she considered a thing long and hard before she done it, wasn't likely to make the kind of rash decision that caused others to question their own judgment.

She wasn't second-guessing herself now, either. It was just that ... aw, come on, admit it — somewhere inside she'd harbored the ridiculous hope that her family would understand her decision to change her will, that they— well, some of them, anyway — would agree with her that was it was the right thing to do.

And her feelings was a little hurt. Okay, more than a little, because it appeared to her that nobody made any effort whatsoever to see things from her point of view.

That's why she'd come up here to the quarterdeck to sleep. Though he'd been gone for more than three decades now, she felt closer to Landon here. She'd slept in the bed here most every night the first year or so after he died, grief so painful she thought it'd stop her heart. Wanted it to sometimes. She wasn't supposed to be running things, making hard decisions about the family and such. That was Landon's job. Well, she'd see him soon, wouldn't be long now. And she'd ask if he thought she'd done the right thing.

Lying in the velvet dark, she let out a sigh that she couldn't hear since she'd taken out her hearing aids, and stared at the skylights in the ceiling, where the storm blacked out the stars and moon, and rain hammered on the glass like a fist on a door.

She wondered how long the electricity would ...

That's when she sensed it. A presence.

Olivia was no longer alone in the room.

Not a single one of her senses offered any proof, and yet all of them were screaming that it was so. There was a presence here. A predatory presence. And for the first time in so many years she couldn't have counted them on her fingers and toes, Olivia Harrington was afraid.

Chapter Sixty-Nine

THE SUDDEN DARKNESS left Jude disoriented and off balance. He'd been poised to hurl Spencer out the open window, but Spencer broke free, and the movement tipped Jude forward and he felt himself falling sideways into darkness.

He could hear Spencer though — off to the right some- where — breathing hard, the sound a gurgle as he drew breath in through his smashed nose and ruined mouth. It was all a disorienting blur. He kicked out and connected with something — Spencer's leg maybe, or maybe the bed railing. He grasped into the darkness to grab hold of Spencer again, but he couldn't locate anything to grab hold of. Somehow, he found himself on the floor on his back, reaching out blindly, searching for anything,

And inside his head, the Other was screeching, *"Kill him! Kill him!"*

Jude was operating in adrenaline-fueled terror, and if he could have gotten a hand hold on Spencer, he'd have choked the life out of him. He didn't care anymore about making Spencer's death look like an accident. In the handful of seconds that had elapsed since he tried to throw his cousin out the window, Jude had acknowledged that he was in a fight to the death. He could not, he *would not,* let Spencer tell the world what he knew. Jude would not go to prison. He would rather die than —

Then Jude felt an iron grip on his upper left arm and was yanked sideways off his knees. His face slammed into the floor painfully and he felt the presence of Spencer above him. Lashing out with his right fist, he connected with some part of Spencer, his side, maybe, or his leg, but he could not dislodge Spencer's grip on his arm.

A voice growled out of the darkness.

"I started to remember ... just flashes, pieces of images, crazy. The clearest memory was your face— with a look of such horror ..." The two men were tumbling around on the floor now, grunting and gasping, wrestling in the darkness, grabbing and hitting and kicking, two furious, crazed animals. "Had to be the instant you spotted the kid ... and the memory haunted me." Jude felt Spencer's fist slam into his belly, knocking the breath out of him. "Because it didn't fit. Your dimple was *so clear* in that memory." Jude could not draw in a breath as Spencer ground out the rest. "It's on your *right* cheek and I couldn't have seen it unless *you* were driving."

Jude struggled to drag air into his lungs, but his diaphragm was frozen by the blow.

"You let me *rot* in prison."

The voice was totally foreign, sounded nothing at all like the young man who'd been looking wistfully at pictures of his gap-toothed little girl yesterday afternoon. It was angry and cruel and cold. And filled with rage.

The chant in his head was that of a banshee, a deranged lunatic.

"Kill him! Kill him! Kill him!"

A wild, Jurassic cry ripped out of Jude's chest. *Who he was,* his soul, pulled Jude Kavanaugh up out of his being by the roots. He could see them dripping blood. The cry left nothing behind but a gaping bloody wound where Jude once had been. An empty space of gore and terror and rage. And madness.

Snarling, Jude reached out into the darkness, grabbed Spencer's arm or leg — some part of him. He opened his mouth and bit down as hard as he could. Spencer shrieked, fought for release, but Jude was a pit bull, shaking his prey in his mouth. He felt blood and skin and muscle in his mouth and kept biting down, making some kind of animal sound that was utterly feral, all trace of humanity gone.

Spencer yanked away his ... *hand.* Jude had bitten his hand. He heard Spencer stumbling backwards, falling in the dark, whimpering, and he lunged at the sound but missed. Spencer kicked out, caught him on the chin and knocked him backwards, his head ringing. Then he heard the sound of Spencer scuttling across the floor like a crab for the door. He couldn't let him get away. Diving blindly, he managed to tackle Spencer, but the smaller man wiggled free and lurched away. He heard footsteps, running. Spencer was running away into the darkness.

Jude lurched to his feet and stumbled after him.

Chapter Seventy

Olivia lay in the darkness giving herself a good talking to! Crazy old woman, thinking there's a Boogie Man in the closet or a monster under the bed—something in the room that she can't see or hear. She'd ought to be ashamed of herself, acting like a ninny.

She paused in her internal tongue-lashing and listened hard, for all the good it'd do her without her hearing aids. Strained to see something out there in the inky black. Didn't hear nothing. Didn't see nothing. Wasn't nothing there!

Except there was.

No way in God's green earth she could know a thing like that, but she did. Maybe getting real old did something to your senses, give you a sixth sense — or seventh, or whatever the number was — to make up for all the others wearing out.

Had to be that. She wasn't alone in the room. She knew it.

"Who's there?" She didn't mean for her voice to quake, but it did.

The question was greeted with the same dark silence she'd launched it out into.

"I know you're here — what do you want?"

Nothing.

But whatever it was — *who*ever it was — had got closer now, was right beside the bed. She could feel him. And maybe smell him, too. A whiff of something burned.

"Go on with your bad self — get on out of here."

She was ashamed of how scared she sounded. And embarrassed. Why there wasn't nobody —

Lightning flashed outside, lit up the room through the skylight. But Olivia saw nothing but white, smelled the sunshine smell of sheets that'd been hung on the line to dry.

Then the pillow covered her face and she couldn't breathe.

GABE SHONE his phone flashlight on Olivia's bed. It was empty.

His heart had kicked into a gallop when that little rascal Chapman said he'd run into Doodle in the hall. Now his heartbeat sounded like a timpani drum in his chest.

"Grandma Liv," he called out. "You in here?"

No answer.

The fat lady hasn't sung yet.

He crossed the room to the bathroom door. Maybe she'd got up to go to the bathroom and the lights went out and now she was stuck in there.

He knocked on the closed door.

"If you're all done, I'll escort you back to bed."

Silence. He opened the door, shown the flashlight all around. The room was empty.

The fat lady hasn't sung yet.

Doodle had been standing there this morning when Chap said Grandma Liv had talked to her attorney in the pantry — about a dissing parrot. He'd heard Chap say that Grandma Liv wouldn't sign the new will — that disinherited the whole family — until *tomorrow*.

Where had she gone? A hundred-year-old woman in the

middle of the night? Had Doodle ... what? Kidnapped her? What for? But where—

The Crow's Nest.

He turned and ran down the hall. The elevator was too slow, so he took the stairs.

~

OLIVIA FOUGHT.

She wiggled and squirmed, tried to turn her head, clenched her hands into fists and battered the arms of the person holding the pillow on her face.

The burst of panic-driven resistance wore itself out in only a few seconds and then she relaxed back into her own pillow. She still struggled to draw in a breath that wouldn't come, though. Instinct. Couldn't help trying to breathe.

But she wasn't afraid anymore.

Jesus, I'm coming home.

~

GABE STOOD in the doorway of the Crow's Nest and shown his flashlight into the room. The man bent over the bed — *who'd been holding a pillow down on Grandma Liv's face* — snapped around toward him, a look of shock, fear, and anger on his face.'

"I's just—"

Launching himself into the room, Gabe tackled Doodle, knocked him backwards onto the bed and then dragged him down onto the floor beside it. He'd dropped his cell phone so he couldn't see what he was doing, but he didn't need to. He lashed out with his fists in the dark, caught Doodle somewhere in the face and he cried out.

Then they were wrestling, rolling around on the floor.

Gabe hit and punched and kicked the writhing figure in the dark, grasped for his neck so he could choke —

A beam of light fell on them, angled downward from the bed.

Maybe he'd dropped his phone on the bed, or maybe there was one on the bedside table.

Grandma Liv was alive.

Fear that Doodle had killed her was replaced with rage that he'd tried to. In the light, Gabe grabbed Doodle's ear and used it as a handle to slam his head into the floor, then he knelt over him, hammering his face with his fists, determined to kill him with his bare hands.

"Gabe, stop," Grandma Liv said. "He's done. Stop 'fore you beat him to death."

That's exactly what Gabe was trying to do.

"Let him go!" she cried. He could hear the anguish in her words. "You can't kill him — he's *family.*"

Her words took all the steam out of him, and he didn't land the blow he had drawn back his fist to deliver into Doodle's bloody face. Doodle was crying, and when Gabe stopped hitting him, he tried to scuttle away on the floor and run, but Gabe grabbed his shirt collar and slammed him back down on the floor.

"I ain't done nothing. I's just getting Grandma Liv a fresh pillow and you come in here … attacking me." He reached up to his face. "You *broke my nose.* I'm gonna call the sheriff, have you arrested for assault. I ain't eighteen yet — I'm a minor. I—"

"One more word out of you," Gabe snarled. "A single word, and I will finish beating you to death."

The boy opened his mouth to speak, closed it, shot a glance at Grandma Liv. "She ain't gonna let you hurt me. Now let me go."

Gabe didn't loosen his grip on Doodle's shirt as he snarled at the boy.

"You get out of this house — right now, tonight. You leave and don't you ever come back. If I *ever* see you again—"

"I got a right to—"

Gabe yanked the boy's face up so he could spit words into his ear. "*Never* come back! I know people who can make a little punk like you disappear. Vanish. Do you hear what I'm saying? I've lost more in a single poker game that it would cost to *erase* you. No body. No funeral. Just no more Mitchell Kavanaugh. Try to murder your own grandmother? I will cheerfully put an *end* to your miserable little life!"

He threw the boy back down on the floor, got a good look at his face in the light. He was terrified. Good. Rolling over onto his side, Doodle staggered to his feet, bounced off the door frame, then ran out into the dark hallway and disappeared.

Gabe got to his feet, suddenly aware of the pain in his bruised hands and scuffed knuckles.

"Grandma Liv, are you alright?"

"Course I ain't alright! If you'd a'got here thirty seconds later, I'd a' been singing with the angels." Her voice was shaky, but she was tough. "Maybe you shoulda waited, then you coulda worked out some deal with Cal at the funeral home — fry one, get the second one for half price."

Gabe didn't laugh because he knew he would burst out crying instead. So he sat down on the edge of her bed and took her hand.

"Thank Chap. I was on my way to Mama's room to—"

"You's going to ask her about that night, wasn't you?"

Gabe was shocked into silence. How did Grandma Liv—

"Ain't no need to be bothering your mama. She ain't well." His grandmother drew in a deep breath. "I'll tell you what you want to know."

"How do you—"

"I was there that night, too. I … seen it all." She coughed.

"You go downstairs and get me a glass of ice water for my throat. Kinda dry. I'll need to wet my whistle. It's a long story."

Chapter Seventy-One

Olivia lay in the bed, trying not to tremble, had to calm herself 'fore Gabe come back.

Doodle tried to *kill* her.

Wasn't nowhere in her mind to put a thing like that, and if she dwelled on it, she would …

She had to get her ducks in a row. She'd bought some time with the I-need-a-drink-of-water ruse. She had to use that time to figure out what she was gonna say.

Where should she start?

There's blood everywhere. Puddles on the hardwood floor, huge dark-red blotches on the rugs and carpet. Olivia knows she'll have to throw them away. She'll never be able to get the stains out.

The screaming just goes on and on, getting louder and louder, and Olivia thinks, no, she's certain she hadn't made that much noise when she was giving birth to either Cyrus or Alex. But she's sure the screams seem overloud because it was so important that nobody hear them. Some part of her mind thinks: That's the way it always works out — when you're sneaking into the house after curfew, you always step on every creaky board in the staircase. If this screaming wakes the sleeping children upstairs ...

Cyrus is as white as a new gym sock, trying his best to comfort the writhing girl on the couch. Girl, not woman. If she is a day over sixteen, Olivia is a three-eyed goat, but the girl doesn't want comfort. She hadn't, couldn't, possibly have planned it out this way, but she sure had grabbed the brass ring when she went into labor right there on the spot, standing in the foyer, yelling at Cyrus, demanding money, threatening to tell Hannah and everybody else in the family about their affair if he refused.

Olivia'd heard the pounding on the front door and had come out to the top of the stairs in her robe and nightgown, looking down at the screaming girl standing beneath the brightly shining chandelier. The girl is drenched to the skin, her shirt sticking to her huge belly, outlining her pregnancy.

Then it all happens at once — her water breaks — right there, whoosh! *The girl is silent for a moment, stops yelling as she looks down in surprise at the puddle of liquid that has appeared on the floor between her feet. Then she staggers forward and Cyrus catches her before she falls. That's when she starts screaming. Cyrus shoots Olivia a look that she catalogues for later — too much there to read at one sitting. Embarrassment. Remorse. Shame. Guilt. Fear. But mostly pleading. Pleading with his eyes for her to help him.*

Olivia doesn't even pause to get dressed, just runs down the stairs barefoot and helps Cyrus get the screaming girl onto the couch in the parlor. She goes to the phone to call 911, but Cyrus steps up and disconnects the call before she has a chance.

"You can't call an ambulance," he cries. "Are you crazy?"

"This girl is having a baby and she needs—"

"To have it. Just like millions and millions of other women in the world have babies every day. This is not a medical emergency. It's childbirth ... it's a natural human function."

"Cyrus, what if something goes wrong? What if there's a complication?"

"Don't you call nobody," the girl gasps. "I don't need no doctor or hospital." Another contraction sinks in its teeth, and she starts screaming again.

"Mama, please ..." Cyrus begs. Olivia looks into her son's eyes and sees the desperation, understands that his whole future is balanced on the razor's edge of this decision. Cyrus Kavanaugh, the heir to the Harrington Circle H Ranch dynasty, is married, has teenage sons ... and he has gotten a girl pregnant, an underage girl.

An *underage* black girl.

A voice comes from the doorway of the parlor. *"Mama?"*

Alex is standing in her pajamas, looking horrified. It is Cyrus's great good fortune that Hannah left this afternoon and will be gone all weekend — has taken their three boys to Houston for her younger sister's wedding. But it's Alex's great misfortune that she chose this night — she's in the middle of her first divorce and needs moral support — to bring her three small children to visit Olivia. The two little girls are asleep in a bedroom down the hall from their older brother, six-year-old Gabriel, who has a nasty ear infection, maybe bronchitis, too. Alex had given him a dose of codeine cough syrup earlier, but said if the fever didn't break soon, she'd have to take him to the emergency room.

A contraction hits the girl and she shrieks, and what happens after that becomes a blur. Blood and screams and curses and more blood. Kneeling in her splattered nightgown on the floor in front of the sofa between the girl's legs, Olivia urges her to *"Push! Push!"* as Alex wipes the girl's sweaty forehead with a cool cloth.

Then the electricity goes out.

Plunged into utter darkness, the girl becomes hysterical and combative — fighting Olivia and punching Cyrus while Alex rushes to the fuse box in the hall. She returns a lifetime later with a candelabra holding seven big candles shining brightly.

"Not a thrown breaker ... the storm must have taken out the power," Alex says. And within five minutes, she has lit the room with half a dozen big candelabras from all over the house, and another dozen individual candles. Then she stands behind Olivia, shining a powerful flashlight. It's as bright as an operating room.

After that, time unhooks from reality and the world is left behind by the engine, just puttering along on a side track until the forward momentum gives out and it stops entirely. Olivia doesn't know how long *the labor lasts. Hours, years. A geologic epoch. Again and again, Olivia is ready to get up and call an ambulance. She's never delivered a baby! But she's seen it, of course, watched over the neighbor woman's shoulder when Mama had Nathan, Roger, and Jeffy. What she remembers about that process is blood and crying out, though, not screaming like this girl. She sees the top of the baby's head. It's there during a contraction, then recedes between one contraction and the next. With every contraction, what she can see of the baby's head gets bigger and bigger.*

She thinks: if that part changes, if the baby stops moving down, she will instantly get up off her knees and go to the phone and call an ambulance, no matter what Cyrus and the girl say. But it looks the same as the births of her three little brothers. And then the top of the baby's head crowns, fills the whole birth canal.

"Get behind her, Cyrus, help her sit up, hold her shoulders." To the sweat-slathered girl, she says, "Push now! Push as hard as you can." The girl's face crinkles in concentration and pain, and she lets out a feral grunting sound as the head begins to ease out. "Harder! As hard as you can. One more time, just one more time."

The girl bears down and suddenly the head pops out like the cork on a champagne bottle and the slimy wet baby rides a wave of amniotic fluid into the world.

And into Olivia's waiting hands.

She grabs the wiggling little thing, almost drops it — almost drops her, it's a little girl — then gets a firm grasp on her body and pulls her out onto the towel Alex has brought.

The little girl sputters once, then draws in a breath and lets out a healthy hiccuping cry that has to be the single most beautiful sound in the world. Alex had the presence of mind to bring a pair of scissors to cut the umbilical cord, a piece of yarn to tie it off, and a washtub to catch the placenta.

She lets Alex and Cyrus take over while the world becomes muffled beyond where Olivia sits on the floor, cuddling the tiny, bloody baby wrapped in a towel to her chest.

After a few little pats on the back and a murmured, "it's okay, I gotcha, you're just fine," the baby stops crying and peers wonderingly up into Olivia's eyes. She stares, doesn't blink, grabs hold of Olivia's gaze and locks onto it and won't let go. She wiggles, her little fists battling the air in front of her. Then she grabs Olivia's finger, clasps it tight and hangs on.

Alex helps the girl to her feet to go to the bathroom to clean her up, which is a useless effort. It's just a powder room, and the girl needs a bathtub — at least a shower. The baths upstairs have those, but the girl is ... disinclined to go upstairs. Disinclined to cooperate in any way, in fact. Is angry, belligerent, and totally uninterested in the baby Olivia tried to hand to her.

Cyrus takes the washtub out through the dark kitchen to the back porch and the girl starts screaming at him when he returns, blames him, rages at him.

"It hurt! I thought that thing was gonna rip me open." That thing? Like she didn't know having a baby was painful?

Olivia takes the baby and a small candelabra into the powder room that's now splattered with blood, lays the child gently on a towel-covered countertop beside the sink and fills the sink with warm water. The baby is tiny — probably not even six pounds — but perfect. Olivia eases the little body down into the warm water and the child instantly stops wiggling ... relaxes and fixes Olivia with another one of those riveting stares. Using a little bit of hand soap— it's all she has— Olivia washes the baby. She cleans away the white stuff — it has a name but she can't remember now what it's called — and gently lathers the black hair on the little girl's head. She has a full head of hair — black and curly.

"What now?" Alex asks from the doorway. Behind her in the parlor, they can both hear Cyrus and the girl — Olivia doesn't even know her name — arguing, their voices getting louder and louder.

"I got no idea."

Alex looks over her shoulder. "The screaming didn't wake the kids, so I guess the yelling won't." She pauses. "She can't stay here." She looks at the baby. "They can't stay here."

"Ain't she beautiful. Look at all that curly hair. You and Cyrus was both bald as cue balls. I had to tape a bow on your head until you were almost two."

The volume and the viciousness of the fight in the parlor escalates.

"This is Cyrus's problem and he's going to have to fix it," Olivia says. "He's going to have to figure out—"

There is a sudden crash from the parlor. Glass breaking, like all the dishes in the china cabinet are shattering at once. Alex turns and bolts toward the sound. Olivia dries off the baby. There's no more yelling and cursing. Just silence. Ominous silence.

She wraps a dish towel snug around the baby, cradles her gently, and turns toward the door of the powder room. Alex is standing there, her face the color of baby powder, expressionless, her eyes huge.

And suddenly Olivia is afraid, as afraid as she's ever been in her life, because she understands that something has happened, something terrible and unfixable, a shifting of the plates in the bowels of the earth, changing the positions of all the continents on the planet.

Pushing past the catatonic Alex, Olivia rushes to the parlor where Cyrus is leaning over the girl — what's her name? — who is lying on her back in the ruins of the china cabinet. There is blood pooling around her ... around her head.

Cyrus turns when he hears his mother enter the room.

"She ... I ..." He runs out of air before he can complete a sentence. "The fireplace poker. She picked up the fireplace poker." Olivia sees it still clutched in the girl's right hand. "Came at me with it, was going to bash in my skull. All I did was push her away. I swear, I swear that's all I did. The footstool was behind her, and she tripped over it and landed in the china cabinet."

Olivia starts to rush to the girl, but she doesn't like the strange, stricken look on Cyrus's face. Suddenly, Alex is beside her, but she makes no move to help the girl either.

"She's dead," Cyrus whispers. That's when Olivia notices the piece of — the broken-off stem of a wineglass is poking into the girl's right temple. Her eyes are open. Staring.

Olivia drops into the chair beside her, holding the baby close, trying to breathe.

The memories of what happened later that night are an incomprehensible jumble in Olivia's mind, with no order of any kind and no sense of the passage of time. Mostly, they're snapshots, frozen scenes and images.

The lights are on, and Alex is screaming for Gabriel, running from room to room, trying to find him.

It is dark. Cyrus and Alex are wrapping a sheet from the linen closet around the girl — the girl's body *— in the golden glow of candlelight. He must have grabbed the sheet on top that has tiny yellow flowers on it, and Olivia thinks she will have to throw the matching fitted sheet away.*

Cyrus is drenched, has been outside in the rain without a raincoat. Alex appears beside him in the bright light of the chandelier — the electricity is back on. Alex is drenched, too, and so is the little boy wrapped up in a blanket in her arms.

"… hypothermia …"

"… emergency room …"

"… Cyrus is driving us…"

Then all is quiet. Olivia takes the newborn baby girl upstairs to her bedroom and sits rocking her for the rest of the night. Cyrus returns before sunrise lights up the bright blue sky. He says Gabe is in the hospital in intensive care — pneumonia and some kind of allergic reaction to codeine. He cleans up the mess downstairs before four-year-old Sydney and two-year-old Brooke wake up, then takes them to daycare at church and returns about mid-morning with baby things — bottles, formula, a onesie, disposable diapers.

He won't talk about what happened. His eyes are vacant. He says he's "taken care of everything."

Olivia doesn't leave her bedroom, just cares for the baby. Her mind won't go out there beyond the moment. Her eyes are likely as vacant as Cyrus's.

When Cyrus returns just before sunset, it is to take the baby.

He's made "arrangements," he says. When he lifts the baby out of Olivia's arms, she feels bereft, hollow.

She doesn't know where he took … his baby daughter … but she finds out later that he left her on the steps of a church. Olivia has no idea what happened to the baby's mother's body. She never asks.

Chapter Seventy-Two

Avery lay where she'd landed, in a heap at the bottom of the stairs with her back against the closed door into the kitchen.

She blinked, tried to orient herself. She'd fallen down the stairs. No, she'd been *pushed* down the stairs.

She had, hadn't she?

Maybe.

More likely she'd imagined that, too, like the footsteps and the breathing. She'd probably merely teetered off balance on the top step and then face-planted at the bottom. A fall like that should have broken every bone in her body and she did hurt *everywhere*. Her left shoulder throbbed where she'd bounced off a wall. Her right knee and elbow had whacked hard into something. But as she lay still, dragging in ragged breaths, it became clear that nowhere did she feel the intense pain of a broken bone.

She wasn't unscathed, though. Stunned seconds passed before she reached up with tentative fingers to examine her nose and lip, the two injuries that hurt worse. Her nose was bleeding. Not gushing, but bleeding, and her upper lip had a vertical cut where it'd made contact with ... the edge of the door frame, maybe. Though temporarily numb, the cut was deep. She could feel where the skin had parted and it, too, was dripping blood down her chin.

Great. A scar on her upper lip— like she had a harelip.

Her whole face throbbed in rhythm with the crashing of her heart in her chest. As the various throbbings separated out, she inched her fingers up to her forehead and felt a serious goose egg forming there. She needed to get ice on it quick or the swelling would black her eye. Both eyes, maybe. Double great. A harelip with two black eyes — that'll be attractive.

Avery understood that bravado was carrying her along, that she really was frightened … if she'd let herself feel it.

And she really did think somebody'd pushed her.

But right now, the need to put ice on her head/nose/lip gave her an excuse not to try to puzzle it out. She got slowly to her feet and opened the door behind her into the kitchen.

The crash and rumble of thunder outside was almost right on top of the lightening that strobed the sky, and Avery could see the brilliant flashes through the kitchen windows. Though intent on making it to the refrigerator and snagging some ice for the growing goose egg on her forehead, she paused when she thought she could hear other sounds beneath the bowling-alley rumble of the storm. No, not the breathing which she *imagined* she'd heard in the stairwell. Nothing so subtle as that.

The hand that'd shoved her hadn't been subtle either, if it'd been there at all. What she heard now sounded like a stampede — a stampede of wounded animals. But where? The walls and hallways echoed, shattering the sound and fragmenting it, making it impossible to tell the direction.

Somebody was coming. More than one somebody, it sounded like. And that more-than-one-somebody was stumbling and falling. She could clearly hear the sounds of bodies hitting the floor and the wall. There were voices, too — feral, animal voices — that didn't sound like any human she'd ever heard.

Clearly, she was listening to a *fight*, not a little punch-and-run dance like she and the cousins used to do through the hallways, racing to some place they'd designated as *ollie-ollie-in-free*. They'd run into each other in the narrow halls, stagger and fall down — giggling like loons, laughing the whole time. And you could tell who you'd crashed into by their voice.

These voices were unrecognizable, making sounds on the other end of the scale from laughter. Grunting, almost growling, men's voices, speaking words too garbled to understand, along with guttural snorts. The melee was coming at her out of the darkness, the sounds getting louder and louder. Whatever it was, whoever it was, wherever it was coming from … it sounded totally out of control. She could get hurt if it rolled over her and she was already banged up enough, could feel her right eye swelling. She needed to get out of the line of fire before —

The lights blinked back on.

Avery squinted in the glare. The rumbling sounds concentrated into the back stairwell, and seconds later a figure tumbled out into the kitchen through the door she'd left open, followed almost immediately by a second figure. The first was propelled by his own momentum into the room, where it crashed to the floor on its belly.

Daddy!

She hadn't thought that word in eight years. But the man lying on the floor was her father alright, and he was hurt — injuries far worse than the lump on Avery's forehead, her cut lip and maybe-blackening eyes. His whole face was a ruin. Blood poured from both nostrils of an obviously broken nose, and his bottom lip was split wide open, sending a stream of crimson down his chin. He was holding his left hand in his right, and blood was streaming down between his fingers.

Stumbling out the door behind him was Jude. His shirt was torn, his face bloody, his eyes wild. He looked *crazy*. He lunged at her father, grabbed his shirt, and turned him over onto his back. Then Jude collapsed, straddling him. Making grunting, growling sounds, Jude fastened his hands around her father's throat and began to choke him.

Avery found her voice then. Her lips thawed and she ran to the struggling men.

"Jude! Stop!"

He didn't even acknowledge her presence, just kept squeezing her father's throat. Her father grabbed Jude's wrists, trying to free himself, and she saw that her father's hand was also injured, a huge portion of the palm of his left hand ripped open, gory meat gushing blood from a jagged hole in the flesh.

"I won't go to prison," Jude growled, his face flushed with maniacal rage. "I won't be locked in a cage. You're not gonna tell anybody it was me!"

Her father's face was turning red, too, a deep purple shade, and blood vessels bulged in his neck.

"Jude, let him go!"

She grabbed Jude's arm and yanked, tried to pull him off, but it was like attacking a statue. She banged her fists on his back as hard as she could, pleading for him to stop. He didn't budge. She had to do something, couldn't stand by and let him strangle her father.

Looking around frantically for something to hit him with, she spotted a black iron skillet resting on a burner on the stove, the skillet Uncle Cyrus had tried to use on Maddie the night before. Taking two steps, Avery grabbed it, then whirled around and lifted it above her head. She hesitated a moment — a blow like that on the top of his head would ...

So she took the skillet handle in both hands and with a wailing cry — "Noooo!" — she swung it like a baseball bat, slamming it with a sickening *whup* sound into the side of Jude's face.

Jude flew sideways and slid across the tile floor until his body connected with the bottom cabinets on the other side of the room. He lay against them awkwardly, on his side, unconscious.

Avery's fingers went numb as the skillet clattered noisily to the floor.

There was a blur of movement beside her then. She glimpsed Grampa Gabe as he raced past her to where her father lay gasping for air on the tile floor. Grampa Gabe knelt over him, lifted him to a sitting position by his shoulders and leaning his body against the bottom of the refrigerator.

"Get me something — a cloth, something," Grampa Gabe ordered. Avery looked around, then snatched a dish cloth from where in dangled over the spigot on the sink and shoved it at him.

"Something I can use to stop the bleeding!" He barked the words and she realized he wasn't looking for a cloth to wipe her father's mashed nose and mouth but for a bandage to use on his mangled hand.

Speaking to his son, a running litany of "it's okay now, you're going to be alright," Grampa Gabe lifted her father's hand up — and stopped. Avery gasped with him, then both their gazes shot to Jude where he lay unconscious against the cabinet. His mouth, face, lips and chin were bloody. A look back at her father's hand and Grampa Gabe made the connection the same instant Avery did. Jude had *bitten* her father, had gnawed a hunk of flesh and gore out of his hand. Like a mad dog.

She opened two or three drawers quickly, looking for more towels, found them, then dropped to her knees beside her father. His face was slightly less red and flushed, but the vessels still stood out on his neck, and she could tell he was having trouble drawing breaths through his swelling throat.

Grampa Gabe took the largest dish towel, folded it over twice and placed it directly on the hand wound, then took the other towels and began to wind them around and around the injury. Avery could only look on helplessly, staggered by what'd happened in the past minute.

Something lay beside her knee on the floor, a crumpled photograph. Either Jude or her father had dropped it. She picked it up, smoothed it out and looked at it. Her own face, much younger, grinned out of the picture at her, a little girl wearing an itchy flower girl dress … *that day.*

She knew her father'd helped go through the family pictures searching for ones of Aunt Hannah to put up for the viewing. He must have found the photo of Avery in one of the boxes and decided to keep it.

She stared at the picture several moments before she noticed what was in the background. It was a sports car, her father's car. It was pulling away onto the road, clearly visible. Just as visible were the two people in the front seat of the convertible. You could see only the backs of their heads. The one on the left side, the driver, had red hair. The one on the right side — the *passenger*— was a blond.

Avery's eyes darted from the picture to her father's face and back to the picture, unbelieving.

I won't go to prison. I won't be locked in a cage — that's what Jude had said when he stumbled into the room. "You're not gonna tell anybody *it was me!*

The reality of what she was seeing — what it *meant* — came together slowly in her head.

The picture made it undeniably clear that when her father and Jude had left the wedding reception that day, *Jude* had been driving the car — not her father. Why would they stop a hundred yards down the road and change drivers? And that meant that when the car had struck a boy on a bicycle less than half a mile from the site of the wedding …

Her mind stumbled over the staggering reality.

Jude had been driving the car that plowed down a ten-year-old child without even slowing down, dragged his body a hundred feet, and left his mangled bicycle in the weeds on the roadside, the front tire slowly turning in the breeze.

Jude had done it. *Not her father.*

Her father hadn't killed that little boy.

Her father had spent eight years in prison for a crime he didn't commit.

Her gaze shot from the picture to her father's face and saw that his eyes were no longer squeezed shut in pain. They were open, and he was looking at her.

Chapter Seventy-Three

THE LIGHTS BLINKED BACK on as Gabriel came down the stairs to get a glass of ice water for Grandma Liv. He flipped off the flashlight app and stuffed his phone into the pocket of his sweatpants, his thoughts spinning so fast they might catch his hair on fire. Doodle had tried to smother Grandma Liv, tried to *murder* the sweet old lady ... and Grandma Liv said she'd tell Gabe the truth about what had happened all those years ago when he dreamed he'd seen a monster.

When he reached the bottom of the stairs, he heard sounds from the kitchen — Avery's voice, alarmed, shouting. He ran across the foyer to the hallway leading to the kitchen, heard Avery cry "No!" and burst into the kitchen on an unbelievable scene. Somebody ... it was Jude... lay stretched out on the tiles up against the bottom cabinets, and Spencer lay in a puddle of blood on the floor with Avery standing over him.

Gabe knelt beside his son, whose face had been bashed in and whose hand ... He looked at Jude's face, covered in gore. Jude had *bitten* him.

He looked up at Avery's face — she must have been in the fight, too. An ugly bruise sat atop a lump on her forehead, her left eye was black, and there was a cut on her upper lip. He told her to get towels for bandages and went to work to staunch the flow of blood from his son's injured hand. He'd have to get Spencer to an emergency room—

"What's going on in here?"

The voice came from behind him. His eyes and Avery's snapped to the door where Cyrus stood in a bathrobe and house shoes. Those seemed to be in order, but the pajamas he was wearing beneath them were on wrong side out, and he carried a crumpled-up piece of paper in his right hand.

"It's all over now," Gabe said. "Everything's okay. The boys" — he looked at the two grown men on the floor, one of them unconscious — "had a little disagreement, that's all."

Then Avery yelled out, "Jude was trying to *kill*" — there was the slightest pause, but Gabe picked up on it — "my father!"

"What was they arguing over?" Cyrus asked, as if he'd just found two little kids wrestling in the dirt, fighting to the death because one of them said the other had cooties. Spencer was still coughing, trying to get his breath back. His face was still scarlet. And his hand ... Gabe would have to get him to an emergency room soon, but in this storm ...

As if confirming his apprehension, a bolt of lightning went off like a flare right outside the window and there was a thunderous *boom*. Lightning had struck something nearby, something close. The wind rattled the house like it was in a hurricane.

"Spencer, can you talk? Can you breathe now, you're not still choking—"

"Was they out chasing Hannah's chickens again?" Cyrus asked as he shuffled their way. His eyes were focused. "I told 'em if they got into them chickens again I was gonna tan their backsides good." Focused eyes used to indicate he was lucid. Not anymore.

Avery held out a crumpled photograph. "They were fighting over this."

Gabe glanced at the picture — it was Avery as a little girl all dressed up in a party dress with ribbons. Cyrus dropped the crumpled paper he was holding and took the picture from her.

"Who's this?" Uncle Cyrus asked.

"It's me, Uncle Cyrus."

"And who are you?"

Avery shook her head. "Look at the background, at the car in the background. That's what matters."

"Right nice convertible, looks like. But I need my glasses to—"

"Look at who's driving!" she cried, her voice rising to near hysteria. "And who's *not* driving."

Gabe snatched the photo away from Cyrus, "Let me see that picture."

It took a couple of seconds — then the car behind Avery in the picture leapt into crisp focus. He couldn't breathe, looked at Spencer, the photo, then back at Spencer.

"*Jude?*" It was the airless whisper of a man whose whole world had just exploded.

Spencer nodded his head slowly.

A great buzzing sound started in the center of Gabe's skull as the implications ... what the picture *meant* bloomed with a blazing white light there.

Cyrus took the photo out of Gabe's suddenly numb fingers, turned to leave, muttering, "I need to get my glasses to—"

He stopped, froze in place, a look of puzzled shock on his face. "And who are *you?*" he asked.

Gabe turned to the doorway to see who—

A woman he didn't recognize stood in the doorway. She was wearing a wet raincoat. The hood was pulled up, hiding her face. But he wouldn't have been looking at her face even if he could have seen it. He was transfixed by the sight of the pistol she was pointing at Cyrus.

"I know who *you* are," she growled at Cyrus. Her voice was

shaking, but she held the gun in a confident, two-hand grip and it was rock steady.

Cyrus glanced back over his shoulder, confused, to see who it was the woman was addressing. Then his countenance changed, and his gaze yanked to the darkened doorway leading into the parlor.

"Hannah?" His was the voice of a pleading child.

"Where's my mother?" the girl demanded.

"Hannah's in … there." He pointed to the doorway, dropping the photograph Avery had given him on the floor. "My beautiful Hannah is … "

"I don't care about Hannah. I'm looking for my mother."

"Who are you?" Cyrus asked.

"Look at me!" She pulled the hood down off her head. You could see freckles, and that she was biracial. "I don't need a paternity test to prove it — you can see who I am." She grabbed a handful of her black hair and pulled it up off her forehead — revealing light roots. *Red* roots! "Where's my mother?"

"Is she a friend of Hannah's?"

The woman snorted. "Oh, I very much doubt that." She took a step toward Cyrus, the pistol pointed at the center of his chest. "You got five seconds to tell me before I—"

"Cyrus doesn't know where she is," said a voice from the doorway leading to the dining room. The woman snapped the gun in that direction with precision and aimed it at Alex. In that moment, Gabe became aware of the changes in his mother that his grandmother had been talking about, as if a veil had dropped off his eyes. She looked like she'd aged ten years. Thin to the point of gauntness, dark circles under her eyes, her face pale. Something *was* wrong with his mother.

"He knew once, but not anymore. Cyrus doesn't remember how to find his way back to his bedroom now."

Gabe finally found his voice and rose to his feet.

"I don't know who you are or what you want, but—"

"I do," Gabe's mother said. "I know who she is." Waving her hand at the gun, she told the woman, "You don't need that. I'll tell you what you want to know."

"You know where my mother is?" The tough, angry tone was gone. There was such yearning and longing in those words that it broke Gabe's heart.

Gabe saw his mother consider the question, deciding how she was going to answer it.

"I know … that you need to stop looking for her. I'm sorry. Your mother is dead."

Chapter Seventy-Four

DEAD, dead, dead.

The word reverberated in Rowan's head, bounced around in there.

Rowan began to tremble. Why wasn't she prepared for that answer, prepared to find out her mother was dead?

"Who are you?" she blurted out to the dark-haired woman.

"Alexandra Harrington. I'm Cyrus's sister."

Rowan's ... *aunt*. Her father's sister.

A thousand questions exploded in Rowan's brain, but she couldn't hold onto any of them long enough to ask it.

"When did she ...?"

"She died the day you were born."

Rowan should have sat down then because suddenly she couldn't feel her feet anymore, nothing from the knees down, like she was standing on stilts. All her fantasies about her mother for four decades ... all futile, hopeless. Her mother hadn't been alive when she was conjuring up any of the images.

. . .

Rowan is nine years old, about to go down the slide at the city park, when she notices a beautiful Black woman coming toward her. The woman is smiling, like she hasn't seen Rowan in a long time and can't wait to fold her into her arms.

It's Rowan's mother! She has come to take Rowan home to live with her and Rowan's father. They live ... on a cattle ranch in ... Wyoming. There are meadows full of wildflowers and butterflies, with herds of horses and mountains painted on the sky, and she has her very own pony, a pinto. His name is Patch and he—

The woman reaches where Rowan is standing speechless, frozen to the spot, waiting to be swept off her feet into a loving hug. But the woman goes right past Rowan. Walks by her and gets down on one knee in front of another little girl. She says something to the little girl but Rowan can't hear it because she can't hear anything. The car horns, the sirens, the birds, little kids laughing. She can't hear any of that. All she can do is stare at "her mother" drawing a different little girl into her arms, hugging her tight, kissing her face. The little girl wiggles to be free so she can run off to play on the slide and the woman stands and looks after her, her face so full of adoration it breaks Rowan's heart. If that'd been her mother, if her mother had come for her, swept her up into a hug, kissed her cheeks and her eyes and her forehead, she wouldn't have tried to get away. She'd have put her arms around her mommy's neck and hugged her so tight she couldn't breathe, and she'd have begged to stay there forever.

THAT WOMAN COULDN'T HAVE BEEN Rowan's mother because her mother had already been dead for ten years!

No! it was unthinkable.

"I don't believe you! How do you know she died the day I was born?"

"Because I was there." The woman named Alexandra paused, gathered herself and turned toward the front of the house, toward the huge foyer with the gigantic chandelier hanging from the ceiling. "I was ... *here.*" She pointed to the foyer. "Your mother went into labor right there, and you were born on the couch in there." She pointed to the room where the woman Hannah had lain during visitation. "We helped her into the parlor—"

"We? We *who*?"

"Cyrus and I and our mother." Their mother — the stately old woman at the funeral who was a hundred years old.

The good-looking bald man interrupted her before she could continue.

"I've been doing the math." He looked at Rowan. "She would have been born about forty—"

"Forty-six years ago, 1976," Alexandra told him.

He gaped at her. "Forty-six … I'd have been—"

"Six years old, yes."

"I was *here* then, wasn't I, when—"

"Yes, Gabe, *that's* the screaming you heard. Her mother down here, in labor."

The man looked like she'd hit him with a wrecking ball.

"But you told me—"

"I said it was all a bad dream, a nightmare. What else could I do? Tell a six-year-old that a baby'd been born in the parlor?"

"What was she doing here?" Rowan demanded of her father.

"What was *who* doing here?"

"My *mother!* She gave birth to me in this house. Why? I was your baby, wasn't I? She was having your baby — you're my father."

The old man looked at her without the slightest recognition in his eyes.

"Are you the woman from the museum? Hannah said you'd be coming by so she could give you the jewelry." He stopped, looked first confused and then stricken."

"Hannah?" He looked around. "Where's Hannah?"

The younger man wasn't interested in what the old man

was saying. He was zeroed in on the woman telling the story, the woman who was his——

"Mama, you made me believe I didn't hear what I heard." He sat down, trembling.

"I didn't know you could hear it. I didn't know it woke you up. You ran away from the screaming out into the yard. Down the back stairs, I guess, through the kitchen. Out into the storm. I was frantic when I couldn't find you. You were sick and you were out in the rain, soaked. All scratched up from the barbed wire by the fence."

"What happened to my mother?" Rowan shouted and the others froze. "She gave birth ... did she die in childbirth?"

"I didn't mean to do it!" The old man cried out so loud and unexpectedly that Rowan jumped and only barely kept herself from pulling the trigger on the pistol in her hand. "She came at me with the fireplace poker and I pushed ..."

"She didn't die in childbirth? Then you ... what? You *killed* her?"

The old man began to pace frantically back and forth across the room, muttering a nonsense monologue. "Didn't. Didn't. Can't let Hannah. Poor Hannah. Never should have. Didn't mean to ... I wanted to get out." He turned and spoke to someone only he could see. "I'm not coming to see you anymore. It's over." Then he looked shocked. "You can't be pregnant!" He began pacing back and forth again, mumbling. "What will Hannah do if she finds out I got a sixteen-year-old girl——"

"She was just *sixteen?*" Rowan choked on the word.

He continued to babble.

"... can't tell Hannah! Given you thousands of dollars. I can't pay you anymore." He put the palms of his hands to both sides of his forehead and pressed. Then his face underwent a transformation. All the tension and fear and anger drained out of it and was replaced by ... nothing. Absolutely nothing. You could look into that old man's eyes and straight out the back of his head.

"What did you do?" Rowan demanded. "You *killed my mother,* didn't you? What did you *do?*"

"He pushed her away, that's all," said the woman, Alexandra. Rowan's aunt! "They were fighting, arguing and she tried to hit him with a fireplace poker, so he pushed her."

"Pushed her? Just *pushed* her?"

"She fell backward, tripped over the footstool, I guess, and fell into the china cabinet and all the dishes and glasses, everything broke, shattered and … the stem on a wineglass with the bottom part gone … like an ice pick. She fell on it and …"

Rowan had been born right here in this house. On that couch where she'd sat with the adorable little boy who talked about slip slops. Her mother had *died* here.

"Who was she?"

"Who was who?"

"What was her name, my mother. What was her *name?*"

"I don't know," the old man said, "but we can ask Hannah. She'll know.

THE IMAGES WASHED over Gabe in waves, a tsunami of images. Blood. Blood everywhere. Had it been real blood, not some fantasy his fevered mind had conjured up out of nothing? Then was the monster real, too?

That image roared up out of his psyche, a shark on the attack, flashing through the water, its mouth open, its teeth ready to eat him alive.

The teeth marks on his arm … the faded scars that ran the length of it where the monster had bitten down but he'd pulled his arm free …

Teeth? Barbed wire? The … *monster?*

"What happened after my mother die — after he *killed* her?"

"Mama took the baby — took *you* into the bathroom and ran water in the sink and cleaned you up. I came to the door and Mama said ... she talked about how beautiful you were with all that curly hair." She swallowed back tears. "While Mama looked after you, Cyrus and I ... we cleaned up the ... you know, there was blood everywhere."

Lightning flashed outside in the raging storm, bleached the color out of the backyard for a frozen moment. It flashed inside Gabe's head, too, in the storm raging there. He watches the internal lightning illuminate the kitchen floor, the black blobs that are really red, puddles of blood, and he runs toward the back door, but he trips. And the monster comes.

"Cleaned up?" Gabe asked, trying to superimpose the reality he was hearing for the first time on the memories of something that really didn't happen at all. Except it did. "How? What do you mean — cleaned up?"

"How many things can cleaned up mean?"

"*Tell me!*" He was shouting at his mother and he didn't mean to. He couldn't help it.

"... towels, old towels ... a mop and a bucket. We put the placenta in a washtub and Cyrus took it—"

Gabe didn't hear the rest of what his mother was saying, something about a sheet. He felt his mouth form words and heard his voice speak them to his Uncle Cyrus.

"You left the washtub by the back door, didn't you?"

But Gabe hadn't willed the words anywhere in the higher centers of his brain, and he didn't hear his uncle's response, if he did respond, because those centers were busy processing images.

Slimy monsters with tentacles, like an octopus. They had teeth, and they bit him. He had the scars from the attack — on his body and on his soul. He'd fallen down when the first one came for him. But as he fought it off, fought to get free, others came slithering out of the shadows, down the walls and across the floor after him.

As the image of the monster flashed in his mind, he grabbed it *and held on.*

He'd never done that before, always willed it away as fast as it'd come, banished it, didn't want to look at it, to see it. But he wanted to now. He even squeezed his eyes shut, willing it to remain there, hot and stinking in a spotlight on the bare stage of his soul.

Not tentacle*s*. *Tentacle.* Singular. There was only one.

And not monster*s*, either. There was only one, the one he fell on. The others were just shadows, reflections of the rain-water slithering down the windowpanes.

He'd tripped over the washtub Uncle Cyrus had set beside the back door and turned it over as he fell. And then he'd gotten tangled up in …

… *the placenta and umbilical cord from the baby that'd just been born in the parlor.*

No teeth. He'd slipped on the mud in the yard and slid into the coil of barbed wire by the fence.

That was reality, what'd really happened, a reality that'd been warped and twisted into an illusion of monumental horror in the mind of a sick little boy with a high fever. He'd created a monster and it had stalked the dark corridors of his mind every day — and night! — for more than four decades.

~

CLEANED UP.

Old towels.

Washtub.

A sheet.

"What did you do with the sheet?" Rowan demanded. "You wrapped my mother in it, didn't you? Her body." She turned to the befuddled old man. "What did you do with my mother's body?"

"Glasses." He turned his rheumy eyes on what he held in his hand, a crumpled-up photograph. "I need my glasses to see—"

Rowan lost it. "*Where is she?*" The words rode a sob out of her mouth as she cried. What had they done with her mother? "Tell me!"

"Cyrus took her," the woman, her aunt, said. "He never said … where he buried her. We … didn't ask."

Rowan didn't bother to ask the old man again, to ask *her father.* He knew once, but not anymore.

"You can't even tell me where she is." It wasn't a question. Her hurt, the bereft feeling, filled her whole being.

"Yes … I can." She saw that … *her aunt*…was crying, too, now. "I didn't see, but later, in the backyard, I … there was freshly turned earth in the petunia garden. In front of the cherry tree."

The young girl with wet hair and a bruised forehead spoke for the first time, like the words were surprised out of her. "Aunt Hannah's koi pond. If they dug up the backyard …"

A rage unlike anything she'd ever felt, greater than any battlefield fury, bubbled up in Rowan's chest. Her father had *murdered* her mother, had buried her body in the backyard — then built a balcony on his bedroom so he could look out over it every morning. And these people … just *planted some more petunias* on top of her unmarked grave and went on with life like nothing had happened, like it was no big thing.

Rowan would kill them all. A bullet between the eyes. Except for the old man. Her father. She'd give it to him in the belly. Gut shot was a hard, slow way to die.

She swung the pistol around to the good-looking bald man. She'd start with him.

A torch of lightning was followed by a cannonade of thunder, and then the room went dark.

Chapter Seventy-Five

GABE HAD ONLY SECONDS — the lights might blink right back on. He launched himself at the spot where the woman — his cousin, his Uncle Cyrus's daughter! — stood pointing a gun at him. The lighted image still formed a negative on his retina. He reached out to grab the gun and got one hand around the woman's grip on it, intent on shoving it to the side. But her reflexes were fast. Instead of trying to pull the weapon free, she dropped to one knee, didn't break his grip but changed the angle of fire upwards — at his chest! Clearly, she knew how to handle a gun — and an adversary — better than he did. Instinctively, he grabbed the gun with his other hand and shoved her hands and the gun downward toward the floor with all the strength in his arms and back. Then two things happened at the same time — crack of thunder shook the whole house, and the gun fired.

Bang!

The sound of the gunshot was masked by the rumble of the thunder, but Gabe felt the gun's recoil, and sensed the passage of the bullet between his spread knees. He was so startled and off balance that he collapsed on top of her. That wrenched the gun from her grip, and he heard it slide across the floor. Then she flung him off and rolled away. An instant later, he heard her bump the table by the dining room door and the sound of the lamp on it crashing to the floor.

The others in the room cried out.

"Gabe!"

"Grampa Gabe!"

"Dad!" That voice was ragged and hoarse. "Are you okay?"

Spencer needed a doctor! That focused the roaring avalanche of Gabe's thoughts and feelings.

"I'm taking you to the emergency room to have that hand seen to. I just need to get a better bandage on it first."

He pulled his phone back out of his pocket, hit the flashlight app, and shown it on Spencer's ravaged face. A moment later, his mother's phone provided another beam of light.

"Somebody turn the light on, I need to find my glasses," Uncle Cyrus said.

"Stand still or you'll trip over something and fall," Gabe said. "Aves, get me more towels. Mama, bring me the candelabra out of the dining room. I need more than cell phone light."

He heard Avery pulling open one kitchen drawer after another.

"You got a lighter?" his mother called out to Gabe from the dining room.

"No. Isn't there a box of matches somewhere?"

"You want to go looking for it?"

"Use the stove."

"It's electric."

"The hot water heater in the pantry then — the pilot light."

"What if the woman … comes back with another gun?" Avery asked with a quaver in her voice.

Well, duh, she'll shoot us, Gabe thought. He realized then

that the emotional blows of the last half hour had *unhinged* him. Get a grip!

His mother returned with candles and took them into the pantry, where he could see the flickering blue flame of the water heater's pilot light sending a golden luminescence to dance in the shadows. She used the flame to light one candle, could use that candle to light the others. When she brought the candelabra into the kitchen, her cellphone flashlight beam played over a lump of darkness where Jude still lay unconscious. He'd best stay that way, because when he woke up, Gabe would — not now. Concentrate on Spencer's hand. He knelt beside his son, and as the light grew with each newly lighted candle, he removed the soaked-through bandages.

"What happened to him?" Alex cried when she saw the wound.

"Jude bit him!" Avery said out of the darkness, handing her grandfather another stack of towels.

"Where's Jude?

"I clocked him with a skillet," Avery said and cocked her thumb toward the shadowed figure lying on his side against the bottom cabinets on the far side of the room.

Gabe placed a thickly folded towel on Spencer's palm. The boy flinched, but didn't cry out, and Gabe knew that had to hurt. He wrapped a long, thin towel around that one and pulled it tight. Then added another and another until Spencer's hand was the size of a boxing glove.

Thunder rumbled again, lightning flashed, and wind battered the house. Maybe he should dial 911 instead of trying to drive to town, but an ambulance would take—

Buzzz!

The sound startled him and he almost dropped the last towel.

"That's a smoke alarm," Alex said, looking in the direction of the sound that was coming from the back of the house. "It'll keep yelling until I take the battery out."

Like everything else in the old house, the alarms weren't exactly state of the art, and they malfunct—

Buzzzz! A second sound joined the first. Another alarm. There was one in almost every room in the house.

"You don't think there's really—"

The blatting of a third alarm joined the first two.

"I smell smoke," Avery said out of the darkness. "Something's burning."

"That woman with the gun, you don't think she—" his mother began.

"She set fire to the house!" Avery finished for her.

Chapter Seventy-Six

Alex was about to tell Avery that she was imagining … and then she smelled it, too. *Smoke.* All she could think was, *Mama won't hear the alarms.* Even if the fire weren't catastrophic, the smoke could be deadly. Thank God the "chimney" wasn't open, but heat would still rise up the staircases to the upper floors and carry the smoke with it.

"Mama—"

"Go!" Gabe said. "She's in the Crow's Nest. Get her into the elevator now while you still can." The elevator would run when the electricity in the house was out, but the shaft would still serve as a chimney to funnel smoke upward. Then Gabe looked toward the dining room where the woman — Cyrus's daughter — had gone. "That fire was set. If I get to it quick, maybe I can put it out."

Smoke alarms were blatting all over the house now. They would set off a stampede — three dozen terrified people in their pajamas bolting in panic out into the pouring rain.

To Avery, Gabe said, "Call 911—"

"My phone's upstairs."

Alex pulled open the magnetic band on her Apple Watch and handed it to Avery. "I need my phone for light."

"Help your father out to the car—"

"My keys are—"

"My car, then. It's at the head of the driveway." Gabe had sold his Maserati, drove an old Ford Taurus. The whole family knew the key code was his birthday. "Get him to the ER at Northwest." Northwest Texas Healthcare system in Amarillo was the closest Level One trauma center. "Make sure the Cactus Creek Bridge is stable before you cross." Cactus Creek would flash flood if three jackrabbits pissed at the same time upstream.

"Take Uncle Cyrus with you."

Avery pressed and held the side button on the watch. When the sliders appeared, she dragged the Emergency Call slider to the right, and a voice spoke from the watch.

"Bailey County 911 center. What is your emergency?"

"The Harrington House is on fire!" Avery cried.

As the voice asked questions, verifying her identity, Alex caught Gabe's arm before he could dash through the dining room toward the smoke.

"Take this," she said and stuffed the safe deposit box key into the side pocket of his sweatpants. "There is enough money there to pay off those psychopaths. Thank your Aunt Hannah."

"What—"

She shoved him toward the doorway. "Go! I'll explain later!" He kept going.

As she turned toward the foyer, she saw Avery bend over her father and hold out her hand. Alex didn't know what'd changed — maybe only that Spencer was hurt. But her heart swelled at the sight anyway. Alex didn't think Avery'd visited him half a dozen times in the eight years her grandson had spent in prison. Maybe she'd never gone at all. She'd been as cold as a glacier to him since he arrived. Maybe …

That, too, would have to wait until later.

Flashlights. There were flashlights … somewhere. No time

to find them, and the batteries were probably dead anyway. But the family members who'd be trying to get out of the house would have cell phone flashlights to guide them. There was that.

Crossing the big foyer toward the elevator in the southwest corner of the house, Alex could hear the sounds of frightened voices from upstairs, loud enough to carry over the ear-piercing blatting of the alarms.

She got all the way to the center of the foyer before the phone flashlight illuminated a cloud of swirling gray smoke. She froze in horror, gasped, and the intake of air started a chain reaction of coughing. The old house's internal gulf stream was funneling smoke up the stairs. The fire must be in the music room — and the chimney *was* open! How could that be? But it was undeniable — you could see the smoke going straight up the grand staircase. It'd pass through the third-floor hall, up the steps and out the Crow's Nest windows. That'd divert much of the smoke away from the second floor bedrooms, of course. But Mama was in the bedroom in the Crow's Nest!

"DID HANNAH BURN THE BISCUITS?" Cyrus asked from the shadows, barely illuminated by the flickering candlelight.

"You stay where you are, Uncle Cyrus," Avery told him. "Don't move."

Alarms were bleating all over the house now, and she could hear a smattering of voices crying in alarm. Leaning over, she held out her hand to her father.

"Can you stand up?"

"I'm good." The words, coming from his smashed mouth, clogged by his broken nose, didn't sound "good."

She wondered if her own eye … *eyes* were black.

He took her hand and got to his feet, swayed, then

remained upright. She'd leave the candles in the kitchen. They'd be useless in the rain. They'd make it to Grandpa Gabe's car by the light mounted on the pole in the backyard. They'd get drenched, no time to go get raincoats —

"Uncle Cyrus, take my hand."

Her father suddenly lifted his arm off her shoulder and lurched toward the other side of the kitchen.

"What are you—"

He said something but the word was garbled and she couldn't understand it.

"What did you say?"

The smoke was getting thicker, not some vague whiff of smoke but like standing downwind of a campfire. How could it get that thick so fast?

"Jude. Gotta get him out."

Avery had forgotten all about Jude!

But her father hadn't. Jude had stolen eight years of her father's life to save his own ass, and yet he … The lump that formed in her throat made it hard to swallow.

Maddie! She was upstairs, too, and …

Avery pushed the thoughts out of her mind. Maddie's hearing was fine. Those smoke alarms were shrieking loud enough to wake the dead and Maddie hadn't even been asleep when Avery left the room. Maddie was strong and young and she would find her own way out of the house. Avery had bigger fish to fry, had to get an old man, an unconscious man, and an injured man out of the house and into the car.

She picked up the candelabra and went to Jude's body. Her father dropped to his knees beside him — either to help or because he could no longer stand up. Avery saw something … not right in the flickering candlelight.

"Bring the light closer," her father said, and she knelt beside him and held out the candles in front of Jude's body. The brighter light confirmed that there was definitely something wrong with Jude. He lay on his side, propped up against the base of the cabinets. He was unmoving, perfectly still.

Her father put the fingers of his uninjured hand to Jude's throat.

"He's dead," her father said.

"*Dead?* How could he be …?"

Suddenly Avery couldn't breathe.

"You mean … I *killed* him?"

"No, you didn't kill him."

Her father pointed to the front of Jude's torn tee shirt. There was a dark stain there on the left side of his chest.

"That's a bullet hole."

"*Bullet hole?*"

"That gunshot. The bullet hit Jude, or hit something else and ricocheted. Right in the heart."

She shook her head in denial, felt tears literally squirt out of her eyes and course down her cheeks. *Dead?*

"Are you okay, Baby Girl?"

Avery had to swallow more tears then, tears that had nothing to do with Jude. She simply nodded because she couldn't speak.

"Then help me up."

She stood and helped her father to his feet.

"Uncle Cyrus, take my hand." She could see the smoke in the air now.

"She did, didn't she?" Uncle Cyrus said. "Hannah burned the biscuits."

Chapter Seventy-Seven

WHEN GABE GOT to the other side of the dining room, the smell of smoke was much stronger. The door into the small hallway was closed. When he shoved it open, he was struck by roiling gray smoke that burned his eyes and sent him into a coughing fit. Smoke was coming out from under the door of the music room and accumulating in this end of the hall. Not a massive amount of smoke, not a very big fire. Not yet, anyway.

But any smoke was dangerous. He needed to keep the smoke out of the dining room, contain it while he put out the fire. He looked around and spotted the heavy dining room draperies. He ran to them, yanked hard. Nothing. Yanked again and down they came, along with the ornate drapery rod that almost clocked him in the head. Good thing Aunt Hannah wasn't buried in a grave somewhere because she'd be spinning around in it — she'd picked those drapes out to match the wallpaper. The ugly Kim Kar-Mashon wallpaper.

Dragging the drapes to the door, he stuffed the fabric into the big space between the door and the hardwood floor — used the rod to jam them in, then left it there to seal it. Then he ran across the dining room to the door into the parlor on the other side, through the big alcove lined on both sides with cabinets where dishes, the good china as well as plastic plates for the little kids, were stored. He crossed through the parlor to the door on the other side into another hallway. When he opened that door, he could smell smoke, but nothing like the back hall. Dropping to his knees, he crawled along the floor where the air was better, all the way to the door at the far end, felt the wood to make sure there was no fire on the other side, then opened it a crack and peered into the hall. He had circled around the music room to come at it from the other end of the hall. There was fire in there all right, but the smoke from it hadn't accumulated this far into the hall yet. Maybe he still had time to put out the fire. Opening the door just enough to enter, he jumped inside and closed the door after him, then ran down the hall to the music room door and eased that door open. He expected to find a small fire there. What he found was a conflagration.

He jumped backward from the heat — the room was lit by bright red and yellow flames spreading out from where four flaming ... *somethings*, balls of fire, were sitting on the oriental rug in the center of the room. He couldn't tell what the things were and there was no way to get anywhere near them. They were surrounded by flames. The fire was spreading away from them over the whole rug, had caught the hardwood floor beneath on fire and was making its way to the furniture and the draperies. Even if he'd had a fire extinguisher, even if he could get to them, it would take more than that to put those flaming *whatevers* out. He was too little too late.

But how could that be? How was a fire this big putting out so little smoke? He watched the smoke rise from the flames. He shown the beam of his cell phone flashlight up. A thick pall of smoke hung down from the eighteen-foot ceiling. Moving smoke. He watched in horror as it flowed across the ceiling and out the vent window above the music room door, across the hall, and into the vent window on the doorway into the parlor.

And from there, it'd cross the parlor, blow out into the foyer, and right up the stairs to the third floor.

The chimney was open!

Someone had opened the music room windows ... and the hallway windows in the Crow's Nest.

Rowan didn't know about the house's unique air flow convection system — the gulf stream. She couldn't be the one who set the fire. *It was Doodle!* When he couldn't smother Grandma Liv with a pillow, he figured to kill her with smoke! When Gabe got his hands on that little punk ...

He shook it off. That was for later. Right now, the flames were too far gone for Gabe to do anything but run from them and make sure everybody got out. Coughing, his eyes burning, he turned around and hurried down the hall the way he'd come to the door into the second hallway. He turned the knob, pushed, but it only opened a few inches and then stopped. He tried again, putting his shoulder into it. The door wouldn't budge. It was ... stuck on something. On what? He'd just opened it five minutes ago and ...

Doodle. He was getting rid of the only witness to his attempt to kill Grandma Liv. He'd wedged something — a chair probably — under the doorknob on the other side of the hallway door.

And Gabe had wedged the drapery rod under the door at the other end.

All the windows on the first floor were covered with decorative metal grates on the outside. The only other door in this hallway opened into the HVAC room and the laundry. There was no window.

Gabe was trapped.

~

ALEX RAN AS FAST as she could across the foyer and into the living room on the front of the house, through it to the Scotland room — decorated in clan tartans, where Hannah held bridge parties. The door on the far side of the Scotland room led to the hallway where the elevator was located.

She got there panting, just that little run. She shone the light through the grillwork door of the elevator and — the elevator wasn't there.

Duh! It was on the fourth floor, in the Crow's Nest. Mama had used the elevator to go there. Alex swore and slammed her hand down on the call button. She heard the elevator machinery begin the crank, lowering the little phone-booth box to the first floor — agonizingly slowly. Alex could run up the stairs faster … no, she couldn't. Not anymore.

Suddenly, the smoke alarms turned off, leaving total silence in their wake. How could *all* the batteries go out at the same time?

"No, please," she whispered. "Not now."

She didn't hear the whisper, of course, wouldn't have heard it if she'd screamed the words at the top of her lungs.

Her hearing could blink back on again in a minute. Or never.

Alex opened the elevator door, got inside, and pushed the top yellow button — Crow's Nest. The machine began to rise. In complete silence. She didn't hear the machinery or the smoke alarms, or her own breathing. She was completely deaf.

The elevator rose up through the southeast corner of the second floor's south hall, where she could see silent pandemonium in the dark hallway. Crisscrossed by dancing light beams, it looked like three dozen people with light sabers were fighting there to the death. The cellphone flashlights didn't light up anything long enough to really see it, just flashed randomly this way and that — a light show at a rock concert.

Buzzz.

The smoke alarms screamed. Voices rolled over each other like tumbling puppies.

"… raining outside! I'm not going out—"

"… broken. The alarms are out, just like the electri—"

"… smell that smoke?"

"Listen to me!" Andy Schaeffer's voice was impossibly loud, could be heard above all the others. How'd he do that? "Out! Everybody out now. No discussion. No going back for car keys or your laptop or an umbrella— *out!*"

He was a firefighter and the others quieted, listening.

They stopped flashing the lights around wildly and focused them on him, standing halfway down the hall in his pajamas. In that constant light, you could see a dim haze of smoke and when they grew still, they could smell it, too.

"Walk — don't run! — to the front or back stairs, whichever's closer. Do it *right now!*"

As the elevator began to disappear through the ceiling of the second floor into the third-floor hallway, Alex could hear him shouting orders, but heard no more opposition, just frightened voices stretched thin and high by incipient hysteria.

COUGHING HARD NOW, Gabe dropped to the floor, trying to think of a way out. Nothing leapt to mind, but the air behind the HVAC/laundry room's closed door would be better than out here in the hall. He crawled to the door, opened it quickly, leapt inside and closed the door behind him. The air was considerably better in here. But he couldn't stay here, holed up in this little room until the smoke or the fire got him.

Safe money's on smoke, he thought, and for a single instant wished there was some way he could bet on it. The moment passed.

Kick down the hallway door?

It was solid oak.

Remove the decorative grates from one of the windows in the study?

Even if he'd had a screwdriver, which he didn't, the screws that attached the grates to the window frames were on the outside of the window. There was no way to get to them from the inside.

Think!

There had to be something! He couldn't curl up in this dark little room that smelled of mildew and fabric softener and die. Not now! Not with Spencer out of prison — and *he didn't do it!* Not with the monster from his childhood finally vanquished. Not with ... he patted the sweatpants pocket where Mama had shoved something. He took it out — a key. What did this unlock that would pay off the psychos who'd threaten to kill him?

Mama.

Mama would say — don't just think outside the box, think outside the box the first box came in.

Dig a hole through the floor to the basement.

Dig a hole through the ceiling eighteen feet above his head.

Punch a hole in the hallway wall.

He froze.

He didn't have to punch a hole in it. There already was one. The hallway laundry chute.

Chapter Seventy-Eight

RISING into the third floor's wide hall, with doors that opened onto the three bedrooms — Olivia's, Cyrus's, and Hannah's — the elevator was swallowed by smoke as thick as pudding. The whole third floor was the chimney that carried smoke up to the windows at the top of the Crow's Nest's stairs. She grabbed a quick breath, tried to hold it as the elevator passed through the chimney. It inched upward. Alex couldn't see, squeezed her eyes shut as the smoke got thicker near the ceiling.

Then the rising car stopped. The machinery went silent.

Alex jammed her finger on the red button again and again. Nothing.

What had happened? The power couldn't go out, the elevator was battery operated.

There was no time to wonder or to try to fix it. The only way to get to the Crow's Nest now was *through* the third-floor chimney — out of the elevator, across the bedrooms, and down the hall to the stairs. Alex dropped to her knees and crawled as fast as she could across the floor beyond the elevator, knees and hands quickly becoming raw. She tried to keep her face as close as she could to the floor where the air was better, but it was still only barely breathable. She strained and fought her diaphragm, desperately trying not to start coughing because she was sure she'd never be able to stop. The world spun around her, sounds growing louder and then softer, and she didn't know if that was the effect of the smoke or Persephone. She crawled through Cyrus's room, then Hannah's, down the hall that ran beside her mother's room, to the stairs at the end of the hall, her eyes squeezed shut, counting the number of rugs she passed over to let her know where she was.

She literally crashed into the stairs in the dark, couldn't hold onto the coughing any longer, and it exploded out of her chest as she clawed her way upward on her belly. Had to make it to … air'd be better … in the hall … smoke flowing out the open windows at the top of the steps.

Who'd opened the windows?

She couldn't stop coughing, couldn't grab a breath in between. She reached the top, couldn't crawl any farther. So she rolled, over and over — away from the smoke pouring out the windows. Hacking and hacking, her throat was raw, but the air on the hallway floor she dragged in between coughs wasn't full of smoke. She rolled onto her belly and commando-crawled toward the bedroom door, her nose inches off the floor. Feeling along the wall, she found the door — and it was closed!

Rolling to the side, she got on her hands and knees and reached up to the door handle. Shoving the door open, she flung herself into the room and scrambled to close the behind her. Coughing ripped open her chest and her head spun in dizzy circles. She didn't so much return to flat on the floor as face plant on it when she couldn't remain upright.

"Mama!" she croaked the word. The air in here was breathable, but she was still gasping, something was wrong with her lungs … all the smoke … she couldn't stop coughing.

"Alex!"

Light suddenly shone in Alex's eyes, blinding her. She tried to tell her mother not to point the phone at her face but didn't have enough air.

"What's burning. I smell—"

"House is …" Cough! Cough! "On fire."

"Oh, sweet Jesus. How—"

"The woman … Cyrus's baby … had a gun."

"Cyrus's ba—"

No air or time to explain.

"Roll off the bed, Mama." Another round of coughing. "Down here … on the floor with me." Crawling toward the light, Avery got to her mother's bed as her mother was about to sit up.

"Don't sit up! The air's b—"

But she was too late. Her mother had already sat up into the ever-lowering level of smoke from the ceiling and she began to cough. Alex reached the side of the bed, got onto her knees, grabbed her mother and dragged her off the bed into her arms, then collapsed backward with her mother on top of her.

Both lay there, coughing.

Time was running out — they had to get out of here, out onto the balcony.

Alex reached up onto the nightstand, snagged her mother's phone, and pulled it down. She shone it around her, locating the balcony doors.

Then the room went silent. Her mother's coughing was gone, the cry of the smoke alarms was gone. She couldn't even hear her own coughing. Deaf again.

***

GABE TURNED his cell phone light back on, and the dreaded "low battery' warning came on. He'd better do something quick, or he'd have to do whatever he was going to do in the dark. He stood and went around the big metal case that surrounded the HVAC unit to the small room with a washer and dryer. He didn't think the family used this one now for anything but kitchen items — tablecloths and napkins. The laundry chute from the outside hall, and the halls on the two floors above, had been installed years — decades — ago.

He shown his light around and his heart sank. This wasn't a laundry room anymore. It was a storage room — a junk room. Stuff was piled on top of more stuff. Old mud boots, an umbrella, the attachment caddy for a vacuum cleaner long dead, and a cardboard box marked simply "supplies" sat on the washing machine. A big plastic container full of who knows what sat on the dryer. Gabe had to get to the wall chute to see if he could try to fit through it, or kick out the wall around it, or ... something. But there were piles of junk everywhere.

In a frenzy of rage and fear, he started digging through the junk, tossing it behind him like he was a dog digging a hole in the dirt. When he got to the chute, behind a rolling kitchen cart missing a wheel, he found it affixed to the wall with heavy bolts. And it was much smaller than he remembered — maybe two feet wide and six inches deep. What could he do with a hole that size?

He slid down the wall beside the chute, defeat and despair tasting like old coffee in the back of his throat. And he could smell smoke. The screen of his phone blinked a red message. Battery power — five percent.

Reaching up to switch the phone off, the beam of light flashed over something in the corner. He pointed the light there, sat looking at what rested against the wall next to a grandfather clock that hadn't kept time since the Eisenhower administration.

Could he …? That was absurd. But maybe …

Shit, what did he have to lose? It was thinking outside the box.

As he stood and walked to the other side of the room, his phone went dead and the room went black.

~

To the balcony. How? Alex's one-hundred-year-old mother couldn't commando-crawl across the room to the double doors.

Alex couldn't pick her up and carry her.

Hard to think. Coughing and coughing. Silent coughing. Maybe her mother was talking to her, no way to tell. Didn't matter.

"I'm going to drag you," Alex said.

If she could.

Grabbing a handful of fabric on the shoulder of her mother's nightgown, she tried to pull in a big breath to hold … couldn't. Couldn't stop coughing.

So she lurched to her feet, up into the bad air, and staggered across the room. So dizzy. The room was spinning. But she managed to stay upright, pulling her mother along behind, her nightgown sliding easily across the polished hardwood floor.

The doors. Sank to her knees. Fumbled with the knob.

The door opened and she fell through it — into pure, damp air!

She couldn't rise, just crawled out across the balcony floor, dragging her mother … should close the door. Can't. Stay low.

Cough, cough, cough.

Through squinty eyes, she could see it was still raining. But she couldn't hear the drops hitting the balcony roof. Couldn't hear anything.

Chapter Seventy-Nine

GABE COULD NO LONGER SEE the two black bags zipped shut, with double handles on top, but he felt around for them, lifted them and carried them out into the smoke-filled hallway.

He began to cough immediately but hurried down the hall to the open door of the music room. In just the few minutes since he'd left, the fire had spread, searing heat radiating out into the hallway. The couch, chair, and draperies were on fire. He could deal with them if he could just extinguish the fire on the floor. He set the two bags down in the doorway and unzipped them.

The one he pulled out of the first bag was swirling combinations of yellow and green. The second was the customary, dignified black. The first bowling ball was Sydney's old one. It was light. The ten percent rule: she'd weighed a hundred and ten pounds at the time and the ball weighed eleven pounds. The second was his old ball and it weighed a hefty sixteen pounds — the maximum weight for amateur bowlers.

Could he hurl a bowling ball all the way across the room to the other side?

He didn't like the odds on that one, but it was his only shot. He picked up the black ball, held it like it was a basketball and propelled it off his chest as hard as he could at the other side of the room. Didn't make it. He couldn't throw it hard enough and it fell three feet short onto the burning oriental rug and was swallowed up by the flames.

He picked up the second ball, started to throw it like he had thrown the first but thought better of it. Instead, he put his fingers and thumb into the appropriate holes and drew back like he was going to launch the ball down a lane. Taking a couple of steps back, he took the stance, as if ten bowling pins were lined against the far wall. He lowered the ball to his side, and then leapt two steps forward and flung the ball out into the room with every ounce of strength he had into his arm … held onto it a second too long so his hand was moving upward when he let it go.

The green ball flew out of his hand, across the room, and crashed full force into the gigantic aquarium.

The aquarium exploded like he'd detonated a bomb in the center, and a hundred and twenty-five gallons of water came gushing out into the room like the Red Sea returning to its banks after the Israelites had crossed. The effect was instantaneous, the flames on the rug sizzled and went out, sending nasty-smelling smoke into the air like blown-out birthday candles. The flaming ball things, surrounded by water, sputtered and went out. He ran into the room across the squishy rug, yanked the burning draperies down, threw them on the wet rug and stomped on the flames, burned his sockless left ankle, but he got the flames out. Then he picked up the soggy drapes and used them to beat out the flames on the couch and chair. The air was full of smoke. He was coughing and his eyes were watering so bad he could hardly see — but he finally did it, finally put the flames out.

He staggered to the open window — that'd be sucking in clean air — and collapsed to his knees in front of it. He couldn't seem to stop coughing, and he was so dizzy he had to hold onto the windowsill to remain upright.

Combustion byproducts and gases. Andy'd talked about that once. Who knew what was in the burning rug — the desk chair had plastic arms.

So dizzy.

The treetops and bushes were red, the light blinking through the rain.

Reflections of the flashing red lights from out front — a fire truck! No, impossible. Couldn't have gotten here that fast. He felt himself sliding down the wall. The flashing lights went out. All the lights went out.

~

ALEX CRAWLED to her mother's side. Olivia lay on her back on the balcony floor, her eyes open, looking around.

"You okay?" Alex asked. Tried to say more, but no air. Just coughing.

She saw her mother's lips move but couldn't hear her response. Duh.

"Can't hear, Mama." She coughed and coughed, felt something inside ... tear from the strain, couldn't catch her breath. "Deaf," she gasped.

Her mother rolled toward her, took her face in her hands. She was talking, but Alex couldn't hear. It was okay, though. Mama was alive.

Alex felt her cheek on the wet balcony floor. Her mother was shaking her. She'd blacked out.

She opened her eyes, could see her mother's lips move, such concern on her face.

"It's okay, Mama." She spoke in little gasps, but she'd stopped coughing. Almost stopped breathing, too. Just shallow breaths. It was getting dark, hard to see her mother's face. "Name's Persephone. Tumor needs an ugly name." Breathing didn't hurt anymore. Nothing hurt. "Bags are packed ... booked on an earlier train."

Couldn't see her mother's face in the dark. She tried to reach out to touch it, but she couldn't move.

"I love you," she whispered — maybe. She hoped she did.

~

GABE OPENED HIS EYES, closed them again, could hear the shriek of some kind of alarm, but far away, now. There was something on his face. He reached up to it and someone pulled his hand away.

"Leave it there," a voice said. "It's oxygen."

Gabe opened his eyes to pandemonium. Lights. People rushing around. Grandma Liv was sitting on the front yard bench wrapped in one of those shiny silver blankets. He was on a gurney, rolling toward an ambulance.

When his rolling ride passed next to Sheriff Ralph Hastings, Gabe reached out, clutched his hand and held on.

The sheriff leaned over him.

"You're gonna be fine, Gabe, just you—"

Gabe ripped off the oxygen mask and tried to talk, but he was so hoarse all he could do was croak — one word.

"*Doodle*…"

He drew in a ragged breath to continue, to tell the sheriff about the pillow and the fire … but the sheriff was shaking his head. "I'm sorry, Gabe. He didn't make it."

"Didn't *make*?"

"Ran off the road, musta been doing ninety in the rain, hit the gas pump in front of that little convenience store and it went off like a bomb! That's how we got here so fast. We already had a truck two miles away fighting his car fire when Avery dialed 911."

Gabe was confused. Must be all the smoke he'd breathed. That couldn't be right, didn't make sense.

They'd called 911 as soon as they smelled smoke — the fire hadn't been burning more than five minutes. It took the fire truck fifteen, maybe twenty minutes in the rain, to get from town to the convenience store where Doodle had wrecked.

Which meant Doodle had wrecked before the fire at the Harrington House even started.

How …?

He let it go.

"Spencer … is he—"

"Talked to Avery on the phone. Your son's gonna be all right, said his hand was a mess, had lots of stitches. They're keeping him overnight to give him IV antibiotics and blood. He lost a lot."

Gabe relaxed back on the gurney, relief washing over him in a warm tide. He looked around.

"You seen my mother? I need to talk to her."

The sheriff's face clouded, had a look that—

"What? What is it?"

"I'm sorry, Gabe …" There was genuine pain in his voice when he continued quietly. "She didn't make it, either."

Gabe felt like he'd hit a brick wall at a dead run.

"What do you mean *didn't make* … you mean she's …?"

He couldn't seem to form the word. After the sheriff told him what had happened, he let them fix the oxygen mask over his mouth again and wheel him into the ambulance without protest. He was crying.

Chapter Eighty

THE WHIRLING TORNADO of reality had been spinning around and around Olivia until she finally told everybody to leave her alone. Mostly they did, left her sitting on the bench beneath the sycamore tree in the front yard waiting her turn for an ambulance, all wrapped up like a Christmas turkey in some kinda shiny blanket, looked like it was made out of aluminum foil. Her middle grandson, Lawson, had shut her down quick when she protested that she hadn't breathed hardly no smoke at all. He'd stood his ground for both his brothers who were … somewhere else. Sam and Millie'd left right after supper, and their grandson, Jude, had got kilt, but Olivia didn't have the straight of that. Jordan's boy Doodle had run his car off the road and crashed into a gasoline pump. But Lawson was here, said Olivia was going to the hospital to get checked out whether she liked it or not and wasn't no arguing with him. Least she was able to convince him to take the others first. Most was just coughing bad, smoke inhalation. Wet and cold, too, maybe some hypothermia. Running out into the rain in your pajamas'd do that to you. But Brooke had fallen on the stairs and broke her arm. Casey'd somehow got a bad cut on her forehead, was gonna leave a scar. Cassidy Schaeffer had gone into labor!

And Alex was dead.

The wrecking ball of that knowledge knocked Olivia's whole soul right out of her body, left her sitting there empty, her insides all eat out, as hollow as an old tree that's been dying for years.

Alex! Couldn't be, couldn't be.

But Olivia seen it. Oh, dear God, she'd watched. She'd been there, and she was at least glad of that. Alex hadn't died alone.

She shook her head violently, like she could fling reality out of her skull, and that's when she seen the young black woman standing between the sheriff and his deputy, her hands cuffed behind her back.

Why, that was …no. Yes! Alex had said …

Olivia didn't even realize she'd got up until she found herself walking across the wet grass and the mud the trucks had churned up. She didn't get fifteen feet 'fore Julianna come rushing over, grabbed her arm like she was falling, liked to knocked her down.

"Where's my walker!" Olivia demanded, ignoring Juliana's bird twittering around her.

"It's right over there to go in the ambulance——"

"Go get it! Bring it here."

Juliana didn't let go, but she did motion for Peyton and Ryan, who clearly thought this whole thing was the grandest adventure ever — Dumb and Dumber — to bring it.

Taking hold of the two handgrips, Olivia felt steadier.

"Go on, leave me alone." She gestured toward the sheriff. "Me 'n him's got private things to talk about."

"Now, Grandma Liv——"

"If you's five, I'd turn you over my lap and bust your butt for talking back. Consider yourself spanked. Now, *go away.*"

Julianna hadn't never heard Olivia talk like that, but her

boyfriend Jamal gave Olivia a respectful nod, then took Juliana by the arm and dragged her away. Olivia liked that young man.

Olivia piloted her walker slowly over the wet ground toward the sheriff. When she got there, she turned it around and sat down on the seat.

"What you got her all trussed up for?" she asked.

Surprised by the question, the sheriff spoke in his most officious voice. "I've talked to your great-granddaughter on the phone. Avery said this woman broke into your house with a gun."

"I have a permit and a concealed carry," the woman said.

The sheriff ignored her. "We found her in your backyard, sitting in the mud under that cherry tree. The preliminary charge right now is arson. There's reason to believe she set the fire and if she did, there'll be more charges—"

"She didn't," Olivia interrupted.

The sheriff gawked at her.

"Set that fire ... she didn't do no such of a thing. I's the one started that fire. 'Lectricity was out and I knocked over a candle."

Sheriff Hastings looked at her as if she'd grown a third eye, but she carried on ahead, pushing through the grief that was eating out her heart because this was a thing that absolutely had to be done right now, and wasn't nobody in the world could pull it off 'cept her.

"Now Mrs. Olivia, there's no way you could have—"

It felt like drawing in a big breath, almost like she could see something in the air, little particles being sucked up and into her. Olivia didn't stand, didn't have to, but she did draw herself upright as she could on the flat seat of that walker. And she fixed the young man with a stare that brought to bear the strength of character from every one of her hundred years and one day of living.

"Ralph Hastings, you listen here to me and you understand what I'm saying 'cause I ain't going to say it but once. The house that got burnt is *my* house — just like this ranch is mine and all the cattle and oil on it, and them shopping centers and hotels — and I don't even remember what all else, but I *do* remember that my family carries a considerable amount of clout in this county."

"Yes, ma'am, you do, but—"

"They ain't no but to it. If Olivia Kavanaugh Harrington tells you she's the one started this fire … you planning on *calling her a liar?*"

"Mrs. Olivia—"

"That wasn't no rhetorical question, son. And don't get that frown mark between your eyebrows. Your daddy and your granddaddy both got that same expression when they's playing poker and they's bluffing. And my Landon won everything but their jock straps. Now you tell Deputy Dog here to take them bracelets off of—" She paused, then spoke tenderly to the handcuffed woman. "What's your name?"

"Rowan Douglas."

The deputy looked at the sheriff, who looked at Olivia, studied her. Then he said to the deputy, "*You* want to call Mrs. Olivia a liar?"

The deputy stepped forward immediately and opened the handcuffs that held Rowan's hands behind her back.

She just stood there, looking at Olivia.

Suddenly, Olivia felt the weight of her grief slam down on her, a weight she couldn't possibly carry. Alex. No! Not her precious Alex.

She hadn't been able to think about it, couldn't think about it. But now it … *settled.* Like sitting down in your favorite chair, it connected, made sense so wasn't no uncertainty no more. All them doctor appointments Alex didn't think her mother knew about. That neurologist in Amarillo, why would Alex be going to see a neurologist … a brain doctor?

Her pale skin.

Her hair falling out

How she ignored what Olivia said sometimes — why, she'd been deaf.

The look she'd get on her face — a desperate look— fear near unto panic … and then despair.

All of it added up, explained what Alex'd meant in the last words she ever spoke.

My bags are packed. I'm booked on an earlier train than yours.

Olivia literally gasped at how bad it hurt! But those weren't her *last words*. Her last words were: *I love you.*

Through the blur of tears in her eyes, Olivia become aware of the young woman standing in front of her, a look of desolation on her face that likely matched Olivia's.

"My only daughter's" — Olivia couldn't stifle a little gasp — *"gone."*

"I didn't do it. I didn't start that fire."

Olivia blew by the denial. Didn't mean a hill of beans one way or the other who started the fire. What was done was done.

"Don't matter. My Alex was already leaving, just didn't quite know how to say goodbye is all."

Olivia swallowed a lump in her throat that was threatening to choke her completely to death. Then she lifted her arms and held them out to … Rowan.

Rowan. Olivia liked that name.

"Come on over here, Sugar, and give your grandmother a hug."

Epilogue

AVERY PICKED up the Texas Tech sweatshirt out of her open wheelie, held it to her nose and sniffed. Smoke. She dropped it back in and stood looking at it for a moment, her mind in such a fog she couldn't manage to focus for long enough to gather her things for the drive back to Lubbock ... where she would "offload" her new best friend, Maddie. Well, there was that, the one good thing bobbing around in the flotsam and jetsam of her family's explosion.

She shook her head to clear it, felt a twinge of pain in the lump on her forehead that had, indeed, blacked both her eyes. Okay, she'd wash the sweatshirt. She'd have to wash all her clothes. But she'd read somewhere that it was almost impossible to get the smell of smoke out of clothing. How could you possibly get that stink out of the draperies downstairs? Grandma Alex would have to —

She literally gasped out loud. Her hand flew to her mouth to stifle a sob and tears streamed down her cheeks.

Avery would never see her Grandma Alex again. How ... how could that be?

"It'll probably take two trips to get all our stuff out to the car," Maddie said from the spot where she sat on the bed, doing something on her phone.

It wouldn't take two trips if it weren't for that idiot duffel bag Maddie hauled around with her everywhere, but Avery said nothing, couldn't say anything, couldn't talk without bursting into tears.

Get a grip.

She was just exhausted emotionally, and physically worn out from a lost night of sleep, too.

"And after all that's happened, we still don't know who killed your Aunt Hannah."

Avery sighed.

"Nobody killed Aunt Hannah." Her voice sounded as tired as she felt. "Those under-the-toenail pictures don't prove a thing. That mark could have been anything."

Maddie blew by her response as if she hadn't spoken.

"We couldn't think of a motive for your Uncle Cyrus to kill her, but turns out he had the best one of all. He couldn't let her dig up the backyard for that koi pond and find the body of the girl he murdered."

Avery's back was to Maddie and she kept it that way because she didn't want to engage with Maddie on any level. Uncle Cyrus had just been babbling, that's all. Just babbling. She certainly wasn't going to tell Maddie what he'd said in the car on the way to Amarillo.

Never again were powerful words you usually regretted, but Avery swore she would never again get talked into …

She let it go, too much to process right now. She needed to concentrate on the essentials. She had to go back to Lubbock — to take Maddie back to school and to sign out for the rest of the week. And maybe she'd drop out this semester, come home, be here for her hurting family. Grandpa Gabe. Grandma Liv. Even pathetic old Uncle Cyrus.

And her *father*. There was still … her father.

"That girl, Rowan … she said she didn't start the fire."

Maddie had put away her cell phone and crossed the room to stand behind Avery. Too close, of course, invading her body space.

Never again.

"Well *somebody* did." Avery felt a flash of anger. "And now my great grandmother is dead."

"Oh, she's telling the truth. She didn't start the fire."

"And you know that how?"

"I know who did start it."

"Who?"

"I did."

"*You* did? Why on earth would ...?"

Avery turned to look at Maddie, and when she took in her face and her countenance, there was something off, something so profoundly odd about it, she lost her train of thought.

Then she saw what was in Maddie's hand. A Bic lighter. Maddie rolled the cylinder with her thumb, and a three-inch tongue of flame shot up into the air. "Most people don't even know how flammable nail polish remover is — acetone. Soak a roll of toilet paper with acetone and it's a torch, a Molotov cocktail."

Of course, she was just yanking Avery's chain.

The hair on the back of Avery's neck stood up.

"Why?"

"Shits and giggles." She paused, then added, "extra points" and burst out laughing. "I wanted to see if that Gulf Stream thing really worked." A crease appeared between her eyebrows. "*Scored* on that transphobic grandmother of yours — she needed to *die!* I'd have burned her alive if I could've. Swing and a miss on her snotty bald son, though." She paused for a beat, then flicked the lighter off. "But mostly I did it because ... I *like* fire."

Avery couldn't seem to draw in a breath. Startled and shocked, yeah, but something else clamped an iron grip down on her ribcage and wouldn't let it move. She was afraid.

I got him back. I poisoned his dog.

"That's not funny," she blustered and moved to take a step around Maddie to the door, but Maddie blocked her path. She was watching Avery's face, studying it intently.

"Yes!" Maddie's eyes had grown bright, but her voice was as cold as a stone on a snowy morning. "That's right. You're getting it. Putting two and two together."

Avery's heart suddenly began to pound like a lunatic woodpecker in her chest.

"Don't try to figure it all out at once. Just make the essential connections. That's all you need."

Avery leapt to the side and lunged toward the door, but Maddie'd been expecting that. She put out her foot and tripped her, and as she fell, Maddie grabbed hold of her ponytail, yanking backward on it.

Pain exploded in the back of Avery's head and her neck snapped in a whiplash motion that propelled all the air out of her lungs in a rush. She cried out, but it wasn't loud enough for anybody to hear.

And there was no one to hear anyway. They were alone in the house.

"Go on … make the connection. You need to know what's coming. I *want* you to know what's coming. I came home with you because I needed to get out of Lubbock alright, but it was to get away from the police." Avery lay on her back on the floor, her head and neck on fire, staring with wide eyes at Maddie, who clearly was getting off on her terror.

"I told you, suicide's hard. Nobody gets it right the first time. You have to practice, study it, make sure there's no way to back out at the last minute."

She paused. "I'm going to practice on you."

Avery made a desperate leap to get up, but the bigger, stronger Maddie was prepared, and as soon as she moved, Maddie drew back her fist and slammed it into the side of Avery's face. She felt herself falling sideways in slow motion.

The world was moving at one-quarter speed. Maddie's voice came from a long way off, bogged down and speaking slowly. Avery hit the floor but didn't feel it anywhere in her body. Her cheek was on fire, blow-torched pain, but even that was set back some. Every movement, every sound, was too slow and didn't match up with the action that'd produced them.

Maddie spoke, but the words formed thoughts Avery couldn't wrap her mind around.

"I'd already picked you out." The buzzing in her ears was growing louder instead of softer, muffling what Maddie was saying.

"… couldn't let you *leave* … came with you."

Maddie reached out and grabbed Avery's right hand, then her left, produced a zip tie out of nowhere and fastened her hands together behind her back. Quick and efficient. Like tying a calf's hooves in a calf-roping contest.

"… trying to scare you … so clumsy you coulda broken your neck and ruined everything … away with it? That's what the duffel bag's for. You'll fit just fine. The other three did."

Three.

Spencer had his daughter back.

An incredibly strange tangle of circumstances he never would have dreamed and certainly couldn't have orchestrated had literally changed *everything*.

Now, he didn't want her to leave for school without … without something. A hug. Yeah, that'd be enough.

Spencer had last seen her in the emergency room and she'd been so kind and caring. They'd had no time to talk on the drive to Amarillo — with freaked-out Uncle Cyrus babbling nonsense about insulin shots and toenails. It'd taken a long time to get Spencer's hand put to rights, and the doctor'd said the likelihood of infection — from a human bite

— was very high, so they'd pumped him full of antibiotics all through the night along with giving him blood.

Avery'd had to take Uncle Cyrus home … and be there for her grandfather and the rest of the family after … what an incredible nightmare. Grandma Alex. Jude and Doodle, too … but *Grandma Alex!*

His sister Casey'd come to Northwest Hospital to pick him up when they discharged him Monday afternoon. They were quite a pair. His face was a smashed ruin, his left hand was bandaged as fat as a boxing glove and hung in a sling. Her whole forehead was bandaged, concealing a gash that'd required thirteen stitches to close. She'd fallen but had no idea what she'd hit her head on. There was such pandemonium, she didn't even realize she was hurt until she was standing outside with everybody else in the rain with blood washing down into her eye.

She mentioned that Avery'd gone back to the house to get her things to go back to school. Casey would drop him off there to pick up his own car — the one he'd borrowed from a fellow parolee who'd been out longer. Everyone else had already cleared out, but there was a chance … a *chance* Avery'd still be there.

From a distance, the Harrington House looked unchanged. The damage had been mostly internal, Casey said. Water damage in all the rooms on the back of the first floor — fire damage in the music room. The study, the hallway, the dining room, and kitchen were a mess of water and the mud firemen had tracked in.

It could have been a whole lot worse, of course. If Grampa Gabe hadn't gotten that fire out … and Andy hadn't gotten the family out. The whole family standing in the mud in their pajamas in the pouring rain. What a sight that must have been!

Casey turned down the lane. The area around the house looked like it'd suffered a mortar attack. Trampled bushes, the yard a mass of gouged ruts from the fire trucks, ambulances, police cruisers. There were no cars but his out in the field beside the yard. Everyone else had already collected their cars and things. Still … Spencer held his breath as they rounded the corner of the house where he could see—

Avery's car was still parked just beyond the back fence!

"You sure you can drive with that thing?" Casey pointed to his left arm and hand in a sling.

"Only takes one functioning hand."

He used it to wave goodbye before he crossed the muddy yard to the back porch, opened the kitchen door and stepped inside. The room smelled of smoke and wet wood. The lights were out, maybe not turned on or maybe never came back on after last night's blink-out. Didn't matter. He could find his way around the big old house in the dark just like everybody else in the family.

MADDIE GRABBED hold of Avery's hair again, yanked her head back, and slipped a plastic bag over it, pulling the bag tight across Avery's face.

Avery tried to suck in a breath and the plastic pulled tight to her nose and mouth. She struggled frantically, desperately, but Maddie rode it out like she was on a bucking bull, held firm and kept the plastic bag in place.

"Wondering what's in the duffel already?"

Avery's hearing wasn't too muffled to detect the snark in Maddie's words. "Water! Plastic bags of water. I haul this thing around and everybody sees that it's heavy and bulky. Then I pour the water down the drain and I can fit whatever I want on top of the empty bags. I'll get Velma out of the back seat floorboard and set her in the passenger seat. Put your Tech baseball cap on her."

There were bright sparkles in the air in front of Avery's

eyes and the volume on Maddie's voice began to turn down. "Then I'll put the duffel in the trunk. Nobody's here, but if I meet somebody on the road, I'll smile and wave."

Now the roaring between Avery's ears had the thundering sound of Niagara Falls and she could barely hear Maddie's words. She wasn't trying to claw the bag off her face anymore because her arms wouldn't move.

"I'll take you to the barn … I already have a spot picked out. It's close to the girl they still say is just 'missing.' I'll leave your car in your dorm lot. When the questions start, I'll say I haven't seen you since you dropped me off at my dorm."

She laughed.

Then the thought surfaced in Avery's darkening brain. It was hard to think, and she lifted the thought ponderously, like she was picking up something heavy. Even as she thought it, it was fading into the gray mist — Maddie'd been planning this all along.

The gray around her turned dark. The dark turned black. Avery was gone.

~

THE DOOR to the room where Avery and her school friend were staying was standing ajar, but Spencer couldn't hear voices from inside. They couldn't have already left yet, though. Avery's car was still outside. He pushed the door open and what he saw was such a bizarre scene he could make no sense of it for a couple of seconds.

Avery was on her back on the floor. Maddie was kneeling on top of her… *holding a plastic bag tight on Avery's head!*

"I'll say I haven't seen you since you dropped me off at my dorm," Maddie said, then threw her head back and laughed. Spencer had heard laughter like that before. It was madness.

Spencer crossed the room in two steps. He grabbed the big girl by her blue hair and hauled her off Avery onto the floor and kicked her as hard as he could, planted the pointed toe of his cowboy boot square in her side, felt the ribs crunch. When she screamed and bent double, he reared back and kicked her again — this time in the face. She flew backward from the blow, the whole front of her face caved in, teeth and nose broken, spitting blood and broken teeth out between smashed lips. His third kick caught her square in the left temple, snapped her head to the side with an awful cracking sound. Maybe he killed her. He hoped so.

~

Sounds. Muffled

A voice. Words.

"Avery!"

Someone was calling her name.

"Breathe, Avery, breathe!"

But she was sucking in a huge breath before she heard the words, filling her burning lungs with air. She gasped in air again and again, heard someone speaking to her but couldn't make out …

There was a familiar scent, unpleasant. She could smell blood.

She opened her eyes and looked up into a face so bruised and damaged it was almost unrecognizable. One eye was stolen completely shut. The nose was mashed sideways, and there were two stitches in the bloated swollen lip.

Her father's shirt was covered in blood. It was all over her, too.

"Avery!"

"How did—"

She couldn't finish the sentence because he grabbed her up into a bear hug so tight she almost couldn't breathe. When he let her go, eased her gently to the floor, she saw why they both were covered in blood. The bandages on his left hand had been torn away. Blood soaked through them and dripped off his fingers.

"What …?"

He looked then, saw the bandages and the blood, appeared to notice them for the first time.

He reached down a bloody right hand and pushed her hair up off the lump on her forehead.

"CPR," he said by way of explanation.

Then he gathered her back up into his arms and held her, rocking a little back and forth, saying words that weren't words into her hair.

All Avery could say was, *"Daddy."*

THE END

Family loyalties and deadly feuds are brought to life in Ninie Hammon's new intergenerational romp through the history of The Cornbread Mafia in rural Kentucky.

Pick Up Your Copy of Fire In The Hole Today

A Note from the Author

Thank you for reading *The Gap*.

If you enjoyed this book please consider writing a review of it on your favorite bookseller's website so other readers might enjoy it too. Just a couple of sentences would mean a lot to me.

Thank you!
Ninie Hammon

About the Author

Ninie Hammon (rhymes with shiny, not skinny) grew up in Muleshoe, Texas, got a BA in English and theatre from Texas Tech University and snagged a job as a newspaper reporter. She didn't know a thing about journalism, but her editor said if she could write he could teach her the rest of it and if she couldn't write the rest of it didn't matter. She hung in there for a 25-year career as a journalist. As soon as she figured out that making up the facts was a whole lot more fun than reporting them, she turned to fiction and never looked back.

Ninie now writes suspense--every flavor except pistachio: psychological suspense, inspirational suspense, suspense thrillers, paranormal suspense, suspense mysteries.

In every book she keeps this promise to her Loyal Reader: "I will tell you a story in a distinctive voice you'll always recognize, about people as ordinary as you are--people who have been slammed by something they didn't sign on for, and now they must fight for their lives. Then smack in the middle of their everyday worlds, those people encounter the unexplainable--and it's always the game-changer."

Also By Ninie Hammon

Cornbread Mafia

Fire In The Hole

Blown' Up A Storm

Ridin' For A Fall

So Shall The Tree Grow

Nowhere, USA

The Jabberwock

Mad Dog

Trapped

The Hanging Judge

The Witch of Gideon

Blown Away

Nowhere People

Through The Canvas Series

Black Water

Red Web

Gold Promise

Blue Tears

The Taken Saga

The Taken

The Changed

The Hidden

The Saved

The Unexplainable Collection

Five Days in May

Black Sunshine

The Based on True Stories Collection

Home Grown

Sudan

When Butterflies Cry

The Knowing Series

The Knowing

The Deceiving

The Reckoning

The Fault

Stand-alone Psychological Thrillers

The Memory Closet

The Last Safe Place

The Gap